# SAVAGE
## Sympathy

# SAVAGE Sympathy

Graham Taylor

Strategic Book Publishing and Rights Co.

© 2015 by Graham Taylor. All rights reserved.

No part of this book may be reproduced or transmitted in any form or by any means, graphic, electronic, or mechanical, including photocopying, recording, taping, or by any information storage retrieval system, without the permission, in writing, from the publisher. For more information, send a letter to our Houston, TX address, Attention Subsidiary Rights Department, or email: mailto:support@sbpra.net.

Strategic Book Publishing and Rights Co.
12620 FM 1960, Suite A4-507
Houston, TX 77065
www.sbpra.com

For information about special discounts for bulk purchases, please contact Strategic Book Publishing and Rights Co. Special Sales, at bookorder@sbpra.net

ISBN: 978-1-63135-406-9

Book Design by Julius Kiskis

22 21 22 20 19 18 17 16 15    1 2 3 4 5

# Introduction

She had been missing all that day and now, as the late summer twilight began to merge into full darkness, real concern was growing.

Bridget Margaret McGuire was last seen talking to a group of villagers outside Maloneys, the last of the five taverns at the Sligo end of town, around mid-afternoon. She had completed her weekly purchases and was returning home from the market. She always enjoyed the two-mile walk from the village to her home on these long summer days.

Bridget and her twin, Kathleen, with their captivating smiles and somewhat shy, yet spontaneous sense of humour, were the favourites of the Bandara townsfolk and the farming people for many miles around.

It was said that even the English, with their traditional contempt for the original landowners of this northern area of the west coast of Ireland, begrudgingly fell to the sisters' all too obvious charm that created such an impact on first meeting them and on subsequent occasions. Bridget and Kathleen, however, were totally unaware of the effect they had on others. The warnings of Big Michael, their doting father, that these troubled times in Ireland were an ongoing threat to the safety of all, were always met with a giggle and a combined reply of, "Ah, Father, who would be interested in two old hags the likes of us?"

Since their mother had died so suddenly when the twins

were only six, Big Michael's world existed only in the close proximity of his two darling daughters.

Big Michael was resting now, but only after many hours spent looking for his daughter, Bridget, by walking the roads that led from the village to their little farmhouse. He prayed that he would find her.

The first of those who walked the fields and searched the rugged coastline merged from the twilight and entered the McGuires' small but cosy sitting room.

"Ah, Padraig, please come in, lad, and rest. Is Kathleen with you, and what news do you bring?"

"Sadly, very little news. Kathleen is outside, talking to those who walked the shoreline. Everyone we spoke to said that this is a very strange occurrence indeed. We are all very fearful."

Kathleen walked into the room. Big Michael noticed a distinct change in his daughter.

"Come, my daughter, sit. Sure, and it's a worryin' time. What could possibly have happened to your sister? Where could she be?"

"Father, oh my God, Father . . ." Kathleen collapsed, weeping as if her heart would break.

Padraig, also with a heavy heart, leapt to her side to hold her and console her.

"Father, I know that even with the help of all the angels and saints, Bridget will not return tonight or any other night. I also know deep in my heart and soul that my sister is not yet dead, but she will not see the dawn. Oh, Father!" Kathleen fell into a beckoning state of unconsciousness held tight in the arms of Padraig.

It was not until just after midday on the next day, the day before the Sabbath, that Padraig Joseph the Older approached the cottage. His son, Padraig Joseph the Younger, and his grandson, Padraig, and two of the coastline farmers were in company with him.

# INTRODUCTION

With a heavy heart, he opened the door and went in. His son and grandson stood by his side.

His weather-beaten face was lined and craggy, and clearly forewarned the terrible news he was about to impart. The horrifically battered and beaten body of Bridget had been found only hours earlier.

Circling gulls had indicated that something was attracting them at the base of Morag, the hilly entrance and rocky foreshore at the entrance to the bay, bringing the first of the searchers to the shoreline. The villagers had gathered, shocked, staring down at the terrible sight below.

Even to the old man's untrained eye, it was obvious that Bridget had been severely violated.

The corpse was carefully covered and taken by horse and cart to the village doctor, and then the priest was notified.

Although Padraig Joseph the Older knew that nothing more could be done for Bridget, he could not allow Big Michael to view the body of his daughter without forewarning. He also knew that nothing would ever be the same again in Bandara.

# Part 1
## Donegal, Ireland

# Chapter 1

Young Padraig lay on the lush green grass at the top of the rise, loving the smell of late summer. He peeped over the brow and looked down at the workers cutting the last of the hay, golden hued in the afternoon sun. Smiling, with the sun warm on his back, he lay happily watching the rural scene.

"Hush now!" he whispered to Jess, his faithful sheepdog.

The top field had always given the best yield, and this summer, the weather had treated them kindly. As he watched, Kathleen picked the last of the hay hand shakings and added them to the impressive haystack. The quality of the hay would ensure the stock would eat well this coming winter, and this knowledge brought a cheerful smile to her beautiful countenance.

She was now in her seventeenth year, small in stature, but as all agreed, the fairest lass in all Donegal, indeed, all of Ireland. Her coal black hair shimmered in the sunlight, reflecting a hint of darkest blue. Normally it draped over her shoulders, but today it was tied back to allow her to work. Her deep blue eyes sparkled, and with her long dark eyelashes contrasting with her perfect clear complexion, only the blindest of fools would disagree that in truth, she was the fairest in the land.

As Padraig gazed down at the peaceful scene, he thought his heart would surely burst. *Ah, Kathleen Mary McGuire, my lovely colleen, this day one week hence I will be the luckiest man in all of Ireland.* Jess licked his hand as if in agreement. He produced the wild flower he had plucked and placed it into the dog's mouth. "Now girl," he whispered again, "off down you go and give to Kathleen."

The dog responded immediately and bounded out through the corn, and with obvious delight ran up to the now resting young lady and sat before her with her offering in her mouth.

"Well now, what is this? Is this the most wonderful dog in all the world, and what does the wonderful dog bring to such as me?" She laughed as she took the wild rose from the dog's mouth. "And pray tell, where could such a good dog's rascal of an owner be skulking, I would wonder? With so much work to be done, he wouldn't be swallowing down the porter at Maloneys now, would he?"

Teasingly, she lifted her skirt several inches above her ankles. "Because if such a rascal was to be hereabouts, it wouldn't be fitting for a young lady to be behaving like a Dublin fisher's wife, now would it? And if this rascally fellow was to be sneaking up behind me, I would surely have to take a big blackthorn stick to him, now wouldn't I?"

"And surely it would not be a fair fight," the voice behind her suggested. "With me bein' such a poor wee man, and you bigger and fiercer than Brian Boru!"

She turned and flung herself into his open arms. The big man held her with such a gentleness and longing, she started to cry with sheer happiness.

"What is this?" he teased. "Does the terrible witch herself be so unhappy to greet the future husband, or will the poor man have to run away to sea?"

"Don't you ever think such thoughts, Padraig Gallagher, or I will truly deal to you." She paused and looked up to his gleaming face, eyes sparkling as if on fire. "I love you more than I could ever believe possible. I would want to die if you were not in my arms each night until God calls us."

"Well, my bride to be, we still have to wait seven more long days and nights before this wondrous happening; now come, let me help you with the forks and rakes and you, you lazy grinning layabouts . . ." he said to the other field hands watching with amusement. "Off you go, and be sure to be at Maloneys tonight and join this poor wretch and drink a porter to celebrate his last week as a free man."

Together they walked from the fields to Kathleen's home. "Father," she called. "We are home! Where are you?"

Her father appeared from his room. Even now, she could not see her father without feeling a deep sadness. Since that direful night last summer, Big Michael McGuire had slipped deeper into a trough of despair. He had lost a great deal of weight, and his frailty and state of mind gave Kathleen much concern. She knew that Padraig also cared for her father, and he had assured her his support for him would not diminish. Their intention was to live in her family home where they could both care for him after they wed.

The death of her mother had meant that the twin sisters had early on adopted the roles of housekeeper and cook. Since the horrific murder of her sister, more and more responsibility fell on Kathleen's shoulders. The fact that Bridget's death remained a mystery only added to her burden.

There were many theories as to the cause. The annual harvest time brought itinerant workers to the region, some being extremely ignorant and crude people who had no respect for women.

Then there were always the traveling people, the true Romany gypsies and the tinkers, both seeking work and some finding trouble, though a few kept to themselves.

While the English landlords and their families and assorted

staff and lackeys were generally contemptuous of the local people, and at times very cruel in their dealings toward their tenants, Kathleen wanted to believe that they were not responsible.

Naturally her friends and neighbours and most of the townsfolk were happy to blame the "bastard English" for any bad happening, from the sudden death of a milk cow to any malaise that may occur. "Such things never happened before they arrived" was the common refrain.

It was true that Robert Bolton, son of the Lord of Blaxton and a member of the English aristocracy, was used to taking want he wanted and getting his own way. He had a bullying nature, and he had made unwelcome advances toward both the McGuire sisters, but with wit and charm, they had suggested to the Englishman that his romantic ambitions be taken elsewhere.

"Come, Father, let Padraig pour you a wee drop of the whiskey, and I will prepare us a supper," Kathleen said, wanting to provide her father with some domestic comfort.

Padraig Joseph Gallagher the Older could still recall the absolute joy when his son's wife, Claire, presented his son, the proud father, with their firstborn, a boy. He well remembered his son explaining to him their decision to name their son Padraig Joseph after him.

When reminding his son there was already enough confusion with an older and younger Gallagher, without adding another Padraig to the Gallagher clan, he was told, "Father, you and I know the difference, my wife certainly knows the difference, those that matter know, but if the accursed English need to find a Padraig Gallagher, any confusion we can give them will always be a blessing."

How prophetic those words were; indeed, the events that would befall the family Gallagher would not be a blessing.

Kathleen McGuire had always been a favourite of the

Gallagher family, and as friendship developed into a much deeper relationship, both Claire and husband, Padraig, were delighted that their younger son, Padraig, would someday wed the lovely young lass.

Padraig the Older simply idolized her and could hardly wait until the day she married his grandson and became one of the family. Fully aware of the failing health of her father, he had continuously assured Big Michael should anything happen to him his now only daughter would be protected by the Gallagher family. And indeed, the grandfather had watched with great pleasure the bond growing between Kathleen and his grandson. Many was the time he teased the young man that Kathleen would carry the shill alee if he should marry her, to which always said, "Ah, Grandfather, indeed, indeed."

Such were the times in Ireland in the late 1700s.

# Chapter 2

Claire and Padraig had two sons. Sean, the younger of the two, whose birth caused complications that in time would prove the family could not be extended, was his father's favourite of sorts. He took after his father, boasting a fine crop of unruly red hair with a temper to testify to all that doubted that the temperament traditionally aimed at those so blessed. And the firstborn, christened Padraig in true family tradition, appeared to take after his mother. Soon after his birth, he developed her fine features and darker complexion, and appeared to most as her favourite, though in truth, both were loved equally and treated accordingly.

As Padraig grew, even before his first birthday, it became apparent to Claire and Padraig that their son was different to the infants of their friends. Sure, he smiled and gurgled and did all the baby things the others did. But when he was quiet, he looked at them with his blue baby eyes almost as if he understood all that was going on about him. As he grew older, he seemed fascinated and was always enquiring, continually seeking answers to questions that he could not yet comprehend. His grandfather spent hours providing him with the knowledge he had acquired in his lifetime.

With the English rulers denying a traditional education to the Irish, frustration and resentment could have resulted had it not been for the Frenchman, Hugo Cohen, coming to Bandara.

Hugo, a Jew and a teacher, had upset the authorities in his local area south of Paris, and subsequent actions had gotten out of hand. He was a very worldly person with opinions both political and religious that had contradicted the supposed teachings of the predominantly Catholic hierarchy in his township. This had resulted in threats to his life.

He had travelled throughout many countries, mixing with the locals and learning their customs and culture. He had developed many skills, not the least the ability to protect himself. While in northern India, he had learned of and become a devotee of an ancient form of self-defence. But it was when he arrived in Paris that he learned of and became adept at La Savate. This form of street fighting greatly appealed to Hugo Cohen, and within a short time, he had earned a reputation of being the best in his region, beating all who attacked him for his beliefs and leaving them with broken legs or ankles. Finally, after receiving death threats, he decided to move on again, and so, after months of traveling, he had arrived in the quiet Irish village of Bandara.

He took up residence in a small room at the back of one of the hostels in town, and strangely, he soon became accepted by the local Irish populace. This was odd in one sense because traditionally, the locals were very suspicious of strangers, especially those who were not Catholic. In fact, he and the village priest became the closest of friends, and all were amused when they spotted the two of them strongly debating matters not normally understood or for that matter not encouraged for local knowledge.

And so, when Father Sullivan suggested to the Gallaghers that Hugo could assist in young Padraig's quest for answers, they readily accepted.

By the time he had reached age five, he had an affinity with animals. Dogs simply loved him. When coming to the village, his parents soon got used to seeing Padraig rolling in the dust with scores of village dogs jumping and leaping all over him, playing as only dogs and children do. Even the wilder dogs that were trained to defend property quickly fell to his charm and could be seen licking and begging his attention. And so, it was obvious that as he grew older, he would become a dog handler and trainer of unique talent.

The Gaelic-speaking lad, who also had a good understanding of the English language, loved to hear Hugo speaking and swearing in French and Hebrew. It became apparent to the teacher that Padraig had a more than natural ability to grasp the nuances of foreign languages. By the time he had reached his fourteenth birthday, the young Padraig was fluent in French, had a full understanding of Latin, could converse in Hebrew, and a passable acceptance of Spanish and Italian.

Yes, Hugo was very proud of his young pupil and loved him as his own son.

By now, Padraig had filled out, and like his grandfather, stood well over six feet tall.

By French standards, he would have been considered an extremely handsome man, with a dark complexion, long black hair almost shoulder length, and piercing blue eyes that always looked deep into the eyes of others.

Working the land and running with his dogs had honed the young man into an extremely fit condition with an athletically built physique. Unlike his younger brother Sean, he shied clear of physical confrontation, not needing to prove to himself that he was the best fighter around. No, Sean, taking after their father, was the family ruffian, as Padraig jokingly called him.

Sean Gallagher could fight. A year younger, but more heavily built than his brother, he had developed a natural pugilistic ability. He had beaten all the would-be-if-they-could-be town champions and a good few out-of-towners. Even the travelling folk had heard of the young lad's reputation, and whilst a few had tried and failed, most had decided it was wiser to stay clear of his lightning-fast fists.

Padraig knew that his brother was more than capable and even thirsted for the opportunity to tear limb from limb the perpetrator of the rape and mutilation of Bridget McGuire.

But since the authorities had done very little to search for her or those responsible for her murder, it seemed most unlikely the young girl's death would ever be avenged.

In fact, all of the Gallagher family had long suspected a cover-up. Certainly, the English aristocracy had distanced themselves from the event, claiming that the "wench" had probably gotten her due rewards.

Everyone had noticed that, not long after the burial, Robert Bolton, son of the Lord of Blaxton, returned to England with two of his colleagues, but nothing was said about it, nor would there be.

The Earl of Blaxton, who resided in Suffolk, had sent his son to Ireland to manage the properties that he had acquired some time back. In all, he owned many thousands of acres of Donegal farmland, stretching from the coast inland from Killybegs down to the town of Donegal and north to Letterkenny and back to the coast.

At first, there was the expected resentment toward the absentee landlord, but as the antipathy lessened and the investment slowly started to show a profit, the earl had decided to send his son to manage the land and push for a greater profit. His son had assured him that he would indeed create an increase in profitability, a very much greater increase, or as he put it, "Those Irish and their lazy and surly attitudes will not be tolerated."

The earl was at first a mite concerned at his son's attitude, but then a large amount of money was invested in this venture. As a number of his friends suggested to him, the young man had the responsibility, and thus, he had the chance to prove his worth.

Young Bolton did have a reputation as a lad with an eye for the ladies, and at times, some rather unsavoury ladies, but of late he had seemed eager to bolster his image as a businessman. And his mother, Lady Constance, did appear much happier in the knowledge that her son was away from the temptations that were all too apparent in London's society circles and seemed to be settling into the challenge that the Irish investment offered.

## Chapter 3

"Ah, 'tis young Padraig, and how fairs the wee fella with only a week to go to the dread of living under the skirt of a wife?"

"It'll be a large mug of stout for you, lad; it's building up you'll be needing."

These and other more ribald comments greeted Padraig as he and Sean entered Maloneys.

The tavern was full of farming folk, field hands, and the usual mix of evening drinkers. The good-natured banter was to be expected as both young men were very popular in the close-knit community and had shared both good and bad times with most.

Their father and grandfather stood at the bar in the middle of this rural mix and beamed with obvious pleasure as their offspring accepted the good-natured "abuse" as tradition bade.

"So, where is the good lady?" his father enquired.

"She will be along a little later as she is attending to Big Michael," replied his son. There was a moment of sadness as the memories returned to that terrible time.

"Come lads, tonight is for the craick; drink these." The barman handed the two young men their drinks. "We toast to the good times ahead, and let us leave behind the bad."

By the time Kathleen arrived at the tavern, all were

obviously the worst for the drink, but so thoroughly enjoying themselves, she accepted her share of the teasing and joined the other womenfolk watching with amusement, all agreeing that the morning would find some very sorry cases.

And besides, she was only too happy to be with her relations and friends to put the finishing touch to the wedding plans seven days hence.

But by the time Blind Hugh O'Neill started his fiddle and the pipes joined in, she was equally happy to pull Padraig to the dancing area and danced gaily to the infectious music the renowned musician played. Soon all the patrons were involved, and those not dancing stood and clapped to the tunes, and all nodded in unison that the couple were a perfect match.

And so, as the evening, or early morning to be precise, drew to a close, the tavern emptied, and staggering and walking sideways, the revellers attempted to make it home.

The clan Gallagher escorted Kathleen to her cottage and left Padraig to bid good night to his bride to be.

"This night one week hence, I will not be walking up that hill." He gestured toward his home. "I will be in your arms."

"My love," she whispered. "I have waited so long; I feel I can barely wait one more week. Now go, before I cause our good priest a stroke at confession if my desires become actions."

"My precious love, I will enjoy these next few nights knowing that they're my last nights alone, because as long as we both live, I can never again be parted from you. When we are husband and wife, I will live every moment with you with a love and devotion that words cannot describe. And nothing, I promise, with my very heart and soul, will ever separate us again."

After again kissing her good night, he left for his home, but felt a little disturbed as a cloud suddenly appeared in an otherwise cloudless early morn and passed over the moon, darkening the already approaching dawn.

By the time Padraig had jumped into bed, he was exhausted, but for some reason, he could not sleep.

The uneasiness he had been feeling of late was unexplainable. He had mentioned this to his mother, and while she stared thoughtfully at him for some time, she finally dismissed it as premarital nerves. It was common knowledge that his mother had "the gift," and certainly in those troubled times, many had sought her help to guide them through their unsettling experiences. It was also thought that these skills had been passed on to her son. Her forefathers had arrived from northern Spain, and certainly there had been a strong Romany influence from whence the knowledge of herbs and potions had been passed down. To her, it was completely normal that the sensitive nature of her firstborn was so apparent. She understood perfectly that when Padraig was training his dogs, they at times followed his unspoken instructions as if he simply willed them to do as he wished.

His brother, Sean, was as tall as Padraig, a towering six feet four inches, but he still needed to fill out. As a fisherman by profession, he always had a ruddy red complexion to match his shock of unruly red hair. Though much wilder by nature, he listened to and was strongly influenced by the talk of rebellion from his father and to a lesser extent, his grandfather.

The family, and in fact, all Catholics, greatly hated the unfair taxes and financial burdens placed on them and the rest of Ireland's tenant farmers. Most of the monies were paid to the absentee landlords living in ease in their castles and manors in England and Wales.

Sean, on his visits home from stints out at sea fishing, would throw his mother a selection of the catch and then sit with the older men of the family and their friends and talk for hours of the unfairness of their status.

Padraig, by contrast, had a live-and-let-live attitude.

But for all their diversity, the Gallagher family were exceedingly close, and none closer than the two brothers.

Padraig finally drifted off to sleep and awoke the following morn to witness the disaster that only well-deserved hangovers can create. Thanks to the intervention of Kathleen, he had not partaken to the extent of the others.

And when shortly after, Kathleen joined them to walk up to the village for Sunday Mass, he watched with great amusement as his mother Claire dished out the appropriate tirades to her sad and sorry menfolk.

"After the midday meal you, you, and you," she pointed to the grandfather, her husband, and her son Sean, "have to finalize the wedding arrangements. The food is to be organized, your best clothing put out for me to prepare, and no doubt, you will have already drawn off the best poteen the still can brew. Now off with you; the walk to the village will soon clear your thick heads."

And so the family, three stumbling, made their way to their weekly obligations to God and Father Sullivan.

The rest of the week passed very quickly, and prayers for a bright and sunny day for the wedding day were answered.

The usual panic in the house of the groom was evident in the household Gallagher. Claire was busily attempting the impossible, to arrange Sean's unruly red mop, and tending to the attire of her husband and his father.

Claire bemoaned, "Ah, now, why can't you all look as wonderful as Padraig?" which only brought the expected barrage of missiles and abuse directed at the smiling groom.

"'Tis spoilt through and through he is and the pet of his mother," Padraig the father joked, "and sure and all we will be glad to be rid of him to Kathleen. She can fuss all over him, and then maybe I can get some attention! Come, Sean, help me with the royal horse and cart for the queen of the house."

And so a little later, Father Sullivan greeted the family with a big grin. He seemed to be enjoying the traditional nervousness of the groom and the comforting support of his brother, the best man.

The little church was packed with well-wishers, the women looking to the entrance for the arrival of the bride, the men mostly wishing for it all to be over so they could start the revelry.

Padraig sat at the front with Sean, wishing for the prompt arrival of his bride.

Suddenly the oohs and ahs announced the arrival of Kathleen and her attendants.

Escorted by her proud father, Big Michael, who appeared much perkier than he had been of late, but still somewhat self-conscious, Kathleen walked down the aisle toward Padraig.

He swayed at the sight of her stunning beauty, and it was Sean who steadied him.

"Steady, brother!" he whispered. Although, he was also captivated by the wondrous sight of the bride as she approached them.

In a trance, Padraig heard the commencement of the service, and as the nuptial Mass continued, his eyes were constantly on the kneeling figure in white beside him.

Then, almost in shock, he realized the priest was beckoning him forward, and then he and Kathleen were standing before him. As he gazed at her while reciting his wedding vows and watching Kathleen repeat hers, he felt his heart beating inside him. *Could I possibly love her more than I do right now?* he thought.

Then Sean handed him the ring to place on his new wife's finger, and when they kissed for the first time as husband and wife, Padraig vowed once again that only death itself would separate them.

The happy couple left the church for their reception surrounded by the well-wishers, all eager to participate in the gaiety. Even in these troubled times, the generosity of their friends was evident. Sean and his fishing companions had provided ample seafood, the foreshore farmers had gathered baskets of shellfish, six butchered lambs cooked close to perfection, steaming potatoes and other assorted vegetables, and Paddy "the Poacher" and a couple of his cronies had "acquired" a sack of fine fat salmon.

All ate and drank copious quantities of ale, porter, and "the good stuff" provided from jars where each was proclaimed by the proud provider to be the finest poteen tasted for a long while.

And thus, the speeches and stories about the poor groom began to be more far-fetched and funnier as the afternoon wore on.

Afternoon stumbled into evening, and the tables were cleared to make way for the music and dancing. The blind fiddler commenced the proceedings by requesting the newlyweds to lead the first dance.

Padraig, with Kathleen in his arms, circled the floor accompanied by clapping and shouts of encouragement before others joined the floor. And so, the happy night drew to an end, but not before Sean arrived with a fine horse and trap to drive them to their home for their first night together.

With nodding smiles from the womenfolk and raucous comments from the men, Sean drove them off, homeward bound.

"What a day, my brother," Sean said with a hearty laugh. "Kathleen, this day will be talked about for years, the day my brother captured and tamed Kathleen McGuire!"

"Hush now, you old fool," she replied. "'Tis you that needs taming, and one day I will be the first to remind you as some poor lass drags you screaming to Father Sullivan."

And so the trap pulled up outside the cottage, and Padraig and Kathleen stepped down.

"Good night, my brother, and thank you for all you did

today." Padraig fondly hugged Sean, and he then accompanied Kathleen to the door.

Lifting her in his arms, he opened the door and carried her into the cottage. Her father was staying with the Gallaghers to ensure their wedding night privacy.

After he placed her on the bed, he knelt and kissed her tenderly. Her arms circled his neck and drew him to her.

"Oh, Padraig, I love you more than any woman could love any man."

As they undressed each other, Padraig eagerly and somewhat clumsily explored those places on her lovely body that he had only dreamed about.

As she guided him and he entered her the first time, he had hardly penetrated her when he unexpectedly exploded inside her. His head and whole body trembled with this newfound passion.

"Oh, my love, my love, my precious wonderful Kathleen," he gasped. "What was that?"

She held him tenderly. "Just the beginning of our new and joyous life together."

## Chapter 4

The rain poured down as it had been doing for the last three days. Robert Bolton was in a foul humour. The gout that plagued both him and his father hadn't eased since the rain had begun. And the expected arrival of Conrad Booth from Ireland had still not eventuated. News that transport from London to Colchester was delayed due to the weather meant little to the notoriously impatient nobleman.

It was well after midday before he heard the coach pull up outside the main doors of Blaxton Hall. Limping with the aid of sticks, he went to the hallway entrance just as one of the servants opened the door to let the travellers in.

"Where in cock-dribble have you been?" snarled the earl. "What kept you so long?"

"Ah! The bloody coach threw a wheel just south of Sudbury, and the road conditions between Sudbury and Lavenham slowed us even more," replied the smaller of the three. "But we are here now, a little damp and sorely in need of a fine brandy."

Conrad Booth stood smaller than five feet, but what he lacked in height was more than compensated with an animal cunning and a ruthlessly cruel nature that matched that of the earl, who he idolized.

Booth had discovered at an early age that he was not attracted to women; in fact, he despised them. And while his sexual preferences were obviously directed toward men, he also had a tendency toward much younger men and teen boys, and very occasionally, younger women.

Standing closest to him, one of his companions, by contrast, was a giant of a man.

Hair Baker, nicknamed because he had none, was more than Booth's protector. He loved the little man and was so devoted to Booth that he would do anything he asked without a second thought. It was rumoured that Baker had murdered more than twenty, all of his victims cut and battered beyond recognition. Baker had been an incredibly successful prizefighter, never beaten, and had a reputation of such cruelty that a lot of those he beat were incapable of fighting again, due to the damage inflicted on them in the ring. He was also Booth's lover.

The third, a cousin of Baker's, was known as Slow. Few knew his correct name and that same number cared. Slow, aptly nicknamed, had an intellect to match. The man was completely ignorant and very seldom spoke, but he possessed a brute strength that was often utilized for the more nefarious deeds instigated by Booth.

Soon they were seated in the study of Blaxton Hall with drinks in their hands.

"Now, what news do you bring from Donegal?" demanded Bolton. "What of the McGuire snip? Is she still as buxom and rare a beauty as her sadly departed sister?" he added with a snigger.

"Before I get to her," Booth answered, "I think your father should be made aware of the increasing tension among the tenants. Many are complaining about the last rent increases, and I've heard murmurings that some are planning to walk off the land."

"I say to hell with them and their complaints!" Bolton spat out. "Maybe a bit of discipline would not go amiss, perhaps a flogging here and there to show these bog-land swine who is in control. The lazy Irish bastards have food on their tables thanks to our generosity. We still allow them to practice their devil-inspired religion from Rome and that against the laws of England. They can still rut in their filthy hovels and give birth to more of their filthy offspring. What more do they want? In fact, a bit of castration here and there would not go amiss," he mused. "Now on that subject, what of the McGuire whore?"

"Before we left, she was preparing to wed that bastard whelp of the Gallaghers," Booth replied. "I told you we should have dealt to him back when you frolicked with the twin sister—him and his high and mighty family.

"You may recall the French Jew. Now there is another troublemaker. After you left for England, he started poking his long snout into the whore's death. He and the senior Gallagher fancy their investigative skills. They kept asking questions, eliminating so-called suspects until they were left with a list of those they claim could have had a motive or were in the area at the time. Needless to say, your name was mentioned on many occasions, as was ours." Booth indicated the other two.

"The fact these fools hate us worked in our favour, that and the greasing of the palms of the local heads of authority, who conveniently pointed out that we, the English gentry, don't meddle with local affairs and the business of the townspeople and farmers other than claiming a fair rent for their land."

The earl pondered these words for a while longer.

"Conrad," he said after several long moments, "I have had for some time now a plan that would increase our incomes considerably. But as you are aware, my father, greatly influenced by my saintly mother, who aspires to a heavenly reward, leans to a peaceable but less rewarding relationship with the Irish. You will agree a united enemy is always strong, but a divided force, each with its selfish agenda, is weakened by petty squabbles. By eliminating the stronger forces, the fools will fall back into line very quickly."

Booth nodded in agreement.

"By this, you intend the demise of the Gallagher family," he stated rather than asked.

"Very much so, and this will allow me the opportunity to taste the pleasures of a certain twin sister. Sadly, though, from what you say, she's been tarnished by the Gallagher whelp. Still, I suppose I have to be happy with one virgin from the family, and now, I'll have the added pleasure of watching young Gallagher witness his young wife entertaining this beast." He pointed to his crotch with a smirk. "This will create much amusement for us all. What say you, Hair, and you, Slow?"

Booth laughed cruelly. "Maybe there will be entertainment for me, also. Perhaps the young Gallagher will enjoy this." He made a crude gesture with his fist and arm.

"Now come, I thirst for the good Suffolk ale; let us be off to drink to our future at the Lavenham Swan. I need to wash away the taste of the Irish taverns."

Lady Constance Bolton watched them depart for the local village from her upstairs bedroom window. The frown on her face conveyed her feelings. She naturally had a mother's love and affection for her son, but she was becoming increasingly aware that much was being secreted from her.

Ever since Chichester had agreed to the transfer of much of Donegal farmland to her husband, which she thought had been extremely underpriced, she had had suspicions that all was not right. She had also been concerned about the somewhat unexpected return of her son from Donegal some time back, not to mention the many so-called business meetings being conducted behind the closed doors of the study. This in itself was strange, but more so the fact that she was not privy to the agendas, whereas her husband normally brought her up to date with the family business concerns.

And she certainly had a distinct dislike for the company her son kept. She also knew that this feeling was mutual, and so she would feign illness and avoid the family banquet later that evening.

## Chapter 5

The rain had not eased, and the three men in the study, nursing their brandies, pondered the weather for the foxhunt on the coming Tuesday.

"Damn the bloody rain! However, back to this damned Irish issue!" spoke the first. "You really do need to reiterate the importance of realizing a grand profit, but not at the risk of alienating the Irish farmers. Your son's bullying method of land management has caused some concern over there. My spies have alluded to a number of incidents that have raised concern among the authorities. Reports of a particularly nasty murder or two, quite out of local character, have them wondering what is afoot. Not for one minute am I suggesting that Robert is involved, but the company he keeps has raised eyebrows."

Thomas, the Lord of Blaxton, stared at his chief accountant. "I am more than aware of my son's worldly ways, if I may put it that way. He is certainly a young buck and somewhat immature, but his behaviour will improve as he grows older, and you yourself have shown me figures that suggest our Irish involvement in Donegal has proved to be an excellent investment. Certainly, my son's management skills are far superior to friend Chichester's business interests in Donegal. Now, let's you and I take a stroll to the banquet room; our new cook has promised a meal fit for our regal majesties, and my blasted foot promises slow progress.

While we wait for my son and his companions to return from Lavenham, why not leave this report for your new assistant to peruse while we choose and sample the wines for the evening."

The Chichesters had become the largest landowners in Ireland. By somewhat dubious means and encouraged by Queen Elizabeth's determination to anglicize Ireland, Sir Arthur Chichester had amassed a collection of estates and other lands in Antrim and Donegal. However, with the ongoing problems of insufficient capital and the difficulty of finding suitable tenants, these land investments had never reached their true worth. This situation worsened after the death of Chichester in 1625. Ongoing responsibility had been passed on to subsequent Chichester heirs based at Belfast Castle, but for varying reasons, there had been little change. In 1708, a fire had all but destroyed their home, causing the family to move to England, thus creating an absentee landlord situation in Donegal.

In 1802, the second marquis, George Augustus, returned to Belfast. A hopelessly inept businessman plagued with debt, he had fled to Ireland to escape his creditors. In the pursuing years, he failed miserably to create a profitable status with his estates. This, coupled with his spendthrift behaviour, only intensified his financial failings, causing him to have to raise additional capital. This situation had not escaped the attention of the Lord of Blaxton, and feigning sympathy and with cash in hand, he seized the opportunity to purchase land at a fraction of its worth, and that is how land in the vicinity of Killybegs down to just north of Sligo and surrounding Lough Erne fell into the coffers of Blaxton.

As to the cash paid, it was quickly squandered.

The assistant accountant, all too aware of the plight of the Irish farming tenants, read through the figures and was quietly saddened at the exorbitant profits his employer gained at the expense of the toils of the true owners of the land. It was bad, and he knew it was going to get worse.

It was true that the turnaround in profits had been due to the cunning business skills of the younger Blaxton and Conrad Booth coupled with their bullish management.

As the assistant accountant worked his way through the financial records, he saw more and more that certainly profits were far beyond fair and reasonable expectations. Furthermore, those who had created the success had given great cause for the Irish to hate the Bolton family.

With a sigh, he closed the ledger and left to join the party at dinner.

"Let us raise our glasses and toast our King!" Goblets were raised and quickly drained.

"A toast to good fortune, and long may good fortune favour us." The glasses were raised once more and emptied with relish.

"And now let me inform my good friends of my plans for future growth and prosperity," Lord Blaxton announced. "While I am most happy with our progress in Ireland, I and some of my learned colleagues are more than concerned with the attitudes of the tenants. We believe that a number of agitators are creating dissent. Already there are reports of troublemakers obtaining weapons, and there have been shooting incidents. The threat of exile means little to these animals. A trip to the penal colonies seems not to deter them."

"Father, my return to Donegal next month will soon settle any dissension among our Irish friends," Robert said. "My trio of colleagues and I . . . " he beckoned to Booth, Hair, and Slow, "have some persuasive techniques guaranteed to quiet those who are stupid enough to start trouble." A malicious smile crept across the face of Robert Bolton as he spoke.

"Yes, I agree," his father replied. "But I do object to breaking the codes of decency. To do so makes us equal to the lawbreaker. However, it is your responsibility, Robert; I have faith in you."

"Now, talk of the colonies brings me to the next topic I wish to discuss. Even if our business concerns in Ireland stagnate, there are opportunities opening on the other side of the world in the lands discovered and claimed for the crown by Captain James Cook. I understand that the lands over there are very rich and fertile, but occupied by the same type of simple, uneducated savages as the Irish—but these brown savages are unclothed, whereas the Irish, at least, do wear clothing. It is said that if you drop a pipe full of tobacco today, a fully ripened tobacco plant will be there tomorrow. While obviously an exaggeration, it seems to me that we should have title of some of this land, and all we have to do is go out there and stake claim to the fairest of these soils for ourselves."

Robert said, "Not we, Father—you. If you think I'm about to commence living onboard a rat-infested raft with sails for weeks on end just to socialize with a tribe of undressed natives in this strange land, you are mad. No, sir! Not me. Not under any circumstances."

Lord Bolton ignored his haughty son. He was used to his outbursts. More wine flowed and then the brandies, and so the conversations drifted from business to the more mundane. It was after two in the morning before each went to his sleeping quarters.

Well after breakfast had been served the following morning, the final meeting took place.

The dreaded gout had claimed two victims, and sore heads for the rest made the mood of the meeting not quite as jovial as the previous days' gatherings had been. However, the main points that had been discussed were re-emphasized.

Conrad Booth, Hair Baker, and Slow would travel to London to await the arrival of Bolton. His intentions were to interview "likely" recruits and then all would travel to Glasgow and by boat to Belfast. A coach would eventually transport them to the Blaxtons' manor in Donegal.

It was Booth, and only he, who caught the expression and smile that crossed Robert Bolton's face in anticipation of what the future would bring. He could not ignore the cold shiver that ran down his back.

## Chapter 6

Kathleen, humming a little ditty, tidied the kitchen area before taking a breakfast of eggs to her bedridden father. Her now much fuller figure suggested that the imminent birth of her first child was only a few months away. As the weeks of her pregnancy passed by, it seemed that Padraig's attentiveness intensified daily. His reluctance to leave her for his working day was obvious, as he left a little later each day.

"Hah, you lazy loiterer, be off with you," she would say, hiding a smile. "There's a new field to be sowed and peat to be dug. This bairn won't be coming along for a while yet. Now away you go."

Padraig had never been so content. The peak of the winter with its Atlantic harshness had passed. Each evening he would sit and watch his wife at the stir-about pot on the fire, delicious smells of simmering mutton, potato, and onions filling the room. Then after the meal, he would sit at the fireside, watching her knit, his two dogs by his side, usually with the bitch's head on his feet as she slept.

Hugo Cohen would brave the cold and spend at least one evening a week sharing the local gossip and insisting that Padraig practice his language skills.

Padraig had, in return, presented the Frenchman with the best pup from one of his bitch's litters, and the two were inseparable.

Hugo had also established a firm friendship with Hugh Porter, the new Bandara constable. In the past, the keepers of the peace had a reputation for corrupt and ineffective policing. However, somewhat prior to Robert Peel's introduction of the Peace Preservation Force in 1814, there were some with conscience who wished an end to lawlessness and who would in time become part of that force. Porter was one of those who strove to end the lawless element that thrived under British rule. Hugo had turned to Porter with his suspicions regarding the murder of Kathleen's sister, Bridget.

Hugo was devoted to Kathleen, and this was greatly pleasing to Padraig, but he never missed an opportunity for a friendly jibe. "You just keep that Gallic charm for the Donegal town maidens, you old frog eater. And you, young Kathleen, stop encouraging the rogue!" he would jest with the Frenchman.

Sometimes on these evenings, Padraig's parents, grandfather, and brother Sean would visit, and the nights would usually end in uproarious banter, resulting in Padraig fussing and insisting that the craick might harm the expectant mother and child.

This would then result in merciless teasing, usually instigated by Sean and encouraged by Kathleen.

These evenings would end with friends and family bidding farewells with their laughter and shouted good nights echoing down the road as they made their way home.

After their departure, Padraig would hold his wife close to him, listening as the sounds gave way to the silence of the night, feeling the beat of her heart next to his, loving her and holding her, and together in their night prayers, thanking those in the heavens for their blessings.

But of late, the young man could not shake the feeling and the hint of sinister happenings that would soon haunt them.

It was on the first day of March that Big Michael McGuire died.

Kathleen was devastated by her father's death. Padraig had never felt so helpless. Michael had faded badly near the end; he was nothing like the big, likeable man of his younger days. His passing was at least peaceful: he had simply fallen asleep not wanting to wake to another day.

While the women of the village did their best to console her, Kathleen's grief was so very evident. She had lost her mother. Her twin had died in unspeakable agony, and now her father had been taken from her.

Even at the wake, the men were unusually subdued. Their attempts to cheer the young Padraig went unrewarded. It would be weeks before normality returned to the young couple's lives. Some claimed it never did.

It was also on the first day of March that Robert Bolton returned to Donegal.

And almost a month later, the impact of his return was evident.

Claire Gallagher answered the urgent knocking at the door. She was greeted by three of the farmers from the next village some eight miles inland. The worried looks on their faces startled her.

"Is your husband in and his father?" enquired the first, obviously very agitated.

The absence of the normal friendly greetings at the door gave those first indications of concern to her. "Aye," she nodded, "come, come on in. Padraig Joseph, we have visitors."

Both the grandfather and son were finishing their midday meal, but rose quickly to welcome the newcomers.

"Paddy Joe, Bucky, and you, Billy Donahue, come sit. Claire, now there's a lass, fetch a brew of tea for our friends here."

As Claire left the room, the two Gallaghers saw the alarmed expressions on the faces of the three visitors.

"Padraig," Paddy Joe said, addressing both him and Kathleen.

"We have had a visit from the English landlord and his men. God help us, Padraig, but Bolton is raising the rents."

"What?" the older Gallagher exclaimed. "When did this happen? The rents are high enough as it is to be sure."

"Indeed, indeed," Bucky Malloy spoke. "The English bastard came to me after Paddy Joe's. They wish to raise the rent by five shillings. Surely to God it will cripple us."

"And you, Wee Billy Donahue, you also?" exclaimed the obviously shaken Padraig Joseph the Younger.

"Aye, Padraig, but it's six shillings they want from me and my brother."

The Donahue property was two fields bigger.

"Bolton told me that all the tenants in Donegal would have to pay the new rents or leave the land," Billy added. "Where would we go? What would we do? In God's name, what can we do?"

All were in shock. The future was now very uncertain. The five men sat shaken and pondering over this grave new threat to their livelihoods.

The stunned silence was interrupted by Claire returning with the tea. She had overheard the conversations, but she feigned ignorance. As she poured the tea, her husband informed her of the bad tidings, adding not only his concern for them, but also for their son and daughter and the new babe on the way.

"If those are the rents for our friends, what will our new rents be?"

That question was answered two days after the initial news broke. Word had quickly spread, but the Bandara farmers were yet to be visited.

The first of the swallows had arrived, also the house martins and the sand martins. The swooping, diving antics in their ever-long search for insects delighted Kathleen. Soon, last year's young would be diving down for clay to build new nests as the mating process began. Last year's little clay cups built under the eaves would soon house the chicks of the older birds returning to take up their traditional residence. She also loved the swifts yet to arrive, as they made a home in the roof, stumbling around with frantic squeaks somewhere under the thatch in their mating.

As she watched with the new spring morning sun warming her, she subconsciously rubbed the now very obvious swelling in her belly. So intent was her study of the birds that she was not aware of the arrival of the strangers until she heard the voices behind her.

Startled, she turned and was quite shaken to find five men approaching her at the rear of the cottage. An involuntary shudder passed through her as she recognized Robert Bolton. Her concern grew when she realized that one of his companions was Conrad Booth. The other three she did not recognise, but the fact that they were cronies of Booth suddenly terrified her.

"Well now, what do we have here?" Robert Bolton enquired. "If I'm not mistaken, it must be the young McGuire. It's married I understand we are these days—well, I certainly hope so," he sniggered. "What with that growing belly and all. I never did get the opportunity to offer my condolences to you regarding the very untimely death of your sister. Most tragic, I understand."

"What do you want . . . wh . . .why are you here?" Kathleen stammered, her frightened glance darting at the five smirking men.

"It's your husband we wish to speak to, is all," replied Bolton. "Now I wonder where he could be. Tell me, Hair, would you leave a sweet young thing like this all alone and unprotected? Who knows what harm could come to a fair lass these days."

Kathleen turned to the man Bolton had addressed.

He just stared at her. He didn't answer the question. He just stared. The brutish size of the man and his cruel ugliness suddenly terrified her.

Screaming, she turned and ran for the open back door of the cottage. Slamming the door behind her and dropping the latch, she collapsed in a cold faint.

Hearing horsemen leaving the cottage of her daughter-in-law, and knowing that her son was out in the fields planting, disturbed Claire so much that she quickly ran the short distance to their home. The front door was unlatched, and she burst through and into the kitchen. Horrified, she found the still body of Kathleen on the kitchen floor. Quickly snatching a cold wet cloth, she set about bringing the younger woman around. As Kathleen gradually came to, she recognized her mother-in-law and broke down into uncontrollable weeping.

When her husband returned home later that day, he was concerned to find his parents and grandfather waiting in the dining room.

Rushing into their bedroom, Kathleen, weeping in his arms, told Padraig of the happenings of the day. As he listened, Kathleen saw an expression pass over her husband's face that turned her blood cold. For the second time that day, she was terrified.

## Chapter 7

Patrick Seamus Maloney was a worried man. He was concerned about the news of the rent increases, first because of his genuine concern for the wellbeing of his clientele, primarily farmers or those whose income depended on the farming sector, but more importantly, his own income, which would be reduced rapidly if the spending power of his customers was reduced in any way.

Of the drinking establishments in Bandara, Maloneys was the most popular, certainly among the predominantly Catholic land workers.

He had gladly offered his large dining/reception area for the meeting organized by the rural people. He had even offered the first drink "on the house."

Padraig Gallagher the Older chaired the meeting, and Hugo offered his expertise to take notes and give input where required.

As each tenant spoke, it was soon apparent that every farmer on the Bolton land holdings had been approached by Robert Bolton and his men, and each tenant indicated that he had rent increases of at least five shillings and more for larger tenancies.

Each tenant that is, with the notable exception of the Gallaghers senior.

Padraig Gallagher was somewhat perplexed at this situation. "My grandson had a visit from them," he said with quiet concern, and quickly outlined the happenings of Bolton's visit, only hinting at the grief it had caused Kathleen and Padraig.

"I can only wonder why they have left us to the last," he added. He did not need to explain that collectively he and his son and grandson now working the McGuire land were by far the largest of the tenants. This was obvious knowledge.

It was wee Willy McHugh who shouted the first of the threats. Wee Willy was mostly a mild man when untroubled, but a total hothead when fired up.

"I says tell 'em to go to hell, them and all the accursed bloodsucking English. What can they do if we all stand united and refuse to pay?"

"Yes!" came roars of support, though notably from the imbibing section.

"Order, order!" Hugo yelled above the clamour. "There is merit in joint negotiation, but I suspect the 'noble' Bolton has not a charitable ear to listen," he added with a hint of sarcasm as the din died down.

"I agree with Hugo," Padraig the Younger spoke for the first time. He had been very quiet throughout the meeting. He was very curious and very concerned about why they had not had a visit from Bolton. He also was concerned that Bolton had called on his son's wife, but had left him and the grandfather alone.

"Perhaps we should all go home and talk to our families, talk among ourselves surely, but most important, let us not talk of rebellion, certainly not until we know the full situation. And maybe Bolton is open to negotiation."

Most agreed that was the most sensible suggestion to end the meeting, and the next was set down for that night the following week.

It was McHugh that the Weasel spoke to. "'Tis a little strange, don't you think, that the Gallagher clan is not asked to cough up the extra. I'm thinkin' maybe there's a favour or two being offered."

"What do you mean?" Willy McHugh replied. "The Gallaghers are with us. They also have as much to lose, if not more," he added, though for a moment the Weasel's words stopped him, but then he quickly dismissed them and walked out.

Sean Gallagher had arrived home from Killybegs on the following Thursday evening. Friday being the traditional fish day, he had brought with him a sack of freshly caught cod. Normally this treat was eagerly awaited, but as the family sat to eat, a sombre air descended on the table.

The family brought him up to date with the news of the meeting, and he was quite shocked and puzzled as to what it all meant. "Why not all join forces and tell the English to go to hell?" was his first reaction.

"Just tell the bloodsucking Bolton none of us can afford the increases. Surely, Grandfather, can't you explain to him that people will end up starving, and some will lose their homes?"

"Apart from scaring Kathleen half to death at our home, they have not been near us," his brother explained. "We expect a visit from them any day now, and until then, there is very little we can do or say. We don't need the worry, what with Kathleen due to have our child any day now."

Sean gave his sister-in-law a comforting smile. "Ah, now, surely you frightened the divil out of them. They are running for mother England to be sure." He winked at her, and his infectious smile made her giggle.

The mood was gloomy, but Sean always had a way to brighten the family, and as he talked of the recent journeys out into the Atlantic and their luck with the fishing, the sadness began to diminish.

And then with the meal over, it was time for the three land-working Gallaghers to begin the planning of the next day's work in the fields in preparation for the rest of the spring sowing.

## Chapter 8

Judge Herbert Throckmorton Squires belched, hastily trying to smother the discretion with a handkerchief. The extremely overweight judge had sat at the bench in Donegal Town for the last three years. His gluttony and love for good wine and expensive brandy had caused him some financial embarrassment at his home in Portsmouth. His long-suffering wife had almost, with some relief, found him in extremely uncompromising circumstances with two dockside harlots. Her family, independently wealthy, had persuaded, perhaps advised, the good judge that his legal skills could be better utilized elsewhere, in fact, anywhere other than the greater Portsmouth region.

And so Squires, heeding their good advice, had moved. By utilizing contacts and calling in past favours, he had eventually met Thomas Bolton, who had arranged his transfer to Donegal.

Robert Bolton and Conrad Booth sat opposite the judge, and when the plates had been cleared from the dinner table, Bolton produced his financial papers.

"It is most important that you understand the situation regarding the tenancies," he began. "You will see from these figures that with the increase of the rents, the overall profits will increase considerably. Now, within these increases, I am able to pass £110,000 into my own personal coffers. However, while this personal profit taking can be easily hidden and not detected, any unfavourable reaction from the tenants could start some busybody looking closer into my dealings."

Bolton waited for a reaction. The judge's eyes gave the signal that Bolton and Booth had been hoping for. Squires's need for money and his avaricious nature played into their hands to perfection. Bolton had no intention of giving the true figure of the monies he intended to misappropriate, but he knew the greedy judge had already figured out what was to be his share of the £110,000.

"Now for my plan to succeed without any hitches, I have set certain procedures in place. And I will need some assistance from your good self from time to time."

He knew there was no need to remind Squires of favours rendered. The judge was only too well aware that Bolton's manipulation had made possible his current status, and only Bolton could end it. Also, the possibility of further riches gave him a pleasant inner glow.

"Whatever assistance I can give is already given," the judge replied, beaming. "There is no need to ask."

"I do indeed thank you. Now here is the outline and my concerns as to the success of the operation." Bolton sat back comfortably and started to spell out his scheme.

"As you are aware, the Irish have a history of rebellion. Most times these uprisings have met with the obvious conclusion. Always they have been started with some deep-rooted grudge and stirred up by some hothead wanting to create a reputation for himself.

"This situation is no different. I have increased the rents to a point where the payments can be met, but they will give precious little in the way of extras. Oh yes, they are affordable, despite what these ignorant peasants claim. They will be able to eat and sleep and have a pint at the tavern, but will have nought left for other spending."

After a weighty pause, Bolton smirked and added, "Like all the other animals, I will allow them to eat, sleep, shit, and rut!" He waited for their appreciative laughter at his joke before continuing.

"Now I come to the question of rebellion. There is only one family with enough intelligence and standing in the communities to unite the farmers. The family Gallagher is respected and has such a following in their communities that they could easily cause us problems, and by that, I mean very serious problems.

"Should the troublesome element within the family start resentment and build from it, I have an answer for them. Even if they don't start trouble in the near future, there is always the possibility they could in the times ahead. I have an answer for that, also, don't I, Booth?" He turned to the smaller man with a malicious smirk on his face.

"I think it would be fair to state that you have a solution to any who dare to cross you," Booth answered, looking pointedly at the judge.

At that, Bolton stood, gathered his papers, and prepared to leave. To the judge he said, "My good friend, I feel we will be delivering some tasty morsels for your judicial entertainment in the not too distant future. I know that you will treat all in kind, bringing swift and appropriate retribution to those stupid enough to stand in my way, and of course, in the way of true English justice and the traditions of our beloved country."

Judge Squires walked out with Bolton and Booth and bade them farewell. He then climbed the creaky stairs to his private room on the first floor. He poured himself a large brandy and watched the two men as they walked down the street to where their driver stood waiting by their carriage.

"Buffoons!" he snarled. "Do they truly think for one moment that I am not privy to their little games?"

He gazed out toward the Atlantic, deep in thought, pondering the inevitable. Then, as if expecting the brandy bottle to reply, he poured another few inches into his empty glass and mused aloud as he watched Bolton and Booth climb into the carriage and disappear from sight.

"In all of history, we've read of those unfortunates who sat meekly under the strong arm of the tyrant until such time as they decide they have nothing to lose.

"Robert Bolton, I see much trouble ahead of you. One day the Irish will find that they have nothing to lose, but oh so very much to win. Watch where you step, young man!"

## Chapter 9

The Atlantic Inn at Killybegs overlooked the beautiful bay and out to the Atlantic Ocean. Sean Gallagher and four of his friends, all fishermen, had just entered the bar to celebrate their arrival from three days at sea. The catch was a good one, and the split after the skipper's take ensured all would take home a fair wage for their families. While the weather had been fair and the seas kind, the work of bringing in the laden nets was heavy going and fit for only the hardiest. All five were tired, but happy and anticipated the pleasure of quenching a hard-earned thirst.

"Well, lads, an ale for each of you," Joseph John the barkeep smiled as he pulled off the last and placed the foaming jug in front of Sean. "'Tis a fine afternoon you've brought back with you and all and tell me of the catch. Is there a small fish for a struggling old man and me with seven mouths to feed?"

"Away with you, you randy old bugger, if you would keep that big fish of yours behind the buttons of your breeches, you'd have no need to worry the likes of us." Sean laughed, throwing a sack over the bar at the barman's feet. "Anyway, these are for your long-suffering wife; tell her I've gutted and cleaned them, and don't dare take the credit for yourself. I wouldn't wish you to get unfair moonlight rewards. You may well end up with another mouth to feed."

And so, as the cheerful banter carried on until well after dark, other fishermen entered and joined the good humour of the now crowded bar.

Most were so occupied with drinking and swapping tales about fish caught or those that got away that the arrival of the three newcomers went largely unnoticed.

One of the three paid for drinks and sat with the other two at the side of the bar.

"That's the one, there!" stated Hair Baker. He nodded toward Sean standing with his friends at the bar.

"Big bastard, i'n't 'e," one of the other two muttered. The second simply grunted.

"True, but he shouldn't be too much trouble; there's three of us."

"He'll go out and take a piss soon; we can get him then," said Slow, but his voice rose at the end, as if he were asking more than telling.

"Perhaps we could also get him after closing," Gypsy Joe "The Blade" Mandino added.

Both Baker and Slow plied their profession with their fists and boots. Gypsy Joe preferred the knife. All three were paid well for their nefarious deeds. They were professionals and were extremely proficient and rarely failed when required to carry out instructions. Their instructions that night were to hurt Sean Gallagher.

By ten thirty that evening, most were well unto their ales and starting to feel the effects. Sean staggered slightly, hiccupped, and slowly made his way to the door. He did not notice the three behind him.

He clumsily fumbled with his buttons, and finally, with a certain amount of pride, watched the great arc rising and splashing over the well-watered weeds at the back of the bar.

He would only vaguely remember later the crushing blow that felled him.

Aware that others would obey the calls of nature, they set to work with urgency.

As he fell, Slow and the Gypsy caught him and held him as Baker piled fist after fist into Sean's unprotected body. He smiled a grim smirk of satisfaction at the sound of cracking ribcage. As Sean fell, the boots went in. The punishment lasted only minutes, but incredible damage had been meted out.

Before others came to the rear of the bar, the three had slunk off into the night.

It was Joseph John who first noticed his friend missing.

"Hey, did Sean go home?" he yelled to the others above the barroom din. "The drunken sot didn't even say good night."

"Nah, he just went out to piss," came the reply.

"He's been a while; maybe he needed to squat," another guffawed.

A shout from the street, however, altered those opinions. As they rushed outside, Sean's comrades were truly shocked when they saw the carnage. He was lifted and carried with great care into the bar.

"Shit, what the hell happened?"

"Get back! Give him air!" Joseph John called out, rushing from behind the bar and nearly throwing up at the sight. He hardly recognised Sean.

"My God, what happened?" he exclaimed. "Bring him through here."

They carried the still form into the lounge and laid him on a couch.

"Quick, rush up and bring back Doctor Reilly," Joseph John shouted, "and for God's sake, don't touch Sean until the doctor gets here."

The din from the bar faded as the word spread, and many concerned faces peered into the room where Sean lay.

A short time later, a muted silence greeted the doctor, who was quickly ushered into the room where the bloodied and still form of Sean Gallagher lay. Peering through spectacles perched at the end of his nose, he quietly examined the injuries.

After several long minutes, he finally spoke. "How did this happen?" He looked from face to face, waiting for an explanation.

Paddy Finnan accepted the role of spokesman and explained that all was as one would expect as the fishing boats returned with the men enjoying the fruits of a good catch and spending accordingly. He recalled Sean going outside to relieve himself, but he and no other could shed any light as to the assault.

Later, Joseph John mentioned to the constable that among the crowd in the bar were three Englishmen, but in truth, he could not identify them as the assailants.

The sun had well and truly risen by the time Doctor Reilly had concluded working on his patient. Sean had not stirred apart from a long, deep moan twice during the night. The expert hand of the doctor had located at least four broken ribs. He was most concerned about damage to lung and kidneys, but could find no obvious evidence. The jaw was cracked and the nose broken. Both eyes were completely blackened and bruised to such an extent that Sean knew he could not open them for a day or two. Both shoulders were dislocated. Fortunately, the doctor was able to put them back in place without too much trouble due to Sean's state of unconsciousness.

Doctor Reilly was most concerned about damage to the brain, but would have to wait until Sean regained consciousness to fully examine him and conclude his opinions.

Strangely, Sean had lost no teeth, and the doctor presumed that the kicking to the head had occurred with the face pushed into the turf.

Finally, exhausted, Doctor Reilly turned to Joseph John, who had assisted with strong coffees and a few small meals throughout the night. "Whoever did this is very skilled in the pugilistic sport. From what I can gather, the assault was completed in less than five minutes. Either the assailants were waiting outside, or they followed him out. Either way, their dirty work was very quickly accomplished. And it would appear mostly without too much noise to attract unwelcome attention. It would also seem that whoever were the culprits, they disappeared without trace. Frankly, this is the work of one or probably more who knew precisely what they were doing. These were professionals. The obvious question is who and why?"

Joseph John's mind was racing back over the evening. "I know most of the people who were here last night. None ever had a bad word for Sean. Certainly none I know would have done that to him. Sure, there is always a fight or two, but always a drink and make up afterward. And none would be stupid enough to pick a fight with Sean. They know he could beat them all, two or three at a time, to be sure."

"Then all I can conclude," Doctor Reilly stated, "is that someone or more had other motives and skills to be able to inflict the damage on the lad to the extent they did. I will have to ask you, Joseph John, is it all right with you if I leave Sean as he is? I don't want to move him. Just leave him until he comes around. Send for me the moment he stirs."

Joseph John replied with unashamed emotion. "Thank you, doctor. I know I speak for us all. Sean will not be disturbed, and I know you will fix him. And when he is fully recovered, you will not be called to fix those who did this. I promise you! You will not be called!"

## Chapter 10

The donkey pulled up outside the Gallagher home, and Paddy Finnan jumped down from the cart. Being a seaman, he was most unhappy on the back of a donkey.

Claire spotted him walking up the path and summoned her husband.

"Padraig Joseph, look, is this not Paddy Finnan?" She couldn't suppress the note of alarm in her voice. "Now what could be bringing him here so early in the morning?"

She had opened the door before Paddy could knock.

"Hey, there, and if it's not Paddy Finnan!" Padraigh the Younger greeted the visitor. "What brings you from Killybegs? How goes the fishing? And where's Sean?" He looked out to the cart. Receiving no answer, he said, "Come in, lad, where are our manners. A mug of tea you'll surely be wantin'."

"Thank you, Padraig Joseph, a tea will do fine." Paddy took a deep breath and said, "Claire, Padraig Joseph, I am sorry to be the bearer of bad news." He sighed and took a seat, and then he poured out the story of the night before.

The shocked family listened in silence.

"I can take you back to Killybegs with me. While you get ready, I will go over to talk to your son, Padraig, and Kathleen. I know they will want to be with Sean when he comes 'round."

Fortunately, Padraig was still at home when Paddy arrived

and was stunned to hear the news of his brother.

"My love, you go with Paddy. Go quick—I will stay," Kathleen said, clearly very concerned. "I will wait here until you return. I fear for the baby on the cart ride."

As the two young men went to join the others, Paddy went into greater detail with Padraig.

"If my brother does not recover . . .?" The hooded threat silenced as they approached his mother. She saw the expression on the face of her son and felt a cold shudder pass down her back.

The journey back to the coast went mostly in silence. Each deep in thought, their fear for Sean was obvious to Paddy, who respected their concerns and concentrated on getting the most speed he could from the donkey.

Finally, they pulled up outside the inn, jumped off, and raced into the bar where Joseph John met them and silently led them in to the side of the couch where Sean lay.

Claire involuntarily burst into wracking sobs at the sight of her son. Her husband, equally shocked, held her tight, supporting her. Padraig the Older could hardly believe the condition of his grandson.

"Who could possibly do this?" He looked over at his other grandson, who stood absolutely still, color draining from his face. His fists clenched tighter and tighter until the muscles stood out on his arms.

As the morning passed, each sat in silent vigil by Sean's side.

One by one, the Killybegs villagers came and offered their support to the family, all vowing that none would truly rest until the perpetrators were apprehended.

It was nearly three o'clock that afternoon when Sean stirred. His first sight was of his grandfather and brother seated by his side. Claire was asleep exhausted upstairs, her husband comforting her.

Joseph John quickly sent a messenger to the doctor, who arrived shortly thereafter.

Obeying his instructions, the others left the room, allowing him to concentrate on his work. Whether it was the skill of the doctor or the strength and determination of his patient, no one dared guess—probably both! However, Sean suddenly mumbled something and moved his head.

The doctor placed a clean wet rag against his battered lips, and Sean's tongue searched urgently for liquid. Holding his head on a slight tilt, the doctor dribbled drops of water into his mouth. Easing his head back, the doctor watched with satisfaction as Sean slipped back into a deep sleep.

He stood and beckoned the family into the room. "It is still far too early to speculate, but I suspect your lad is fighting his way back to recovery."

Padraig knelt by his brother and kissed him lightly on his forehead, and holding his hand gently, whispered in Sean's ear. "My brother, I am here. If you can hear me, bear witness to this pledge. I will find whoever is responsible for this, and I swear on the suffering you are enduring that I will make them pay. There will be retribution. I will make somebody pay!"

Before he could rise to his feet, Padraig felt a slight pressure as he held Sean's hand in his. He knew then that his brother would recover, and he gave a comforting light squeeze in return.

The family gathered outside, Padraig gladly accepting a ride back home to be with Kathleen and inform her of the tidings. The remainder of the family preferred to stay with Sean in case there was a change for the worse.

*****

Robert Bolton was in great humour that morning. "There's

nought to beat a hearty breakfast with good company and great news. Tell us again, Hair; tell us how that first hit felt. And he went down the first time—ah, if only I was there. The cocky big bastard won't be strutting for a month or two, eh!"

Hair, with his limited speaking skills, gave a description of the brutal assault the night previous. With occasional interjections from his thug colleagues, Bolton was satisfied that his task had been completed.

"Now, Booth, tell me. What news of the Weasel? Pray tell me if the skulking little vermin has done as we told him."

Booth gave Bolton the information required.

"Well, I suggest matters are well in control," Bolton said with smug satisfaction, "and we can now wait and see what our Irish tenants do next."

Doctor Reilly was truly amazed. Not a week had passed, and Sean had recovered sufficiently to be transported back to his family home. And thanks to the fussing of his mother and an everlasting supply of good Irish broth, he was soon able to rise from his bed and walk unaided.

He was not able, however, to attend the next tenants' meeting and was content to remain home and be spoilt by the attention of his mother and sister-in-law.

Prior to the commencement of the meeting, the news of the attack on Sean had spread, and all had enquired as to his wellbeing. Their concern lightened as Padraig informed them of the special attention his brother was receiving. Feigning jealousy, he told outrageous tales, exaggerating the recovery while masking his true feelings.

His instinct told him the attack and the reasons for that night's meeting were linked, and he did not want his concern to show. And when Hugo announced the commencement of the meeting, the news that followed did little to alleviate that concern.

Virtually all of the farmers closer to Letterkenny had been visited by Bolton and Booth and told in no uncertain terms to pay the increases or expect the worst. What the "worst" entailed, they had no idea, but they knew that the future would be bleak.

As each tenant spoke of his encounter with the English landlord, the clamour increased, and Hugo had to continuously call for order.

"Silence!" he finally roared, having had enough.

After the din abated, he spoke again. "You are all obviously very upset and concerned about your futures. But all this shouting and yelling gets us nowhere. Now let us quietly look at the facts, as we know them. First, the law is on the side of Bolton. As the properties belong to him and his family, he can charge what he wishes. Regardless of any outcomes, whether beneficial or otherwise, you have a choice: You can agree to pay, or you can walk away from your farm. Should you refuse to pay, you invite the consequences.

"I cannot nor will not advise you to stand in refusal. However, should you wish to do so, you must stand undivided. Together in unity, you may persuade the Boltons to see reason. If not, your combined strength may undermine his desire to pursue further action.

"Now I suggest you quietly form groups and discuss these conclusions. You may wish to vote any outcomes. And you will need to choose a leader." With that, Hugo sat down and the groups began to form.

Padraig the Older sat with him and watched the groups and at times listened in on the animated discussions. "Hugo, my friend, I am extremely worried," Padraig said. "The talk of rebellion grows. Even my own son is talking of defiance. My old bones are just not up to all this madness."

"Yes, these are worrying times. You do know that the blasted Englishman will not relent, and he has the judge in his pocket and some particularly nasty henchmen to do his dirty work. It could well have been his doing that caused young Sean's injuries, but for what reason, I don't know."

Their musing was cut short as the groups started to break up, and Willy McHugh stood and called out. "We have all had our say, Hugo; we now wish to advise you of our decision."

"What is your will, then, men?" Hugo said and sighed in weary anticipation.

"The proposal is to stand united against the ruling of the landlord."

"So be it. My final advice to you all then is as follows. First, elect yourselves a person you trust to be your leader and spokesperson. Second, and most important, any further decisions must be jointly made and agreed to. Finally, follow and obey the instructions of your elected leader.

"If there is nothing further to add, I propose this meeting closed until this night week. That will give you all an opportunity to think about who you wish to lead you. When we meet again, that election will then take place.

"May God guide you in your choice, and I pray he will protect us all."

## Chapter 11

A slight breeze stirred the branches of the tree outside their bedroom window. Claire turned over again, trying to get back to sleep without disturbing her husband snoring peacefully by her side. Padraig and his father had returned from the farmer's meeting obviously very worried about the turn of events, but she had sensed a feeling, almost of elation, as if her husband welcomed the opportunity to stand against the unfair demands of Bolton.

She was very much aware of his feelings regarding the Boltons, and in fact, the English in general, and while she understood the reasoning behind the hatred, she had tried to teach toleration to both her sons and a sense of understanding that not all those on the other side of "the water" were cut from the same cloth. And while Sean was adamant that all the English were the bastards from hell, Padraig was much more prepared to learn and understand the variances of different nationalities.

Long before Robert Bolton had arrived in Donegal, his father, Lord Thomas Bolton, and Lady Constance had visited their new land holdings. During their stays, Claire had met them both, and although their conversations were infrequent, she found Lady Constance to be a lady of good humour, who had a kindness about her that belied the locals' perception of the English gentry.

Robert Bolton, however, had only confirmed to all once more

that the English were not to be trusted. He had destroyed any good relations his parents may have formed. Claire certainly disliked the younger Bolton, and her deep inner senses had warned her of the depraved nature lurking behind the sneering and confident countenance of the man. She strongly suspected a link between him and the murder of Bridget McGuire. Furthermore, she recognised the aura of evil emanating from the man and could only expect the worst from him and what was yet to come.

The bleating of sheep, disturbed by the passing of a fox through the meadow, stirred her again, and she felt for the comforting reassurance of the Rosary beads. After some minutes of praying to the Virgin Mother, she finally succumbed to sleep.

The early morning fog had still not lifted. Padraig the grandfather had risen and stoked up the coals and warmed himself while his son and Claire slept on. The old collie beside him, warming by the fire, watched with one eye as the old man filled his pipe and puffed contentedly. Satisfied all was well, the dog sighed and went back to sleep.

"Hey, wake up, you lazy old beggar, let us walk on over and see if my grandson is awake yet."

Together, the old man and his dog ambled up the field and over to the cottage, taking the longer route, not noticing the two horsemen riding toward the family homestead.

Claire had heard the back door of the farmhouse close and the dog bark excitedly at the prospect of stealing a morsel from the dogs next door. Deciding to rise and let her husband sleep longer, she pulled some warmer clothing over her and walked into the living room. Eerily, the mist had just parted a little as she peered through the window to the path leading to the road. A cold shudder went down her back. Sitting silently in their saddles staring at her were two men. The mist closed, and they disappeared.

She ran into their bedroom. "Padraig, Padraig, wake up. I

# SAVAGE Sympathy

think we have visitors."

Her husband stirred. "What is it, woman?" he grumbled. "Can you not let a poor man sleep?"

While gathering his clothing, he noticed the shocked look on his wife's face, and the first instincts of alarm brought him fully awake. "Who are the visitors?" he asked, although he felt he knew.

The not at all friendly hammering on the door confirmed his worst suspicions. Robert Bolton had arrived.

Padraig Joseph opened the door. The two Englishmen stood there.

"Good morning, I trust this early call has not inconvenienced you?" one of them said.

Claire heard her husband's reply. "Not at all! It is early, but I am sure we can offer you a hot drink of tea. Please, will you kindly come in. Claire, it is our landlord himself come calling. Prepare some tea for us all."

Claire watched with trepidation as the two men followed her husband into the room.

Padraig saw his grandfather walking over the field to join him. Always an early riser, he was keen to feed his dogs and commence the training on the younger pups. His reputation as a dog trainer had spread wide, and while he hated parting with his young dogs, he knew his training guaranteed the buyers a dog of excellent pedigree that was good with the sheep.

His grandfather watched with pride as his grandson whistled and called and the dogs obeyed his every command. As he walked up, the animals ran over to him, barking and scrambling for the treats he had brought with him.

"Grandfather, you undo all the hard work I have put in this morning," he joked with obvious affection. "Just look at this lot. You spoil them rotten, now they won't obey a word I tell them."

"Kathleen," he called out. "Look who's here!"

His wife, who had also heard the barking and realized the grandfather was there, came out and attempted to hug him.

"Now, now, careful there. We don't want any harm done to you and the baby, do we?" Padraig the Older said teasingly.

She gave him a kiss on his cheek. "I have never felt healthier, Grandfather; indeed, and I need to be, looking after himself there, running after him, doing the cooking and washing. It never stops, and now I suppose I will have to rush off and feed the both of you."

Together, arm in arm, the three walked over to the back door, Kathleen giggling with enjoyment at the attention she was receiving.

They had only just sat down to drink their tea when the front door burst open, and Claire rushed in.

"Mother, what . . .?" Padraig said, but he couldn't get another word out.

"They are here!" she gasped. "Robert Bolton and that other horrible one! They are talking to your father, please both of you, come, come quickly. Kathleen, I'm sorry to startle you, I'm so frightened. Please, quickly, come quickly."

Rising, the two men followed Claire to the door.

"Please stay here, Kathleen," Padraig said to his wife. "I will be back as soon as possible. Do not worry—I will not be too long at all."

Grandfather and grandson walked over to the farmhouse and went into the living room. The three men who were seated there, waiting, as if they had all the time in the world, looked up when they arrived.

"Father, Padraig, come, sit! I think you already know our visitors. This is our landlord, of course, and this is Conrad Booth. Gentlemen, my son and my father." Padraig indicated to the newcomers. "And of course, this is my wife Claire."

After a moment of silence, Robert Bolton cleared his throat and spoke.

"You have little or no doubt as to why we are here. You are, of course, aware of our visits to the other farmers, and you well know of the increases in rent. But why did we leave you to last?" He looked at each in turn. "I have a proposition I need to discuss with you. I hope you will find the following beneficial to us all."

Claire stared at Bolton. The aura of evil that she had so readily noticed earlier was almost overpowering as it circulated throughout the room.

Bolton's disarming smile did little to reassure her that his intentions were honourable or honest, and while his charm and manners were obvious, she was aware of his devious background and knew not to believe or trust a single word he uttered.

"I know and fully understand your dislike of the English and the tenancy agreements regarding your traditional farming lands, but there is little I can do to alter the situation; however, I can offer a solution to ease the burden in your case." Bolton watched them all closely.

"I am aware that there is a meeting in a few days' time to elect a person to lead a group of dissidents. First, let me strongly assure you that I will not tolerate any who oppose or disobey my rulings, and secondly, I will destroy any who attempt to do so. However, if this supposed leader were to take a more understanding role in his responsibilities and strive to create a harmonious relationship between the tenants and myself, then I would respond in kind."

A nervous silence was the expected reaction.

Bolton continued. "Now, let us take this further. If, for example, you, Padraig Joseph, or you," he nodded toward the older Gallagher, "were chosen as the leader, would you have the blood of your comrades and friends on your conscience? Would either one of you instigate a decision that would create certain swift and merciless retribution to those involved? Or would you suppress the talk of rebellion and seek a much safer alternative?"

Padraig Joseph turned to Claire. "Wife, would you please take warm milk up to Sean and see to his care."

In the ensuing silence, Padraig Joseph stared at the ceiling of the room. As soon as Claire had gone to attend to Sean, he turned first to his father, then to his son, and then he spoke to Bolton in a low and deliberate tone.

"I have no idea who will be elected. I cannot speak for my son or my father, but I will swear now, on the deaths of my ancestors, that if I am chosen, I will do all I can to achieve a life of fairness and decency for ourselves and our comrades. I also suggest to you and your kind to think again if you feel that you can keep us, the Irish, downtrodden and the simple lackeys of the English. If the time for rebellion is ripe, then you have nobody to blame but your selfish, greedy, and uncompromising selves. No, Robert Bolton, I would never take a safer road. I, Padraig Joseph Gallagher, proud son of my father, am not a coward. I do not and will not ever stoop to accept the treacherous hand of an Englishman in any arrangement, business or friendship. You, Bolton, and this devil's carrion with you, leave my home now. If your shadow or that of your hirelings ever darkens my land or that of my family again, it will be the last time. Now go!"

Bolton stood, his face a seething mask of fury. Without taking his eyes off Padraig, he said, "Come, Conrad, we are not welcome or worthy in a house of fools."

As they walked from the house, Bolton turned and shouted back at the Gallaghers. "Walk with care, all of you. What happened to your fish-stinking son of his mother whore was a warning, your first and your last. Do not give me cause to return.

If and when I do, there will be no pleasantries. And as you do not appreciate my generosity, take notice, you are now liable for the tenancy rent increases."

He and Conrad mounted their horses and rode away.

## Chapter 12

Padraig lay in bed, feeling Kathleen's breath in his ear as he held her in his arms. The events of the morning had shaken him, and he did not want to distress her with the full knowledge of the contents of the conversations, particularly so close to the birth of their child.

"I can feel our baby kicking," he murmured to his wife. "He will surely be a fine big lad."

"You mean the kicking of our new daughter?" Kathleen giggled.

"Oh, to be sure, it will be myself who will be the slave to two demanding witches should that be the case."

"Oh, and it's a witch I am now, is it?"

"Indeed, you set up magic and stole my heart and soul when I wasn't looking."

"And what magic did you use to steal mine then, Padraig Gallagher?"

"My sweet, sweet precious love, no magic could ever capture one so beautiful as you. I could love none as I love you. I would count the grains of sand on our shores in despair if I were to lose you. Nothing would have any meaning in my life. My life would have no purpose . . ." He paused, thinking, and then not wishing to continue on those dire thoughts.

"Tush, my silly man. I am here and will be until I am an old

# SAVAGE *Sympathy*

hag, and it's well rid of me then, you will be wishing. Now let me give you a butterfly kiss and hold me off to sleep."

Her long dark eyelashes lightly whispered against his cheeks. He smiled in complete contentment. So very deep in love, they fell asleep in each other's arms.

Claire Gallagher also lay in her husband's arms. She, however, was not content. Claire was extremely worried. While his snores indicated a deep untroubled sleep, she knew that her husband's outburst and threats earlier that day had severely inflamed the serious conditions concerning their community, and the trouble that would follow would have long-lasting repercussions. The dreams that had been causing her distress in recent nights now threatened to be real, and instead of lacking substance, the patterns and the dark sinister apparitions now held great fear for her wellbeing and the safety and future of her family.

While trying to confide in her confessor, the good priest had simply dismissed her concerns as mere superstitions and had admonished her to trust in God and put away such dangerous works of the devil. "To help cleanse these thoughts, pray part of a Rosary for your penance. Go in peace, my daughter." And with that, he was on to the next confessor.

But peace was far from Claire's mind. She wondered what Bolton was planning and what would be the reaction to the happenings of that morning. Finally, she drifted off into a troubled slumber.

Bolton crept quietly up the stairs and entered their bedroom. He ran the blade over his open palm feeling the keenness of the cold steel before he silently sliced the skin, causing a thin slash of blood. His tongue caressed the scarlet flow as his lips lightly touched the blade.

Standing over Claire Gallagher, he raised the knife to plunge it deep into the sleeping woman's unprotected bosom.

As the knife started its deadly descent, a flash of moonlight lit up the room. Claire opened her eyes and screamed.

Padraig Joseph awoke at once and sat upright, peering into the darkness. Turning to his wife, he held her shaking body, realizing she had been dreaming, but suddenly afraid for both of them.

"Please, I beg you, my husband! Let us leave here at once. Wake up Sean and Padraig and Kathleen. We must all leave now. We can go to Dublin, to my cousin. Please, please, I implore you."

"Hush now, enough of this talk of leaving. This is our land. No bloody land-stealing Englishman will take what is rightfully ours."

"Padraig Joseph, please listen! Bolton intends to kill us all. His pride will not allow him to overlook yesterday. No land is worth the loss of my loved ones."

"Claire, you have had a bad dream. We can talk about this in the morning. Sure and it will all be different in the day."

But no amount of talk or consoling would calm Claire. Deep down in her soul, she knew that she and her family were doomed. It was just a question of when.

The farmers gathered for the election meeting. The Gallagher menfolk had arrived, certainly against the wishes of Claire. Padraig and Kathleen had been told of the dream, and while concerned, both had dismissed it, although Padraig did have some misgivings because he shared his mother's Celtic instincts. However, he was certain that his faith in family, strength, and the deep bond that held them together would stand firm against all opposition.

Word of the confrontation had spread rapidly. Some were secretly pleased that at last the Gallagher family had been brought in line with the rest. But all were concerned at the threats to the family. And while most agreed that unity would repel any opposition to their livelihood and way of life, there were some who were secretly frightened and wished for a safer solution.

"Again, let me impress on you all the importance of choosing your spokesman wisely," Hugo Cohen began as the meeting commenced. "I pray that your elected leader is one who genuinely cares about your communal concerns, but most important, can liaise on your behalf in an intelligent and authoritative manner that results in fair and equal decisions that benefit all parties.

"With that in mind, in an orderly manner, please let me have your nominees."

A stocky farmer from the Eastern region stood. "I nominate Willy McHugh."

Two stood at the same time. "You first," Hugo indicated to one.

"I nominate Padraig Joseph Gallagher the Younger," stated Willy McBride.

"That was my nominee, also," confirmed the other.

Five in all were nominated. The ensuing silence indicated that all were satisfied with the nominees.

"I will give you ten minutes to think about the men who have been nominated, and a vote for the most popular choice will take place. This man will be your chosen leader. Think and choose wisely."

In the short time following, Hugo approached his friend, Padraig Joseph the Older. "Padraig Joseph, are you happy with your son being chosen as a nominee? And more important, how will you feel if he is chosen as spokesman?"

"There is little doubt he is more than capable to be a leader of any group. But with his outspoken feelings concerning the English, I have grave misgivings about him being the leader at this time. I am also extremely concerned he will take a personal stand against Bolton, and this position of power will give him too much confidence to take on the earl."

"Exactly my feelings," Cohen murmured in grim agreement. Then, seeing that the groups were breaking up, and the men seemed to have made their decisions, Cohen raised his voice and addressed them.

"I call your attention. Please give a show of hands to each of the nominations. You are allowed one vote only. As each name is called, please raise your arm."

"Willy McHugh!" Twenty-one arms were raised.

"Padraig Joseph Gallagher!" A good half of the gathering stood as one.

The formality of announcing the names of the other three was completed.

"Gentlemen, I announce your choice of leader," Hugo Cohen finally announced. "Padraig Joseph Gallagher the Younger has been chosen as your elected leader. Padraig, I offer you my congratulations. If I may, I wish to offer you some advice before inviting you to stand and speak. We have some good men here tonight. Should you need advice in any future decisions, I trust you will call on the collective support of our friends. Gentlemen! I offer you your chosen leader!"

Padraig Joseph stood and walked to the table where Hugo had taken his seat. "My friends, I thank you for your confidence."

Hugo listened as Padraig Joseph spoke about forming a committee, starting with those nominated earlier that evening. He spoke in general terms regarding their joint concerns about the tenancies and Bolton's rent increases. Then he appealed to the farmers' loyalty to Ireland.

"But what are we to do about these cruel and unnecessary increases? This is our land—the land passed down to us from generations of our forefathers. We and those before us were born on this, our land. Did King Henry and his English thieves have the right to take from us our birthright? Do we pay, or do we refuse and stand united against Bolton?"

Hugo could sense the underriding current of unease and realized Padraig Joseph was pandering to the farmers' dissatisfaction with the terms of their leases. He watched as Padraig whipped up the mood of the farmers to a fierce intensity, and then he lowered his voice to barely more than a whisper.

"My fellow countrymen," Padraig said, and the farmers all leaned forward, now completely mesmerized by the words spoken and not wishing to miss any. "My friends, my countrymen, we are the heart and soul of our land. Our blood has watered our crops." Padraig gradually raised his voice until his words rang throughout the room. "It is our flesh and bones that have fertilized and enriched our soils. Our wives suffer, and our children go hungry, as the bastard foreigners steal from our mouths and live in the lap of luxury while we men can only dream of what could be.

"The law is the law of the greed of Henry the King. He and his equally greedy and scheming daughter, Elizabeth, have destroyed the very backbone of Ireland.

"Are we to die with the memory of what was and yet still could be?

"Or will we fight and die united, standing as one, as we drive the filth of England back into sea. To the men of my country I state, I will stand! Who will stand with me?"

Hugo watched in amazement as all stood cheering, yelling, and punching their clenched fists upward in shared defiance.

The din gradually died down when Padraig indicated that they should again be seated. "My friends, tonight the future of Ireland is in our hands. The time is truly right to reclaim our birthright. We will now dictate the terms.

"While all will share the responsibility, I will ask the following to remain after the meeting so that our planning can commence. You will all have your part in due course. Our enemy will no doubt become aware of our intentions, but we must keep them guessing as long as possible."

It was some considerable time later that the gathering finally broke up, and the defiant ones made their way back to their families.

All who attended were beginning to hope that finally their prayers soon would be answered. Even those that did not pray joined with the rest, hoping that at last Ireland would again belong to the Irish.

One, however, was happy for another reason. The Weasel would now have news to take back to Bolton.

## Chapter 13

The Weasel let himself into Bridey Kelly's hovel after the farmers' gathering at the tavern. The two cabbages and bag of potatoes satisfied Bridey, who, in turn, satisfied the Weasel. The urchins that Bridey had brought into the world, all from various fathers, would have food for a day or two or until another caller banged on the door and disappeared behind the sacking that shielded the sight, but not the grunting and groaning sounds that emanated from their mother's bedroom.

Bridey had been in particularly good form this visit, and by the time the Weasel had escaped from her ample proportions, found his trousers, and tripped his way out and up the track to the road, he was much later than he intended.

The Weasel had acquired his nickname because of his sneaky, slinking manner of suddenly appearing in company, listening, and leaving with information he later used to his advantage.

He was especially skilled at targeting the few women in the community who were devoid of morals or without manner of income. He wasn't too concerned about the lies he told his long-suffering wife, but was most worried about the reception he expected from Hair, who had been waiting for over an hour at the appointed place to give him a ride to the rendezvous with Bolton and Booth.

He finally reached the crossroads where Hair sat. Two horses grazed peacefully by the roadside as he staggered breathlessly to the waiting man. Hair stared at him.

"You stink! Don't come close to me. If the horse doesn't like the smell of you, you walk to the manor."

Without another word and no backward glance, he mounted his horse and trotted down the road, picking up speed and maintaining a steady gallop in an attempt to make up for the time lost. Good fortune favoured the Weasel. His horse was either in good humour or wished to be alongside the other two. They made good time and soon galloped into the manor courtyard and dismounted.

"Wait here." Hair entered the manor and strode into the study where Bolton and Booth sat waiting.

"By the smell of the bastard, I would think the stink of rutting explains his lateness," Hair said without waiting to be spoken to.

"Send him in," Bolton said.

The Weasel entered and shuffled around in the silence.

"Sit," Bolton ordered. "You have kept us waiting too long as it is. The news you bring of last night's meeting had better please us, or that unpleasantly odorous object between your thighs will feel the steel of the Gypsy's blade."

The Weasel quickly relayed the events of the meeting. Questions from both men confirmed that their predictions were well founded.

"It is as I forecasted, Conrad. With one or two exceptions this Irish rabble are without backbone. If they are without a competent leader, they are as wandering sheep who will obey our wishes. They may not like it, but they will obey nonetheless.

"Just look at the hovels they live in. Their manner of dress is an insult to we who dress properly. It is right and just they be deprived of education. Do the hogs seek learning? Do the cattle wish to improve their status? No, of course not. And these lowly animals, the Irish, are even lesser than the beasts I refer to. Look at this pathetic creature." He gestured dismissively toward the shaking Weasel.

"He is most happy and only too eager to sell out his fellow citizens for an hour or two of humping a harlot—our very own Celtic Judas Iscariot."

Booth grinned at the cowering man. "Now, don't be too hard on the poor fellow, Robert. He has provided us with the information we need. And he is certainly aware he has much work and a good deal more information to provide us."

"True, but now let us attend to this problem of their newly elected leader. I misjudged this Irishman, Gallagher. I figured he would be tempted by our offer to live in the relative comfort of lesser tenancy rentals, but I suppose he is not. More fool he. Tell me . . ." Booth spoke to the Weasel again. "Just how much support do you think Gallagher can expect, and more important, how far will the local farmers go in an attempt to rebel against me?"

"Most will go along with him so long as they see no threat to them," the Weasel replied, making an effort to sound confident and authoritative. Booth and Bolton could despise him all they wanted, but he had been at the meeting, and they hadn't. They needed him. "These Irish believe in safety in numbers. A few of them are more stubborn than most and will stand alongside Gallagher. They will fight for what they believe in. Gallagher has convinced them that to fight is true and noble. They believe that they have an ancestral birthright to Irish land, and you do not."

Bolton was quite surprised at the Weasel's synopsis. Realizing he had been too harsh in his treatment of the man, Bolton changed his tone. "Come, my good fellow, I have been a little too concerned over this matter. I did speak to you out of turn. Thank you for your excellent report. I want you to return to the village and keep your ears and eyes open for any further information. Send a messenger to me as soon as you have anything to report. Here, take this." He tossed the Weasel a small leather bag of coins.

A very relieved Weasel left and hastened to the waiting Hair with the horses.

As they trotted from the manor, Bolton turned to Booth. "I look forward with great relish to the entertainment of watching Mandino slicing the wretch from arse to throat. But for now, let us consider the information he has given us and make appropriate plans to combat this Irish rabble. Fetch the Gypsy; we will need him to recruit some suitable persons. He can take Slow and Hair up to Belfast with him and visit the localities he enjoys. Those hog pens are full of villains, all with the correct pedigrees for the job at hand, if you gather my meaning." He paused to snort a derisive little laugh at his joke. "Conrad, my friend, I look with delight to our future, but I suspect the future for some will be short lived."

Booth left the chuckling Bolton to fetch the Gypsy and set about finding recruits.

Sitting and savouring the day's first whiskey, Robert Bolton mulled over his plans and ambitions, but especially his longing to be gone from this place he loathed. Bolton was a man totally without conscience. He always succeeded in whatever challenge he attempted because he always got his way. He had total confidence in himself and his ability to take what he wanted, regardless of the consequences. He needed to amass great fortunes and own title to land in both the old and the new worlds. He needed money to finance his ruthless, greedy ambitions. The Irish tenants would provide that money. He would squeeze every last penny from them, and he would allow no one to stand in his way.

For a moment, he let his thoughts wander to Kathleen

Gallagher. *No longer a virgin, my dear, unlike your now deceased sister, but still worthy of some entertainment,* he mused. *But not until you rid yourself of that hideous lump you are carrying.*

He poured a second whiskey.

## Chapter 14

Padraig woke, and not wishing to disturb Kathleen, lay and listened to the songbirds outside their bedroom. His wife had had a troubled night's sleep as she attempted to find a more comfortable position. Obviously, her very pregnant state was causing discomfort, and he could only hope the birth of their first would soon eventuate.

Jess, the sheepdog, had heard movement and gave a little bark to alert Padraig that she was certainly awake and also needed attention. With a smile, he quietly slipped from the bed and gathered some scraps from the previous night's leftovers.

He went outside to greet his pet. "Now, who is this dog wanting some attention?" The dog wagged her tail and commenced rubbing herself against Padraig's leg. "And so a good dog demands some treats, does she now?"

Padraig sat and quietly fed her little morsels, to which she responded by licking his fingers in appreciation. "Come now, let us go, and check your pups."

Together, they walked to where Jess's brood lay. She proudly stood watching as her master picked up and tickled first one and then the rest of the wiggly puppies. "Ah now, and it's a wonderful sight we have here, Jess. I just hope they train up as well as their mother and indeed their father. Who knows, we could have another champion sheep dog here."

A scream broke the morning stillness startling both dog and master.

"Kathleen!"

Padraig leapt to his feet and sped to the house, bursting in and racing to the bedroom where his wife lay beside their bed from which she had appeared to have fallen.

"Fetch Claire, please Padraig, help me back onto the bed and run for your mother."

The night had been another long one for Claire. She had again tossed and turned. Strange shapes and faces had blended in with familiar faces in her restless dreams. Tortured and frightened eyes stared, and open mouths screamed silent cries, pleading for release from the agonies they were suffering. Helpless, Claire tried in vain to reach their grasping hands and pull them from their pits of despair. Not quite understanding, she saw visions and dimensions of the past and frightening visions of the future. The constant reminder of blood spilled in past conflicts in the land of her birth insisted her subconscious awareness that she must do all in her power to protect her family.

Then out of the swirling mire of her visions, the sneering countenance of Robert Bolton suddenly appeared. He stared right through her and deep into her heart. Crying out, she pleaded that he spare her family, knowing all was in vain, and her pleas for mercy would be ignored. Smiling, the grim specter emanated a depth of depravation and evil far beyond her total understanding before it slipped from her sight.

Claire had slipped back into the security of sleep, but not before she witnessed the last of the visions. She saw figures of men and women yet unborn without faces, their souls searching in despair for their promised paradise. She watched as countless restless spirits proudly gave their mortal lives for the lands they wished to free while those unworthy, well-dressed savages took from them all they wished to steal with no sympathy, only savagery—savage sympathy.

Her husband had lain deep in sleep throughout the night, certainly with the assistance of many pots of fine porter. But it was he who awoke first at the sound of his son bellowing from beneath their window.

"Claire, come on woman, what ails young Padraig?" He tripped from the bed and hastened to his waiting son.

"Father, please," he gasped breathlessly. "Quick, wake Ma, and come up to our house. I fear for Kathleen. I'm thinking her time is nigh upon us. I think the baby is here."

The commotion had indeed woken Claire. Hearing the words of her son from the bedroom, she called down to him. "Go back to Kathleen, my son—I will be there as soon as I dress."

With a smile, she added, "And don't worry . . . everything will turn out just fine," knowing her words would not be heeded. She was also trying not to worry; it seemed the baby was early. She had estimated the birth to be at least another month away.

A short time later, Claire arrived to find Kathleen relatively comfortable with a relieved Padraig by her side. "We have to have the false alarm or two to truly prepare you for fatherhood," she said to Padraig, and laughed as she hugged him and prepared to return home.

On the short walk back to her cottage, a cold shiver went through her. She scanned the landscape, searching for hidden eyes, but all appeared peaceful.

## Chapter 15

Bolton stared at the rabble of men drinking around the tables in the barn he had allocated as their living and sleeping quarters.

Those from the London slums had met with the Bristol dockland thugs and sailed to Dublin before traveling up to Donegal. A few days later, they were joined by an equally nasty looking bunch from Belfast who were predominantly Scottish.

"Mandino and Hair have done well. I swear, I don't think I could have recruited a more likely collection of ruffians to match these."

"Not a one among them that a mother will own up to as her own," Booth murmured.

"Time to address them then, Conrad."

Booth walked over to a wagon and helped Bolton up, and both men stood watching the crowd of ruffians, commanding their attention. Booth raised his voice to be heard over the din and called for silence.

"Right, you lot. I wish to introduce you to Robert Bolton." Bolton inclined his head. "But first, for those who have not met me, my name is Conrad Booth. You already know Hair, Slow, and Gypsy Mandino. Gentlemen, please stand for Robert Bolton."

In silence, all stared up at the saturnine figure looking down on them. All felt a tremor of fear pass through them. All recognised that this man was truly evil.

He spoke. "First, I welcome you to the manor. You have agreed to the conditions of being at this fine abode, and you will do what is required of you. I now warn you of the consequences should any of you choose to disobey me or refuse to carry out my orders to the letter. As members of a private enforcement force, you will be expected to put your life on the line to protect your colleagues as you obey my orders.

"You will kill as instructed, and you will maim as instructed. You will burn and destroy property as instructed. You will be feared with good cause.

"You have already agreed to the terms of payment. I now give you further good news. A bonus will be paid for the right ear of any who oppose you. Of course, I do refer to the ear of one who will no longer need it.

"You may use the women as you wish before you kill them. We want no more siring of trouble-making Irish swine. I see you all smiling with relish at the job to be done. Good.

"Now, a warning: Should any of you choose not to obey orders at any time, the Gypsy will be asked to display his special talents. His knife will deprive you of your manhood before you die a slow death."

Bolton watched his words sink in to those below him. A smile on his sardonic features did little to reassure the now very alert and attentive group that precious little charity would be granted from this man. The aura of evil emanating from him sent shivers down their spines. These thugs had met many men who were bad to the very core. Indeed, most of them strived to equal or surpass that.

"Excellent," Bolton continued. "We understand each other. Now, I will tell you why you've been hired. My family and I own most of the land in the northwest of this country. The tenants who farm this land are planning to rebel against us. They refuse to pay their rents and intend to steal our property. This will not happen. All will have one chance and one only to agree to my terms. Should they refuse, we will change their minds with consequences that they will not find pleasant.

"I understand that some among you have firearm experience. You will find an excellent armory of the finest new flintlocks and pistols to utilize your skills. Blades of the keenest steel are available for those who enjoy bloodletting face to face.

"Finally, remember this: These people are breaking English law and attempting to make fools of us. I will not tolerate this behaviour, and I will punish all who try.

"So, my friends, drink up, and eat well, for tomorrow you will learn of your tasks."

Bolton and Booth returned to the manor, leaving the unruly rabble to their eating and drinking, all boasting of their deeds of the past and the villainy they were eager to participate in on behalf of their new employer.

"Well then, Conrad, my friend, I am impressed with your stout fellows. I somewhat suspect our Irish friends won't be. We will nonetheless need to plan carefully. I want all talk of rebellion and those responsible for instigating trouble squashed swiftly so that all the crops are established and all monies due to me can be paid without further problems. We will commence calling on our tenants before the end of this week."

## Chapter 16

Kathleen watched with fondness from their back door as Padraig fussed with the pups. She smiled to herself as she rubbed her swollen belly. "Soon, my little one, you will be playing with your own little puppy."

Claire had calculated the birth to be in four weeks or less, and Kathleen was enjoying the special attention from the family, particularly from her husband, who would not allow her to do any of the household chores until the baby was delivered, and she was back on her feet again.

"'Tis truly spoilt I am to be sure," she said to the little one inside her. She giggled to herself.

Then suddenly she gasped. A shock of pain speared through her. She held the side of the doorway for support and called out. "Padraig, Padraig, help me!"

Her husband jumped up and ran to her, assisting her to their bed. "Stay still, my love, I will run and fetch my mother."

In no time, he was back with Claire who promptly attended to her daughter-in-law.

The concern on Padraig's face was so obvious to Claire, and she smiled, understanding and loving her son so very much. "'Tis too early to be worried now, Padraig. These early pains are normal. The babe is not due for at least another three or so weeks. Now go and make a brew . . .make yourself useful," she scolded her son.

However, the smile disappeared as more pain showed on Kathleen's face.

"Padraig, would you boil up a larger quantity of water, just to wash Kathleen's face, you know," she added, keeping her voice calm, but she couldn't hide her concern.

"Is all well with her?" Padraig stammered. "What is happening?"

"Her water has broken," Claire explained. "I think you might be a father sooner than expected. Kathleen, your labor has commenced."

The first of the contractions soon confirmed Claire's prediction. She quickly gave her son instructions to bring the items she would need to assist in the birth.

By now, his grandfather had arrived, his father not being at home. The expected arrival of his first great-grandchild excited the older Padraig, but his assurances that Kathleen was in the best of hands and care did little to calm the expectant father, who rushed and fussed until he was firmly, but kindly pushed outside.

"Go and see to your pups, and we will call you when we're ready," his grandfather said.

Sometime later, Claire paused for a rest and drink. The contractions were now ten minutes apart and regular. She estimated the birth to eventuate in an hour or so. "Not long to go now," she said to the old man relaxing and enjoying the moment.

It was some time later, as she looked out to the yard that she smiled to herself, catching a glimpse of her son, loving him in this his first foray into fatherhood, remembering her great pain in bringing him into the world.

"Ah, 'twas worth it all . . ." she mused when a sudden cry caused her to rush to Kathleen.

"I think it's coming! Oh God, it hurts so much . . . help me .

.. help me."

"Padraig!" The old man called out to his grandson. "I think it's time."

Together, they stood outside the bedroom, not daring to look, trying hard to ignore the unfamiliar sounds. When suddenly they heard a quick slap and the unmistakable sound of a crying baby filled the room, they nearly crumpled in relief.

"Oh, dear sweet Mother of God, it's a wee girl, it is to be sure," they heard Claire cry out, and then the sounds of the baby's first cries filled the house with new life.

"Padraig, come and see," Kathleen called in a weak, but satisfied voice.

Padraig was numb with shock, and by the time he entered the room and began to recover and respond to both the congratulations of his grandfather and wanting to hold his wife and the new baby, he didn't quite comprehend his mother's concerned comment.

"I don't understand; the wee mite should be bigger . . ." Claire said, and then, "oh, my God, there's another!"

In absolute shock, Padraig stared as slowly another tiny head started to show.

"Push!" Claire coaxed. "Push, sweet darlin'! There, there, more . . . and again . . . and again . . . yes, that's it, my girl!"

Again, the room echoed to the indignant cries of not one, but two little babies.

"Well, who's the clever girl then?" an excited Claire enquired of her daughter-in-law.

Dumbfounded, Padraig could only look first at the baby he held, then at the baby his mother held, and then at his totally exhausted wife.

"Come hand me your daughter and go to Kathleen," Claire said. She held both babes and watched as her son walked slowly to his wife's side.

He knelt and took her in his arms, and as the emotion of the moment gradually sank in, he started to weep. Kathleen held him, kissing his head, his face, trying to dry his uncontrollable tears. Oh, how she loved him.

"Now then!" she whispered. "Maybe I can hold one of our babies."

Claire passed both newborns to their mother and gazed with pride and love at her family.

"Come." She gently took the grandfather by his arm. "Let's leave them together."

## Chapter 17

Hugo and Padraig Joseph the Younger sat watching as the tenants milled into the meeting room at the back of Maloneys. The ales were particularly sweet as they toasted to the new additions to the family.

"Here's luck to you, Grandfather, and long may you remain one." Hugo raised his glass with a smile. "Have the twins been named yet?"

"Hah," Padraig Joseph laughed. "Kathleen yelled at me when I suggested Padraig the Fourth. I think we will have no more Padraigs in this family for some time. They are talking of Mary for the wee girl and William for the lad. 'William?' I said. However, 'tis fine, and she has relented for Joseph as the name for the wee lad. But you know women, that could change at any time, at least until the good priest gets his hands on them. Speaking of which, the christening will be on Sunday after Mass. You will be there of course."

"Oh, to be sure, to be sure," Hugo replied, mimicking the local Irish accent. "*Supriste!*" he suddenly exclaimed when he saw a commotion at the doorway to the room. "Is that Peter McAllister? Look, Padraig Joseph, he is covered in blood."

The two men raced to where three men were surrounded by agitated farmers.

Indeed, two appeared badly injured, and the third had

collapsed to the floor. All were covered in blood and moaning in extreme pain.

"What in God's name happened? Who did this?"

McAllister, obviously very shaken began to explain. "I left to meet up with Michael and Liam at Brogan's Mill about four hours ago. We were traveling on my cart and coming down the rise toward the Killybegs road." He paused to gather his breath.

"As we reached the trees before the road, a man came out and grabbed the horse. Others came out of the trees and told us to get down off the cart. The first man asked where we were going, and were we heading to Bandara. I said that maybe we could carry some but not all with us. They laughed and then grabbed Michael. Before I knew what was happening, some of the men started to beat him with fists and staves. Me and Liam jumped down to help, but some others held us down and beat us. One man told them to stop beating me and said they needed someone to drive the cart to town to warn the rest of you what would happen to troublemakers. They thrust me from them, and I fell over. I couldn't get up in time to stop them from kicking and beating Michael and Liam. They threw them onto the back of the cart and told me to get in and get moving." He looked over to Padraig Joseph and Hugo.

"Who were these men?" Padraig Joseph demanded.

"A big man, an Englishman, said that all the farmers who didn't pay their rents would receive a thrashing and to tell all those who disobey the earl to expect visits from them."

"Would somebody run and fetch Hugh Porter," Hugo interjected.

As one of the onlookers rushed off to find the constable, the others tended to the injured farmers. Padraig Joseph called Hugo and some of the more responsible farmers to one side.

"We need to talk about this before the meeting," he said.

Constable Porter arrived shortly after and joined the very worried farmers. After listening to a summary of the events, he pulled aside Hugo and Padraig Joseph to have a private talk with them.

"Quite frankly, I am not surprised," he began. "I have heard rumours of troubles brewing from some of the Donegal town constables. Not being Irish, these thugs don't have much sympathy for the local farmers. I suspect they're being paid by Bolton and therefore will side with the English over any issue."

"A pox on the bastards," exclaimed Padraig. "To be sure, we do not want their help. We can support ourselves, and we will fight back, but can we expect interference from them?"

"Worse," replied the constable. "I would expect the judge and the Donegal constabulary to come down hard on any issue they consider to be against their ideals, and it is common knowledge that the good judge is one of Bolton's pawns. He obeys all of his wishes and commands."

"So where do we stand?" demanded Padraig Joseph.

"Legally you must do as Bolton requests. It may not be right or fair, but you must obey the law."

"English law!" Padraig Joseph snorted.

"I agree, but still the law nonetheless," said the constable.

Aware of his friend's quick and fiery temperament, Hugo suggested, "Perhaps we should commence the meeting of the farmers. With Hugh as an observer and possibly an advisor, we will be able to judge the feeling of the people and make some plans as to where we turn next." All agreed and shortly afterward, the meeting commenced.

By then the doctor had attended to the injured men, and there were mixed emotions in the room. Some were obviously shaken by the attacks; others were visibly enraged.

After much agitated discussion and some legal advice from

Constable Porter, it was decided that a group representing the farming would approach Robert Bolton to reach an agreeable solution.

Padraig Joseph and Hugo were chosen, as were five farmers of steady composition and even temper. They would ride to the earl's residence the following day.

The Weasel slipped out as the meeting was breaking up, and the farmers were standing about chatting among themselves over final details of the plan.

Sean, now back on two feet and enjoying an ale at the bar behind the meeting room, spotted him leaving, but it was much later that the significance of the Weasel's early departure hit home.

Bolton watched as Conrad Booth spread the remains of the eggs on a slice of fried potato, placed it in his mouth, and chewed with obvious relish.

"Ah, this Irish country living! Way too grand for the likes of those." He nodded to the gathered men loitering outside on the grassed area in the front of the manor. "I wonder what our visiting party will make of them?"

"No doubt we will find out in a very short time," Bolton replied.

Indeed, the two had hardly finished their tea when Hair walked in. "A couple of carts and some men on horseback are on their way up the road."

The two men stood. "Now this should be most amusing." Bolton smiled to Booth and Hair. "Come, let us observe their arrival and ensure their welcome is a warm one."

Some minutes later, the riders approached the manor with apprehension. Two men were standing on the steps, feet planted firmly, arms folded, glaring at them as they rode up. Behind them stood twenty burly men radiating pure aggression.

Hugo had no doubt that their presence was to intimidate. A stab of fear shot through him.

One was dressed completely in black. His expression was cold and disinterested. The other was dressed somewhat flamboyantly in black and red silk, and he was smiling at them, but there was no warmth in that smile.

The horses sensed the heavy tension and stepped nervously. The mounted men glanced at each other with apprehension, unsure of what to do next, each waiting for the other to break the silence.

Finally the man in black spoke. "And what brings you to my humble abode this fine morn, pray tell? You, Padraig Joseph Gallagher, as I recall the last time we spoke, I had the distinct feeling that I was most unwelcome at your home, and I seem to recall a reluctance to discuss certain matters of important business. What could you possibly want to say to me this day?"

Clearing his throat nervously, Padraig Joseph spoke. "Yesterday, three of our friends were attacked. I have good reason to believe some of your men were responsible." He glanced at the men behind Bolton who moved menacingly closer.

"Can you point out those heinous villains who perpetrated such an act?" Bolton replied with heavy sarcasm. "And, may I ask, why should I be held accountable for your friends stumbling upon wandering traveling vagabonds?"

He looked at the menacing mob. "Now, which of you naughty boys did bad things to these men? Come now, confess."

Hoots of ribald laughter greeted the request. This was followed by amused silence.

Turning to Padraig Joseph again, Bolton said, "Perhaps you have come to suggest how you wish to pay your rents, and perhaps you have with you the first instalment."

Then, with a sudden change of tone, he said, "Listen to me very carefully, Gallagher. You and your worthless kind will pay to me my dues. You will have the payments ready at the last day of this coming week when my collectors call. Should you decide not to do so, I will drive you and your contemptible kind off my land and into the Atlantic if need be. And I will replace you and all who disobey with good English and Scots farmers who will appreciate my land and work it in a manner befitting those who have a true love of the soil. Now be gone and warn your compatriots of my words."

Turning to his thugs, Bolton pointed and commanded, "You! Tear them apart if they are not off my land by the time I reach my study. Come, Conrad, we have better uses for our time."

Padraig Joseph was shocked at the threats. He now realized that he and all of his kith and kin were in great danger, not just for the present, but for possibly the rest of their lives.

Hugo, also numbed with shock, reached down from his horse and grabbed the reins of the first cart. "Go, go!"

The carts and riders suddenly turned and bolted from the manor followed by howls of delighted laughter and jeering from the chasing mob.

## Chapter 18

"It was almost as if they were expecting us."

"But if so, how would they have known, Da," Sean replied to his father's comment.

Hugo also had been quietly thinking about the happenings of that morning. Placing his jar of porter on the bar, he finally spoke. "If Robert Bolton was responsible for the assault on McAllister and the others, and I'm certain he was, then he would have had a fair idea that we might visit, if only to show some concern. But I do agree that he acted as though he was expecting us."

A large group of worried farmers had met at Maloneys to hear how the meeting with their landlord had fared. Being a Saturday night, farming folk and others from all the outlining areas had made a point of coming to Bandara, and all were now extremely worried about their future, and most fearful of Bolton's dire warning.

Comment followed comment, and after most had voiced an opinion, Padraig Joseph called for silence. "It would appear there are only two options."

When he spoke in the silence that followed, his words left little doubt about his feelings, and all realized that another page of Ireland's bloody history was about to unfold.

"We have the choice of bowing to the cruel and greedy demands of foreign interlopers, or we stand united one and all and fight these bastards man to man."

Padraig Joseph paused, searching the faces of the men listening to him, looking for any who might show weakness. Satisfied that he now had their full attention, he continued.

"You all know that the land you live on is your land, land that has been farmed for generations by your forefathers, every sod of soil tilled with sweat and pain to produce crops, to provide food for your families—homes built to provide shelter and comfort for your wives and children.

"You have bred livestock, cattle, pigs, horses, and donkeys; all yours, yes, my friends, all belonging to you, or so it should be! But this will never be because of the actions of the thieving deceit of King Henry. For over two hundred and fifty years, our people have been suppressed by their regime and the rulings of the royalty of England. The time has come for us to tell the bloody English to go to hell!"

Shouts of, "Hear, hear!" rang through the tavern.

"Tell them to get their stinking arses off our land, or we will drive them into the sea and back to their own country. Are we man-to-man weaker than them?"

"No!"

"Will we bow to them and crawl as worms frightened to stand up to them?"

"No!"

Padraig Joseph paused for effect. "Join me, stand alongside me, and fight for what is rightfully yours."

"Hear, hear!"

Sean and brother Padraig listened with pride as the words of their father stirred their blood, fuelling passion and emotion among all the farmers.

"Father, I will stand with you and fight 'til I fall," Sean spoke out for all to hear. "Damn the filthy bloody English!"

The rest of his words were drowned by roars of agreement.

Sean turned to his brother. "We'll show 'em, little brother, me and you and Da, and maybe Grandfather."

With fists raised high in defiant salutes, Sean and the farmers shouted their support for rebellion.

"But what of my wife and son and daughter?" Padraig murmured. "What could happen to them?"

*****

If Father Sullivan had knowledge of the troubles, he gave no indication, his Sunday sermon delivering the traditional message of God's love in return for obedience and commitment to the faith.

He concluded his sermon by telling his parishioners of the addition to the community of the Gallagher twins. He congratulated the proud parents and advised the congregation of the christening to be held immediately after Mass.

And so, as the waters trickled over the heads of William Joseph and Mary Bridget Gallagher, the Catholic community of Bandara was increased by two.

The womenfolk fussed and chattered, and the menfolk hopped about impatiently waiting for Maloney to open his doors at midday.

It had been agreed that the bad tidings of the previous day would not hinder the gaiety of this very special day, and Padraig, Kathleen, and the twins were the centre of attention until a very tired mother called a halt and begged to be allowed to return home.

Sean lovingly assisted his sister-in-law up onto the cart with the twins, and as Padraig gathered up the reins to depart, the crowded bar emptied to see them off.

As they trotted away, Claire watched until her son and family finally disappeared from sight. The sudden haunting cry of a crow flying overhead caused her to shudder. Deep inside her, sinister warnings were developing, warnings that she had no understanding of, how to cope with, or how to help those that she was certain would need help, but from whom?

Turning to rejoin the others, her eyes met her son, Sean's. For the briefest of moments, that understanding flashed between them. Sean would remember that moment for the rest of his life.

*****

For once, the Weasel felt comfortable. Bolton and Booth had accepted his report with gratitude.

"My dear fellow, you have done well." Bolton smiled. "So the fools intend to defy me, you say. I find it hard to imagine any of them succeeding in defeating any of my men in any form of fisticuffs. Some are big lads, I grant you, but none has the gutter experience of my slum dwellers. You have already witnessed the damage that Hair and Slow can inflict. Likewise, Mandino and his friends have no peers when it comes to their skill with the blade.

"These Irish fools have absolutely no organizational skills. They will blunder in disarray until they get off my land or pay my dues.

"We commence calling for our payments in a few days' time. I suggest you make yourself available to bring back any tidbits of information I may find useful, for which I will be most grateful. Conrad has a small token of appreciation for you; be assured the rewards will be much greater when all is complete."

After the Weasel departed, both men raised glasses, smiling in anticipation of what lay ahead.

Somewhat later, Bolton sat alone, his mind wandering back to the day he had claimed Bridget McGuire for his own, albeit for the briefest period of ownership. He had watched her chatting amiably to a group of local wives outside Maloney's tavern.

He subconsciously rubbed his groin, feeling the erection, as the memory of the beauty of the lass aroused his desires. Since first sighting the twin sisters soon after arriving in the North West of Ireland, his fantasies surrounding Bridget had reached a point that he knew were almost beyond his control. He had spoken to her on a number of occasions, and while she had treated his approaches in a polite and courteous manner, she had given no indication that she was interested in anything but a polite acquaintance. Her sister was very smitten with one of the local farmers' sons, and he was aware that his own jealousy and the lust he felt toward both young women were almost beyond control.

His wild imagination showed him images of both women satisfying his sexual fantasies in orgies of passion that surpassed anything the sluts and harlots he employed had ever achieved. He would awake from dreams at night wringing with sweat, his body aching, demanding release from the uncontrollable longing and coveting for the maidens.

One day, he would resolve the situation, one way or another.

He remembered watching as Bridget tossed her head back, her hair flying in a halo of beauty, giggling and then laughing out loud at some story told to her, her long tresses falling across her shoulders, her infectious laughter delighting her friends.

At last, she had picked up her market basket and started homewards.

With his head cocked to one side, Robert Bolton smiled. "I wonder whatever did happen to her?" he murmured, and picking up his glass, he roared with laughter. "Oh well, one down, and soon, the other to be mine!" The heinous laughter echoed throughout the manor.

## Chapter 19

Hugo Cohen had suffered anti-Semitic abuse for as long as he could recall. He was so obviously Jewish, his features the butt of ridicule even when he was quite young. He had tried everything: ignoring the taunts, walking away, hiding from the bullies, and hoping it would cease. When it became obvious that he would forever be victimized, he decided to stand up to his antagonists.

His local Irish friends now wished to do the same to Bolton's thugs, but he knew only too well that they were hopelessly inexperienced and no match for those ruffians, who were highly skilled in brutal confrontation. Hugo also realized that he had precious little time to prepare them. But he had to do something.

"First, let me talk to you about my past and tell you of troubles and situations I have found myself in, and how I managed to escape with bones intact and once or twice with my life."

Hugo addressed a group consisting of Padraig Joseph, his sons Sean and Padraig, and a mixture of farmers and a few fisher folk. The latter, when hearing of the dilemma their friend, Sean, had found himself in, had quickly volunteered to help.

Hugo told of his experiences, explaining that when much younger he had learned, often the hard way, how to fight and beat even the most hardened and feared fighters. He told them that eventually he had earned respect, and those who he had beaten had taught him skills that were unheard of among the troublemakers and bullies he would confront.

"Today I intend to teach you, *mes amis*! There is little hope of a peaceful resolution with Bolton. I suspect that his men are spoiling for a fight, and they will expect to win. Under normal circumstances, I would expect them to do so. They are tough, hardened men, seasoned and very experienced in brutal combat, and I suspect, killing. And quite frankly, none of you would be a match for them. Already, Sean here has suffered from their actions. However, I intend to bring in some equality, that is, if you are interested."

Smiles and nods of assent gave Hugo the indications he was searching for.

"Good. Now let us assess our strengths. First, I suspect that as hard-toiling fishermen, you are very strong. Likewise for those of you who are shepherds and land workers. You are probably very agile and strong as well. In the next few days, I will hone your strength and make you men not to be reckoned with.

"I will instruct you in methods of man-to-man battle that will truly amaze you and will certainly come as a great surprise and shock to our enemy. I will also instruct some of you in skills with the knife, but no, not just an ordinary knife. I will introduce you to my little friend here."

Hugo then produced a knife with a blade that curved in an arc, razor sharp, but only a few inches long, and as he handed it around, few doubted the damage it would inflict.

"There are not many who know of this and how to use it, but those who do win most battles, as you will quickly find out when I teach you. I have only six of such blades, so I will select from you the six who will show me they have the ability and the desire to become a student. But those six will also have to prove that their strength and fighting ability is greater than the rest.

"We will commence your training once you have spoken to your families and agreed to be part of our group of rebellious Irish fighters. Indeed, my friends, it will be a mark of honour to be called Irish rebels." Hugo smiled in grim humour.

"Before we commence training, I must give you the severest of warnings. Both Padraig Joseph and I have every reason to suspect that someone is passing information about the farmer's meetings to Bolton. This spy is almost certainly one of the tenant farmers. We have every reason to believe that he is not one of you. However, should I find out that indeed one of you is either that person or is passing information about our activities to Bolton or any of his men, you will regret ever having met me."

Silence filled the room as Hugo let his words sink in. "Secrecy is our motto," he said. "We begin our training tomorrow."

Later that night, Padraig lay with Kathleen in his arms, their two beautiful babies sleeping peacefully in their cot alongside the bed.

He had spoken to his wife, holding her tight as he explained all that Hugo Cohen had talked to them about earlier that day.

"Ah well, my wee fighter!" she had giggled. "'Tis the terror of the North West, we can name you, you and Sean. And me, poor little me, what will become of me? Surely now, nothing will happen to me with two such feared fighters to protect me and our wee ones."

Soon after, Padraig felt his wife fall into peaceful slumber. Sleep escaped him. The thought of being separated from his beloved Kathleen and now his little ones was so unbearable that he wondered what would be said if he excused himself from the meeting with Cohen when he did awake in the morning. What would his father, brother, and friends think of him if he chose to protect his family at home?

When he gradually drifted off to sleep, his dreams of a happy past were brutally invaded by nightmares of a future so horrific that he had never could have imagined it.

## Chapter 20

Padraig opened a sleepy eye; his brother snored softly alongside him. As he looked around him, he spotted Hugo stirring the previous night's embers. The tripod supported a metal pot warming a gruel that smelled inviting.

"Ah, the first one awake. Come lad, you can help with the breakfast. There is tea if you want it." He pointed to a pot.

Just as the sun's first rays lit up the eastern skies, Hugo banged the pot, calling out loudly to the sleepers. "Up, up, come now, stir yourselves. Move your lazy bodies, it's way past time to begin your day."

Some moaning and groaning commenced before the men assembled one by one and began to eat.

"Now listen to me," Hugo Cohen began. "I need your full attention. I want to divide you into four teams of five men each. As there are nineteen of you, I will make up the number in one of those teams. I have placed equipment for each team at the base of the dunes. You will meet me there in twenty minutes. You will wear your shoes or boots and light clothing. I advise you to relieve yourselves thoroughly before we commence; you won't want to carry surplus weight." He finished with a smile.

Good-natured moans, groans, and grumbling dissent began as each man stirred to action.

Hugo stood watching as the Atlantic waves washed onto the

sands of the beautiful Irish coastline. He walked from the cart track that meandered from the farmlands down to the flat sands where his training would commence.

On both sides towered sand dunes, evidence that peace and tranquillity were not always the case, as the wrath of the Atlantic very often replaced the calm with storms that shaped the sands into the heights that he would use to toughen these farmers and fishermen and turn them into an elite fighting force.

Hugo watched, smiling as finally the nineteen stood before him. "I will arrange your teams." He then selected men and showed them where to stand. He placed Sean in one team and Padraig in another.

"You will notice that you've been disbursed into teams of equal weight and height, man for man. This is important, as you will all learn to utilize the strengths of your team to compete against the other.

"Each team will have a leader. This leader will not be selected. He must earn the right to lead. Your leader will be chosen by his determination to lead. By midday, he will be the last man standing. We will begin with simpler challenges and increase our training to more difficult challenges. Each training session will begin thus."

Hugo pointed to a distant point far up the beach to the north. "During the night, I placed four rags on four sticks. Each team will run and bring a flag back. I will set the pace and gradually build up speed until you are running at full pace as you return here. Now we begin."

The twenty men set off. Long before they had reached the flags a mile or so away, some were gasping. Hugo urged them on. Half eventually reached the flags with the rest straggling behind. Hugo was the first to arrive, his breathing only a bit more labored than normal because he was in such peak physical condition. Padraig,

Sean, and a few others were not far behind him.

"*Bonjour, mes amis,*" Hugo laughed. "Now the race begins." Grabbing a flag, he raced back down the beach. "Who is with me?" he called out.

Both Padraig and Sean grabbed a flag. A slightly built fellow named Danny snatched the last. They took off after Hugo.

After the first furlong or so, Padraig had gathered him in, the other two not too far behind.

Hugo picked up the pace. Padraig stayed with him. They reached the halfway mark. Hugo sped up again.

"Can you stay with me? I think not!"

With a furlong left, Hugo felt in control and settled into a full driving pace like a well-built racehorse galloping with ease on the hard-packed sand. Suddenly, he heard Padraig alongside him.

"Good-bye, my friend," he said to the shocked Hugo.

Together they ran, locked together, both gasping for breath. Neither showed intent to slow the pace. The others were now far behind them.

With about a hundred yards to go, Padraig put in a final burst and sprinted forward. He hit the finishing line, a mark scratched along the sand. He fell over the line and lay in the sand, exhausted.

Seconds later, Hugo joined him. He stood bent over, hands on hips, regaining his breath.

"Well done, Padraig! You ran well. My most sincere congratulations to you. Now, where are the others?"

When the stragglers arrived, Hugo addressed them like a drill sergeant.

"With the exception of Padraig and perhaps Sean and Danny, the rest of you are pathetic. We will now commence with the dunes. We will find out who are men and who are babies. You will have noticed that each flag is a different color. So far,

Padraig's red flag is the flag of honour. It is your job to ensure your flag is also a flag of honour. Let us begin."

The Maghara sand dunes that had been formed by the relentless Atlantic winds were continually changing shape, some as high as sixty feet, but all consistent in that the loosely packed sand made them difficult to climb without slipping backward in an effort to reach the tops.

For the next hour, Hugo drove them up the sand dunes and chased them back down. Eventually, he felt they could not continue, and he called a halt. "You may rest for a short time, and we will then begin your support training." He walked away and left them lying groaning in the sand.

A sharp whistle stirred them a little while later. He stood in the ocean in ankle-deep water. "Come!" he beckoned.

Hugo was well aware of the respect the Irish had for the sea, most fearing the pounding Atlantic waves. He also knew that very few could swim, certainly none who would brave the surf.

Lying in the sand, stretching from the water's edge up the beach lay ropes, each about one hundred feet in length. Alongside each was the colored flag, now with the stick firmly embedded in a small wooden log.

"I shall now measure your bravery. First, you must rescue your flag, and maybe you will have to brave the sea and rescue your comrades.

"I intend to hurl the wood with the flag out into the sea. One of your team members will wade out into the water while holding the rope and bring back the flag; the rest of you will hold the rope and ensure the outgoing tide does not take your team member away. I want you to select the one from each team who will chase the flag. I will go for my white team. Are you ready?"

Sean, still smarting from his brother's victory in the run, raised his voice defiantly.

"I will go for the blue team. We'll soon find out if my brother is a fish or a rabbit!" He laughed.

"The red team will return first," Padraig replied, "and on my return, I will have to drag your worthless self and the blue team with me." Padraig laughed goodnaturedly and whipped up the support of his teammates by calling, "What say you, red team?"

"Never!" shouted Danny, egged on by his teammates. "The black team will be the victor!"

"Then let us begin, and we shall see whose strength and agility matches his boast!" said Hugo. "Please strip off all clothing. You will be naked so that you can move through the water like an eel."

Hugo was aware that the Gulf Stream flowed not far-off the coast of Donegal, and thus, the warmer waters coming from it would not cause too much discomfort.

A little apprehensively, the men obeyed, looking around self-consciously at the others until all stood ready.

Sniggers of embarrassment were followed by comments of a ribald nature that soon had all in fits of laughter that broke the tension.

"Tie on your ropes," Hugo commanded after the merriment had settled down, happy in the knowledge that the first foundations of team bonding had begun.

He showed them a knot that didn't tighten, but allowed full body movement. Attached to each block of wood was a corded piece of rope. Hugo picked up a long supple wooden rod. Placing the tip into each circle of rope, he hurled each flag far out into the water, beyond the first of the pounding waves.

He ran naked into the water, chasing after his flag, with the rope trailing after him. "Who follows me?" he yelled back to the others.

Together as one, the others hit the water. Hugo was already in water up to his waist and diving under the first wave. Sean was pushed over by the force of the water and washed back into Padraig, and both floundered to regain their feet. Meanwhile, Danny floated up and over the waves and soon found himself in deep water, but close to his flag. He glimpsed the swimming Hugo, and while not possessing his skills as a swimmer, Danny managed to paddle over and grasp the flag. Raising it high, he yelled back to his team. "Drag me back, lads. Haul me ashore."

Gleefully, they pulled on the rope, and soon they stood alongside the laughing Hugo and his team.

A very disgruntled and half-drowned Padraig and Sean were dragged from the water by their teammates to be greeted by hoots of derision from those on shore.

"You will both have to replace your flags before you join the victors," Hugo said to them sternly, pointing to the distant flags floating out to sea. "The rest of us will eat."

Sean and Padraig suppressed the urge to groan in dissent and set to work immediately, the rumbling in their stomachs driving them to get the job done.

After they had all eaten and rested, Hugo called them together.

"I am well pleased with our first morning. So far today, you have learned the importance of teamwork and how supporting each other can achieve so much more than individual effort. You have overcome and conquered your fears. You have found that you can extend the strength of your body beyond what you would have thought possible.

"We will work on these skills later again today and for the next two days. If I am satisfied that you are ready to take on the next challenge, we will commence your more serious training that will help you trounce Bolton and his ruffians once and for all. But before then, we have much to do. We will now start again."

Groans of disbelief and negative banter were silenced by the quiet leadership of Hugo, who simply walked toward the next challenge and waited for the men to follow. Without another word, they rose to start the afternoon sessions.

By the end of the first day, the men were exhausted, and all collapsed onto their makeshift beds too tired to moan at the promise of an early start at dawn. They were used to greeting the day while it was yet dark to tend to fishing nets and farm animals, but this was a different kind of work altogether.

During the next two days, Hugo took great care to push them only as far as their bodies could tolerate. Alternating various routines and gradually allowing them to conquer their fear of the ocean, his recruits had found new levels of fitness and actually enjoyed the pleasure of learning to swim. They particularly enjoyed the fun of diving into the waves only to be washed back to shore, laughing and spluttering as they were dumped about, but always under Hugo's watchful eye as he searched for dangerous undertows that could drag them into danger.

They awoke on the fourth morning, again to a beautiful dawn. Indeed, the spring had been kind to them without a hint of rain, only clear cloudless days.

"I am well pleased with your progress," Hugo began. "I am now confident we can begin your serious training. Today, you will learn to protect yourselves and if need be cause harm to those who would harm you. And should you have to, you will learn how to take the life of those who would kill you."

He marked out a circle roughly ten feet in diameter.

"Sean, we will commence with you."

He threw Sean a length of black thorn, one of many branches he had collected from the trees that grew alongside the shoreline. "Now, I want you to come at me and smash me on the head with your club."

Sean caught the club and frowned. "No, I cannot do that . . ."

"You are right, you cannot, but can you try? Try your hardest, but you will end up kissing the sand. And remember, once inside the circle, only the loser goes out, and *mon ami*, that will be you."

Smarting at these words, Sean warily circled the Frenchman and then struck.

Suddenly, he was face down on the ground. He rose, spitting sand, angry at the howls of laughter from his mates. Again, he hit the ground, only this time a little harder. Dropping the club, he charged, aiming for Hugo's midriff. He felt his legs buckle behind him, and then Hugo had him in a vicious headlock, his arm tight around his throat, forcing his upper body back.

"Sean, I could now easily end your life." He relaxed his hold and allowed the very dazed young man to recover.

"You see that size in battle counts for very little. It is what you do with your size that counts. You have all witnessed just some of the skills of *la savate*. I discovered this unique fighting art while trying to survive the attacks of anti-Jewish antagonists in the back streets and alleys of France and the Mediterranean seaports. Translated in English, *savate* means boot and *chausson* the slipper.

"As you all witnessed, I used both to dispatch poor Sean here. In the coming days you will learn this art. Gentlemen, shall we begin?"

Padraig missed his wife and newly born twins so very much and ached to be with them again. But also, as he explained to Sean, he was enjoying finding his way around the new skills he was learning.

# Chapter 21

"y lords and ladies, may I welcome the Lord and Lady of Blaxton, Lord Thomas and Lady Constance," the doorman announced.

They made their grand entrance into the ballroom already quite full of a gathering of the elite from the surrounding London counties.

"Ah, Bolton, old chap! And, of course, your wife, the beautiful Lady Constance." They were greeted by one of a group standing in the spacious room.

"How are things in the lovely county of Suffolk?"

"Fine, fine," Lord Bolton replied. "The spring barley and wheat are well established. We will have a goodly and bumper crop, I wager. A few kind showers and a fine warm summer should ensure a healthy profit for the growing season."

The spring ball was the foremost social event in London, and invitations were issued to only the rich and the influential, and to those who were allied in maintaining the growth of the coffers of society's elite.

The men were attired in the latest London male fashions, and the women wore their most beautiful gowns and finery.

The young cocks strutted and preened, each plying for the attention of the daughters of the gentry in the successful gaining of the hand of one to escort to the dance floor.

The banquet consisted of the fattest fowl, the best of beef, pork, and game, the freshest catch from the ocean, and assorted fruits and vegetables brought in from offshore markets, all accompanied by the finest wines, ales, and brandy available.

With the banquet completed, the women sat sipping champagne, catching up with the latest scandal and smiling at the antics of their sons and daughters. The men, of course, retired to discuss business over the traditional ports and brandies.

"Gentlemen, Lord Porchester will address us this evening. He has much to tell you of foreign investment and opportunity."

The portly figure of the lord stood. "I am aware that many of us own land in Ireland and the returns continue to be good, but as an investment, there is always the ongoing risk of unfavourable weather and the unpredictable moods of our Irish tenants." Lord Porchester paused as a murmur of polite response rippled throughout the room. "Quite frankly," he continued, "I wish that we could replace the lot with good English stock; however, that not being practical, we should turn our attention elsewhere.

"Currently, we have in excess of twelve thousand English ships plying the world's oceans, and we are trading with most of the New World. But there still remain many lands untouched, islands recently discovered still virgin in vegetation and game, and peopled by savages unfit to reap the land's bounty. You are all aware of our great explorer, Cook, who was savagely killed by these natives. You may also be aware of the land he discovered in the southern reaches of the Pacific and claimed for the heads of our realm, and of course, us.

"Unfortunately, the bastard French, Spanish, and Portuguese also want to lay claim to our newly discovered land, just as the Dutch have claimed much of the African continent and continue to cause us considerable embarrassment and thus have a strategic advantage over us.

"For these reasons, we plan to sail to and colonise the land east of the great continent of Africa.

"The heads of the brotherhood that we all belong to have long been concerned with another serious matter, that of the continuing burden of overcrowded jails and the serious problem of an increasing number of criminals joining their ranks. Gentlemen, we don't want or need this filth in England; we want a society free of murderers, thieves, pickpockets, and vagabonds.

"We therefore propose that we empty our jails, scour the streets, and pick up any of those we don't want in our country and pack them in ships and send them to these new lands.

"This serves the dual purpose of ridding our shores of these animals and colonising our new land. It will also act as a major deterrent to our European neighbours.

"As these new lands are cultivated, and in time become viable, we will then step in and claim them as ours and share the bounty equally among us."

A silence ensued as this exiting news sank in, and then moments later, the men forgot their usual stiff upper lip and erupted in cheering. When calm settled, several of the men had questions.

Lord Porchester said, "I have invited a small number of ships' captains here this evening. I have suggested they mingle with you and answer any questions you may have and generally give you the benefit of their experiences in these and other waters. I introduce to you Captain Arthur Phillip."

"Thank you, Lord Porchester," Captain Phillip said, and he stood to be heard by all. "Captain James Cook was indeed a great captain and a great man. His achievements will forever be etched in history. No navigator explored the Pacific as thoroughly as he did, nor made discoveries so momentous or important. In the name of His Britannic Majesty, he laid claim to the largest land mass in the Southern Hemisphere, the island continent known as New Holland. Thanks to the good captain's considerable skills, this vast land, with all its hidden wealth, lies waiting for those who will claim it."

Captain Phillip continued his presentation, fielding questions and generally creating immense excitement.

It did not take long for the realization of new wealth to sink in. After Captain Phillip finished speaking, he and the other captains found themselves fending off the eager opportunists.

Most of the questions were related not only to the island continent, but to the other islands in the South Pacific, but as information was limited, the replies only left them more intrigued and more determined to be the first to lay claim to the imagined riches awaiting them.

"What say you, Bolton?" Porchester murmured into his friend's ear, having taken him aside to light a new cigar. "Look at them, like greedy little roosters around the grain bin."

"Quite true, Porchester," Bolton replied. "Indeed, quite correct, but the potential for wealth is incredibly great. Certainly if the new lands offer similar finds of gold, silver, and other riches such as those found in the Americas, I would be happier to invest my time and money there rather than in Ireland."

"You make an excellent point, Bolton. How are things in Ireland? I am continually having problems with my Irish tenants."

"Likewise." Bolton said the word with such disdain that it sounded like a growl. "As it happens, the Lady Constance and I intend to travel to Ireland toward the end of summer to help supervise the harvests with my son, Robert."

"And how is the young bounder, a terrible young rascal as I recall." Porchester smiled.

"At times he is a bit of a handful, I'll grant you that. He is ambitious, but I am happy to report that he runs our affairs in a professional and profitable manner."

Changing the subject, Bolton said, "Allow me to introduce

you to Captain Phillip. He is a remarkable young man with a wonderful future ahead of him. I hear that the admiralty have their eyes on him, and there is talk of a huge opportunity that he could be offered."

*****

As Lord Bolton and Lady Constance rode home in the carriage, he told her about the riches in the New World.

"My dear, I believe that the knowledge made available to us this evening will alter our lives and change the destiny of our wonderful country forever."

Lady Constance gave her husband an assessing gaze, somewhat bemused at his enthusiasm to continually search for further riches, but deep within herself, she was saddened at the thought that his gain would most certainly be at the expense of others.

## Chapter 22

"Top o' the morning to you, Padraig Joseph Gallagher the Younger! Get down from your horse. I'll allow you to go no farther."

The words in Gaelic came from a concealed place in the trees along the roadside.

"And a fine day it is to you also, Patrick Malloy." The reply came also in Gaelic.

"You cannot go any farther. The madness might strike you, too." Patrick Malloy emerged from the bushes.

"Madness!" Padraig Joseph smiled. "And indeed, what is this madness you refer to?"

"Your two fine lads and those others down there at the beach at Maghara I am telling you about. 'Tis themselves and that Frenchman friend of yours that are acting as if the divil himself has claimed them. 'The Madmen of Maghara' my wife calls them."

A puzzled Padraig Joseph alighted from his horse.

"Oh yes, completely mad they are," Malloy continued. "I have forbidden Maretta to go nowhere near them. As naked as babies they are, charging up the sand dunes, then back down again and jumping into the sea with not a cloth on a one o' them. Shouting like banshees! And into the sea, I tell you."

"Well now, this I must see," said Padraig Joseph. "Come, show me."

Together, the two men walked the mile or so to the dunes and scanned their eyes up and down the beach. They eventually spotted a group of people near the stream under the trees.

As they approached, both Sean and Padraig grinned and shouted gleefully to their father.

Hugo also welcomed the two newcomers.

"You have chosen a fine time to visit, my friend. Come, view the warriors. I would ask that you settle quietly and allow them to demonstrate their new skills." They watched as Hugo selected two men and beckoned them toward him.

Suddenly, both stiffened.

"Excellent!" Hugo smiled. "The triangle of intent. What action will you take?"

Both men circled warily, then, as one seemed to attract the attention of Hugo, the other sprang. Suddenly, Hugo was on his back in the sand, both men astride him, their hands raised above his head in a menacing manner.

"Well done. Padraig, an explanation for your father is in order, I believe."

"We have been taught that in conflict, if an opponent shows any form of triangle in his arm, he is about to produce a weapon. We must then strike first. Hugo's hand had gone behind his back, his arm bent into a triangle shape as he went for a knife. You saw what happened."

"Phee!" Patrick Malloy exhaled, obviously very impressed.

"Right lads, I want you to go for a run to the end of the beach and back while we have a talk."

Both men watched amazed as Sean and Padraig moved off at a fast pace.

"I can hardly believe what I am seeing, Hugo," Padraig said, shaking his head in disbelief.

"Mad, I told you, mad as March hares!" Patrick exclaimed

"Now, what tidings do you bring?" Hugo asked.

"Not good, I am sad to say. Three days ago, Bolton's men arrived at farms inland from Letterkenny. All were told to pay the new rents. They either could not or would not. That night, their doors were bashed in, the men were beaten, and their furniture smashed. A couple of the young lads were badly hurt when they tried to help their parents.

"The constables were called, but offered no help or sympathy for that matter. Our local constable, Hugh Porter, is still of the opinion that they are being paid off by Bolton or his magistrate."

"Is it only the inland farms or have there been others?" Hugo enquired.

"At this stage, they are the only farms we have heard of, but there could have been further attacks last night that we have yet to hear about. Now that this has started, I think we can only presume the worst. Bolton did promise that he would tolerate nothing but complete obedience and compliance to his orders. He will settle for total submission only."

Padraig was silent for a moment before adding, "In some respects, I am sorry I allowed this to go this far, perhaps we should have tried to negotiate with Bolton or at least tried other ways to prevent this."

"Padraig Joseph, is this the rebellious firebrand I am listening to? No, my friend, this Englishman would have pushed and demanded more and more. He never would have been happy with a compromise; from the first time I met him, I suspected he was a sadistic tormenter happy only when causing major discomfort for others. I must say with regret that for some reason he has targeted you and your family as the central point of his attention.

"No, my friend, stand firm. You will have to defend yourself. You will have to stand strong and remain determined to do all in your power to fend off this threat, and when you do, peace will return to our region. However, let me make you this promise. I will do all I can and more to equalize the odds and perhaps turn them in our favour."

"And you can be certain that us coastland people will stand firm with you, also," added Patrick Malloy. "These lands were always our lands and will stay that way so long as I draw breath."

Their conversation was interrupted by the arrival of the first of the runners.

Padraig Joseph and Patrick watched as the five raced almost in a straight line to be the first man back. Close behind them were the others.

Hardly believing his eyes, Padraig Joseph watched as his two boys drew away from the pack and sprinted the last fifty or so yards, then pulled up alongside them, barely breathing hard.

"I suspect that this little bunch of renegades will do much to assist in our equalizing," Hugo said with obvious pride, "but to utilize their new skills, we must plan with complete precision. No one but us will know what they have learned here. When they have completed their final training, they will return home and act as if nothing out of the ordinary has occurred.

"I have pondered long and hard, and I have chosen a group of men who will be involved in the planning of the defence of our properties, but more importantly, a strategic force that will assist our lads to perform to the best of their ability and allow them to show their new fighting prowess. Padraig Joseph, I will ask you to approach the people on this list." Hugo produced a page with names on it.

"Please memorize these names, and then destroy this list. I want you to call on each and invite them to meet with us at the destination shown."

Hugo smiled and said, "Patrick Malloy, I do like your description of my men. They will be known among us as the

Maghara Madmen, a name I suspect they will grow to use and love with great affection. Yes, a madness consistent with cunning, determination, and fighting skills certainly unheard of before in these parts and maybe new to our English friends. Now, with the greatest of respect, I would ask you to bid them your farewells; we have a bit more work to do before I return them to their families."

## Chapter 23

"I care more for an ugly fat whore with the pox than I care for these peasants," sneered Robert Bolton.

Judge Herbert Throckmorton Squires peered over his spectacles at Bolton. "Come now, dear boy, one should perhaps be a little more kindly disposed to these wretched people, what?"

The weather had at last turned, and the full fury of a summer storm had made the dirt roads a quagmire.

Both Bolton and Conrad Booth had attempted to arrive at the judge's office for the meeting dry and in fine humour, but the driving rain and wind had resulted in both facing the judge in foul tempers.

After a warming tea, the judge opened the business proceedings.

"The good King Henry's charter clearly defines that you are legally entitled to a fair rent, and his delightful daughter, Elizabeth, when she became queen, made it perfectly obvious that while she shared your disdain for these people, she did alter the charter, but as most would agree not in the interests of the Irish people.

"However, I feel that your hatred for the Irish does not fully allow you to beat them mercilessly into the soil and starve them off their land—your land, sir," he quickly added.

"Indeed, I would not waste good piss on them if they were on fire," said Bolton. "But I demand what I consider a fair rent, and the increases are justified. I intend to collect them in the manner that I see fit, regardless of what they or any authority says otherwise."

"I have prepared your legal notice as you requested," the judge said, handing him the parchments, not wishing to debate the matter further. "It states just as you ordered. But I am certain that instead of meeting the demands, the tenants will react most negatively toward them, and you can expect an angry reaction."

"Good. Then let it be so. The foolhardy ones will overreact, but some will toe the line. The foolhardy I will squash as the worms they are, and those who comply will be allowed to remain on the land so long as the rents are paid on time and in full each month. Quite simple, as I am sure you will agree." Bolton smiled, again without a hint of goodwill in his eyes.

"The notices will be delivered starting tomorrow, and the night callers will visit if the tenants do not respond as instructed."

The judge said, "I have noticed that you have not increased the rents in the Sligo rural regions, and there seems to be few problems there. May I enquire as to your reasoning for this?"

"Selective monetary information gathering." Bolton grinned slyly. "And besides, as I have stated time and again, the farms in this region bring in bigger yields and can afford the increases."

Seeing that it was pointless arguing, Judge Squires turned his attention to the other matters at hand.

When the meeting was over, Bolton and Booth made their way through the wind and rain to the tavern, cursing the inclement weather. With drinks in hand, they joined the men seated at the dingy rear of the smoke-filled room.

After exchanging the usual pleasantries, Bolton turned his attention to the swarthy Spaniard. "I have a job that is perfectly suited to your talents, Mandino." He explained in detail to the now fully attentive trio sitting opposite him.

Displaying milky white teeth as he smiled in anticipation, the Gypsy replied, "This task is a simple task; when would you like us to complete it?"

"This weather has settled in for at least another three, maybe four days, I am told," Bolton replied. "Perhaps three nights from now. The wind and rain should cover any noise that would alert our 'friends' to your actions."

"Consider it done. Yes?" Mandino turned to the other two men next to him.

Both nodded, lifting their glasses in agreement.

As forecasted, chilling winds and consistent drizzle greeted Bolton the following morning as he walked to the barn where the men were assembled, five of whom had been selected to carry the proclamations, which he handed to each.

"Your instructions are to call upon the tenants allocated to you. You will ensure you speak to the head of each household and read to him and his family the words of the proclamation. You will have the protection of four colleagues, but I doubt that the tenants will cause too much trouble at this stage.

"You will ask that each either give an assurance to pay in full or part thereof the monies owed to me. To refuse will invite retribution, and you will make it abundantly clear that the retribution will be swift and without mercy.

"You will be calling on only the larger properties at this point, and as these begin to fall in line, the smaller farms will follow. As you are aware, we have already started the warning process on some of the more distant smallholdings. Now, we will capitalize on those warnings. I wish you good luck, gentlemen."

# Chapter 24

Padraig Joseph and Hugo prepared to address the assembled farmers and tenants.

It was noticeable to Padraig Joseph that his two sons and the others from Hugo's select group preferred to stay together.

Hugo watched this with a knowing smile.

"They are now men—your sons and their friends. I have prepared them to protect their land and their families. They will not let you down. The time has come for you, as the chosen leader and spokesman of your people, to stand for what you believe to be fair and just. My men and I will support you. Talk to your people, Padraig Joseph; unite them and give them the pride they so rightly hunger for."

Padraig Joseph Gallagher looked around the large, crowded room attached to the tavern, watching as those before him stared back at him in anticipation of the words that surely would have such effect on the shared future that awaited them.

"The time has come, my friends," he began. "This night we make a choice. Will we be a lackey, a slave to the realm of England, forever bowing to the wishes of the uninvited and unwelcome demands of those who have stolen land from us—land that belonged to our fathers and their fathers before them? They want to take the food from our mouths and the mouths of our hungry children, and yet we must watch, as they grow fat and gloat over us.

"We lie in our beds at night cold and with hearts broken and listen to our babies cry, our women afraid of what the next day will bring. Our women watch as their spirits and the spirit of their men are stolen along with all the decency and all that we love as a family, with nothing given us in return. They have stolen everything from us. We have nothing: No dignity . . . no self-respect . . . no manhood!

"We are less than the mice and vermin that fight for the scraps of food under their tables—our food, the food that we pull from the sea and plant with our own hands, while they laugh in our faces."

One of the men called out, "You speak the truth, Padraig Joseph!"

Padraig nodded, but continued unabated. "They forbid us to follow the teachings of our church. They forbid us to educate our children. They forbid us to be who we are—the peoples of Erin. Yes, my fellow countrymen, tonight we no longer choose to lie down in dirt and indignation as cowards and accept forever all that the English do to us: rape our country, destroy us as an Irish nation . . . Together we say enough, damn you! Get from our land. Go back to your shores. Give us back our dignity. Give us back our homeland. Return Ireland to us, the Irish."

Padraig Joseph stood there in the now sudden silence.

"Enough!" one man echoed in reply.

"Enough!" another repeated vehemently.

He recognised Sean's voice and the voice of another. And then as one, all the men stood to their feet yelling, "Enough! Enough!"

The timbers of the old building fairly shook as the shouting and stomping and clenched fists punching the air continued unabated for some time until Padraig Joseph raised his arm and called for order.

The din gradually died down.

"Throughout the history of Ireland, tyranny has caused much bloodshed and the loss of innocent life. I stand here tonight not as a tyrant, but as one who is asking for justice in the name of the Irish people. History will testify that we rebelled, yes rebelled, but only against the tyrannies of the kings and queen of England. We had no choice!

"If we must fight, then fight we will, but we fight only to put right the wrongs and injustices done to the Irish people.

"If we must fight, then so be it, but we will fight only to claim what is rightfully ours and to protect and defend our properties and our families." Padraig Joseph paused. Looking slowly from left to right and then to the rear of the room, he suddenly yelled, "Who will fight with me?"

Again the room erupted as each man stood and shouted his support for the cause of justice and freedom.

Padraig Joseph raised his hands to calm their enthusiasm. "As you know, all the king's troops that were here making our lives miserable are now in America fighting another colonial cause, but there are still the local constabulary to contend with, and Bolton has quite an army of his own to do his dirty work. But I promise you that we will have a little surprise for any who attempt to force us from our land.

"Bolton's men have already started their dirty work. To ensure that we and our families are protected in the future, we will have to be ready to defeat them and to do to them as they would do to us."

"Hear, hear!" the men cheered.

"I have done enough of the talking," Padraig Joseph said, his voice sounding a bit hoarse. "Next, we will put you in groups based on the region of our beautiful country that you call home.

Hugo and I will give you further information and advise you what to do when Bolton or his men come to call."

For the rest of the evening, both men talked with each of the groups, and as earlier agreed, told them only what was necessary for them to know, but putting into place the strategy they had planned.

Later, Padraig Joseph sat with his two sons and Hugo sipping an ale.

"They are still unaware of where you were and what you were doing during your training sessions on the beach," Padraig said quietly to his sons. "And we intend to keep it that way until the time is right to strike."

*****

The Weasel could hardly contain his excitement. The information he had for Robert Bolton could result in a nice little purse and who knows what else.

Bolton was enjoying a later than usual breakfast when he was told of the Weasel's arrival.

"Send him in, and ask Conrad to join us."

The Weasel told them about the meeting the previous night and how the tenant farmers were swayed by the powerful oratory of Padraig Joseph Gallagher. When he added that all the farmers were in favour of rebellion, the earl's countenance darkened.

Booth, sensing the mood of his friend, fired question after question at the Weasel as Bolton sat in silence, listening attentively.

Finally, he said, "You have done well. Conrad, this report is well worth a few shillings. Please pay our friend his money, and when you return, I would like you to bring Mandino with you."

A short time later, the three men sat in the earl's study.

"When you return from tonight's task, I have another job for you," he said to the Gypsy. "I understand that one of your men is particularly adept with the garrotte."

Mandino smiled. "Si, señor."

"I have a small concern that seems to be growing into a larger problem. The root of this problem needs to be . . . shall we say, eradicated."

Observing the look of puzzlement on the Spaniard's face, Bolton explained what he wanted done and was pleased when Mandino nodded his head enthusiastically in agreement.

## Chapter 25

Padraig missed Kathleen and the twins more than he had missed anything in his life. During the beach training, when the opportunity allowed, he visualized being with them in their home with Jess and the pups clamouring around them. He ached not only from the pain of the exercises, but from the pain of separation, and while he was sad to leave his comrades, he could hardly wait to return home.

At night before falling asleep, he pondered how best to announce his arrival, whether by stealth—sneaking in and surprising them—or bursting through the door shouting, "I'm home!"

However, Hugo had ended training early to allow them time to stop off at a small roadside tavern on their way back to their homes, and as the loaded wagon pulled up, Padraig begrudgingly joined the thirsty brigade at the small bar.

"Don't fret so, brother," Sean said with a hearty clap on Padraig's shoulder. "Before Kathleen is finished with you this night, you will wish you were back here with us." Sean laughed.

More ribald comments followed from the others, and soon Padraig realized he may as well enjoy the moment, and of course, the ales.

Too soon, they heard Hugo shouting above the din. "Attention, *mes garçons*! We must go now. The storm is moving closer, and poor Padraig has had enough time away from his bride."

When Sean and Padraig were dropped off, the commotion caused by the shouting and laughing of their friends brought Claire rushing out of the house to see what the ruckus was about, and soon Kathleen came out to join her.

Padraig fell, rather than jumped, from the wagon and, oblivious to all the banter, he ran to her waiting arms.

Later, as they sat eating their supper and tending lovingly to the little babes, Padraig tried to tell Kathleen of his experiences while away, but all he truly wished to do was tell her of his love for her and how much he had missed her.

He also felt that while he had learned a great deal, and he was now a different person than the young man who had begun the training program, he would have preferred to stay away from the violent path his friends were eagerly looking forward to.

Although Kathleen had been willing to allow Padraig to make love to her so soon after the birth, he realized that to do so would cause her discomfort and pain, and so he had declined. However, that night as they lay together, she eased herself on top of him, and tenderly and so gently, he entered her. As she felt him begin to climax, she took his big hand and guided his forefinger to where he massaged her slowly and then increasing until she began to cry out loud and then louder, and as her passion climaxed, Padraig, moaning in ecstasy, released his love deep inside her.

It was much later, as Kathleen lay fast asleep in his arms, loving her soft breathing against the side of his cheek and listening to the little ones give an occasional snuffle, Padraig suddenly felt a cold fear descend around him. "God, please don't take them from me," he whispered softly.

He had no idea why this dire feeling should fall over him; he knew only that to lose his loved ones would be to lose his mind, his body, and his very soul.

The silence of the night was broken by the sound of an owl outside their bedroom window, and Padraig suddenly felt very alone and very afraid. Tenderly holding Kathleen as close as he could without waking her, protecting her, listening to those night sounds, he gradually drifted off to sleep.

He saw the woman in his dreams. He was sitting on the sands of a shoreline so different to any he had ever seen. She was dressed in a white gown with a white hood that covered her head. When she slowly pulled the hood back from her face, he gazed into her eyes so piercingly blue, but filled with sadness.

Her face, so very beautiful, reflected that sorrow. As she stared at him, tears welled in her eyes and coursed down her cheeks to her gown.

Padraig extended his hand to her, but as he did, she suddenly disappeared.

He awoke in the morning with the memory of the woman stark and vivid in his mind's eye.

He left the bed where his beloved Kathleen was sleeping peacefully, and he walked down to greet Jess. He spoke quietly to her and gently tickled behind her ears, and again he felt that deep feeling of dread. Sitting with his dog's head on his lap, Padraig suddenly began to weep. Sobbing uncontrollably, he felt Jess stand and lick the tears that were falling down his face.

It was some time before he could gather his senses, and then only because he heard Kathleen attending to one of the twins. He rose and went to join her.

## Chapter 26

Sean arose from his bed when he heard the first sounds of the morning songbirds.

With the storm still having not abated, he decided to ride into Killybegs and talk to his fellow fishermen since they wouldn't be at sea today. He needed to explain to the captain and crew why he would not be available as a regular crewmember for some time in the future.

After saddling up one of the family's two mares, he went into the house and bade farewell, promising to return the next day.

With the wind blowing the rain full into the face of both horse and rider, the journey was not as pleasant as it normally would have been, and Sean was much happier as the little fishing village came into view.

From the top of the hill looking down onto the harbour he could just make out the tied–up fishing boats through the misty rain.

After stabling the horse, he walked to the house of his friend, Lonny, who was also the owner of the boat.

He quickly warmed up over a cup of hot tea and began to explain why he had been absent for the past few weeks and why he could not be relied on for much of the remainder of the summer.

"Summer," Lonny replied, looking with disgust at the dismal cold rain. "'Tis more like midwinter. Still an' all, it should clear in the next day or two."

The friends chatted a while longer, with Lonny showing great concern as Sean explained the predicament he and his family were in.

"Do you think that the beating you took not so long back was related to all this?" Lonny enquired.

"There are those who think so . . . yes, perhaps."

"Well, if there is anything we can do to help, you only have to ask," Lonny said, and he added with a sly smile, "While you are here, though, you can help me do some work on the nets."

"Gladly I will help you, but on one condition." Sean grinned.

"Aye, lad, agreed, I'll set them up later in the Atlantic Tavern."

With the nets repaired, the friends joined several other fishermen, and together they roundly cursed the weather gods while downing mugs of creamy fine porter.

The drizzle and sea mists created an eerie atmosphere outside the tavern, and the day was darkening early, so Joseph John lit the lamps to bring some warmth and light into the drinking area. Noticing three newcomers entering the tavern, he left the fishermen and went down to the other end of the bar to serve them.

The effect of the good beer had improved the mood, and with voices raised and hearty laughter ringing out, no one noticed the English accents of the men ordering drinks from Joseph John.

As they turned and carried their drinks to the side of the bar, the barkeep returned to Sean and his friends, who noted the guarded expression on his face and immediately felt their hackles raised.

"I say Sean," Joseph John said under his breath, "don't make it too obvious, but when you get a chance, take a look at those three who just walked in and ordered. They were in here the night you were beaten."

Appearing to be talking to Lonny, Sean peered over the shoulder of his friend. In the dim light, he could just make out the features of the three.

He could see that one was completely without any hair on his face or head. Another was dark and quite ugly, with a cruel countenance. The third was sitting further in the gloomy darkness, so he couldn't really see too much of him.

He could, however, tell that they were all big men. And he did notice that all three were staring right at him.

"Problem?" Lonny enquired.

"Not yet, but I think there may well be sometime soon," Sean said quietly.

"If they're the ones who beat you, I don't think they'll be game to start anything this night, not with all you lads around." Joseph John said this to the eager faces of the fishermen, who now realized there was a hint of trouble in the air.

"You know, lads, I think I might just walk on over and say hello."

With the bravado of a good few porters, Sean started across the room. The three men watched him closely, sitting motionless.

"It's English, you are then?"

They sat in silence staring at him.

"You wouldn't happen to be three of Robert Bolton's men now, would you?"

Again, silence.

"Now presuming you are puppets of Bolton, and not pretty ones I tell ya, then may I be asking, are you the cowardly scum who would attack a man behind his back?"

"Did you piss in your trousers then?" This snarled reply came from the man in the shadows.

"Would you like to stand up here and repeat that?" Sean spat in his direction.

The confrontational words had not escaped the fishermen, who had moved closer and now stood behind Sean.

Hair finally spoke. "On your territory and with us outnumbered,

I don't think so." He waited a beat and added, "But you will get yours, and I will be the deliverer."

"That'll be enough." Joseph John pushed through and stood between Sean and the seated men. "I'd take it kindly if you three got the hell out of here. You and your lot are not welcome here, and I'm telling you to leave and don't come back."

They slowly rose and made for the door.

Looking back, Hair said, "Remember, Irishman, I'm coming for you."

"And I'll be waiting." Sean smiled darkly.

★ ★ ★ ★ ★

"What time do you think it might be now?"

"Close to two hours after midnight."

"Good, then let's move."

Gypsy Mandino and the two Scots moved from the cover of the trees. The lamps they carried threw enough light to guide them through the misty gloom. The house was in darkness, and they made no sound as they crept past and made their way to where they knew the dogs would be sleeping.

Just after Kathleen let Jess out to enjoy the night air and escape the pups for a few minutes, the slightly built Macgregor sneaked into the backyard and tossed the poisoned meat toward the back door. He watched with satisfaction as Jess gulped the unexpected treat and went back inside.

As the lamp lit up the inside of the house, Mandino could make out the motionless form of the sheep dog. The pups lay by her side, obviously disturbed by the strange cold stillness of their mother. Their frightened eyes looked up around them, and they whimpered softly as they tried in vain to snuggle under Jess's unresponsive body.

## Chapter 27

Just before dawn, Kathleen awoke and fed the hungry babes while Padraig slept on.

When he woke, the sun had broken through the surly clouds, and as he looked out their window, he could see that the bad weather of the last few days had finally cleared.

He turned and gazed at his wife lying in a halo of black tresses, who, after feeding the twins, had fallen back to sleep.

For some minutes, he lay there staring at her, the memory of their lovemaking still fresh in his mind.

The twins fed and contented slept peacefully in their cot by their bedside.

Gradually as the new day's sun began to warm the room, Padraig thought of turning over and cuddling up to Kathleen.

The bad memories of the troublesome dream faded, and the time spent with Hugo and his comrades no longer seemed as important as his responsibility to his family took preference.

*Ah*, he thought, *better see to the dogs.*

He rose and quietly dressed without disturbing his sleeping family.

As he walked down to where Jess would be with her puppies, he stretched and yawned. "Where's that good dog, then?"

Puzzled, he stood there for a moment. Jess was always sitting close to the doorway to the room where she slept with her young, waiting to be with her master as he walked into the room.

As he turned to walk outside, he looked to where the newly washed baby clothes sat folded on the table.

He froze in horror.

His beloved dog, disembowelled, lay with her intestines and blood staining the babies' clothing. Her puppies, with their throats cut, were lying beside her.

Padraig stood staring and then closed his eyes, hoping that when he opened them again this nightmare would have gone away. Slowly he sank to his knees weeping. "Oh, my God, how do I tell Kathleen?"

Numb with shock and shaking badly, Padraig placed the bodies of his beloved animals in a blanket and carried them into the barn. Tears still fell on his hands as he dug the graves to bury Jess and her pups. "Who did this to you? Why?"

As he patted the last mound of earth in place, he thought of the bloodstained washing. He dropped the spade and went quickly to hide the washing before Kathleen could witness the horrific spectacle.

"So, who is looking for more rewards then? Surely the man doesn't do the woman's work unless he wants something, now does he?" Kathleen stood watching him with a cheeky smile.

Padraig let the washing fall to the ground, and he walked toward his wife. He put his arms around her and held her tight to him.

"What's wrong, Padraig, talk to me. What's happening?"

"I don't know what's happening, I know only that evil is all around us," he murmured, and then she realized he was choking back tears.

"Come, my beautiful love, we need to go down and talk to my father, but first I have to tell you of a terrible happening, and my heart is breaking at the very thought of it."

As Padraig turned to place the washing where his wife would not see it before he told of his discovery, he looked outside at the surrounding trees, searching for hiding eyes and the fearful threat they now posed to his beloved wife and children.

★★★★★

Each holding a babe in his or her arms, Padraig and a tearful Kathleen burst into their parents' house, startling Claire as she was preparing breakfast.

"What's wrong? Padraig, why is Kathleen crying?"

"Where's Father? I need to see him."

The very unusual curt reply shook Claire.

Frowning, she replied, "He and your grandfather are out in the barn."

"I'm sorry to tell you this, Mother—Jess and her pups have been killed. Please look after Kathleen and the babies."

Carefully placing the baby girl in his mother's arms, he rushed outside and ran to the barn. "Father, Grandfather!" he called.

Both men were focused on reshoeing one of the horses when they looked up, startled at Padraig's sudden arrival.

"A fine morning to you, son, or is it?" enquired his father.

As Padraig poured out the sad story, his father's face hardened.

"The filthy bastards! It has to be that bloody Bolton, the bastard."

"How is Kathleen?" his grandfather asked. "She will be heartbroken."

"Grandfather, she is very, very upset—and afraid."

"Come. I think we should all go inside and see to our women," he replied.

The three men returned to the house to find Claire still trying to console Kathleen. Seeing Padraig, she jumped up and ran into his arms. He held her tight.

Claire had prepared a large pot of tea, and they all sat down and began to search for answers as to what to do next. After much deliberation, it was decided that the three men would go into town and talk to Hugo and maybe the constable.

"I have to say I'm not surprised," began Hugo. "I have been waiting to see what Bolton would do to your family. No doubt at all that he is behind this; he was just biding his time, and now that he has struck, he will increase the pressure until he squashes you all."

"So, what do we do next?" Padraig Joseph the Older enquired.

"By these actions, and presuming it is the work of Bolton, he will expect you to react or to submit.

My real concern, young Padraig, is that he or his men entered your home and did these vile acts without raising alarm from your dogs or waking you." Hugo looked at the father and then at the grandfather.

"I shudder to think what this morning could have been if they had gone for Kathleen and the babies."

## Chapter 28

"Gentlemen, you know what you have to do."

Robert Bolton stood up and stretched. He had spent the last half hour or so enjoying a pot of coffee while discussing the tenancy situation with those he had chosen to lead the collection groups.

"As agreed, you will take your men and demand the outstanding rents due from your allocated list of farmers and tenants.

"You will advise that they have until mid-afternoon to collect the monies and pay you when you return at that time. You will also advise them that you will return each week about the same time and collect that week's rent.

"There will be no more warnings or dilly-dallying around. Failure to pay will result in immediate eviction. In those cases where you feel it is necessary, you may burn their hovels to the ground—if need be, with the tenants inside.

"This will have the added effect of a severe warning to those whose properties are worthy of saving and must pay up or else.

"I think you will all agree I have been more than fair. I am entitled to what is rightfully mine, and I have the right to claim it."

He paused and smiled, adding, "Oh, and don't forget your bonuses. Those that show true aptitude will be rewarded accordingly. Shall we call them 'blood bonuses'?"

He chortled, and the others sniggered in derision at the hapless Irish. "So, gentlemen, off you go a-merrily collecting. Good luck to you all."

A short time later, in fine humour, Bolton and Booth watched as the riders and wagons departed with their motley crew of thugs.

However, as they passed through the gates of the manor and turned inland, hidden eyes were watching.

"Follow at a distance being careful not to be spotted. Bring us back word of the places they visit. Go swiftly now."

As riders slipped quietly from their hidden places, Hugo mounted his horse, beckoning to the other two.

"Come, we will ride and join the others at the meeting place."

The Brackey River meanders down from the highlands gathering moisture from the Atlantic rains and from the low cloud cover of mist and fog. At times, it is a raging torrent, at other times a smallish river that winds its way over rocks and falls, forming pools where salmon gather before heading upstream to spawn.

In a field alongside one such pool, the men had gathered and lay around in the lush grasses enjoying the mid-morning warmth.

A delighted yell of triumph sounded from the water's edge.

"That backside of an ass, 'tis ya brother, Sean Gallaher," one of the men muttered. "The lucky beggar has landed a fat sea trout, I wager."

A confirmation of his prediction came flying up from the stream and landed on the bank, flapping and glistening in the sunlight.

"And I'll soon have another to join that one on my plate tonight!" came the happy comment from the river's edge.

"How do you put up with the swaggering arrogant oaf, Padraig?"

"Ah, Danny, 'tis the price of being the intelligent one in the family I have to admit," Padraig said goodnaturedly, but his smile belied the sadness that rested heavy on him.

Sean had arrived back from Killybegs, and hearing of the death of his brother's pet animals and witnessing the grief in his brother and sister-in-law Kathleen, he had become enraged. It was only the soothing influence of their mother that had gradually calmed him, but not before swearing a bloody oath of vengeance.

"The bastards will pay, Padraig. We will find them and do what it is necessary. That I promise you!"

The sound of galloping horses approaching interrupted their conversation.

"This will be Hugo."

As the men jumped to their feet, the three riders galloped through the trees and down onto the field, dismounting before their horses stopped moving.

"Greetings to you, comrades!" Hugo called. "Come, gather around. We have much to discuss and plans to put into place before the day grows old. So first, I want you to form into your groups as we have practiced."

The young men swiftly obeyed and waited for further instructions.

"Excellent. Now select your weapons."

All the men complied and then stood quietly. Some held blackthorn staffs, which were long and thick at one end and thin enough to hold and wield at the other. Others held a shorter but similarly fashioned version. Both weapons would inflict great damage, but would not splinter or break. Some of the men had chosen cudgels.

"Knifemen, step forward," Hugo commanded.

Six men walked to the front of the assembled groups.

Hugo handed each a small sack. Inside the bag nestled a knife with an unusual shaped blade. Hugo had first discovered the Shabaria while living in the Jordan River region. The razor sharp curved blade, while acceptable for everyday use, was essentially a fighting weapon and unique in providing self-defence.

"Men, I am entrusting you with a fighting weapon of great importance. Skilled warriors have used these knives for many centuries. Much blood has flowed as this beautifully crafted blade has ended the lives of countless thousands over the ages. You have had limited training in the art of close hand fighting with your knife, but you will develop new skills in combat and become even more proficient. I wish you luck as the spirit of your Shabaria protects you and licks the blood of those who would do you mortal harm."

Hugo had watched his men very carefully on the sands of Maghara. After great consideration, he had chosen those to whom he would entrust a Shabaria blade. Not one of the young men had been in any confrontation that could be regarded as life threatening, with the possible exception of Sean.

He was well aware that there were experienced killers among Bolton's force, who would end the life of one of his friends without a second thought. And while all of his men could now hold their ground and wield their clubs with skill and ability, he knew that the earl had superior weaponry, certainly firearms, and a variety of knives.

But he was aware that few could match him in frontal confrontation, particularly in the fighting skills he had developed in the deadly arena of the dark and dingy back streets and alleys of the slums of Paris and Marseilles.

He had passed on these skills to his young and willing army of country Irish lads.

"In a short time, we will learn how Bolton's men intend to inflict harm on our farming friends. Today, you will test your training, as you protect those families and repel the invaders. On this day, you will walk tall and bring pride to yourselves and your people.

"Now, until the riders return with the information we require," Hugo continued, "I want you to fall into your formations and familiarize yourselves again and again with our battle strategies."

While he was addressing them, Padraig Joseph arrived and watched with Hugo as his two sons practiced hand-to-hand combat with their comrades. While worried about the outcome, he was somewhat relieved to see their precision, and pride overcame concern.

"My friend, you have done well," Padraig Joseph said to Hugo. "My sons will not let you down, nor will any of these good Irish lads."

"They won't let *you* down, *mon ami*," Hugo replied.

The first rider rode in a little later, followed soon after by the other two.

Padraig Joseph heard Hugo call to the eager young band of fighters to mount up or board the wagons. A shiver of trepidation went through him.

"My God, what have I started?" he said to himself.

He knew that only time would tell.

## Chapter 29

James John Burke lived with his wife and five children in a small thatched-roof home that had housed generations of Burkes since old John Burke had built the solid stone house during the reign of King Henry.

Mary O'Brian had fallen in love with the huge, but gentle giant of a man and promised to raise their children in the peaceful tranquility of their home nestled in the beautiful little valley so close to the fresh running water of the stream. James John was a resourceful man, utilizing all that God had gifted them in the way of natural fertilizers and regular rainfall to guarantee them a steady supply of vegetables for the family and plenty of grain to feed the animals and chickens that scratched around the house and fields.

Big James John and Mary were farmers, happily raising their children and living in peace and harmony with the land as their forefathers had done before them.

Indeed, as far back as James John could recall, the earlier generations of Burkes had all refrained from felling the majestic oak trees on their property. These magnificent trees stood so proud, protecting the family and their home from the elements. All over Ireland, trees had been cleared for timber and to make way for pasture and sowing fields, but this one small area had remained tranquil and serene under its giant canopy.

Many had heard James John remark, "Surely the wee folk need a home and all, and its best to let be what is free!"

But Mary Burke could see visions of their home engulfed in flames and her family's charred remains lying in the blackened rubble of what was now a terrible reminder of those halcyon days of old.

When Bolton's men left that morning, promising to return that afternoon for the monies they did not have, she had collapsed into the arms of her husband, with her younger children whimpering in fear at the sight of their mother's distress.

Five very large and ugly Englishmen had left little to her imagination as to what lay in store for her personally if their demands were not met.

As she sat concealed under the old oaks on the other side of the wooded area at the back of their home, she prayed to God and the Blessed Mother for the protection she so desperately craved for her and her children huddled close to her.

The buggy pulled up outside the house. The five men sat silent, alert, and looking around them.

"All too quiet, ain't it?"

"You don't suppose they run off?"

"Shut ya bleedin' mouths," snarled the reins man. "Look, the front door is ajar. You, Freddy, come with me."

The two men alighted from the buggy.

The other three watched as the two carefully approached the door.

"Hey, in there—if you don't come out, we're comin' in."

A few more moments of silence passed.

"That's it. I've had enough." A raised boot smashed against the door and halted it as it rebounded back.

As the noise reverberated around the clearing, the first man charged through, followed close on his heels by the second.

When the echoes of the invasion diminished, a sullen silence descended around the house. "What in hell's goin' on?"

The remaining three men on the buggy sat perplexed, wondering what to do next.

"Bloody 'ell. I bet the bastards are havin' it off with the missus."

"I dunno, it's all too quiet, i'n't it. Should have 'eard the odd scream or two."

"Sparrow, you stay here with the buggy. C'mon, me and you'll go see what's happening."

Cautiously, the two made their way to the now fully open door. Peering inside, only silence greeted them.

Beckoning to his colleague to follow, the first man slowly eased himself into the house. The second followed.

Sparrow watched and waited. The only sound he heard was the afternoon song of a blackbird high in a tree alongside the house. The horse snuffled and shuffled her feet in agitation at having to stand so close to the grass and not being able to graze.

"Hey, you in there!" Sparrow finally shouted.

Silence.

"What's goin' on? Do you need any helping in there?" Sparrow again yelled out, but this time without too much enthusiasm.

A few more minutes passed.

"If you're not out in two more minutes, I'll go fetch Bolton."

A full fifteen or so minutes passed. Sparrow was now more than concerned; he was scared. He had felt eyes peering at him, eyes that did not belong to his friends, who now appeared to have deserted him.

"That's it. I've 'ad enough."

Pulling at the reins, he turned the horse and trotted her off at a quick pace to put distance between him and the house that had swallowed Bolton's enforcers.

Sometime later, Sparrow turned the badly lathered mare into the manor house driveway and pulled up in front of Bolton and a small group of his men.

Looking first at him and then at the empty buggy, Bolton quietly asked, "So, where are the others?"

Sparrow stuttered out his story, and to his amazement, Bolton simply ordered him to take the horse and buggy to the stables and care for the horse.

When he pulled into the stable yard, two other drivers greeted him and quickly informed him that they'd had the same experience at the farmhouses they had visited.

In the manor house, Conrad Booth and Robert Bolton were discussing this unexpected turn. "Personally, I don't blame any of them," said Booth. "I probably would have done the same. Besides, I suspect they were deliberately left alone to send back some sort of warning. What should we do now?"

"Separate them from their lower parts, to begin with," snarled Bolton.

"We first have to identify those who are responsible, then locate them, and give them our special kind of justice. But let's not forget that we also have to find out what has happened to our brave bunch of professional debt collectors, who have so far collected nothing." Booth added this last bit with dripping sarcasm, but his comment was greeted by stony silence at first.

Finally Bolton spoke. "This we know: the three places where the incidents occurred. Presumably, we will find some evidence that we can follow. And certainly we know who lives in these three hovels, so we can at least compel them to talk.

"There is still plenty of daylight, and with the long twilight tonight, we may get the answers we require. The weather appears to be staying dry, so go and round up those who are still with us and give the orders to mount up and prepare the remainder of the wagons. Also, have my stallion saddled. Then instruct them all to meet me out front."

Bolton turned and stalked out of the room. He headed straight to where his gun collection was kept.

The centrepiece of his collection was a matching pair of medallion-encrusted Doune pistols that had been given to him by the Duke of Sutherland. Beautifully crafted and deadly accurate, the pistols were the pride of his collection, and Bolton treasured them above all others.

Selecting the two pistols and ammunition, plus a long-barrelled musket and loading equipment for all, he felt a surge of excitement at the thrill of confrontation and the expectation of what lay ahead.

He dressed, positioning the loaded pistols in specially designed pockets in a knee-length black coat, and then he walked out, musket in hand, to where the assembled men waited.

He called to Hair Baker and Slow to join him and Booth.

"I don't know just how good this rabble is at resistance, but I do know I can count on you. Before this day is out, I want those responsible for today's outrage very dead, and you, Hair and Slow, I want you to personally assist me in their demise.

"Mandino, you and your men stay here with Conrad, and look after the manor until we return. Now, let's ride. You, Sparrow, lead us back to the Burke place."

★★★★★

The wagons, each carrying five or so men, and the seven mounted men approached the top of the rise. Bolton could see down through the tree-lined lane that ran to the stream and then up to the house. In the early evening light, he watched an older woman and two younger lasses struggling with pails of water as they climbed the hill up to the house, water slopping over the side of the pails.

Smiling in grim anticipation, he gave the order.

"Ride them down!"

With much shouting and hollering, the horses were spurred into action, and the chase was started.

The three water carriers, hearing the commotion, turned and saw the danger and dropped their pails and ran for the safety of the house.

The first of the riders at full gallop came to the end of the lane before fording the stream in pursuit of the three. Because of the din, none heard the command.

"NOW!"

Suddenly, two ropes were pulled taut from the cover of the trees on both sides of the lane, one a foot from the ground, the other six feet higher.

The first horses hit the lower rope and hurtled toward the water, catapulting their riders headfirst into the rocks and gravel.

The following horses and riders hit the higher rope, hurling them backward.

Unable to stop, horses and wagons surged into the chaos, stomping and smashing horse and rider alike.

"GO!"

From the trees and undergrowth, the Irish resistance fighters sprang, each swinging a large blackthorn club or pikestaff, piling into the moaning men, clubbing bone and flesh into total submission.

"ENOUGH!"

Circling the carnage, Hugo and his men surveyed their handiwork in silence. The only sounds came from the terrified horses struggling to their feet, and the feeble cries from the broken and badly injured men who were conscious. The rest lay as they had fallen.

"There they are, my two good friends." Sean pointed to Slow

and Hair.

Hugo walked to where Bolton lay barely conscious.

"Drag him over here." He indicated to two standing close by.

They obeyed, and Bolton gave an involuntary gasp as the pain from their inconsiderate handling wracked his body.

Hugo glared down at the Englishman and said, "I have no sympathy for the plight you and your friends find yourselves in. You have received probably less than you intended for this and the other families you came to call on this day. I suspect the lives of those families mean little to you, and your intentions were less than honourable. So, the question I ask is this: What do we do with you now?"

Eyes simply dripping with hatred stared back at Hugo.

"Padraig, Sean, and Liam, you and the lads separate those that are badly hurt or worse from those that can stand. Bolton, I intend to treat you and your men as you would not treat us—this time at least. I will show you the mercy that you would not show us, but only this once.

"However, if you threaten any of the Irish people, or in particular, the family Gallagher ever again, I will personally kill you. Do I make myself clear?"

Bolton stared at him, then turned his head, and watched as his men tried to gather themselves together.

In considerable pain, he finally managed to stand. "You must do as you must do. So must I." He spat some blood out of his mouth onto the ground at Hugo's feet.

"So be it," Hugo replied, unfazed at Bolton's display of contempt.

"Come. Let us be gone," Bolton snarled. "Those who are able can take care of those that need help."

Without another word, he climbed onto his stallion after much struggle, staunchly refusing help, and his defeated party piled into their wagons and drove away rather quickly, Hugo observed.

As they melted into the woods, Sean paused alongside Hair and promised, "Englishman, it was I who bashed and spread your ugly nose across your face. It was I who kicked my big Irish boot up your arse. And it will be I who will send you to hell if you show your shit ugly face near me again—you and that filthy creature." He pointed to the hapless Slow covered in blood, trying to get to his feet.

He then turned, and whistling a little ditty, went to join his friends.

Hugo turned to Padraig standing close to him and said, "Let us enjoy this, our first taste of victory, but I am certain Bolton will not be so easy to tangle with the next time."

Padraig nodded, but said nothing.

## Chapter 30

Gypsy Joe Mandino could hardly believe his eyes as the bloodied and soiled Robert Bolton rode his slightly limping stallion up to the manor. Five or so in similar condition followed. Even more stunned, he watched as the wagons used to transport the others turned into the barn stable yard. Those men who needed help were aided by others in a not too dissimilar condition. All were bloodied with gaping cuts and wounds from head to toe.

Unaided, Bolton slipped from the saddle, almost stumbling, and addressed the Gypsy.

"Don't just stand there staring, you stupid fool. Get the others and help them." He indicated to those behind him. "Then harness up a wagon, take anyone who can walk, and go fetch those we had to leave behind. I suspect we may be burying one or two."

Bolton's eyes darted around at the scruffy lot of them. "You, whatever your name is, go with the Gypsy."

He then staggered into the manor, almost colliding with Conrad Booth.

"What . . . ?"

"Never mind what!" Bolton interrupted. "I want to know who, how, and when these ignorant peasants could not only offer resistance, but do so and succeed. Furthermore, I want that bastard

Weasel brought to me first thing in the morning. He had better have answers, and perhaps more important, he better have a good reason for why he did not give us this information earlier."

*****

Both Padraig Joseph Gallaghers, grandfather and son, listened as Sean and Padraig told them about the events of the day. Scarcely believing the news, each reacted differently.

"That'll show the Englishmen what we're made of!" Padraig Joseph the Younger chortled with delight as Sean enthusiastically told and retold how he had gained revenge for the beating he had taken from Hair and Slow. "They'll not come back for a second helping to be sure." He raised his glass and swallowed a large portion of fine Irish whiskey in triumph.

While Padraig Joseph the Younger celebrated their victory, the older Gallagher was somewhat reticent. His only remark was, "And it's all to you, me fine boys, and you, Hugo; you did well, by God you did well."

Both Claire and Kathleen had joined the victory celebrations, and although now approaching two o'clock in the morning, there seemed little likelihood of a halt to the proceedings—at least not until the drink ran out.

Few, if any, of those who had delivered such a telling blow to Bolton's men had left, none wishing to miss a single moment of the afterglow of victory.

But neither Claire nor Kathleen could help but notice that while Sean and his father relived each moment with great gusto and cheered wildly as each of the other lads told of their moment of glory, his brother Padraig was strangely silent.

It was some time later that his grandfather spoke to him. "My grandson, you don't seem to be enjoying this night as the others are doing."

"Oh, indeed I am, Grandfather, indeed, I am. I am only worried of what Bolton is thinking right now. I know he will not let this pass. I know that at this very moment, he is plotting his revenge, and he will exact a terrible retribution, but on who, Grandfather? Will it be us he targets?"

Claire could not help, but overhear her son's words. She then knew that her worst fears and the horrible premonitions that had so frightened her would soon be upon them.

Just before the sun rose and the skies began to lighten, the house emptied. Tired but happy young men made their way home. Hugo had thankfully accepted the offer of a bed and now snored with the combined assistance of many tumblers of assorted whiskeys and ales.

As Claire lay alongside her sleeping husband, the memories of her son Padraig and his wife walking from her home were deep within her. She could still see Padraig holding a babe in one big arm, the other around the shoulders of Kathleen as she held the other babe close to her in her right arm. As they walked up the hill to their home, she had watched until they were out of sight.

Tears welled up and ran down her face into the pillow. How soon would it be before her world no longer existed? How long before the evil that she knew was so near visited and destroy them all?

Kathleen watched her husband place the babies in their sleeping cot. The tenderness that such a big man could display when handling his little ones never failed to amaze her. That same tenderness and gentleness when he touched her during their lovemaking gave her a longing to be in his arms and never leave him.

"My love, there is something that bothers me. You were so quiet when your brother and your friends told of their exploits. It was almost as if you were not there."

Padraig stared at Kathleen. Finally he spoke.

"Oh, indeed, I was there, and surely I did the damage to Bolton and his men. But Kathleen, my love, I can lay no claim to pleasure in my actions. At first, I thirsted for the opportunity to break open the heads of the English, who would do much to hurt us. I wanted revenge for what they did to Jess and her pups. But when will it stop? I know full well that Bolton will return, this time with more men and more arms and more hatred of us, the Irish. He won't stop—at least not until we are all beaten into submission and with the probable death of many of those close to us.

"I also know full well that my father and brother ache with the anticipation of another and yet another opportunity to let English blood flow.

"If I refuse to fight with them, I am a coward and not worthy of the love and respect of my family and friends. If I fight and thus bring pain, anguish, and possibly even death to you and to those I love so much, then who is the winner and who the loser and at what terrible price?"

Kathleen stood by her husband's side and cradled his head to her bosom.

"Ah, now, surely the good God above will be looking over us and sheltering us from danger. He would not have allowed those beautiful wee ones to come into our life and then take them away from us now, would he?"

Later, as Padraig drifted off to sleep, Kathleen's words stayed with him.

Would he take their two beautiful babies from them?

## Chapter 31

The early morning screeching of the crows woke her, but her husband slept on. While others called him by his nickname, she addressed him by his birth name, Arthur. The Weasel hated his Christian name and ignored it when used by anyone but his wife.

While secretive by nature, his wife preferred secretive to sly. Arthur had been particularly silent of late. When questioned as to his whereabouts, he would shrug and murmur, "Ah, just doin' tings."

So, the smashing of fists on their door so early in the day alarmed her, but it did not really surprise her. "Arthur! Arthur, wake up!"

Stumbling from their bed and hastily pulling on his trousers, the Weasel tottered to the front door. Half asleep, he peered out at the three men standing on his doorstep staring at him.

"Come with us. Now!"

He was suddenly grabbed, and before he could give any resistance, the Weasel was dragged to the waiting horses. The horsemen galloped off with the Weasel barely hanging on to one of the riders.

Gradually, as his pleading questions were met with stony silence, he realized they were headed for Bolton's manor. He also realized he was in trouble, but he had no idea why.

The horses galloped up to the manor, and he was dumped unceremoniously at the front entrance.

He looked up and saw Bolton staring down at him. His premonitions of danger were confirmed as he noticed for the first time that Bolton's normally immaculate veneer had changed terribly. The doctoring of the previous day's damage had done little to hide the wounds he had collected.

"Get inside!" Bolton demanded. "Move your slimy carcass."

The Weasel was pushed and shoved up the steps and into the house. His eyes darted around the palatial room and saw Bolton easing himself into a chair; several others sat waiting in the comfortable furniture clustered around the fireplace.

"You have been paid well, Arthur; in fact, very well to provide me with any information that pertains to the Gallagher family and their rebellious ways." Bolton paused and stared at the now visibly shaking Weasel. "Well?" Bolton prodded him for an answer.

"I don't know . . ."

"What don't you know, imbecile! Do you mean to tell me that you don't know that these stinking Irish bastards have their own private army? Those same filthy bastards appear to be very well trained and are now laughing at their very obvious cleverness at dishing out what they consider a considerable victory. We suffered not only an embarrassing loss of dignity, but most of us are now nursing injuries, some so severe that at least two of my men may not survive this day, and you tell me you don't know.

"Well, Weasel, let me tell you something you do know. Unless I receive information that points me to the instigators and all those who participated in this sorry debacle, I will personally cut the throats of those vermin you call your children and turn your wife over to those who suffered yesterday. They, I promise, will show little mercy. Do I make myself clear?"

"Yes, yes, I think so . . ."

"You only think so!" roared Bolton. "Then think of this. As you watch the demise of your family, you will be thinking of how I will kill you and how slowly you will die. Now what do you think?"

"Tell me what you want me to do, Lord Bolton."

Bolton spent the next hour explaining exactly what he expected from the badly shaken man, and then he sent for the Spaniard.

"Take this fool to Bandara. It being market day, I expect a large turnout in the village. As the day progresses, most will retire to the taverns where tongues will start flapping and much will be revealed. Weasel, you will listen and bring back as much knowledge as will save your sorry life.

"Mandino, ensure that you are not seen by the villagers when you meet him later this evening. Then return him to me. Now go."

*****

Judge Herbert Throckmorton Squires peered over his spectacles and successfully hid a gloating smile.

"And pray tell what misfortune has been laid upon you?" the judge enquired of the two men now seated in his office. Secretly he wished that whatever had happened to Bolton had been somewhat more severe. He had no opinion of Conrad Booth one way or the other.

"The misfortune you refer to occurred as honest revenue collectors were going about their business. And I assure you that the misfortune will be returned tenfold to those who participated in the assault on my collectors and myself," replied Bolton.

As the judge listened to Bolton's account of the previous day's happenings, he couldn't help but feel certain sympathy for the plight of the Irish farmers.

"I did suggest to you sometime back, my good fellow that even the worm doth sometimes turn. Surely, you didn't expect these people to succumb to your perhaps extravagant demands without some form of rebuttal.

"I could point out that in other parts of Donegal, and indeed other counties, collections are made without incident. Certainly the Irish are far from happy, but there appears to be a much more peaceful coexistence in those parts."

"Let me remind you," snarled Bolton, "your position here is to make our presence in this godforsaken excuse of a country a bit more acceptable. By which I refer to your legal opinion, where, correct me if I am mistaken, allows me to collect land taxes for land that my father and I own and that for some insane reason the Irish lay claim to.

"As I understand by English law, I am allowed to use force, if necessary, to pursue that claim. And as the local constabulary, indeed those not on the other side of the Atlantic, fighting another lost cause seem most reluctant to help, then I am entitled to enlist my own legal collectors."

"Ah, is that a statement or a question?" enquired the judge.

Conrad Booth shuddered as Bolton rose to his feet and stared down at Squires.

"I have had just about enough of you, this blasted country, and those that populate it, but most of all the asinine stupidity of those that live on the lands that my father and I own.

"Now, my good fellow," Bolton sneered sarcastically, "listen very carefully. I intend to use force to achieve my ends, considerable force. Your responsibility is to ensure that whatever steps I take are to be seen as legally correct. In short, some may suggest I am taking the law into my own hands. You will always, without exception, present a case of an honest businessman conducting himself in an honest and ethical business manner.

Do I make myself clear?"

*****

Sometime later, Judge Squires sat quietly sipping tea and puffing occasionally on an unlit pipe. The departure of Bolton and his colleague Booth an hour or so earlier had left him with many unanswered questions. His legal knowledge and his own insalubrious background had given him more than enough experience to realize that Bolton's behaviour was far from normal. This he had been aware of for some time.

Young Lord Bolton reeked of exaggerated egotism, mental instability, and the patent inability to conform to the gentlemanly code of honour befitting his station in life. Judge Squires wondered if Bolton suffered some sort of lunacy cleverly hidden as ruthlessness. Even the hideous possibility of syphilis had not escaped him.

One thing was certain: Bolton had a motivation far removed from the simple occupation of landowner. The judge was certain that time would reveal an obsession that he and all his wily ways could not put a finger on.

"Gertrude!" he called out to his secretary. "I need to dictate a letter to you."

## Chapter 32

The continuing fine weather had been very kind to the growing crops. Beautiful sunny days and every third night or so, a gentle swing of breezes would bring in a shower or two.

This was reflected not only in the variety, but also the quality of fresh fruits and vegetables available on the market stalls. The good humour that invariably went hand in hand with this kindly seasonal environment was also very apparent.

Claire and Kathleen were being happily charmed by one of the regular traders, a rather loud and pushy merchant but not without charisma.

"C'mon, me darlin' wee angels, you'll not find better apples than these. Firm and sweet as yourselves, I'll wager. And I'll charge you lots less than those pirates farther down the line for lesser fruit. Your husbands will wonder in awe at your cleverness to put apples like these on your table this night."

"Ah, now, you cheeky beggar," laughed Claire. "All right then, let us have a bagful and also some of those pears."

As they left with their produce, they giggled as he commenced his call to attract new trade from the next housewife out enjoying market day.

"Get your apples and pears 'ere, me dears. Don't you dare go off to those thieves over the way."

While they were both frugal, the women loved to browse the shops, and Kathleen was always the target of a mix of local affection and flirtation. She always blushed suitably and returned the comments with appropriate replies that referenced her fine husband and two sweet babies, who were being cared for by a trusted neighbour this day to give her a bit of break and a fun afternoon with her mother-in-law.

She and Claire also made sure that as the markets drew to a close around three in the afternoon, they joined other women in the ritual clamor for end–of–day bargains. They all then made their way to Maloneys to meet up with the menfolk.

As they approached the tavern, it was obvious that Maloney was doing a roaring trade with drinkers both inside and out. Pushing and shoving their way through, Claire and Kathleen eventually found their husbands surrounded by a great many of fellow imbibers.

The women were immediately paid much attention by all the men before being rescued by their respective husbands.

"I have missed you," Padraig said, smiling, as he kissed Kathleen gently on the forehead.

"Oh, to be sure, and just look at yourself, not a care in the world, while your mother and I are out doing the hard work," she replied with a mock stern reply.

"Is all well?" Claire enquired of her husband.

He quickly told her of the response of the villagers and the other farming folk who had come to town for the day, highlighting the points that all had a newfound confidence in their stand against Robert Bolton and his thugs.

Also, several recruits who had heard of the rout had volunteered to join the ranks of Hugo's fighters.

"Who knows what may develop?" Padraig Joseph added. "There is talk of this spreading throughout Donegal and even down to Sligo and maybe even farther afield."

The Weasel had been dropped outside Bandara earlier in the day. As his wife and offspring planned to visit Donegal Town the next day, he did not expect any interruption to his investigations.

As he visited each drinking establishment, he mingled with the patrons, keeping his eyes and ears open. He was stunned to learn of Hugo's success and even more astounded that his men, sometimes referred to as Hugo's Heroes, could establish themselves so quickly and efficiently into such a fighting force so secretly that few knew of its existence.

By late afternoon, as Bolton had so accurately predicted, the tongues were loosened by copious quantities of alcohol. As the Weasel deciphered fact from absolute fantasy, it became apparent that there was now a real threat to the ambitions of Bolton.

In fact, the Weasel could sense the definite prospect of the local land being returned to the rightful owners—the Irish families who had farmed that land for generations. And where would that leave him?

Thoughts of grabbing his family and escaping from the region were an option. Deserting his family and thus being able to move more quickly was another.

But if he did that and Bolton triumphed, he would lose everything. He certainly could not return.

However, if his information aided Bolton to the extent that the victory was in large part due to him, then the Weasel could rightly expect suitable compensation. Indeed, a true dilemma it was.

He was suddenly aware that the afternoon had moved into early evening. The thought of being late for his rendezvous with Gypsy Mandino sent an immediate shiver down his back, but the prospect of learning as much worthwhile information as possible was also of importance or so he thought.

And so, he made one last stop at Maloneys again.

He had been there earlier, and his eavesdropping on the Gallagher clan had provided him with the bulk of his report for Bolton.

As he walked through the entrance, he noted that the bar had thinned out a little, some having moved on to other taverns or departed for home. He glanced around slyly, taking note of those still enjoying themselves. Good-natured voices, louder than the norm, caught his attention, and he realized that they were coming from the Gallagher family and friends. It became obvious they were about to depart, and the traditional backslapping farewells were taking place.

Eventually the group made its way to the door.

"Hey, Sean, ya ugly old ass, ya!"

"What ho, lads. What brings you to these parts?"

The newcomers were obviously seafarers, fishermen like Sean, and appeared to be old friends.

Sean introduced them to his family and added, "If you wouldn't mind me staying on here for a little longer, I'll be having a few wee small ones with the lads."

As the family departed, Sean and his friends brought more ale and decided to go outside to drink. The Weasel followed.

Feigning drunkenness, he staggered along and pretended to fall onto the grassy verge not far from them. Certainly, he was well within hearing range.

"You all right there, then?" one of them asked. His only response was an exaggerated, inebriated snore.

"He's had many too many!" laughed another.

"Sean! What's all this we are hearing about a battle with those bloody English interlopers, then?"

During the next half hour, what the Weasel heard confirmed much of what he had learned earlier that day. And then the information he knew would save him made its way to his ears.

"But how did you know where to find the bastards? And how were you to know where and when to strike?"

Sean explained to his friends how Hugo had trained a fighting force to compete with any enemy, and he and his brother were part of the force.

And then, not realizing that he was releasing key strategic intelligence to listening ears, he told of Hugo's plans to be aware of all Bolton's comings and goings with his spying campaign.

"Naturally what I'm telling you is for your ears only. I know you lads won't be messing about, now."

"Sure and all this chatter is thirsty work, time for another."

The drinkers returned to the bar to recharge their jugs, and a smug Weasel snuck off into the dusk.

It didn't take him too long to reach the outskirts of Bandara, and shortly after that, a mile or two from the village, an approaching horseman indicated that the Gypsy had returned for him.

*****

The Weasel was led into the study where Bolton and Booth sat smoking cigars and drinking brandy.

"I invite you to join us, Mandino. I suspect that if this wretch has done us proud, we may well have some specialized work for you. So, what do you have for us?" Bolton enquired of the Weasel. "I'm sure I don't need to reinforce my promise to you this morning."

As the Weasel stuttered his way into what he had heard, Bolton suddenly realized that the little snitch had surpassed his expectations.

"Slow down, man, slow down. Conrad, fetch him a brandy. I suspect he might possibly deserve it."

After gulping down the contents of the glass, the Weasel continued. When he had completed his report of the day, the three men sat in silence, each deep in contemplation.

Bolton looked over to Booth. "Conrad, I believe our friend has done well, very well, in fact."

Turning to the Weasel, he continued. "I will also have more for you to do. In the meantime, not a word to a single soul, or I will have yours. Mandino, give him a ride back home to his wife, a little more gently this time." To the Weasel he added, "I will require you back here in the morning. Don't be late."

"Conrad, finally we can plan a great deal more confidently. What say we have a brandy to celebrate our good fortune."

The excitement of the report and the contents of a bottle of France's finest gave both men plenty to discuss. Finally, Booth yawned and suggested they retire and continue their planning the next day.

# Chapter 33

He mixture of alcohol he had consumed combined with the mortification of defeat at the hands of the Irish had greatly unsettled him. He had tried to fall asleep, but sleep just would not come. In desperation, he had stuffed the Oriental mixture into the pipe and lit up. As he inhaled, he knew that he would either pass into the peaceful expanse or the ghostly hallucinations would revisit from the past.

As the purple drapes closed and turned blood crimson, Bolton drifted off, aware now that the latter would apply. The curtains slowly, so slowly, drew open, and the horrific memories revisited him.

His horse snorted and stamped her two front feet impatiently.

He had been watching for her departure from the village. He knew she loved shopping at the markets, and on fine afternoons, she particularly enjoyed the walk to her family home two or so miles from Bandara.

He had been unable to keep his eyes off the beautiful McGuire lass since first spotting her at the market the first time he had visited Bandara shortly after arriving from England to manage his family's concerns in Donegal.

He had spoken to her on three different occasions, and while she had been polite and friendly, he could not decide whether her captivating, yet introverted, response to his approach could be considered encouraging.

He was infatuated with her. He could not accept any reaction to his advances other than total compliance. Each night he would toss and turn, his desire for her overpowering him. His vivid imagination would conjure up countless scenarios where she would satisfy even his most bizarre sexual ambition. Sleep would finally release him from his obsessive desires, leaving him lying in a mess of sweaty wet blankets.

Even in the distance, he could see her toss her shiny blue–black, shoulder–length hair, and it set his heart racing.

Giving the reins a shake, he started the mare down the dusty dirt road to meet her.

"Well, good afternoon, Bridget McGuire." Pointing to her market basket, he added, "And tell me, did the market traders fall to your beguiling smile and let you have them at the true price?" Jumping from his mount, Bolton commenced walking alongside her.

"Ah, indeed, sir, you jest, but I suspect that both buyer and seller were satisfied."

"Pass me your bags, and I will tie them to the saddle. It will save you carrying them."

"'Tis no trouble at all; I truly would prefer to carry them myself."

"I insist," Bolton all but demanded. "You are aware of who I am and how much I can make your existence so much more pleasant."

"Oh yes, I am very aware of who you are, and also how much trouble you can cause if you wish. I beg you most kindly to leave me be."

"Well, we are the perfect little madam, aren't we? What is it you have against me?" Bolton demanded. He could feel his blood rising at her rebuff.

"I have nothing against you personally, but surely you would hardly expect me to react sympathetically to the treatment we receive from the English landlords, and you being one of them. Now, I have asked you to leave me in peace. Please do so."

A surge of rage suddenly engulfed Bolton. "You stupid little wench!" He raised his right hand high and chopped down savagely at the nape of her neck. As she collapsed, he scooped her up and threw her effortlessly over the mare.

With only stone fences and fields around them, Bolton knew that he had no witnesses.

He leapt up into the saddle, secured her to it, and spurred the animal into a fast gallop. Hauling on the reins, he turned the mare's head to the coast, and the horse responded and settled into a full gallop.

Bridget recovered once or twice to see the ground flashing by beneath her. The first time she fainted from a combination of fear and the blow she had received. The second time she received another sharp rap on the back of her head.

"Keep still!"

Even if she wanted to move, the strength of the man's hand holding her against the pommel of the saddle was a deterrent.

The nausea created by the physical ill treatment and the bouncing of her body suddenly resulted in her losing the contents of her stomach.

"You filthy bitch, ah look at my jodhpurs. You will regret ever waking this day."

Some minutes later, Bolton tugged on the reins and slowed the horse to a halt. Bridget was tossed to the ground.

The grassy area where she lay sloped slightly toward the edge of a high cliff face that dropped down to the stony shoreline far below.

As Bridget slowly gathered her senses, she heard the sound

of seabirds and realized that she was close to the coast, but far from help. She looked up to see Bolton staring down at her from his horse.

He eventually spoke. "Well, Miss McGuire, what do I do with you now?"

"Please take me home to my father and sister."

"Bridget McGuire, you have brought this on yourself. You see, if you had used the intelligence God gave you, you could now be planning to become the lady of the manor. Instead, your stupid pride has landed you in this predicament.

"We could have shared so much together. You would have learned to respect me, as well as my position as a peer of the realm. And in return, you may, perhaps, have been able to put this sorry existence behind you and become a lady of nobility."

He dismounted and walked to her side.

Sitting on his haunches, he reached for the top of her bodice and unexpectedly ripped it down, exposing her white breasts.

"No, no. Please don't do this. Please God, don't do this to me."

"God? Did you call me God? Interesting! What I have in mind would be considered most ungodly." Bolton's tone was callous and unfeeling. "There are two ways of doing this. We can enjoy our experience with your cooperation or without it. What is it to be?"

The cold comprehension of the plight she was in triggered her next move.

Without hesitation, she sprang at Bolton, her fingernails searching for his eyes. He fell back, the sudden attack taking him by surprise. She grasped a nearby rock and lunged at him, aiming for his head. She heard him grunt as she hit him, and he fell to the ground stunned.

She started to run, having no idea where to run to. The cliff suddenly appeared in front of her. Panicked, she turned and ran full into Bolton. Savagely, he struck her again and again. Mercifully, she dropped lifeless, unable to fight back anymore.

A cold breeze greeted the badly beaten young woman as consciousness slowly returned.

Terrified, she became aware that she was lying in grass, fully unclothed. She peered through eyes that were now slits due to the blows she had received. She could make out Bolton standing over her naked.

She cried out in mortal fear, calling for help that would not arrive. In vain, she tried to cover herself with her hands.

Almost in insane harmony, a chilling laughter joined her screams, only to be replaced with a frightening and equally insane giggle.

"Hush! Be quiet. Your prayers were heard and have now been answered. Let me explain. Your God and my devil have entered into a liaison, not unlike a marriage, and I am now about to consummate that union."

He fell on her, forced her legs apart, and plunged deep inside her, ignoring her wretched screams.

She had never known pain quite like it; the degradation and humiliation she was suffering was beyond any feelings she had ever experienced. Finally, he shuddered and lay on her, exhausted.

In the far-off distance, she thought she heard him yell, "You filthy, bitch whore, this is all your doing!"

She felt herself being dragged through the grass. She thought she could smell wildflowers. She really didn't care. She wasn't even curious as she felt her body being raised.

She didn't cry out as he flung her over the cliff face. The angry cry of disturbed or curious gulls also went unheeded. Life left her battered and grossly abused body as it crashed onto the jagged rocks below.

Bridget Margaret McGuire was no more.

Thomas Bolton cried out in his sleep. He thrashed and tossed and turned, kicking out at visions that taunted him relentlessly.

Conrad Booth was wakened by the commotion and rushed into his friend's room. He gently held him, drying the perspiration from his head. Slowly Bolton returned to reality.

"Did she visit you again?" Booth enquired. "You do know she is not worthy of you."

Tormented eyes stared out at Booth.

"It will not end until her twin joins her. And she will, perhaps with more gratification, but this I promise, her twin will join her."

Bolton lay back and drifted off into a deep and untroubled slumber.

# Chapter 34

Bolton had summoned those he wanted for the assembly. They all sat around the large banquet table, waiting for his arrival. There was little conversation, primarily because few had anything positive to talk about. And none wished to be caught in dialogue when Bolton arrived, thus risking the ire of that unstable man.

Booth arrived first, uttering a terse good morning. Bolton arrived shortly after. To the total amazement of those seated, he appeared to be in extremely high spirits.

"Good morning to you all." He seated himself at the head of the table. "I have two statements to make," he began. "They reflect on two errors of judgment: theirs and mine. First, mine. I have learned a valuable lesson. I will never underestimate a foe again. The good news, gentlemen, is that I can correct my error.

"Now let us discuss their mistake. They had the opportunity to defeat their foe, I speak of us, and they stupidly failed to strike the killer blow. They wounded us, in some cases almost fatally, but as you can see, most of us lived to fight again! My friends, this gives us the opportunity to sup the sweet nectar of revenge."

Bolton allowed a moment for the murmur of agreement to ripple around the table.

"I have devised a strategy that I will now confer to you. But before I do so, I wish to highlight my immediate objectives. The harvest this year will be the best for many years. As a result, I will recoup my revenue losses with probably an increase due to, ahem, unplanned expenses.

"I will certainly root out and destroy those who planned and carried out this rebellious action.

"And finally, I will put firmly into place a policy that will terrify all who wish to oppose me or interfere with my business in any way." Bolton sat back and beamed to those seated around him.

"Which of you has the first question?"

"Can we expect reinforcements?" Hair enquired, trying to hide the apprehension he felt.

"Indeed, as I speak, Mandino will have reached Belfast or close to it. He knows of a specialist group, who is most experienced in the field of their expertise. If all goes well and Mandino is satisfied that they fulfil my expectations, they will be with us in due course. And Hair, you will have the pleasure of witnessing the dying breath of the Gallagher pup," he added.

"When do we strike back?" another asked.

"Good question. We lull them into a false sense of security, and then we hit them when they least expect it. We won't be moving for at least two or three weeks, which means that you who have suffered injuries will have time to recover."

"Have you thought how best to strike at them?"

"Oh indeed!" This brought another derisive smile from Bolton. "Nothing has occupied my thoughts since the debacle; allow me to answer that fully."

For the next two hours, the discussion continued until finally Bolton called a halt.

"Gentlemen, you all know what is required of you. In the following days, you will concentrate on becoming fit and ready for when we commence our campaign."

*****

Sean Gallagher had arrived home late the night before and was annoyed at being hauled out of bed with an aching head.

"Your father is calling for you," Claire admonished him. "Hugo and your brother are also here."

After throwing a basin of cold water over his head, Sean felt a little better and made his way to where they sat.

"Just look at yourself!" his brother joked.

"Padraig, if I had what you have to go home to, I wouldn't need to feel this way," he replied, throwing a friendly punch at his brother's shoulder.

"Hush, lads, I think you need to listen to Hugo," their father interrupted. "He has a bit to talk about."

Hugo nodded and smiled pensively.

"I share your ill humour, Sean, mon ami. Some mornings I think I should change my ways, but then . . . *C'est la vie*. But to matters at hand! I would surely love to be a fly on the manor wall. I would give much to know what Bolton will do next. But since we do not know, we must prepare for any plan that Bolton will devise.

"In some ways, I suspect that I may well rue the day I had the opportunity to kill him and did not do so, but . . ." He shrugged his shoulders.

"Maybe they have had enough," Padraig suggested. "His men did take a severe beating."

"I would like to think so. But I am confident that if they do return for a second bout, my tactics will be enough to end it once and for all."

Sean groaned. "Does that mean more of your torment on Maghara Beach?"

"Yes, it does, my good man, but with a greater emphasis on weaponry and your ability to take the life of another."

Claire involuntarily shuddered. Without the men noticing, she left the house and walked up to Padraig's home to be with Kathleen and the children.

It was later in the morning when Padraig entered their home and saw his mother visiting with Kathleen.

"Mother, we wondered where you had disappeared to. We were worried; you never said a word."

Claire looked up at her son, the man who was no longer a boy. A deep sadness descended over her.

Recognizing all was not well with his mother, Padraig sat and looked into her eyes. "What ails you?"

"My son, my son, I love you more than I love life itself. But I fear that our future days together are not many . . ."

"What do you mean?" A knot of alarm coiled in his belly.

His mother gazed at him for a few long moments before speaking.

"For some time now, I have had trouble sleeping. Visions appear, frightening images, and whether I am awake or asleep, they haunt me. Your father laughs at me when I tell him about them, so now I don't bother. But Padraig, it is all so real. I have never told anyone this, but I knew that you were going to lose Jess and the pups."

"What?" Kathleen and Padraig exclaimed at once. "Surely, no!"

"I saw a dark man, who spoke in a strange tongue, looking up at your home from the barn. As the rains stopped falling, he stood in silence staring, just staring. He then went and dragged the dead body of Jess, and dripping with blood, he snuck into your back door and dropped it onto your table. He laughed and cut poor Jess so that her insides tumbled out. He then went back out and brought in the little pups and placed them around their dead mother."

Claire broke down and cried in utter grief.

Padraig held his mother and tried to sooth her. "But that couldn't be, Mother; surely this was a dream that happened after . . ."

"No, no, no. Padraig, Kathleen, I have had other dreams, other images too terrible to tell about. You must take the children and run. Go to Dublin, anywhere, just go."

"Mother, we will not run from our home and family. We will face the threat, any threat, and you know I will allow no one near my wife and children."

"Padraig, I have had another dream I fear to tell you about. I have seen you walking in deep despair in a strange land—a land so strange, the living creatures are like nothing I have ever seen before. The people are so frightening, and you are among them. Kathleen and the little ones are not with you. You are so alone. Please go away from here, go now, I beg of you. Kathleen, please heed my warnings and go."

"Mother, even if I wanted to, we cannot leave now. Sean and I are to go to Maghara Beach tomorrow to improve our skills to protect you and the others who need our help. Sure and all, I am worried and have been for some time. I am not like Sean. I do not enjoy the confrontation as he does. But I feel I cannot let Hugo and my father down. But would it help if you stayed here until I return? I know my father would approve."

"If Kathleen agrees, so be it. I would love to help with the little ones."

## Chapter 35

King George III had succeeded his grandfather George in 1760. During his reign, madness and the toppling of Prime Minister William Pitt the Elder by the Whig party had resulted in men of mediocre talent performing in his cabinet.

Parliament, as such, refused to listen to the concerns of America, which had duly led to the Revolution. As a result of this crisis, most of England's fighting force and constabulary had departed for the east coast of America. This, coupled with the growing dominance of France, had allowed those from a privileged background to realize that the only thing impeding their greedy ambition was the weak resistance of the locals.

Hugo Cohen suspected that Robert Bolton's father was closely connected to George III, and hence the manner in which Bolton ignored all codes of decency. Hugo had also reasoned that, should Bolton die, his death would be seen as murder. The wrath of English hierarchy would then descend upon them.

His plan was to instruct his recruits to use subtle and uniquely defensive methods to protect their homeland rather than launch an all-out war, which he knew they could never win.

Thus far, his efforts had been successful, and the Irish lads had been apt students. Hugo was very pleased with his team of young men.

"*Tres bien,*" he said to the elder Gallagher men. "Your boys and their friends have surpassed my expectations."

The three friends had watched as the twenty-three resistance fighters commenced jogging from their end of Maghara Beach and gradually increased their speed. When they reached the other end of the beach, they then turned and sped back to the starting point.

"I could barely run a quarter of that distance," Padraig the older muttered, obviously impressed.

To the gasping runners Hugo said, "Go and drink and return back here."

The two older men watched and listened as Hugo addressed the runners while they relaxed on the warm sand.

"It is with some gloom I talk to you this day. When we left here to face the English the first time, I was confident that you would do well, and you surpassed my expectations. We had surprise as our ally. Bolton and his friends had no idea that we were waiting, and indeed, no idea that we would damage them as we did.

"He will not allow this to happen again.

"We would be absolute fools to think that he will not strike back, and it would be fatal to be ill prepared. I will instruct you to the best of your ability, but sadly, I suggest that we may not fare as well next time.

"I have every reason to believe he is searching for hardened and seasoned fighters—paid killers, evil men without scruples who will rejoice in spilling your blood. The sadness I feel is the knowledge that if and when we leave here again as fighters, some, maybe all of you may never again enjoy another day of celebrating your birth.

"You all have families and responsibilities to them. I will certainly not feel offended if any of you want to return to your homes."

Hugo paused, and before he could say another word, Sean

leaped to his feet and shouted, "Never! We are Irish, and Ireland is our home. None of us will turn as cowards and desert each other and our homeland. We will fight and destroy the English as they would destroy us. We are ready. Prepare us!"

"Is this the feeling of you all?" Hugo asked.

As one, twenty–three men stood and raised their fists in defiance. "We are ready!"

Their eager response easily reached the listening ears of the hidden watcher high up on the sand dunes.

"You were previously taught weapon skills," Hugo said. "Now you will learn how to concentrate and take the life of an enemy. You will become a specialist as you master the art of the staff and the blade. Go collect your weapons, and split into your fighting teams."

Each selected his weapon of choice, *maide ceathrun* or *crann bagair*. All were to be proficient in skills with the quarterstaff or cudgel.

For the next three hours, Hugo advanced their expertise from their traditional ability to protect themselves to combat level. At times, he stepped in and pointed out an error in judgment usually resulting in the participant lying flat in the sand.

"I am not trying to shame you, but to show you what your enemy will do to you, only he will make your mistake fatal."

Midday, they stopped for rest. Father and Grandfather could hardly believe what they were witnessing.

"These men are only just starting," Hugo said with obvious pride. "When you return in a few days' time, you will have every reason to be proud of them—that is, if they can keep up," he added with a smile.

The weather turned bad during the night, but that gave no respite to the training, which continued for the next two days, each day increasing in intensity.

On the fourth day, the two older men returned. They had difficulty recognizing their son and grandson. In fact, all twenty-three young men were weather worn and unshaven, but all looked like men with a purpose.

As they lined up and greeted the elder Gallaghers, Hugo called out, "Now we will let them judge if you have improved. Sean, Padraig, Danny, and Liam, come forward with your weapons."

He waited as they came forward. "Sean and Padraig, show us what you have learned."

Both men shaped up to each other, and suddenly Sean lunged with a quarterstaff. Padraig sidestepped and aimed a vicious blow at Sean's head with the cudgel.

Padraig the Older gasped.

But the cudgel missed by an inch as Sean dropped to his feet, then swiftly turned, and swung the staff in an arc, aiming for Padraig's midriff.

Padraig appeared to dive over the staff in a somersault, landing on his feet, and as Sean turned to face his foe again, a knife appeared in Padraig's hand, and he lunged for his opponent's groin, stopping before the blade struck home.

"Good God Almighty!" Their father cried out, completely unaware of his blasphemous outburst. "They could have killed each other."

"That is correct," Hugo replied, not without a hint of pride in his tone. "They are now trained to kill or show mercy. The circumstances will dictate the conclusion."

Both brothers were now holding each other, laughing uncontrollably.

"You will think twice before you attempt to chide us now, Father," Sean said, pulling his father to him with affection and clapping his hand on his back. "But let the others show you what they can do."

The balance of the day was taken up with further demonstrations of their new skills in hand-to-hand combat.

"And now, we prepare for the final test," Hugo announced. "As we discussed earlier, one of you will leave for your home. After fifteen minutes, your chosen assassins will follow you and attempt to kill you before you arrive at your destination. As Padraig is the overall winner of this day, his brother and Danny will both have the pleasure of attempting to deprive his poor suffering wife of his companionship this night.

"Those others of you who were also winners will have fifteen minutes before your two assassins attempt to kill you. Good luck, and we will learn the results of 'kill or be killed' tomorrow over ales."

As they dispersed, the Weasel quickly left his vantage point and faded into the gathering twilight.

## Chapter 36

Kathleen glanced out the kitchen window toward the sunset. Even at that late hour, the sky was vividly ablaze with violet, scarlet, and gold. As she gazed at the wondrous sight, she all but missed the unkempt figure leaping over the stone wall and running alongside the front of their house. She watched, puzzled, as he appeared to melt into the long grass at the base of the wall and disappear from sight. She almost went out to investigate, but the memories of recent bad goings-on stopped her, and she thought it best to stay put and watch for further movement.

Some minutes passed, and then two shapes appeared out of the gloom and peered around the gateway toward the house. They moved cautiously through the entrance to the path and snuck toward the house.

Suddenly, with a hideous scream, the stranger launched himself from the grass and leapt onto their backs. They crashed to the ground. And then, to her amazement, they rolled around in the dust, laughing hilariously. Astonished, she watched the wild sight, and gradually she recognised the three men.

Engrossed in their epic battle, none of the three saw Kathleen approach until the cold bucket of slops landed on them.

Indignation was quickly replaced by shame, as the silent figure stared down at them, right foot tapping the ground leaving no doubt as to her feelings.

"Oh, me darlin' . . ." Padraig stammered.

"Don't you me darlin' me," she yelled at him. "And you, just look at the sight of you!" She pointed to her husband. "Get you and you two down to the stream, and don't dare return until you are scrubbed clean. Get!"

Duly admonished, Padraig sheepishly returned somewhat later. Sean and Danny, not daring to face the wrath of the furious wife, left him to it.

"Cowards!" he called after them as they headed down the lane.

He couldn't see the big grin all over Kathleen's face, as she watched from the window, and it had disappeared when he walked in to face her.

It was only later, much later, as she feigned sleep that his pleading finally reached home, and she turned over and put her arms around him and pulled him to her.

"Oh, but you're the bad thing—now start showing me how truly sorry you are!"

★★★★★

The next morning, Hugo, Padraig Joseph, and Grandfather Padraig sat nursing their ales on Maghara Beach as Padraig and Sean welcomed their comrades to learn the outcome of the previous evening's mock kill exercises. As each downed their drinks with obvious relish, it was apparent that a strong bond had developed among the twenty-three.

"You should have seen Sean run!" Danny said. "And then she grabbed Padraig by the ear and dragged him inside; poor wee man didn't have a hope!"

Howls of laughter followed the conclusion of the highly exaggerated version, according to Danny.

The three older men could not help but notice the stance of

the younger men. All stood prouder and stronger. They were men with a purpose! Gone was the shuffling uncertainty of youth, now replaced by an inner strength and understanding of the responsibility they shared and fully accepted—to restore their land back to the rightful owners, the Irish.

Hugo had arranged for the meeting of his men to be conducted behind closed doors, and he had ensured that no one could overhear his plans and strategies.

"There are a number of certainties that I want you to be aware of. Bolton will show no mercy in his attempt to achieve his objectives, and he will take no prisoners. He will have gathered new forces, and as you have noticed, he has guns. He and his new recruits will use those and any force at their disposal to defeat us.

"Remember, a gun will only fire once! You must make certain that before a trigger is pulled, you are already taking evasive action. Then, before the gun is reloaded, you have dispatched the firer. Use your agility and speed of foot to ensure that their aim is continuously untrue. If he has you in his sights, you are dead.

"I would be lying to you if I suggested that all will return from battle unscathed. With immense sadness, I can only say that in all my life I have never loved folk the way that I love you, and I dread the thought that even one of you will be taken from us.

"But this I promise, whoever falls fighting against this enemy, his loss will be avenged with a severity that knows no equal.

"I only make one request before we talk of strategy. In line with your religious upbringing and your responsibility to your parents, please talk with my good friend, our parish priest, and be aware that God's blessing is always with you."

*****

Both good and bad news travel fast. And certainly the word that Bolton needed recruits had travelled far.

Even before those from Belfast had arrived, men had been calling at the manor offering their services, dangerous men, who cared little for the lives of others and were only concerned about the payment they received for services rendered.

Bolton derived great pleasure in interviewing the hired killers and listening in fascination to their litanies of horror. Ireland and its troubles had attracted those that fed on the pain of others. Child molesters, rapists, and murderers were commonplace, especially as the only policing that was in evidence could be bought for so little— that is, if a constable could be found who cared.

And Bolton had all those who represented law and any form of order firmly on his payroll.

The promise of bounties, and the fact that Bolton showed no concern for the Irish tenants and their families, fired the imagination of the mercenaries, and they salivated at the promise of sexual fulfilment as a bonus. That Bolton was happy to allow them to slake their lust only encouraged their collective wickedness and drew them closer to him.

He heeded not the cost of keeping the men fed and housed. Indeed, they were well happy enough with quantities of ale and cheap wine, and it was as easy to feed ten as it was twenty.

And so, when Mandino and the balance of the men arrived from the north, Bolton had a force that would destroy the rebellious might of the Irish. He was certain of this. He then began to select and position those he knew were capable of achieving his ends.

The Weasel's latest information gave him great confidence that the overall strengths of his hired men and their superior weaponry would crush the Irish at the first confrontation, and he could barely wait to gloat.

His consuming hatred of the Gallagher clan and his overwhelming desire to have the twin of Bridget McGuire was so strong he had to be careful it did not cloud his judgment. He knew that Conrad Booth was aware of his feelings, but not the depth of his resentment nor the extent he would go to satisfy his craving.

## Chapter 37

He now had thirty-seven, able-bodied men who sat or lounged around, waiting for his arrival. From them Bolton had selected those he felt had leadership qualities. Two who had impressed him were Scots; they had an absolute hatred of any who were Catholic and an historical abhorrence of the Irish. Tommy MacFetridge and Willy Mason were big tough men and certainly commanded respect. They were also skilled in most forms of combat and had no qualms taking the life of another, whether in battle or merely to settle a squabble or argument.

MacFetridge had a huge mop of coarse, uncontrollable, red curly hair that would never see a comb nor did he care. A similarly unruly strip of eyebrow all but hid two piggish eyes that while crossed did not seem to impair his sight. Like Mason, he always wore a kilt into battle, but this day had chosen a ragged top that showed off his massively muscled torso. His trousers had also seen better days and his huge feet were housed in well-worn boots, but as weapons, they had pulverized many an unfortunate's head.

Willy Mason, by contrast, was dark, also with long, unkempt hair, black, thick, and greasy that dropped down over his shoulders. Like MacFetridge, he was a tall man, but much thinner. He walked with a permanent nervous gait, always looking from left to right, his sneaky eyes continuously searching for a threat to his well-being. This day he wore the same clothing that he had been wearing for the last week or more, and it was noticeable that only his friend chose to be near him.

But Bolton cared not for their unsavoury aroma; he had chosen them simply because when they grunted an order, the rest obeyed immediately.

Conrad Booth had made it perfectly clear that these two were never to be invited into the manor, and he pointedly stayed upwind of them both when having to be in their vicinity.

These two would control the enforcement team, and Bolton had made it perfectly clear he cared not a drop of spit how or what methods they chose to do so.

He, with Mandino, Hair and others that had been with him from the outset, would make up the monetary collection party, as he put it.

Gloomy clouds partially hiding the sun had greeted the beginning of yet another working week. Rain was still some way off, but time was of the essence to cut and gather the crops before the wet weather set in.

Padraig Joseph rose from his breakfast table to leave for the fields, but stopped short at what he saw out the window. A group of seven riders had pulled their horses to a halt outside the Gallagher home. The riders sat in silence, watching and waiting for a reaction from the household.

Robert Bolton had heard breakfast preparation noises as the house began to greet the day. He thought he saw a face at one of the windows. Amused, he waited. Only the horses snuffled, nibbling at the grass growing beyond the stone fence side of the house. The only other sounds came from the thrushes and blackbirds singing their delight as they hauled up big fat worms from the gardens.

Some minutes later, Padraig Joseph Gallagher the Younger came from the rear of the house and walked toward them. As he reached the front gate, he stared at each of the riders. His father appeared and stood by him.

Eventually Padraig Joseph spoke to Bolton. "What brings you here, and what do you want of us?" His voice displayed no emotion.

"Such a cheery greeting on such a beautiful morn!" Bolton replied with a sneering, sardonic smile.

"Just state your business and get to hell."

"My business is to claim what is mine, Irishman. To date, you owe me twenty-seven guineas, and the property that your brat and his woman live on owes me the same. The question I now ask is, how do you intend to pay me?"

Padraig Gallagher stared at him for a beat, assessing him.

"Englishman, I and mine live on the land that has belonged to the Irish for centuries. On account of your fornicating King Henry, who could not and would not keep his meat in the royal larder, you wrongly assume that we are supposed to bow and accept royal thievery.

"We may have meekly complied in the past, but I say, no longer. This is our land, and from now and forever, so long as I and mine live on it, we will stand and fight for it. You and all the other English and oh so noble landlords can return to your land, and leave us be."

"Gallagher, you are a foolish and stupid man. However, I will grant you your wish. I will allow you to stand and fight for your land for as long as you live." He produced a chortle of snide laughter.

"Oh," Bolton added, "Your rudeness almost made me forget the other point of my visit. It has transpired that a particularly brutal bunch of nasty ne'er-do-wells has taken it upon themselves to attack and lay waste to the outlying homesteads. They are being not at all nice to the womenfolk, and I understand the younger ones are really taking their fancy.

"Now in my infinite kindness, I was about to explain that part of the monies you should be paying me could be retained by you and the other families for protection from these vagabonds."

He paused, watching the reaction his words were having.

"And on our way to visit you this day, I heard the sad tidings that a family or two some ten miles from here had an unpleasant visit from these men only last night."

He turned his horse's head to depart and signalled the others to follow.

"It is such a pity that when you do die, it will be with the knowledge that the blood of all these people will have been shed as a result of your ignorance and stupidity. I bid thee farewell, at least until we meet again."

Both Gallagher men watched aghast as Bolton and his posse took off at a gallop. His parting words slowly began to sink in.

"What in God's holy name have I started?" Padraig Joseph Gallagher the Younger whispered.

The songs of the thrush and blackbird had also stirred the sleeping family farther up the country road.

Kathleen Gallagher gently ran her finger up the nape of her husband's neck. He gave a little involuntary shudder.

"Beast!" he muttered.

She gently kissed his ear and blew softly.

"Beast," he muttered again, only this time with a slight gasp in his voice.

She giggled. "I wonder what I can find down here? Ooh, and what is this?"

This time he turned and gazed up at her, his eyes eating up her beauty, staring at her in wonderment.

He opened his mouth to speak, but she lightly touched his

lips with her finger.

"Ssh . . . I have a little secret I have to tell you! I meant to tell you last night, but my big lazy man fell asleep on me."

He smiled at her.

"It is so lonely for the twins, I have felt for some time they should have a little play friend." She paused as her words slowly made sense to her husband.

"What! When? What do you mean?"

His words were smothered as she kissed him again and again. And so gently, ever so gently, he entered her, loving her.

★★★★★

Claire Gallagher had watched the morning's surprise encounter and heard most of the words between her husband and Bolton. But it mattered little; she already knew. And she also knew as she watched her boy and his beautiful wife walk down the road toward her home. She knew about the little one in her womb.

And she also knew of the days to come. She willed the tears not to flow. Claire felt she had cried her last drop anyway.

## Chapter 38

Two days had passed since Bolton's visit to the Gallaghers. It seemed to Padraig Joseph and Hugo Cohen that neither of the two district constables appeared to be too concerned about the shocking tragedy that had befallen the O'Reilly and Deaker families. Hugo Cohen actually suspected that they might have known what would happen prior to the murders.

Both constables had traveled over from Donegal Town to visit the scene and view the carnage.

The remains of both cottages were still smoldering, occasional spirals of smoke drifting up from where the thatched roofs had been. Only the stone walls remained. The wooden doors and window frames had been destroyed by the flames.

Hugh Porter, the Bandara constable, had been transferred to Belfast some weeks back—all too conveniently, it was thought at the time. And so it was the village priest who had been first called on to do his holy work, dispersing the blessings and oils on the dead. Only old Tommy O'Reilly was still capable of receiving the comfort of the last rites, and he died immediately after the final blessing. He was incapable of telling what had happened.

It was mid-afternoon the previous day, as the Gallagher family and Hugo Cohen, who had quickly arrived after being told of Bolton's call, were seated, waiting for confirmation of Robert Bolton's grim threat. No one was surprised when a messenger came from the priest.

A nearby neighbour had heard the commotion during the night, and then seeing the flames, had made his way through the darkness, and witnessed the horror. Too terrified to move, he had waited and watched 'til dawn. As the skies lightened, they left on horseback and in wagons, laughing and chortling at the carnage and devastation they had caused.

The neighbour, not owning horse or donkey, had run and walked until he fell, exhausted, through the door of the priest's home.

The good father had quickly harnessed pony to trap, and together they had returned to what was left of the two homes. But before he left, the priest had instructed one of the townspeople to take the sad news to Hugo and Padraig.

With Sean over in Killybegs, Hugo quickly explained what he wanted, and brother Padraig set out to gather up the rest of the lads and get word across to Sean. By the time Hugo and Padraig Joseph arrived at the cottages, the poor priest was wandering around, trying to find if any had survived.

Old Tommy's son was lying outside, his head smashed by a heavy cudgel. They had dragged Tommy's wife outside, and when Padraig Joseph saw what had been done to her, he bent double and threw up.

It appeared that their two boys, not yet fifteen years old, had attempted to fight back. Both had been hacked to death by knife and axe.

Together, the three men and neighbour walked over to the Deaker property.

Benjy Deaker and his wife had only been in the region for just over a year. Hard-working people from Dublin, they, their two daughters, and son had cherished the challenge of breeding stock and growing vegetables from their gardens.

All five were dead—slaughtered. Again, as the priest attempted in vain to bring some dignity to their mutilated corpses, it was apparent that all five had been subjected to the most unimaginable treatment. In shocked silence, the four men arranged the five bodies side by side, then knelt by them and prayed.

As Padraig and Hugo explained to the constables the terrible sights they had witnessed the previous day and how the bodies of both families had been taken back to the village for requiem Mass and burial, they were both taken aback by the disinterest of the two.

"So, what action do you intend taking?" enquired Hugo. "Have you any idea who could have done such a thing?"

"I'd be thinking that whoever did so are long gone by now. T'was probably the travellin' folk that come along lookin' for easy pickin's," one replied.

"Just look at the tracks they left when they ran away. Why don't you follow those and make enquiries?" Padraig Joseph suggested angrily.

"Har, indeed, and I'm sure that the same tracks will soon disappear into the comings and goings of normal traffic. No point in following that line."

It was obvious to Padraig that nothing would be gained by further discussion, and he stalked off in disgust.

His mood was only slightly improved by the sound of approaching horses, and he was cheered by the sight of his two sons arriving on a trap accompanied by three others on horseback.

The normal good-natured banter was missing as the five lads alighted and learned the details of the happenings.

Sean and Padraig could not help but see the bloodstains that were still in evidence, and they were visibly shaken by the sight.

"Who could do this?" Padraig asked.

And without waiting for an answer, they walked down the road a short ways from the ruins.

"Look, here is where they left. There must have been a fair number of them. Their tracks indicate at least a dozen or more."

"Hey, you!" yelled one of the constables. "Enough of you, you be minding your business, and get back out of here and go home where you belong."

"This is the first time either of you has showed concern," Hugo snarled. "Maybe you don't want to find where these tracks take us. Possibly, they could lead to the Englishman's manor. Then what would you do?"

"Padraig, carry on, lad. Sean, follow him, you and you other three. Then meet us back home later. But take care and do nothing other than observe."

"As for you two, there is nothing to be gained by spending any more time in your illustrious company; come, my friend, let us go." Hugo and Padraig Joseph left the two constables staring after them as they rode off.

The trail led exactly to where their father had predicted.

"Father," Padraig concluded, "Sean and I both agree that there was no attempt to hide their way back to the manor. It seems to us that Bolton intends us to know."

"That is exactly as I see it also," Hugo agreed. "It confirms Bolton's statement to your father and grandfather that this terrible happening is indeed a warning that Bolton gets his filthy way or . . ." His voice trailed off as his memory revisited those awful scenes just hours back.

He glanced over as Claire came and placed her hand on her husband's back and rubbed his shoulder. She had never seen him so broken, but she understood that no normal person could see what he had seen and be unmoved by it. The grandfather was equally disturbed.

Hugo was very aware that his strength and character would need to be their anchor and solace.

"My friends, it is essential that you listen to my words." He paused to get their full attention.

"Padraig Joseph Gallagher, the path you chose was to be a leader for your people. That choice was to lead them from the oppression of the English. You were aware that there would be casualties, and now there have been. Choose to allow your conscience to be troubled if you must, and I blame you not if you do so. But sadly, this will not release you from your promise to free your countrymen and women. Whether you are successful in the end is not the question, though I firmly believe you will be. The true definition of your leadership is to create a reality in the minds of the Irish people that they have the right to freedom and the ability to claim that independence.

"Even if you are not successful, you will have created the dream. Others will take up that challenge and follow your example, and one day Ireland will indeed be free. And on that day, the Irish people and history will recall those who believed in and led the fighters, yes, the freedom fighters who fought for and gave this country its rightful independence.

"Now my friend, stand and be that leader."

Turning to the two young men, he said, "Come, Padraig and Sean, we have much to do."

Both lads went over to their father and put their arms around him. Together, the three stood as one, their bond strong. Padraig Joseph looked at his sons with pride swelling his chest. And then he turned so that none could see the tears that ran down his face.

Sean's farewell words echoed through the silent room. "Hey, Da, stay strong. You hear! Stay strong."

## Chapter 39

The village of Bandara had never known a more somber time. Due to the conditions of the bodies and the violence associated with the deaths, the traditional wakes were bypassed. The hastily built coffins lay side by side in the church, and a communal rosary would be said for all.

The church was packed with mourners with many more outside. It was obvious to all that Father Sullivan had been very badly affected by his own personal involvement with the tragedy, and at times, it showed during the Mass and later at the burial grounds.

There was no gaiety at any of the packed drinking establishments either. Quiet conversations centred on how and why, but more importantly, what might happen next.

It was apparent to Hugo that the Gallagher family stayed close together during the morning and later in the afternoon at Maloneys, and he understood why.

Father Sullivan sitting next to Hugo enquired, "Is all well?"

"I suspect Padraig Joseph is feeling that he is responsible in some way," Hugo replied.

As friends, he knew he could confide in the priest, and he told of the happenings at their home, but even he was surprised at the reply.

"The workings of God at times baffle me. I watch those that

follow and obey blindly, I grant them absolution for their sins, and they put their trust in the Divine Being yet again." The priest paused and thought for a while.

"And then I have to explain to them that God works in peculiar ways when I'm asked why he allowed these poor innocent people to die in such a horrible manner. I will pray and trust in God's goodness that he will not allow Padraig Joseph to lose faith, but will guide him and give him the strength to overcome all obstacles in his way."

"Father, please ask God not to overlook me when he's passing out all this strength and assistance, because I and those young men over there will need all that he can give."

"Hugo, I will pray long and hard that these killings cease and all come to their senses. But I know in my heart that this will not happen. Just look at your young men; they ache to avenge the deaths of their friends, and you, sadly, have to teach them how and hopefully not lose their young lives as they do so."

"Thank you, my good friend," Hugo said to Father Sullivan. "I will pass on your blessings when we meet later this evening."

Most of the mourners returned to their homes, but there were still those who wished to drink the sad night away. Hugo arranged for the use of one of the upstairs rooms.

He and Padraig Joseph gathered with the entire Maghara Beach fighting force.

Sean and brother Padraig confirmed that the tracks of the murderers had lead toward the direction of Bolton's manor, and while that was not proof positive, it was most likely the manor where the killers were housed.

Hugo looked around the room crammed with the young combat force.

"To be successful, we need to be certain that the men we hunt are those responsible, and we need to know their strengths and their weaknesses. We cannot allow any further killings. I propose that we keep a lookout posted close to the manor to observe all that goes on, particularly if any large groups of men leave. I, therefore, need volunteers to become spies."

Hugo and Padraig Joseph smiled as every hand was raised.

"Thank you, but I need only three. Two to observe and one fast rider to bring us back the information. I will choose another three to replace the first three and so on. Each three will work as a team, continually monitoring all movements at the manor. Each rider will have the services of the fastest horses available. You will ensure that those at the manor are unaware of your presence. We will also have to stay together until further notice.

"Padraig Joseph has suggested we use his barn as a base so you will need to return to your homes and pack the necessary rations and supplies for at least a week and probably longer. You will obviously bring with you the weapons you have been trained to use.

"My young friends, you are very aware that I have complete confidence in you. You have already tasted a victory of sorts. You certainly dealt with and dispatched Bolton's last horde of scoundrels, but I feel certain that he has replaced them with an evil and competent force of villains. Your assignment will be much more difficult, but I believe you can accept the challenge and win with honour. However," Hugo paused, and when he spoke again, he did so very slowly, letting each word sink in.

"I have spoken with Father Sullivan, and he has made himself available for you to visit him and talk to him if you have any doubts as to where you stand with your Catholic faith. I do not need to add that you should also be in a state of readiness if indeed the worst should happen, and you depart from this life."

★★★★★

Robert Bolton raised his glass and laughed heartily. He swallowed the contents in one gulp and demanded another. As soon as his glass was filled again, he stood unsteadily.

"Let us toast another to our newcomers, hey! Not here ten minutes and already these ignorant peasants are pleading for protection. Ha! Begging not the protection of that blasted Gallagher, but mine, I tell you, mine!"

Earlier that day, his collectors had called on tenants quite some distance from Bandara. It was true that the seditious mood that had been prevalent prior to the murders had changed. Fear had replaced the farmers' bold dreams of independence. They had paid as much as they had to the collectors and assured them that the balance would be paid as soon as the late summer crops were sold.

MacFetridge and Mason sat with Hair and Slow, all four showing the effects of excess imbibing.

"I propose a toast to you who have showed that we are not to be trifled with!" Bolton again raised his glass. "What say you, Conrad? A few more strikes and even the Gallagher family will fall in line or die!"

Booth smiled wryly. "Indeed, indeed. And when do you intend to hit the Gallagher family?"

"I think just a little more softening is called for. Why deprive our men their pleasure. I am sending the collectors closer to Killybegs and then to Bandara. The ones who refuse to pay will have a call from those two." Bolton nodded toward the big Scots.

"And what of the family Gallagher?" Booth looked directly at Bolton. "In particular, the pretty young wife of the Gallagher pup?"

Bolton smiled. "I feel that a personal visit would be appropriate. Yes, Conrad, a personal visit to give the young lady the opportunity to express her concern and how she can correct the rudeness and inhospitable behaviour of her husband and his family. And Conrad,

I assure you that one way or another she will!"

The revelry continued until well after the sun had set. Gradually the drinkers either staggered to their beds or collapsed where they had sat.

Heavy rain clouds had commenced building offshore, and before dawn had rolled in, soon after sunrise, the rain began.

The two men, who had saddled their horses, had done so with aching heads, and as they rode from the manor northwest toward the village of Bandara, they cursed the inclemency of the weather.

"Bleedin' stinkin' rain!" moaned one to the other. "We oughta be back in our cots like the others."

"Yeah," the other grunted.

Neither saw the two horsemen following silently behind them. The sound of the rain and the conditions concealed them from discovery.

Not in any great hurry, they eventually pulled their horses to a halt outside a farmhouse.

When the door opened and the farmer appeared, one spoke.

"In accordance with the powers bestowed upon me by the courts of England, I am here to collect the outstanding monies owed to your landlord Robert Bolton. A refusal to pay all or a fair portion of these monies will result in dire action on behalf of the owners of this property. I am instructed to advise you that if necessary, you may be evicted, this property will be taken over by the legal owner, and new tenants installed. What say you?"

"Get off my land—*my* land, you hear? And tell Bolton that my family and I will never leave our home, this house that has been the home of generations of my forefathers. Be gone before I take a blackthorn to your skinny hide!"

Shortly after the two had departed, there was another knock on the farmer's door.

After a brief conversation, the young rider mounted his horse.

"To be sure, Hugo Cohen will be with you shortly," he said, turning his mount into the rain and trotting off.

The collectors made two more calls with much the same reaction as the first.

"I doubt Bolton's mood will be the same tonight as it was last night. But then, he may well enjoy releasing the Scots and their murderous lot again." He shuddered, though not at the cold or the rain.

## Chapter 40

As if with a mind of its own, the mood of the Atlantic had changed, and the heavy rain had turned to dense fog, which crept farther inland from the coast, and the early morning sun could do little to penetrate let alone disperse it.

Led by local lads well used to the vagaries of these seasonal conditions, Hugo and his men had little trouble finding their way to the Lynch farm.

Tommy Lynch, whose father had been visited by Bolton's collectors the previous day, was relieved to see his home intact. Normally a very humorous lad, and always the good-natured recipient of jokes from the others in Cohen's young band, he was most concerned when hearing about the threat to his family.

"Hey, Tommy boy!" His father greeted him as they pulled up outside the farmhouse. He had obviously slept little the previous night, and his relief in seeing the arrival of his son and the others showed.

Padraig and Sean strode over and both shook hands with the farmer.

"Good to see you again, Padraig and Sean Gallagher, and the rest of you. Tommy, go tell your mother to boil up some tea. Come on in, lads."

Gradually, all went in and bade good morning to the others in the household, and finally warmed by the brew, they settled indoors or out to await further instructions from Hugo.

*****

Bolton's head ached, either from the excess of drinking or the inconsistencies of the weather, and he felt he had a fever. He certainly did not feel like leaving the warmth of his blankets.

Calling out for Conrad Booth, he settled back on his pillows.

"I feel as if a horse has kicked me in the head," he moaned to Booth, who simply smiled and nodded with exaggerated sympathy.

"I don't really feel up to riding today. But we need to follow up on those cursed peasants from yesterday!"

"Simple," Booth stated. "Why have a dog and then do your own barking? Your private army of primates appear more than capable of doing what is required without your leadership. Send them."

"You are so right, dear friend. They boasted enough last night about their prowess in conflict. Would you be so kind as to pass on these instructions, and then let me die in peace!"

"I think not," Booth laughed. "The devil looks after his own," he muttered to himself as an afterthought.

"What was that?" Bolton enquired.

"Nothing . . . nothing at all." Booth left the room to speak to the Scots and to pass on the orders.

MacFetridge and Mason had agreed that horses and carts would not be needed.

Indeed, a groan had gone up when they announced to the assembled band of ruffians that a "wee jaunt" to the three farms to follow Bolton's orders would simply increase the eagerness to complete the task.

Just after midday, Bolton had arisen from his bed, and covered with a day gown, watched as they prepared their arms and gathered for his final instructions. Even with an aching head, he was amused to find that the highlanders had changed into their kilts.

"A bit damp up there!" he mused to Booth.

Both Scots carried a targe. The highland shield was crafted from oak planks with tooled and embossed leather and decorated with brass studs. A nasty steel spike emanated from the central boss. An arm loop secured the targe with a wooden handgrip, enabling the shield to be used for defence or as an offensive weapon. Both also carried a twenty-inch, single-bladed knife called the highland dirk.

A double-bladed axe hung from the shoulder of each, both sides honed razor sharp, so keen that facial hair could be removed with ease, not that either ever considered using them for that purpose. The axes were for killing.

"Not overly pretty, are they? You wouldn't want to wake up and find one of them in your bed one morning, would you?"

"And then, maybe *you* might!" he added with a hint of sarcasm, remembering the comment made earlier by Booth, with strong reference to his sexual preference.

Aware that he owned the only firearms in the district, Bolton felt that as the North Country men were extremely skilled in traditional weapons, they were more than adequately armed and capable of eliminating the poorly equipped Irish. And the sooner the better.

He then began to explain exactly what he wanted from them. "It is very straightforward," he concluded. "They pay, or you play."

As they trotted off in the direction of their violent destination, he watched until the fog at the end of the lane swallowed them up.

Even with the guidance of the collector, who had ridden to the Lynch farm the previous day, the party lost their way on numerous occasions, and it was an extremely ill-tempered lot that eventually found the road leading up to the farmhouse.

"It never got this bad back home," Mason snarled. "Filthy bloody place!"

"Steady!" MacFetridge muttered. He stood quietly surveying the lay of the land ahead of him.

Normally at this time in the late summer afternoon, the farm would be a hive of activity. However, with the swirling mists, an eerie silence hung over the farmhouse and the fields around it. From where they stood watching, the house almost seemed to disappear as a particularly heavy cloud rolled in.

Not a bird sound came from the surrounding area, not from the few trees or the fields. Normally a crow would be perched on either one of the stone fences separating the fields from the roadside, expressing disapproval of the gathered fighting force.

"So, where are they?" MacFetridge muttered to Mason.

Slowly, they approached the farmhouse. They circled the house and found nobody.

"Willie, you charge through the front door. Kick it in if need be. I'll go through the back. Take three men with you. You," he pointed to two men close him. "Come with me. The rest of you spread out and bring to me anybody you find. Do them no harm—not until I tell you!"

Hair Baker and four others walked toward the stone wall fence to look over the meadows. As he peered over the fence, he failed to see the men lying flat at the base of the wall. He made only a slight grunting sound as the sharpened tip of the spiked pike spear went through the base of his throat and up into his skull. He stood there, anchored by the pike staff now jammed into the ground.

So sudden was the attack, the other four noticed nothing until the first looked over the fence and saw the motionless men lying there. His sudden gasp was cut short as Sean Gallagher stood and swiftly jerked the man's head back and sliced his throat open from ear to ear. The gush of blood flooding out and the gurgle of the dying man shocked the other three, and before they could recover, they were smashed to the ground by heavy cudgels. But if any mercy had been shown before, none was given this time.

As they fell, their faces no longer recognizable, those responsible for the murderous blows were joined by others of the rebel group, who streamed over the wall, screaming blood-curdling taunts as they each eyed a foe and charged forward.

Those standing in the roadway were swamped, and as they put up meager resistance, they were also dispatched with ease, some by blade or pike, others with the deadly blackthorn cudgels.

Stunned and now very frightened by the horrific sight before them, the remaining five men standing, witnessing the carnage in front of them, turned and fled to the safety of the house, colliding with those inside trying to get out alerted by the din.

"Get oot the way!"

MacFetridge stood mesmerized by the sight before him.

Twelve of the party Bolton had sent lay dead or dying.

Hugo Cohen, the Gallagher boys, and the rest of the rebel band stood drawing deep breaths of air, some doubled over, recovering from the demands on their bodies.

Gradually as one, they stood proud, defiantly staring up the farmhouse. Apart from a bruise or two and no more than superficial scratches, they were unharmed.

Tommy Lynch could contain himself no longer. "Get from my house, you cowards!" he yelled.

MacFetridge and Mason stood quietly, staring back at them.

Secure in the knowledge that his family were safe with friends in Bandara, he called out again.

"You cannot stay there forever! You will have to come out sometime. And then you will join them in hell." He pointed to the bodies lying in the road.

Slowly, the highlanders moved back into the house, still silently eying their enemy. The door slammed, and almost immediately, the misty fog intensified.

Tommy Lynch turned to Hugo Cohen. "Not yet, Tommy," Hugo spoke quietly. "We surround your house and wait for our moment to strike."

Hugo's men sat or stood waiting patiently for his order to finish their task.

## Chapter 41

Thoroughly lost and very frightened, one who had survived the attack finally arrived outside the manor. He had witnessed the massacre of Bolton's men from some distance up the road from the farmhouse. As soon as he saw the Irish burst over the stone fences and commence the slaughter, he panicked and fled.

But now, he was even more afraid of Bolton and his reaction to the news he would impart and with good reason.

Bolton listened incredulously as the sorry tale was related to him. "Dead?! You say half of them have been killed by the Irish?"

"Yes," he replied.

Conrad Booth watched and listened with a wry smile.

After gleaning all the information he could, Bolton dismissed the man and turned to Booth.

"Well, you were right on one count. I sent the dogs, but they couldn't do a man's job. It appears barking is all they were good for. It's much too late to do anything now, but come first light, you and I will go and see for ourselves, and then we will determine what action I need to take. Someone will have to inform Slow that his lover is no longer with us. I suggest you go and talk to him and inform the balance of the men to be ready to leave, fully armed, come morning. I will inspect and choose suitable weapons for the two of us to use."

Without another word, he turned and stalked off.

Conrad Booth walked over to the men's quarters. After spending some time consoling Slow, he called over to a young man and beckoned to him to follow him outside.

"First thing in the morning, I want you take this message to the honourable judge. He will be most interested in this news."

Booth began tousling the pretty young man's locks and added, "That is, after I send you from my bed!"

*****

"What the hell are the bastards up to now?" MacFetridge asked of Mason.

The gloom of the day had finally faded into the night's darkness. Both had been waiting for the darkness to make their escape. However, with some trepidation, they watched as Hugo and his men moved about.

They had watched from the windows of the Lynch home at the activities of Hugo and the triumphant band, who went about their preparations.

They had obviously raided the woodshed as fires attempted to penetrate the gloom. These fires, about seven in all, had been lit in a circle surrounding the house. Between the fires and the house, they could make out the sentries standing at attention, obviously making any escape from the house very difficult. Others lazed by the fires, warming themselves, making no attempt to stifle their delight at the predicament the highlanders found themselves in.

Taunts and laughter reached their ears from time to time, intensifying the hatred the two had for the Irish.

"I will cut their balls off and stuff them down their Papist throats!" Mason snarled.

"Yes, but first we have to get out of here and get back to

Bolton. We need to even up our forces a bit. Bolton has muskets and guns; we will see how that lot measure up with lead balls flying at them," MacFetridge said quietly.

Turning and nodding to the others packed in the farmhouse behind them, he whispered, "Later, when the Irish tire of their banter, we will bust out of here. We will catch them off guard. We will send these cowards out to tackle those sentries, and during the confusion, you and I will escape into the night. Fight only to protect yourself, and remember, we run tonight to fight another day."

Mason nodded in full agreement.

MacFetridge had found a jug of potato spirit—poteen.

"Ahh, how can ye drink this evil brew? Willie, have another swallow." He passed the jug.

"At least it puts a warmth in the belly. Pass it 'round, to them. It may well put a fire in their guts!"

He sensed that it was approaching the midnight hour. Whatever moon there was could not pierce the cloud and mist. Looking out the window into the murk, he could see the fires still burning, though not as bright as before. He noticed still bodies sleeping close to the embers.

The sentries stood silent, staring at the farm, waiting for any movement before alerting the sleepers.

"I think we should wait a little longer; the fight today will have taken its toll. Tiredness should also start to weaken the sentries."

Another hour passed.

"Willie, shake them up!" Quietly, MacFetridge explained the plan to the now fully alert men.

"As ye pour oot the door, one by one you attack a sentry each, man on man. Willie and I will be in support behind you, me oot the front door, Willie oot the back. As each sentry falls, we attack the rest as they come at us. It will be easy as they will be trying to recover from sleep. Now position yourself. Half of ye be at the back, the other half there at the front door. I will smash this jug onto the hearthstone there. When it smashes, that will be your signal to attack."

"Willie!" He pulled his friend back. "Stay by me," he whispered.

"As they engage the Irish, you stay by me, and we will protect each other as we run for it."

The silence of the night was shattered as the jug smashed.

Immediately, men poured out into the night. The first ran at a sentry, his axe held high. As he slashed it down onto the sentry's head, there was no resistance. The body simply crumpled to the ground. The wooden staff holding it upright fell with the body.

Stunned, he hardly felt the steel of the pike ripping up and into his belly. The second man lying concealed at the foot of the targeted sentry finished him off with a savage blow with his cudgel.

"It's a trap!" The scream came from somewhere in the dark followed by a ghastly gurgle.

The night was suddenly lit by the fires springing to life. Clusters of hay, liberally doused with spirits, burst into flame as they hit the embers of each fire. With their backs to the flames, the Irish were not affected by the unexpected flare–up. Not so those from the farmhouse.

As they shielded their eyes to concentrate their sight on their enemy, they were hit on all sides by the Irish.

It was over almost before it began. As the light from the fires began to die out, bunches of hay were lit, and with the aid of several lamps from the farmhouse, the Irish searched for survivors.

There were none.

However, as the search intensified, it become apparent that none of the bodies were those of MacFetridge or Mason.

"They escaped!" Hugo said to Padraig and Sean. "And in this darkness, we will never find them."

"And that poses another problem. They will be with Bolton by dawn—that is, if they don't get lost. Either way, Bolton will be insanely furious when he finds out about this night. He will be here soon after first light, and this time his guns will certainly place the fight to his advantage."

"I agree," Padraig stated. "I am in favour of moving out and returning home to rest up and prepare for what he will do next. What say you, Hugo, Sean?"

Looking at the victorious band of his friends, Sean suddenly felt an emotional charge he had never felt before. He saw the exhaustion moving in, and the lads starting to wilt. He felt like never before that he wanted no harm to come to a single one of them.

"Agreed, Padraig; come, brothers, for we are now all brothers—blooded brothers of the battle to free our country."

Hugo smiled in agreement. He was also very proud of those blooded brothers.

Together, they rescued their weapons and stripped the bodies of weapons.

"Not only can we utilize their weapons, but we deprive the enemy of them as well," Hugo explained.

"Can you believe it? I think the sun will be shining by the time we get home. The weather is clearing. An omen, eh, brothers?" Sean laughed.

## Chapter 42

Padraig Joseph and his father looked through the doors of the barn where the victorious young band lay oblivious to all that had happened during the previous night.

The bad weather had gone, the sun was shining without a cloud to be seen, and the warmth of the new day ensured that no cold discomfort would waken them.

"Their innocence has been taken from them," the older man muttered quietly.

Both his grandchildren had arrived back at the house not long before the songbirds had greeted the day. Both were very tired, but joined with the others as they told and retold the story of the conquest. He could hardly comprehend how Hugo had devised the strategy of using the bodies of the dead in such an ingenious way. Even more astounding was that they had suffered not even a minor injury, although Hugo would only insist that good luck had favoured them.

While Sean had insisted he bed down with his comrades, all fully understood and shooed Padraig home to his obviously very worried wife and their babies.

"Dare I dream to think this is all over?" Padraig Joseph asked of his father.

"I would give all the rest of the years of my life if I thought God would intervene and put a halt to this greed and destruction, but sadly I think not," the grandfather replied.

The stench of death reached the nostrils of Bolton and Booth as they approached the Lynch farmhouse. The sight that greeted them as they rode closer shocked Booth, but Bolton gave no indication of his thoughts.

Conrad Booth had been very concerned that a similar fate awaited him, and he was most relieved to find that only the dead were there to welcome them. They had met MacFetridge and Mason a mile or so from the manor on their return to safety.

Bolton showed no obvious reaction as he listened to their story of how they had survived, but the others had not. The fact that they showed no sign of injury intrigued Bolton.

"What do you make of their tale, Conrad?"

"Either they are extremely skilled or exceedingly lucky," Booth replied with heavy cynicism.

Bolton had provided wagons to transport the rest of his force either dead or maimed. He instructed those onboard to spread out and search for survivors or any trace of the Irish.

Sitting on their horses upwind, they watched as the men rummaged around the bodies and were not surprised to hear the worst.

"Not a one alive!"

It was very obvious that from the battering the bodies had received, none could have survived. Booth watched as Slow eventually found the corpse of Hair Baker. He watched, fascinated, as the huge man sank to his knees and held the body of his friend with a tenderness that belied the brutishness of the man. Great tears appeared to roll down his face. He picked up the body and walked effortlessly to the wagon and laid the body tenderly on the floor of the cart.

"What the hell is he doing?" Bolton exclaimed. "I don't want any of this lot near my manor!"

"I suspect he wants to give his friend a send-off, maybe to hell, but a burial nonetheless." Booth smiled at his attempt at dark humour. "On that point, what do you suggest we do with this sorry little mess?"

"That, Conrad, has been on my mind, also. I am of the opinion that, as the Irish created this disarray, then why don't they tidy it up, what?" He raised his eyebrows in amusement.

"I had intended to burn the house down. Wouldn't it be amusing to watch the reaction of the pathetic tenants when they find the stinking state their charred farmhouse when they return home?"

"Onto the wagons!" he yelled to the men. "We're heading back to the manor."

Without another word, he spurred his horse and rode off. Booth shrugged and followed.

On their return to the manor, Bolton ordered MacFetridge and Mason to his study. Not allowing either to sit, he stared at them both. Finally, he spoke.

"Explain to me, if you will, how you managed to survive the slaughter when all the rest of my men died and with nary a scratch on either of you."

Both men shuffled their feet nervously and dared not look up.

"I am waiting."

Finally, MacFetridge stuttered, "The . . . the . . . the . . . Irish . . ."

"Silence, you buffoon!" Bolton roared.

"I was there. I could clearly see what had happened. The Irish simply outfoxed you. And I strongly suspect you hid until it was safe to run and save your cowardly hides."

Toying with a pistol, he suddenly pointed the gun at the worried MacFetridge. He pulled the trigger and the lead ball winged past his head, clipping off the tip of his ear.

"The only reason I do not put a bullet between your eyes is that I intend you to have one last chance to save your sorry lives."

With blood pouring down his face, discoloring his beard, the highlander watched and waited for Bolton to finish.

"You will go with the Gypsy, both of you. Mandino and his men will take you to the Gallagher home. I understand from my spy that the French Jew and his band of Irishmen that made such fools of you have made their base in the Gallagher barn. When the time is right, you will sneak into both farmhouses and kill the Gallagher men.

"You will kill only the old man and his son. And you will kill the two brothers Gallagher. You will not touch either of the Gallagher women. Do I make myself clear?"

Both highlanders nodded their assent.

"Remember, you succeed, and you live. Fail in any way and I will hunt you down and your death will be slow and very painful. That is, if the Gypsies don't slice you to ribbons before I get to you."

Bolton waited for the appropriate reaction.

"Good. Now go. Mandino will let you know when he is ready to leave."

After they had departed, he called for the Weasel. After a short discussion, he dismissed him, and as his name suggested, the Weasel slinked out.

*****

*A delightful morning, as only an English morning can be!* Lady Constance Louise Bolton smiled to herself, toyed with her coffee cup, and then took another sip. She had not intended to listen to the conversation that her husband was conducting with his secretary. She had overheard the raised voices and recognised concern in her husband's words. It was quite apparent that the letter that had arrived from Ireland contained news that had clearly upset Thomas Bolton, the Lord of Blaxton.

While she was aware that her son had ambition, she was also thoroughly aware of his ruthless nature and his total disregard for the unfortunate who might stumble in his way.

"I cannot believe what I am reading," Thomas Bolton said to his secretary. "I trusted him to handle my matters with dignity and respect for the tenants. I did not expect this!"

"He is, perhaps, a might headstrong, m' lord," the secretary replied.

"Good God man, headstrong?" Thomas Bolton laughed without a trace of humour. "It would appear that rents have not been collected for some time. I am aware that the Irish were unhappy, but had been paying. Now apparently my son has increased the rents to a point where the tenants have rebelled. And quite frankly, I probably would have done likewise in their position."

"You are, of course, going to Ireland, m' lord? I will attend to matters, and perhaps you can leave earlier."

"Thank you, my good fellow. But the Lady Constance is looking forward to the early autumn ball; we cannot leave until after that. Neither you nor I want to face the inevitable rage of a woman deprived of showing off her new frock at the season's first social event.

"And besides, I have meetings with my business colleagues regarding the investments in the new lands in the South Pacific.

"No, we will leave as planned. After we have enjoyed the pleasures of the ball, we will depart."

Lady Constance heard them stand, ready to leave the room. She quickly moved from the hall and walked outside.

"New frock indeed," she snorted. "I will have a new frock whenever I want one! But I wonder what my son is up to?"

## Chapter 43

Bolton could not quite understand it. He had been to many burials, and indeed, he'd been responsible for a few in his time. But to witness the grief of Slow as he bade farewell to his friend, Hair Baker, was astounding, at least to him it was.

Slow had approached him late the previous evening when the wagon had returned from the Lynch farm. In his stuttering fashion, he had begged to be able to bury his friend on one of the hilltops overlooking the manor fields.

"And presumably you will want to put a cross on the gravesite?" Bolton had asked with masked amusement.

To his surprise, Slow had stuttered a yes.

So Hair Baker was laid to rest, looking out toward the Atlantic with a wooden cross placed on the mound to remind those who were interested that this was his last resting place.

Bolton smiled as he spoke to Mandino.

"A wooden cross! I wonder if he above or his so-called saints welcomed their wayward son back or sent him down below?"

Mandino chose to remain silent.

"What! Don't tell me you are developing a conscience?"

Bolton looked at the Gypsy, who slowly turned to him and replied. "On two occasions, you have sent forces to strike down these Irish people. On two occasions, you have failed. In this most recent attempt, all but two were killed. Perhaps, he above and his saints have intervened in their favour."

"Absolute nonsense! Why, you yourself succeeded in getting close to the Gallagher pup, and you had him at your mercy. Maybe I should have given you instructions to take care of that pup along with the other pups you cut up."

"Sí, sí. But, Señor Bolton, you did not, for you had your reasons, and it is not for me to question; only to obey. You pay, I obey, hey?" He laughed.

Bolton looked intently at the swarthy Spaniard.

"You're a good man, Mandino. No, I do not object to paying you the blood money. You earn every shilling. And yes, you are right, I did underestimate these blasted Irish and their Jew saviour. But how long do you think they would last leaderless?"

"What do you have in mind?" Mandino asked.

"The demise of the rebel Gallagher, and likewise the death of his two meddling sons and their Jew leader," Bolton said. "And any others who should get in the way," he added.

"I should have some news soon of their whereabouts and hopefully their future plans and movements. Some of my men will create some diversions to keep them occupied. It may well be that during these diversions I rid myself of the Gallagher brothers and their leader, Cohen. And in particular, I will savor viewing the corpse of the tall dark brother, Padraig Gallagher."

Cohen and Padraig Joseph were enjoying their ales at Maloneys. They had walked into the village earlier that afternoon. Both felt that after their victory, calming down was needed more than a celebration.

But the ale still flowed. The word had certainly spread, and as the doors opened and each new drinker arrived, much backslapping and good humour flowed.

"'Tis truly a foin job youse be doin! The bloody English will be goin' back with their tails tucked right up their arse."

"Ah now, right enough, Willie McBride. It's a good job surely enough," said Padraig Joseph. "But it won't be over until their tails are on a vessel returning to their accursed country."

Few noticed, however, that while Sean was very much the centre of attention and thoroughly enjoying it, his brother was a good deal quieter.

It seemed to Padraig that he had only been home to his wife and the twins a brief moment, and suddenly, he was separated from them again. In truth, he understood only too well the importance of defeating the English and banishing them and their cruel injustices served upon his people. But his heart was not in it—taking the life of another. And while he had killed only one, and that seemingly in self-defence, his long standing Catholic beliefs questioned these actions.

But mostly he hated being separated from his wife and family.

Dusk was descending and the door opened again and two strangers entered. They approached the bar.

"A fine evening to you both; what would you be having?" the barkeep enquired.

"Your best ale. It has been a long journey and a thirsty one."

"Strangers, then, and what parts are you from?" The barkeep set the ales in front of them.

"Wexford. We have heard of the victories of the Donegal people over the English and wish to meet those responsible and congratulate them on their courage and conviction. Pray tell, where may we meet their leaders?"

"Indeed, you are in luck! Sean, Take these two men over and introduce them to your father and Hugo Cohen. They are up from way down Wexford way."

"Wexford! A long way from home. And you wish to speak to my father? Come, follow me."

Pushing through the throng, he reached Hugo and Padraig Joseph.

"Hey, Da, Hugo . . ." Pointing to the two men, he continued. "These men are up from Wexford and wish to talk to you."

Sean watched closely as the two men approached and put out their hands in a show of friendliness. He relaxed as the four men shook hands and sat.

"We're brothers—John and Michael Murphy. We have heard great stories of how you have stood up to the might of England and beaten them, and we are in awe of your triumphs. Now we wish to learn from you. We also want to make a stand and send the swine back to where they belong."

"Would be rebels then are you?" Padraig smiled. "Then this man is who you should be talking to, Hugo Cohen. He is responsible for all that has happened. He singlehanded took those young men there, drinking their victory ales, and turned them into the fighting force you have heard of."

"Not so," Cohen replied. "This man Padraig Joseph Gallagher, the father of the red-haired rogue that brought you to us, is the man you need to listen to.

"His dream to free his land from all who would do harm to his people has captured the imagination of all and now it would seem yourselves. Listen to him, and dare to dream his dream. And then, maybe you and all of Ireland can unite and tip those scum into the sea and send them back to where they belong."

Padraig Joseph smiled and said, "I'll save my speech for another day!"

Hugo clapped him on the back and said, "He certainly knows how to stir us to action. But first, we must show some hospitality. You will need to bed down soon for the night. Come, we will arrange some beds for you both. And I would like to introduce you to Padraig's two boys, Sean, who you have met, and his brother, also named Padraig."

Hugo added with a sardonic grin, "I don't know what it is

with you Irish. Absolutely no imagination when it comes to naming your offspring."

They pushed their way to where the loudest of the noise emanated from.

"Sean, Padraig, and the rest of you louts, we would like you to join us in welcoming these two. This is John and Michael Murphy. They are from Wexford and want to take part in the cause to free Ireland."

To the Wexford men he said, "Sean and Padraig are the lads who've shown us how to put the pike to the English."

The newcomers settled into true Donegal hospitality, and more ales flowed as the stories of the victories were shared by each of the young men.

Gradually, they realized that a rebellion in Wexford could happen, and they too could rid themselves of the blight of the English. Michael and John Murphy at last relaxed, and yes, they too began to dream.

## Chapter 44

"I love you, I love you, I love you. As God, the Blessed Virgin, and their son Jesus are my witnesses, I could not love you more than I love you."

Kathleen looked into Padraig's eyes as she listened to him. He had arrived home late the night before a little worse for the drink he had consumed. He had woken her as he stumbled into bed. Almost frantically, he had made love to her, apparently unaware of her desires. She had held him as he quickly climaxed, and then he had fallen asleep.

This morning, however, the memories had returned, and crestfallen, Padraig had begged her forgiveness for his bumbling behaviour.

"Hush," she whispered. "I know, and we love you, too."

"But I have so much I want to tell you, to ask you what you think. I am torn between so many loyalties."

Gradually, Padraig poured his heart out to the woman he loved so dearly. He told her of his reluctance to be part of Hugo's fighting force any longer. He told her of the repugnance he felt as he killed for the first time. He told her of his love for and dependence on his deep Catholic beliefs, and how he felt that killing the English, despite how ruthless and despicable they were, was a betrayal of those beliefs. He tried to explain to her his fear of betraying his father, his brother, and his fighting comrades.

"But above all this," he said, "I am so utterly frightened that some terrible happening will take you and our children from me."

She listened, holding him tighter and tighter. She could not tell him that his mother had forewarned her of her son's feelings. At the time, she had put it down to what she thought was Claire's witch-like qualities. Surely not a bad witch, but Padraig's mother was different from the rest of the women in the village, albeit a good woman. Indeed, it was Claire who had insisted on her two sons developing good reading and writing skills. She had encouraged Padraig's love of different languages and his ability to master them and speak eloquently in each.

Yes, Claire Gallagher knew many things, and she certainly knew her son. Deep down, Kathleen suspected that Claire knew more than she was prepared to tell. But no matter what the future would bring, Kathleen would support and love her big husband unconditionally.

"Hush," she said again. "Whatever you need to do, you will do, and I will be standing right alongside you."

And with her beautiful, sparkling blue eyes flashing, she asked, "And how sincere is your apology? The wee ones are still asleep. Perhaps you can show me how sorry you truly are!"

Later that day, Padraig, Kathleen, and the twins made their way down to the family home.

Padraig introduced her to the Wexford men, who were seated at the table with his father, grandfather, and brother. Hugo was addressing all and paused as they entered the room.

"Is this an angel brightening up an already beautiful day?" he asked with Gallic charm.

"Oh, such lies." Kathleen giggled. "You sit and join the men, Padraig. I will go help your mother prepare the midday meal."

"Padraig, we were just talking about our early days and telling our friends here about how all you lads developed from young men into seasoned fighters."

"And extremely encouraging this amazing tale is," Michael Murphy stated.

"If we can do just half as well when we return home and instruct our men accordingly, I am confident that we too can turn the tables on our uninvited foe."

"Padraig, we have decided that we will return to the beach at Maghara," Hugo said. "We will spend a day or two showing our friends our methods so that they can pass on that knowledge to their men. We will also increase our skills to the next level." He paused, lowering his voice.

"We feel that we have weakened the resolve of Bolton and his men sufficiently to be able to deliver the killer blow. We have decided to wipe out all that remain of Bolton's men, and, of course, Bolton himself."

"And this, who knows, could begin the cleansing of Ireland," John Murphy solemnly declared. "We may well be witnessing the elimination of all who threaten our country's sovereignty."

*****

Judge Herbert Throckmorton Squires was extremely ambitious, but very devious. He had absolutely no liking for Bolton, but greatly respected his guile and ruthlessness. He also feared him and fully understood his fate should Bolton ever discover his collusion with Conrad Booth.

Booth had arrived with the papers he had prepared for Judge Squire. All he needed was the signature that would bind them and secure the judge's commitment to realize Booth's ambitions.

They were both fully aware that the English decree set by King Henry VIII giving title of traditional Irish land to the English had been causing major concern to both English and Irish, but for obvious different reasons. Indeed, in many parts of

Ireland, their efforts to persuade the Irish to return a profit had failed miserably. Some of the absentee landlords had sold title to other English investors, who hoped to do better. Such was the case with Thomas Bolton, the Lord of Blaxton.

Both Judge Squires and Conrad Booth had seen firsthand the results of Robert Bolton's attempts to pressure the local Irish to respond first to his requests and now his demands. They were well aware that causalities would occur, and were not at all surprised at the outcome.

"It is precisely as I predicted," the judge declared, wiping the remnants of snuff from his nose. "One way or another, Bolton will die, either at the hands of the Irish, or as you suggest, one morning he will simply not awaken. A combination of the Oriental pipe and French brandy can be fatal, you know." He sniggered. "One would never know one's throat was being cut, would one?"

"Yes," Booth replied quietly, "and you may be equally certain that the combination of snuff and brandy can result in the same should you attempt to swindle me out of my share of the titles, once all has been completed." There was no doubt as to the outcome should he feel justified.

"Have you had any indication of when the Lord and Lady Constance are due?"

"Actually, I have," said the judge. "Word arrived only yesterday. They attend an annual ball in London and leave shortly after. They should be here in less than a month, and such a pity they won't be returning, yes?"

"Yes, a pity, I agree," was the reply from Booth. "Indeed, such a pity!"

"Now, before you leave, you have, ahem, signed those papers?" The judge indicated the documents.

"Yes," Booth replied.

"Good, good. Excellent," the judge muttered. He was silent for a few minutes as he thoroughly perused the papers. "All is in order. Needless to say, you won't let these documents fall into the wrong hands, will you?"

"Hardly!" Booth replied, and he stowed the papers in his satchel.

*****

The Weasel had followed the party, as they made their way down the small country lane, heading to the coast. He had been in the tavern as the brothers from Wexford discussed the resistance efforts with the Gallagher family and Hugo Cohen. He had overheard enough of the conversation to report back to Bolton. He practically salivated as he pondered the reward he would get for his efforts.

He would inform Bolton of the antics of the Jew and his team of rebels when they commenced their work on the sands at Maghara.

Eventually, the main party reached the gap between the sand dunes before moving out onto the beach proper. The Weasel had trouble keeping up, as the pace they set soon had him gasping. The two from Wexford also appeared to be troubled, but managed to keep with the party, but they fell onto the dunes to recover and swallowed big gulps of water from the jugs to quench their thirst.

Cohen and his men were totally untroubled, and to the unbelieving eyes of the Weasel, they stripped off their clothing and plunged into the sea.

A little later, they all emerged, laughing and pushing each other in jest, as they dried off and put their clothing back on.

Hidden at the peak of one of the sand dunes, the Weasel spied on them, as Hugo put the young men through various fighting maneuvers. They produced staffs and pikes and clubs of different sizes and shapes and squared off with each other, lunging and parrying, dodging and sliding from attacking blows.

It seemed miraculous that no one was hit or hurt.

After a while, they stopped and settled on the sand to rest. Cohen stood in the middle, talking and gesturing, occasionally addressing the two Wexford men.

"I wonder what them are talkin' 'bout," the Weasel muttered to himself.

Sometime around mid-afternoon, they broke up, and he watched, as they set out looking for driftwood. It wasn't too much later when the wood was dumped where fires had obviously been burning before.

Others returned with clumps of black-shelled mussels, while some had collected cockles.

As the sky began to cloud over, a cool breeze sprang up, and the fires were lit.

The Weasel suddenly realized he was starving. The aroma of steaming shellfish wafted up and around the dunes and eventually reached him. He could smell charred mutton, and his mouth drooled in anticipation of food he would not taste.

The sound of the breaking surf could not drown out the happy chatter of the contented and well-fed men.

Now feeling most miserable, he decided it was time to leave and face the long trek home.

"I'll be damned if I wait any longer. His self will have to be happy with what I tell him." So saying, the Weasel slipped quietly down the dunes and soon began the homeward journey.

## Chapter 45

A strong bond of friendship had developed between the Donegal people and the Wexford brothers. The camaraderie and enthusiasm that the brothers Murphy had witnessed during the day, as the men practiced their manoeuvres, inspired them to such an extent that they also wanted to join in and learn more about fighting with the pikestaff.

As the day ended and the night began to draw in, the fires were built up again. As all settled in around the warmth, they told more of their background.

Hugo and the Gallagher family had listened with great interest as Michael and John Murphy had told them their story at the tavern that first night, but the other members of the party had not heard and were amazed to discover that both were priests.

Both were Wexford born and both were well traveled. John had studied in Spain and Michael, much to Hugo's satisfaction, had spent some time in France.

Father Michael was the parish priest of Ballycanew and Father John a curate in Boolavogue. A close friend, Bagenal Harvey, was studying law and supported the ideal of government reform and emancipation. All three of them were men of liberal principles.

Ever since Queen Elizabeth had instigated the law that gave aristocratic Protestant English families ownership of traditional

Irish lands, unrest had been building up.

Outbreaks of rebellion, such as in the northern province of Ulster thirty-eight years after her death, had enflamed the issues until Oliver Cromwell's military campaigns squelched any further uprisings.

While there were many examples of fairness by English landlords, by and large, cruelty and total disregard for the general wellbeing of the Irish were the accepted practice.

Both Fathers John and Michael had witnessed firsthand relative peace and harmony in Spain and France, and they felt certain that the same could be achieved in the country of their birth. With careful planning and fighting skills, such as they were witnessing this day, they felt that this goal could be achieved.

"And what will the Wexford people do about this, then?" one of the lads asked.

"I do suppose much will depend on what develops here in Donegal over the next month or so," John Murphy replied.

"The defeat of Robert Bolton and his thugs will only give confidence to ourselves and others who wish to defy the English," Michael added, "and who knows, all of Ireland may well stand up and demand freedom and be prepared to fight for it."

"But what if we don't succeed, and Bolton defeats us?" Padraig Gallagher asked quietly.

"What! Did I hear you right?" demanded Sean. "You listen to me, brother Padraig, and listen well. I will not hear of this word, defeat. And how can you sit there and even contemplate such a thought? How can you?"

The sudden fury from Sean Gallagher stunned the others.

Attempting to soften the outburst, Hugo interjected.

"While none here feel that this will happen, perhaps if such a tragedy were to occur, it would give the English a huge cause for elation and create so much despondency that it could set back other Irish causes months, even years. But this will not happen, will it?"

Michael Murphy also attempted to defuse the now volatile situation.

"Padraig, of course, does ask a fair question. It is better to be prepared if such a thing occurs, and if it does, we will arm ourselves and fight another day. Remember, Bolton has been beaten twice and badly, and he will come back a third time. Certainly, this time he knows your strengths, and now he will be bringing in his. But for now I am tired; sleep beckons, and I suggest we all settle down for the night."

As the stars and the half-moon bathed the sleeping camp in soft filtered light, only Padraig lay awake, looking upwards, listening to the breaking waves surge up onto the sands of Maghara.

A vision of strange, unclad dark people had been haunting him. He was standing on a stark, treeless brown land, alone. He longed to be with Kathleen. He simply ached with desire to hold his babies. Tomorrow, he would talk to his father and Hugo. And yes, he would surely talk to his brother Sean.

★★★★★

Pat McHugh had watched the party make their way down to the sands the previous day. Because of the remoteness of his property, he had had virtually no contact with the collectors. They had called twice some time back, but where his home was situated, he could see miles up the valley. Long before they had arrived, he and his wife had gathered up all the children and disappeared into the hills behind the property until it was safe to return home.

He was in total support of the defeat of the landlords, however, and waited with great anticipation for the regular visits of Hugo and his men to the beach for their training.

Very little that occurred in his locality escaped his notice, and certainly any strangers, or for that matter, local people, who visited the area, gathering shellfish, could not do so without him or one of his many children becoming aware of their presence.

None of the local people would even consider going down to gather mussels without yelling out a cheery, "How are ya, Pat?" or stopping to chat for an hour or so.

It was for that reason that when the Weasel snuck past the first time, it had caused Pat some concern. He just did not like the Weasel, but country courtesy insisted upon a civil greeting or even a nod in recognition.

But it was plain to Pat that this was out of the ordinary.

Hugo and in particular, Sean and Padraig, had stopped and chatted for a while earlier on the previous day. They had introduced the two Wexford men to him and amiably passed on idle gossip regarding the North and the South before trotting off down to the beach.

He observed the Weasel some minutes later, slinking past, following behind, and this time he followed him.

He watched as the Weasel climbed the high dunes and settled down to spy on the men training on the beach.

"What the divil's he oop to?" Pat muttered.

After a while and with no further movement from the Weasel to observe, he got bored and wandered back up to his home. Later when he returned, the Weasel was still lying there, spying.

"'Tis surely strange!"

He watched as the Weasel suddenly got to his feet and slid down the dunes, before making his way back up the valley.

And this time, Pat followed him.

Hugo had instructed that on their training days various duties were to be allocated, and not wanting to be left out, John Murphy volunteered to start the early morning fires and brew the tea.

The morning started out clear enough, and as the priest sat staring out to sea, silently saying his prayers, watching as the embers started to glow, he could see clouds gathering way out on the horizon.

Sean, the seaman, had said the previous night that he could smell rain, and sure enough, it looked as though his prediction would prove correct.

Hugo explained to John Murphy that his strategy for eliminating the Bolton presence would not take place until later in the month, so John and his brother agreed it would be better for them to return home. Meanwhile, they planned to pass on the information about the resistance efforts with their own people and other Irish folk they happened to meet on their journey home.

Hugo also promised assistance from himself and the ever-eager Sean in the year to follow, after their work here was completed.

It was obvious to the priests that thorough planning and great care were needed to make their stand successful, and this would take time.

As the warmth of the fires reached out, and the smell of freshly brewed tea touched the noses of the sleepers, they gradually arose to greet the new day.

"Sure and I said there would be rain today," Sean bragged with a smile. "These old farm boys wouldn't know nought. Come on, little brother, rise, and greet the day."

Apparently, the angry words of the night before were forgotten.

Hugo looked out to sea. "Yes, Sean, I suspect you are right. That red sky tells us the weather could turn nasty. Let us pack up and return to Bandara before it hits us."

It was on their way up the valley a little while later that Pat came out to talk to them.

Hugo's face darkened when he heard how the Weasel had been skulking about spying on them.

"This explains much," he said in a quiet, even tone. "While we've always seemed to be one jump ahead of Bolton, I've had the suspicion that he had a great deal more information about us than he was entitled to. This means that we will have to re-evaluate our situation."

He thanked Pat for his vigilance, and they recommenced their journey homeward.

It was just before they came into view of the village that he suddenly stopped and turned to the others and smiled. "Like all bad news, we can turn it into good. I have an idea."

## Chapter 46

Thomas Bolton, the Lord of Blaxton, was in fine form. All was in readiness for his trip to Ireland, and his good wife, Lady Constance, had made certain that the kitchen staff had prepared the foods and drinks they needed for the journey. Their personal servants would accompany them to tend to their every need.

The brandies were superb, as was the whole evening's food and wine, as he sat back with a glass in one hand and a fine Caribbean cigar in the other.

"I understand you depart later this month?" Lord Sydney enquired.

"Yes, indeed. I have had troubling reports from our business manager, who attends to matters concerning our estates. The blasted Irish have been causing problems, and while the endeavors of my son to correct the same have largely been unsuccessful, I feel that with a little more diplomacy and effort, we may well finish with a profitable status by the end of the harvest."

Lord Blaxton paused to sip from his glass.

"So, it's partly a pleasure trip, but more a need to teach my son some business sense and sort out this Irish concern. But old chap, tell me more about the convict issue here in England. It is an absolute disgrace that we should have to contend with the criminal element of society to begin with. Sending them all off to the colonies is a great idea. I congratulate you heartily."

"Thank you," Lord Sydney replied. "But in fairness, William Pitt believed that the idea had merit, and in my position of both home and colonial secretary, our prime minister has given me all the support I need."

"Tell me more of this Botany Bay," Lord Blaxton enquired. "Sounds all very far-off and rather exotic, but let's hope not too exotic. We do not want our villains and vagabonds to have too pleasurable a time there, what?" Lord Blaxton chuckled, thinking himself witty.

"Well, it transpires that a midshipman named James Mattra on one of Cook's voyages into the Pacific spotted the bay while off the coast of New South Wales. He suggested to that buffoon Lord North that this new land would be an ideal location to deport not only our criminal element, but also those who oppose our political idealism; in fact, apart from our loyal servants and those deemed worthwhile, we could simply pop the lot in a ship and export them to this far–off land. Good idea, what?" Lord Sydney laughed.

"And Pitt obviously likes and endorses the proposal?"

"Indeed, old chap, indeed."

"Do not forget that I want to be involved in any possible financial return in any of the Pacific ventures," Thomas Bolton, Lord of Blaxton, insisted.

"Of course. And there will be much in the way of rich pickings. Of that, you may be certain. The whole plan of sending these worthless scum to settle the new land and then open the way for us once the time is right is an excellent one."

*****

The Weasel sat opposite Robert Bolton. He had told of all

that he had seen down at Maghara Beach. Bolton responded most positively.

"I really must say you have done an excellent job," he purred. "And these strangers; you have no idea who they are apart from they appear to hail from down South?"

"All that I have told you about them, I overheard in the tavern the other night."

"Mmm. I suspect that the news of these so-called victories of the bloody Gallaghers has traveled far, and these two want firsthand information from them and the Frenchman.

"But from what you have told me, I don't think there will any further victories. What say you, my sneaky little friend?"

The Weasel nodded in vigorous affirmation. "Indeed, sir; oh, yes indeed."

"And now a reward for a job well done. I will fetch some coins for you from Booth's office. Please stay seated."

Bolton walked down the hall to his manager's office.

Earlier that day, Conrad Booth had suggested he travel to Donegal Town with the cook and one of the servants to purchase the provisions. Bolton had readily agreed as he also needed to stock up the depleted spirits cabinet.

"Damn and blast!" he exclaimed. "What the hell!"

He had tripped on a loose board partially concealed by a carpet. Almost tumbling to the floor, he grabbed the side of a desk to support himself.

As he bent down to replace the loose timber, he spied what appeared to be a set of papers bound with a ribbon.

"Now what is this, pray tell. I wonder . . ." As he opened and read, his face darkened. "That bastard . . . that treacherous filthy bastard." He stood, absolutely furious, becoming more and more livid as he read on the papers. "I'll kill him. I'll cut his perfidious heart out and slice his body into tiny pieces and feed them to the pigs."

Gradually he calmed down, and then he began scheming.

He folded the papers and tied them with the ribbon, then replaced them exactly as he had found them under the floorboards. He put the carpet back into place and went to the drawer where he took out the coins for the Weasel's reward.

"There you are, my friend," he said, returning to his office and handing the coins to the Weasel. "Sometimes you truly do not know who your friends are. But at least I can trust you, my sly little comrade. Can't I?"

Completely perplexed by Bolton's mood, the Weasel left, scratching his nit-infested head. "Strange . . . 'tis very strange." Then looking up at the darkening sky, he muttered, "I'd best get a move on."

As Sean had predicted, the rain began to fall.

*****

Hugo had reasoned that the Weasel would have now been to and informed Bolton of their activities on the beach at Maghara. He agreed with Sean that the weather would turn bad and stay that way for at least three, perhaps, four days.

He felt justified therefore in allowing all his men to return to their homes. This would also give them a chance to help bring in the back end of the summer harvests. However, he needed them to return before the weather cleared again.

This also allowed him and Padraig Joseph to spend some extra time with the priests before they commenced their homeward journey back to Wexford.

After Padraig spoke briefly to his parents, he turned toward his home.

Sean guessed that his brother was deeply concerned and troubled, and he decided to walk back with him. Neither was too concerned about the rain nor getting wet.

"Hey, little brother, I know only too well that you hate being away from Kathleen, and I can fully understand this, but you do know that you have a responsibility to protect her and the twins. You also have a responsibility to finish what we have started and pledged to finish. We have to destroy Bolton and any other threat to the freedom of our families and our people."

"Sean, I understand, and I agree with you. But I have no more stomach for killing. You and the others may call me a coward, and you may well be correct, but I just cannot lift another weapon and take another life. I simply love Kathleen and my children too much to allow the hatred of these strangers to interfere with my feelings toward them. In fact, deep down, I probably don't even hate them. I do not like what they do here, and I do not like what they do to our people, but hate them? No, I do not truly hate them."

"What! This is madness. What will our father say when he hears about this?" Sean was incredulous.

"Yes, I know. And again, I can only agree with you."

"Padraig, I know you are not a coward. What would happen if Kathleen's life was threatened by the enemy? And remember, these are the bastards that killed your bitch and her pups."

"I would die in my attempts to save all three, Sean, you know that. I just do not want to take part in any sort of organized fighting. I am only truly happy when I am around my family. I have a splendid new young collie that is responding well to my training, and I want to spend time with him also."

"When do you intend to tell our father and Hugo? They will be more than a little angry."

"True, Sean, and I expect this. But remember, we also have a heavenly Father, and my conscience keeps telling me that what I am doing is wrong. I understand that you feel it is all justified and proper. I don't."

"So, you simply stand by and let this English swine trample on us and treat us like dirt?" Sean was growing more exasperated by the minute.

"I can only do what I must do," Padraig replied quietly, but firmly.

The two brothers stayed silent, both deep in thought, as they arrived outside Padraig's home.

"Come inside and dry off."

"No, Padraig. You go in and be with Kathleen. No doubt I shall see you tomorrow."

"Sure. But please, Sean, say nothing of this. I will talk to Father in the morning."

Sean turned and walked back down the hill in the now pouring rain. His shoulders hunched to ward off the wet, it appeared to Padraig that his brother carried the weight of the world on them.

As Padraig walked to his home, Kathleen opened the door to greet him, hugging him, and kissing him in welcome, and all his resolve and decisions now felt fully justified.

"Look at yourself, you're wringing wet. Come and sit by the fire, and I'll fetch some warm dry clothing for you."

"Ah, and look here," Padraig said, spying his twins in their little cot. "Two beautiful little babes I have, and I see a fine brave dog, looking after my little ones."

Padraig picked up his baby daughter and held her to his face, smelling her sweet baby scent.

He put her down and picked up his son and cuddled him, too. Then he stood by the fire, warming himself, occasionally bending down to rub the dog behind his ear.

Kathleen entered the room, holding a bundle of clothing. "Here, take off those wet clothes and put these on, and then you can sit. I'll bring over the stir-about pot, and you can tell me all the news."

"Mmm. I am so hungry I will eat the lot."

As Padraig ate, he told his wife of his conversation with Sean and his decision to talk to Hugo and his father.

Kathleen stood and went to her husband. Holding his face in her hands and looking intently into his eyes, she whispered, "I love you, oh, my beautiful love, I love you so very, very much. You must do what you think is right. And always remember: God and the Holy Mother will never let any harm come to us."

Then, as an afterthought, she smiled at the watching dog. "And you, the big brave dog, you will protect us all now, won't you?"

Padraig looked on. A feeling of dread abruptly hit him. He could not explain it. He knew only that a terrible threat of imminent danger hung over them.

## Chapter 47

The storm had set in, and already the Atlantic winds had intensified so much that it was unsafe to walk about due to flying tree debris.

But the priests had to meet with the southbound coach leaving from Donegal Town, and so, sadly, the farewells were made, and they bundled up to escape the wind, as they boarded the trap for Sean to commence the drive.

"Well, at least the harvest was completed and all the hay stored." Father John stated this merely for something to say because his heart was heavy, leaving his new friends.

After both priests had given their blessings, particularly to the little ones, Kathleen and Claire gave them a hug.

"We will see you again, never fear," Father Michael Murphy said, giving Claire one last hug.

"Sure, and it's only the sadness to see you go," Claire replied. No one knew of her true feelings. She was much too frightened to speak of her fears to either of the priests.

Later that morning, Claire sat with her obviously troubled son.

Kathleen was feeding one of the babies, and she looked on with concern.

"Please tell me what worries you, my son."

Padraig quietly told his mother all that he spoken about with Kathleen the previous night.

"I am aware that the villagers talk about you as if you have power and knowledge that they do not possess, Ma."

"You have it also, Padraig," his mother replied softly.

"What do you mean?"

"Your skill with languages, your ability to work with and talk to the animals, and the way they respond to you. And yes, while you pretend to ignore it, there is a strong purpose for you to be in this life. My son, I am not certain if it is right for me to tell you this. But I have seen many visions, and these hazy apparitions have revealed to me a man, a great fighter, and a saviour to many people, strange people. These people are like no persons I have ever seen. And my son, that liberator is you."

While Padraig looked on at his mother in stunned silence, the words that she dared not tell him and the apparitions she had seen, but could not describe would stay with her until she died.

She could not tell of the angels of death that would be her son's constant companions.

With a sigh, she said, "But I think it is now time to talk to your father and grandfather. They are both out in the barn. Go to them."

As Padraig walked from the room and out of the house, Claire went and picked up the other baby. She also walked from the room, but Kathleen was too busy to notice the stream of tears flowing from the older woman's eyes.

Padraig Joseph listened intently to his son's words. At first, he was extremely angry, but a warning glance from his father silenced him.

"You have thought long and hard on this, lad?"

"I have indeed, Grandfather, I have."

"Well, then, there is little else to be said." The words of disappointment were most apparent in Padraig Joseph's voice.

"I wonder what Hugo will say when he hears about this."

The young man simply shrugged and sat in silence.

A sudden barking broke the mood, and the three men looked to the barn door as a sheep dog burst in, followed by Kathleen.

"Ah, and here's the good boy then." Padraig smiled, ruffling the dog's ears.

"He's a good one, that dog," his grandfather concurred.

"Aye, and I need to work him even in this weather. Come on, boy. Let's go."

Together, he and Kathleen walked from the barn with dog in tow, leaving the two older men sitting in silence.

Finally the grandfather spoke. "Do not think harsh of him. When I was a younger man, I also loved your mother, as he loves his Kathleen. And it broke my heart when she died. You were only four years old at the time. And I have missed her every waking moment of my life. Please, my son, be patient, and he will be more of a son to you than you will ever realize."

*****

The storm had altered the plans of Conrad Booth. Instead of arriving home around mid-afternoon, it was much later in the day before he returned to the manor and attempted to enter the house without letting in too much windswept rain.

"Rather late, but understandable, I guess."

Robert Bolton stood warming himself in the drawing room.

"Damn this bloody weather!" Booth exclaimed. "Donegal Town is also getting a hammering."

"Yes, I suppose it would. And pray tell, did you happen to spot the good judge by chance?" Bolton asked.

"Indeed. We had lunch together, and he asked after your health. To which I replied you were well, apart from the mood you woke up to this morning." Booth laughed a little.

"Well, that mood changed," Bolton said, looking immensely

pleased with himself. "In fact, my mood changed very quickly. I had a visit from our little friend, the Weasel."

Bolton told Booth all that he had learned. Watching him very closely, he added, "I took some money from your desk to pay him. I hope you don't mind."

"Of course not," Booth replied. "Our little Judas must collect his pieces of silver."

Booth detected the deliberate note in Bolton's voice and wisely decided to ignore it. His eccentric behaviour had seemed to be worsening with his compulsion to feed his addiction. But that matter would be resolved in the not too distant future.

"But of greater importance," Booth said solicitously, "what do you intend to do with this information?"

"This weather has altered my plans somewhat, but when it clears, I will be arranging a meeting of sorts, a pleasant little soiree on a beach—well, hardly pleasant, I'll wager, not for the Irish scum we will meet there."

"Oh, tell me more," Booth demanded.

Bolton told him what he had in mind, but he left out some important details. He certainly could not tell Booth what he had in mind for him. Booth would soon find out. Indeed, he would!

After Booth left, the Gypsy walked in.

"You summoned, my lord," Mandino said, and then he laughed. His droll tone didn't escape Bolton's notice.

"Know your place, Spaniard!" Bolton answered, and it almost sounded as though he were teasing the man. "A glass of wine?" he offered.

"If I may join you, then, of course," the Gypsy replied.

After settling down and tasting the wines, Bolton finally spoke. "This blasted weather has dampened my plans a bit." He paused and tasted another mouthful of wine. "I have had a chance to think about other matters, and this inclement change could, in fact, benefit me greatly."

Mandino watched Bolton closely.

"I have every reason to state to you that when this weather comes good, we will see the demise of the Gallagher clan."

"Oh! And what of our original plans?"

"Not too much change. You and the Scots will still make your visit to the Gallagher home and finish matters there. But I will lead the rest of our men to where I am certain we will locate their rebellious scum and do away with them."

"And may I ask—what of the wife of the young Gallagher and their babies?" the Spaniard replied.

"I will take care of them. You are not to go near them or their home. You can do what you wish with the older Gallagher woman, but I have plans for the younger one."

Mandino decided not to press the matter further.

"You mentioned the fighters. Where do you intend to deal with them?"

Bolton explained how the Weasel had discovered their place of training and how he would conceal his men and wait for them.

"But how will you know when they will be there? They are most elusive, and they seem to be very well organized."

"That will be their downfall. You are correct in your assessment of them. But their leader, the Jew Frenchman, is the key."

Bolton explained how he would use the information the Weasel supplied and set the trap accordingly.

"Yes, you are correct when you say they have developed skills, excellent skills, in fact. But they still cannot cope with that weaponry." Bolton chortled as he pointed to the gun cabinet.

"No, the muskets and my guns will soon settle this, and there will be no further opposition to my demands."

## Chapter 48

No matter how hard the rains fall, the Sabbath must be honoured, and Sunday the village church was full as always, though the steamy atmosphere bore witness to the dampness of the parishioners' clothing.

Padraig and Kathleen had managed to keep the little ones dry, and they lay snuggled under the warmth of their parents' clothing.

"One blessing, we don't have to sit and kneel and kneel and stand," Kathleen giggled.

"Shh! Heathen!" Padraig teased.

He looked at his baby daughter nestled in his arms and watched as Kathleen lightly smoothed the new black hair that had so recently started to appear on his son's head. She licked her finger and tried to make a little curl, but to no avail. He watched enchanted as she smiled at her failed attempt.

He again realized that his decision to stay with her and not go with his brother and the others was the right one.

He looked directly at the statue of the Blessed Virgin and nodded his head.

"You blessed me with my family, Holy Mother. I cannot betray your kindness and desert them now, can I?" He silently prayed his gratitude.

The evening before, he had met with Hugo, the parish priest, and the others at Maloneys. Hugo, as expected, had been most understanding.

"Padraig, you indeed do have a responsibility and that is to protect your family. And when we depart after the sky clears, you will ensure no harm comes to not only Kathleen and the babies, but also your mother and grandfather. This old codger can look after himself." He laughed as he nudged Padraig Joseph.

The priest had also added his comments.

"You don't want to be gallivanting around the hills when you have the little ones to look after, quite surely," he said, not revealing his true feelings regarding the forthcoming conflict. While he loved Hugo and the Gallagher family as his own, he could not turn his back on his Catholicism and endorse the killings even though there was sufficient reason to consider it right and proper.

And he was most happy that at least the young Gallagher had prioritized his responsibility and intended to stay by his wife's side.

Padraig's thoughts were interrupted when the priest called for the blessing prior to the conclusion of the Mass.

"Lord, we give you thanks for the success of this year's harvest. And now we ask for your blessing."

After the service, the parishioners milled around, waiting to dash for cover, as the rain slackened off.

Hugo and the Gallagher men had been sitting, enjoying the afternoon. Even with the rain falling unceasingly, the good ales had accentuated the Sunday mellow mood.

"Ah well, the fields will love the watering, and it will be easier to plow them before the winter sowing."

"Indeed, Sean, and it will not be yourself that will be doing the work. It will be the likes of ourselves," his father stated.

Padraig laughed at the banter between his brother and father. All the emotion of his decisions to separate himself from the rebels and remain with Kathleen faded for the time being.

"And when will the good ladies be joining us?" Hugo suddenly asked.

"Time enough!" Padraig Joseph replied.

"'Tis women's work that they are at, talking and the like, planning other ways to make a good day unbearable. But then a clever man like yourself, Hugo, wouldn't know about things like that, being without a woman's clutter and free from the harness of marriage."

"Ah, Father!" Padraig began.

"Shush, brother, time will tell, and one day you will remember this day," Sean joked. "You will say, 'My brother and father were right.' Hear me well."

Hugo suddenly stiffened.

"Here he comes. Don't turn around! He's just walked through the door."

As expected, the Weasel had done the rounds of the drinking establishments and finally found his way to Maloneys.

While appearing to be engrossed in conversation, Hugo watched the actions of the man ordering a drink at the bar. Like the creature he was named after, the Weasel slyly glanced around the room, his eyes continually on the move.

"What's he doing?" Sean asked, his back to the bar area.

"He's looking around to see who's here. Let's give it some more time. Now that he has found us, he won't be going too far, and then you give your little performance as planned."

"I do hope you are right," Padraig Joseph sighed softly.

"Oh yes, he won't be going too far. Not until he has found out what we want him to hear," Hugo smiled.

Their conversation was interrupted by the arrival of the womenfolk.

"Well, well, and what do we have here?" Hugo stood and welcomed the new arrivals.

Padraig went to Kathleen and gave her a quick hug. Claire went and sat next to her husband on the chair that Hugo had vacated.

After a brief conversation with Kathleen, Padraig said, "Sean, do you mind driving us home? The babies need their sleep."

"Not at all. I can then concentrate on slaking my thirst without those looks I get from my brother's wife."

Kathleen gave him a playful push.

"Just you wait until the day some poor lady gets you, and then you will know!" she laughed.

"Never!" Sean laughed. "Now come, and let's be off."

"My grandchildren!" Padraig the Older smiled.

Hugo watched them depart. He also watched as the Weasel followed their progress from the bar and then turned back to his drink.

Sometime later in the afternoon, Sean returned and sat with a group of men that the Weasel recognised from the beach at Maghara. Again feigning unsteadiness on his feet, he partially stumbled his way to where they were seated and sprawled in a chair not too far from them. He then mumbled to himself, dribbled a little, and pretended to fall asleep.

Sean watched from the corner of his eye and nodded to his friends.

Gradually, their conversation appeared to be a bit more spirited, and then Sean lowered his voice, but still loud enough for the Weasel to hear. "Are you all ready for when this blasted weather clears up, then?"

"Aye, Sean, indeed."

"This time we will destroy Bolton and his kind."

"And do we return to Maghara, or do we stay at your father's barn?"

"We return to Maghara. I would say this weather will clear

in a day, maybe two. We will meet at our barn to collect our provisions and then spend two days practicing manoeuvres. After the second day, we will rest at our camp on the beach and leave during the night to strike Bolton at his manor as the sun rises. The moon will favour us as it is near to full again."

"So, when the weather clears then! Come, lads, we will drink to the death of Bolton."

The Weasel didn't budge. He waited until the young rebels had finished their drinks and decided to move on. He then stood and made his way from Maloneys to visit a friend in the village. He would stay the night and make his way out to Bolton's place when he woke tomorrow morn. He could almost feel the touch of the silver that Bolton would give him, maybe even gold. Either way, the monetary gratitude would certainly ease the seasonal problem of having to find food for himself and his wretched family in the long, cold winter months.

As for the young rebel group and the Frenchman? Well, they were deserving of what they would receive from Bolton. The Gallagher family had never considered him. No, they would get what they deserved.

## Chapter 49

The weather seemed to have calmed. The driving winds and belting rains had gone, but the clouds were still very black and threatening. It was the absence of noise that woke Conrad Booth.

As he gazed out of the window with a steaming cup of brew in hand, his thoughts returned to the previous night. Bolton had been extremely quiet. He had spent the latter part of the evening intermittently sipping on a large brandy and then gulping down a few good swallows of ale. He had also taken most of his guns from the gun cabinet, broken them down, cleaned them, and returned them to the cabinet.

His fingers had caressed the fine walnut stocks, as a lover might stroke the breasts of his beloved. Booth watched, as Bolton ran his hands along the shining silver barrels and back, lightly testing the trigger action, locked in complete fascination with his weapons.

All this in relative silence, completely ignoring any who might venture close by, they being the footman, who had brought in some late evening snacks, and of course, Booth himself.

Finally, Bolton had seemed satisfied that all was in order and retired to bed.

The following morning, staring out at the depressing moody weather, Booth suddenly realized that the strange fellow Weasel had materialized out of the gloom. He was talking to one of the men, who had wandered up from their quarters.

"What brings you here this gloomy morning?" Booth asked, as he went out and approached the two men.

"It's himself, the master I'd be lookin' to see," the Weasel replied.

"It could be some time before he comes down for breakfast," Booth replied.

"I can wait," said the Weasel.

"As you wish," Booth replied, and he went back into the house again.

"I'll be damned if I'm going to risk his bad liver by attempting to wake him," he muttered to himself, but was most surprised and somewhat startled when suddenly a beaming Bolton appeared.

"And top of a funny old morning to you, dear friend." His voice gave no hint to the excesses of the evening before. "And is that our feral friend I hear outside? Now there's a good fellow, would you mind sending him in? Pop him into my study while I fetch a hot tea."

Shaking his head in wonder, Booth went back outside and said, "He'll see you now."

The Weasel scurried in behind Booth, and they went directly to Bolton's study.

"And so, what news have you brought me?"

The Weasel sat facing the smiling Bolton, who was seated behind his desk. He really couldn't figure whether he preferred a snarling, nasty Bolton or the apparently jovial person smiling at him, knowing that at any moment that mood could change him into the vicious, violent person he knew so well.

Choosing his words very carefully, he told all that he had seen and heard at the tavern and gave a collective summary of his day at the village. The more Bolton cross-examined him, the happier he became.

"And just when do you think the Jew and his Irish rabble will make their way to this little gathering at Maghara?"

"Certainly not until the weather has cleared," replied the Weasel.

"And in your most learned opinion, just when do you think that will happen?" Bolton enquired.

"Ah, now. You see, it's the lull that we are having, as if the storm gods are taking a wee rest. By midday, the winds will be back, and we should have a fair old blow for another four to five days, and then the weather will hold fine, at least until the full autumn cold sets in."

"So four days it is. Four days to prepare for a massacre on Maghara," Bolton laughed.

"Do you like that, my fine Mr. Weasel? A massacre on Maghara—now that does have a ring to it, what?"

"Ah yes, indeed it does, indeed it does," the Weasel replied, though not quite sure what he was agreeing to.

"And now for you, I offer a token of my appreciation." Bolton tossed him a bag of coins. "And you will receive more, but only on completion of the total annihilation of my enemies. I want you to be here in three days' time. You will lead my men and me to this Maghara place in time to prepare a surprise for the Irish, one they sadly won't live to regret. Come, I will organize a pony for you to ride home on, so that you will miss the start of the rain. And then you can return bright and breezy in a few days."

Astounded at Bolton's good humour, he stumbled along by his side to the stables and soon, hardly believing his good fortune, he cantered off in the direction of his home.

Bolton had spied Mandino and invited him to meet him up at the manor later toward midday. The Gypsy followed the butler into the drawing room, where Bolton was standing at the gun cabinet.

"Ah, Mandino. Come, let me show you some of my very special possessions."

He handed him a flintlock rifle. "This is an Austrian Maurer. Look, see these folding sights. It is a feature of this particular weapon, and in the right hands, it can hit a target from some considerable distance.

"And this!" He handed to Mandino a German Wideman shotgun. "Only a single barrel, as you can see, but at close range, certain to blow the guts of some poor unfortunate all around the countryside. And with the blessing of Diana, goddess of hunting, engraved here." Bolton pointed to an engraving close to the locking mechanism.

"But this is my personal favourite." He produced a pair of pistols, and placing one on the table, he handed another to the Spaniard.

"I had the great pleasure of meeting the designer of these, a John Twigg by name. He had a workshop in Charing Cross and became friendly with my father, who persuaded him to set up in the more fashionable Piccadilly Circus area with his new partner. As a way of showing his appreciation for his much-improved business, he presented these to my father, who handed them on to me. Observe these four barrels. A shot can be fired by each of these two cocks; then, by a simple turn of this catch, these two priming pans are released, which then allows me to fire the lower two barrels.

"Can you imagine the shock as I fire one barrel, and when an ignorant Irish peasant thinks my firepower is gone, suddenly three more shots follow. And with this matching pistol, the strong possibility of eight, certainly six of the bastards die."

Mandino handed the pistol to Bolton, who returned both to the cabinet.

"Now, my friend, I have a great deal to talk to you about."

Bolton quickly told Mandino all that the Weasel had informed him about that morning.

"But there is one thing that causes me considerable concern. I may hate the blasted French Jew, but I do respect his canny survival instincts. He is no fool. So how does a bumbling Irish farm peasant learn so much from such a clever man?

"Simple! Our little snitch is either part of the conspiracy, or he has been fooled, and false information is deliberately being leaked to him, knowing that the fool will report to me, and I will be mislead. Well, that will not happen, I tell you!"

Mandino nodded. His shrewd mind fully understood and agreed with Bolton's assessment. "So, what do you plan to do?" Mandino asked.

"If they expect us to attack them, then we will. But we will attack when they least anticipate a strike. They have chosen their battlefield well. As we come down the only road to the beach, they can strike at us from the cover of hills, gullies, or trees. Then they can run back down to the beach, expecting us to follow, then head up through the dunes and hills, circle back onto the road, and hit us as we return home. Very clever!"

"I agree. Quite a plan. So, what do you intend to do?"

"I have finally found the perfect place for our brave Scots warriors. Buried alive."

"What!" exclaimed the Spaniard.

Bolton told Mandino what he had in mind. He clapped his hands in delight.

"Bravo! No one will escape. But what do you have in mind for the older Gallaghers and the young one's wife and babies?"

"Oh, I have very special plans for them. You will still take care of the two older Gallagher men and the mother. And by the time you have had your pleasure, I will have finished off the Jew and his men and returned to have my way with the young wife."

Mandino smiled in anticipation.

"No one, no Irishman or woman, will ever stand in my way again," vowed Bolton.

"Back to the matter of the battlefield: I want you to go and prepare a selection of targets. Position them at varying distances from the barn doors, so that if the rain does return, we can fire in relative dryness. Each man will show his skills with the rifles. I will select the best among them. They will be my riflemen, using those." He pointed to the rifle racks.

"And a special reward for those who excel. Later today, the whore wagon returns from Belfast. The finest shots get to fire first as they have first choice of the ladies."

Bolton and Mandino roared with laughter.

## Chapter 50

Hugo, Padraig Joseph, and his father sat together, warmed by the fire, sipping their hot drinks.

"This weather has certainly turned much colder, but still when it breaks and the sun returns, it will warm up again."

"I have never heard anyone, in all my travels, who is so preoccupied by the comings and goings of the weather conditions." Hugo laughed good-naturedly at the comments of his friend. "In the taverns I hear of the 'good drying winds,' and this subject will go on for hours."

"A slight exaggeration, but I do agree there is much to be discussed in the topic of the drying winds," Padraig smiled. His father nodded sagely in agreement, also with a smile.

Hugo truly loved these people. He simply could not understand how anyone could treat these kind, simple folk so harshly.

They loved their land and what they could produce from it. They certainly placed tremendous stock on family values, not dissimilar to the French. And he fully understood why Padraig Joseph was prepared to fight for the right to live in dignity and peace and harmony with all.

But his heart was heavy with the knowledge that all could be lost, including the lives of those now very close to him.

When the rains and the winds died down, Sean drove his mother and brother Padraig and Kathleen into the village to stock up on supplies before the bad weather returned. Sean also had a list for a substantial supply of provisions needed for their trip to Maghara.

The twin babies slept peacefully, having been lulled to sleep by the quiet voices of the three men. Padraig's new dog dozed close by, every so often opening one eye to check that all was in order, before drifting off again.

Hugo suddenly changed the conversational mood. "My very dear friends," he said, "I must ask you this."

The others looked at him and waited to hear more.

"It troubles me deeply. I must be absolutely certain that you realize the truly fearful risk that is soon to be about us. If our young men and I fail in our quest to rid you of the English and their power over you, and they demand retribution as Bolton no doubt will, are you prepared for the worst that could happen?"

"Hugo. I understand what you are saying," Padraig Joseph hastened to add. "But I have no doubt in my mind that you will destroy Bolton and his invaders. So, there is little to be fearful of. And as a result of your victory, we can take our fight to other parts of our country and gradually release Ireland from the greed of the English. No, my friend, God is looking after us all, and he and right will prevail. Please do not fret. Am I right, my father?"

Padraig the Older paused before he spoke. "I also have complete faith and trust in you and your valiant group of young men."

"Then there is nought more else to say other than to confirm together our final plans. Sean is of the opinion that we will have cold wind and rain for three, possibly four more days." Hugo waited for confirmation.

"He is the seaman in the family. I suppose I will have to agree with him," said Padraig Joseph. "Do you think that treacherous Weasel has spoken to Bolton yet?" he added.

"Oh, most certainly!" Hugo replied. "Just as we hoped, and no doubt he will have claimed his blood money."

"But tell me, both of you, what do you think Bolton's reaction to the news will be?"

Hugo watched the younger and the older man thinking about his question.

Finally, Padraig the Older answered. "Were it me in Bolton's position, I would be thinking long about the Weasel's story. I would consider much of it to be accurate, but I would also be wondering why so much information that has been secretive up until now would suddenly become common tavern talk."

Hugo nodded. Looking to the younger Gallagher, he said, "Padraig!"

"I don't think the Englishman is all that clever. You have out-guessed him twice already. Why should we think differently this time?"

Hugo was silent for a moment or two and then answered. "I am afraid I side with your father, Padraig. We have reason to believe that he has a ready arsenal of firearms that he has yet to use. I am certain he will arm his men this time. He will do all he can to annihilate us. He will stop at nothing.

"I truly believe that for us to destroy him, we must outthink his every move."

Taking a piece of charcoal from the fireplace, Hugo drew some markings on the wooden tabletop.

"I hope Claire doesn't get back too soon and catch me at this," he grinned.

"No matter, it will wipe clean."

"All right then," Hugo began. "This is a rough map of the road down to the Maghara beach. The families who live close to the area will advise us of any movement by Bolton. Let us presume that we arrive at the beach before them, and we should, and we will make our move as soon as the weather allows.

"Now, as bait for our self-made trap, we know that Bolton will follow the road down to attack us, thinking we have no escape. We will position men far back from the road in the bushes and long grass. And, of course, we will use the stone fences to place more men where possible.

"They will make no move until the signal is given.

"At best Bolton now has no more than twelve, perhaps, fifteen men. Even if half of them have guns, we will target them first and kill them.

"Then the men at the beach will attack them head on. And as those on both sides strike, and we close down the flank, they won't be able to retreat up the hill to safety. Sadly, though, this time I have every reason to believe that we will lose some lives."

Padraig Joseph nodded in agreement. "I share your distress. It will do no good to the families who lose a son that their loss will be for the benefit of Ireland, my own son included."

"No, it will not," Hugo said in a quiet voice. "So, what do you want me to do?"

"I want you to lead my son and the sons of my people to smash these devils and destroy them as a lesson to others that would invade our land."

"So be it!" the Frenchman solemnly declared.

★★★★★

They called him One-Eye Smith. But his one eye was superior to the two eyes of the others that could not match him in the target shoot.

While the sound of gunfire reverberated around the back of the barn area, it masked the sound of the wagon that clattered up to the front of the manor.

Conrad Booth interrupted the shooting competition to tell

Bolton his "guests" had arrived.

And so, with howls of laughter and vulgar comments, Bolton began his prize giving.

"The overall winner of the shooting competition is One-Eye Smith. Please select your lady of pleasure."

As jugs of ale were poured, Smith chose a rather pretty young lass, and to the hoots and hollers of his comrades, he made off with one hand grasping a jug of foaming beer and the other around his "prize."

Gradually the rest of the ladies were mated off, and the poor unfortunate losers of the competition would have to wait until either the luckier ones fell asleep or tired of their companions and settled down to the drink.

The madam, a Londoner and an old friend of Bolton's, retired to the house where a lavish meal had been prepared.

"It seems much has changed since we were last here," she observed.

"Oh, indeed it has, Rose, indeed it has," Bolton said. Between various dinner courses and drinks, he told her of all that had happened.

She noticed a considerable change of mood between Booth and Bolton, but declined to comment on the obvious coolness of their relationship.

But later, much later, as they lay together, recovering from her very vigorous lovemaking, she enquired. "Things don't seem to be as friendly between you and Conrad."

At first, Bolton declined to comment, but as their intimacy had created a trust between them, he decided to answer. "I have discovered items that would suggest that our man-loving oddity has a traitorous bent. It could well be that our friend Booth may not be with us too much longer—he and another that I believed loyal. Yes, it should prove to be an interesting few weeks ahead of us."

"Oh, who's the naughty boy, then! Now, are you ready to be a bit naughtier?" She giggled.

But as the night progressed, the face of Rose became the face of Kathleen Gallagher.

"Soon . . ." he muttered. "It won't be long now."

Naturally, Rose completely misunderstood the words she heard.

## Chapter 51

The plan was very simple, and to the ruffians listening to Bolton, it appeared to have no flaws. Though all were most likely suffering from the excesses of the previous night, none showed any sign of emotion other than the greedy grins of expectation of spilling blood and taking the sovereigns for doing so.

The rain was still pouring down, and while chilly, it was still not excessively cold. This was a concern to Bolton, not that he really cared about the Scots, but he did care about their effectiveness when they arose out of the sands.

While the Scots had been coerced into volunteering, Slow was adamant he wanted to be part of the plan. His simmering hatred for the Irish, due to the death of Hair Baker, gave him only two options, to kill those responsible or die trying. He just did not want to go through the rest of his life without the companionship of his friend.

The three would be insulated from the cold by wearing a layer of sheepskins with the fleece to keep the body warm. That and a cloak of oil-skinned hides wrapped around them would act as a lagging to ward off the effect of dampness and chill. They would then be buried in the sands of Maghara.

Timing was the key. For the scheme to work, all had to be in position before the Irish arrived at the beach. Bolton knew that the Jew had spies all around and he had to secret his men out of sight or he would fail.

When he attacked, if their flank was not covered, the Irish could simply run down the beach and up the hills and be gone to fight another day.

With this escape route covered, they were effectively surrounded. Even if, as he expected, the Irish were to send another force down the road behind them, his superior firepower would be too strong for them.

But the rain had to cease before the dawn for his men to get to the beach without the local farmers spotting them.

Returning to his study, Bolton spied Conrad Booth walking to his room.

"Ah, Conrad. I wish to talk with you."

Together they walked to Bolton's office.

"Please be seated."

Bolton noted that Booth seemed somewhat ill at ease.

"Perhaps you wish to discuss something with me. Maybe there is a problem that I need to know about."

"None that I know of," Booth replied.

"Then let me pose a scenario. Some time back, I heard of a landowner who discovered his most trusted aide, his accounts clerk actually, was secretly plotting behind his back. It happened that the clerk knew of matters that could be used against his employer in a court of law to avail himself of monies he was not entitled to.

"Now the question I ask you is this: If you were that landowner and you discovered a situation as I have described, what action would you take?"

"Having never been in this situation, I cannot answer," Booth hedged.

"Hmm . . ." Bolton mused. "Then tell me, what action do

you think I would take?"

Booth suddenly realized that Bolton knew much more about Booth's dealings with Throckmorton than he let on, or he was bluffing to determine what information Booth might share unwittingly. He thought for a moment and answered. "For a start, only a fool would try to take advantage of you! And secondly, I would imagine that if a situation did occur, then your legendary attitude of fair play would come into effect, and you would allow reasoning to determine what happened before taking action."

"And if a trusted friend was that fool?"

"Then one never knows what would happen. But why would a friend do such a thing?"

Bolton stared deep into Booth's eyes before replying. "Well, then, let me tell you what the landowner I referred to earlier did.

"The following morning, the cook found the traitorous fool. His eyes had been taken out. He could not see to make this mistake again. His tongue had been cut off. He could never talk about this again. His ears had been severed from his head, as a testament to the evil he had listened to.

"His hands had been chopped off, as a warning to others who might take what was not theirs.

"Now, what do you think of that?"

"Robert, why are you telling me all this?" Booth countered

"It always worries me when a person answers my serious questions with another question. It suggests, perhaps, that the person may have something to hide. You wouldn't hide anything from me, would you?"

Before Booth could reply, Bolton stood up quickly from his study table.

"But enough for now. Tomorrow, we have a battle to fight. It is way behind time to catch up on some sleep. Rest well, my friend, sleep well."

Conrad Booth stood and followed Bolton out. He knew he would not sleep, certainly not this night. The warning was clear. One of them would die, and it certainly would not be him.

★★★★★

Hugo and Padraig Joseph smiled at Sean.

"And if you're wrong?" Hugo asked.

"With a belly full of porter and a smile from a sweet, wee lass, yes, I have been known to make an error in judgment a time or two, but with the weather, never!

"Look yon to the coast. See that break in the clouds way out. That tells me that behind that is the last of this bad stuff."

The heavy rain had eased and occasional showers and drizzle were all that was left from the deluge that had been with them for the last five days or so.

"Well, if you are right, then we can expect the men to start arriving in the next few hours."

By mid-afternoon, Sean's prophecy proved correct. And as the skies cleared, gradually the men arrived.

With five hours of daylight left, the last of the fighting force joined the others in making final checks of their weapons.

Padraig joined his brother and the young men. No words were needed. All felt cared for by their friend. Padraig certainly cared for each and every one of them.

"I could go . . ."

Before he had finished, Sean placed his arm around his older brother. Looking into his eyes, he explained, "We have talked this through long and hard. We don't need you with us, but the family and Kathleen must have you close by. You have a greater responsibility to them than you do to us."

"But . . ."

"There are no buts, Padraig," Hugo said, echoing Sean's

sentiment. "I will be secure in the knowledge that you are here with these, my adopted family. I want to be confident that all is protected here until our return. And you will do just that. Protect them all: Kathleen, the babies, and your parents and grandfather."

Padraig nodded. "It will be done."

"Excellent!" Hugo then raised his voice. "We depart in ten minutes."

★★★★★

The Weasel looked down at Slow.

The four men had dug three trenches in the damp sand, each one about four to five feet deep. The two Scotsmen were lying in the trenches, waiting for the sand to be packed around them.

"Are you sure you're comfortable?" the Weasel asked.

He looked up at the late afternoon skies.

"Do your work, damn you!" muttered MacFetridge.

The Weasel shoved sand over the first Scotsman and patted it down firm. He then positioned small chunks of driftwood around his head as markers and large, thick hollow reeds into his mouth for breathing tubes. Over his face and around the reeds, he placed a piece of thin homespun cloth. He scattered a few loose layers of sand over the head with only the three protruding reeds giving any indication of what lay buried there.

"I can hardly be seeing if it's yourself down there," he said, but of course, there was no reply.

Finally all three were concealed. He brushed the sand smooth and stood back to survey his handiwork.

He walked briskly down to the water's edge, brushing his hands behind him, leaving no marks on the hard-packed sand, and then he made his way to the distant headland where he climbed to a vantage point and settled in to wait.

★★★★★

"Hey, there, Hugh Malloy, and how are you, now that the rain has gone?"

"Fine, fine," came the reply. "Hello there, Hugo, and young Sean and Danny and all the rest of you lads. Now don't be telling me it's down to the water you are heading for." He shook his head in bewilderment.

"Aye, indeed we are," Sean replied.

"Tell me," Hugo said. "Has anyone else been down this way today or during the rains?"

"Only a silly old fool and perhaps his friends would be thinking of a thing like that," Malloy replied, glancing at the large number of men lined up behind Hugo and Sean. "And I certainly did not venture my head out until hearing the clatter of you lot coming down. No, none that I am aware of passed this way in the last day or two."

"Hugh, we need your help," Hugo began. "I expect that Bolton and a party of his men will be following us down in a very short space of time. You know of the troubles we have had with them. This time we intend to finish it all, once and for good.

"I want to position some of my men back up the way a bit, hidden behind the stone wall and the trees. I certainly want you and your family to stay well clear of us and them. I want no harm to come to any of you."

Hugo then went on to explain what he had in mind.

After sending six of his men back up the road again, Hugo and the rest of the party made their way down to the sands of Maghara.

"Well, we will have no problem gathering firewood for the fires," Sean said, looking at the mass of driftwood thrown up on the beach.

"No," Hugo replied, looking up and down the deserted sands.

Apart from a dozen or so gulls happily gobbling up the remains of smashed mussels and other assorted damaged or dead fish washed up from the storm, the beach was deserted.

"Sean, break out some of the dry turf and start the fires. I want to climb to the tops of the sand dunes and have a good look around. Danny, you come with me. We have seen no sign of Bolton, and I find it hard to believe that with all the bait we have supplied him, he has not snapped at the hook in some way or other."

Both men were away for an hour or more, and by the time they returned, the sun had long gone over the horizon and only the glow of the heaped up fires and the starry night skies gave any indication of light.

Sean looked up with an enquiring glance as they approached.

"Nothing!" Hugo said. "Nothing to suggest that apart from ourselves there is anyone else around. If this is true, we should expect Bolton to arrive sometime in the morning. I would not expect him to attack at night. It would be too risky.

"So, I want to set up sentry fires a hundred yards up the beach and also down the beach toward the headland. I want two sentries posted at each. These will be changed at four-hour intervals.

"I doubt very much that Bolton will come at us from either end of the beach. Even if the Weasel did help him, he would not be able to bring his men through the steep, hilly terrain with ease. No, Bolton will come at us down the road we use.

"And even with his guns, our ambush should prove too successful, and we will overpower them."

Hugo gave the instructions and eager hands quickly responded to build the fires and take the first shifts of sentry duty.

Sometime later, he looked up and down the beach. He could see the fires burning brightly with two sentries at each.

"Well, my friends, we cannot do much more than wait. I want you all to settle down and try to get as much sleep as possible. And please pray . . . pray very hard to your God that he smiles down on us tomorrow."

## Chapter 52

The crossing had been particularly bad. With the ship heading into violent winds, Lady Constance had been seasick from the time the boat had left the coast of England.

So, it was with considerable relief, as she sipped another cup of water, that she could see the welcoming sight of the Northern Irish headlands in the near distance.

She smiled up at her husband who had been most concerned at her continuous retching. "I am feeling so much better," she said. "At least now that I can see dry land."

"My poor dear, I felt quite helpless, not being able to assist you in any way," Lord Thomas Bolton replied.

The ship docked with relative ease, mainly because the winds had dropped, and they were sheltered from the westerly blow.

As they disembarked, they were very happy to see the coach waiting for them.

"Good afternoon, my lord and lady. Not such a pleasant voyage I suspect."

"Good day to you Johnstone, old chap. It's good to see you again, and no, it was a very nasty trip indeed."

"May I suggest, m' lord, with the weather still unsettled and all, would it not be a good idea to rest up in a nice inn and allow the good lady time to recover before the trip across to Donegal?"

"An excellent proposal. I was about to say just that. Lead on, my good fellow. A glass or two of fine brandy will quickly wipe away the memory of that dastardly sea trip. What say you, my dear?"

"Yes, but please take care as you load my baggage, Johnstone. I have brought with me some wonderful finery."

"Yes, my lady. Yes, of course," Johnstone sighed, as he went to fetch their luggage.

*****

Robert Bolton stood up in the stirrups and looked down the few hundred yards of the road before it commenced its winding way down to the beach at Maghara.

Assembled behind him, his heavily armed men rested.

They had left the manor not long after midnight, and while there was sufficient light, some had found the going hard, tripping at times with the burden of the weaponry.

"It's all bleedin' right for 'is nibs up there on 'is 'orse 'n' all, in it?"

He had smiled as he listened to the moaning.

"And it were all bleedin' right, as you enjoyed the whores I gave you, weren't it?" Bolton replied, mimicking their accents.

The snickering that followed gave him the assurance that his men were primed for the challenge that lay ahead of them.

"And the ladies will be back in another seven days, but only for those of you who earn the sovereigns that I will be paying you."

Bolton sat patiently. He was supremely confident his careful planning would result in the demise of the Irish farmers who had challenged his rightful authority. He felt a delicious stirring in his loins as he thought ahead to the death of the ones he hated so fervently and to the expectation of what lay ahead when he finally had Kathleen Gallagher pleading for his mercy.

Dawn was about two hours away.

Mandino and Philippo Montoya would be closing in on the Gallagher homes.

Down on the beach, Slow and the Scots would be most relieved to rise from their sandy trenches. Bolton smiled in anticipation.

Padraig Gallagher stirred. He knew his restlessness was due to worrying about his brother and his friends.

Kathleen moved in her sleep, and he felt comforted by the warmth of her arm as she flopped it over his chest and then cuddled up closer to him. He then drifted slowly back to sleep.

He did not hear his dog stir and go over to the window where he peered out into the night. He had not heard the sounds that had woken the dog, nor had he heard the animal's low growling. And he had not seen what the dog had seen—the furtive movement of the two men as they passed his house and snuck down the lane toward the home of his parents and grandfather.

*****

Slow was the first to move.

He had lain perfectly still for such a long time, but gradually, the urge to turn onto his side became irritating, and then as the discomfort grew, a form of panic began to set in. He fought it off as long as he could, but the sand began to trickle through the cloth and onto his face.

He could breathe perfectly well, but only while he was still. The urge to escape grew greater and the dread stronger.

Finally unable to take any more, he thrust his head up and out into the still night. Spitting the reeds from his mouth, he drew in huge gasps of welcoming, fresh clean air and slowly relaxed his head onto the sand.

"What was that? What was that noise?" Matthew Murphy, one of Hugo Cohen's young men, stood up and looked around. "Did you not hear that strange sound then, Michael?"

"No, I can't say that I did."

Both men stood and looked up and down the beach.

"Where did it come from, Matty?" Michael asked.

"I don't rightly know."

Both men had been on watch for three hours, and while neither would admit it, both were quite weary and half-asleep.

"Well, the sun shouldn't be too far from rising," Matthew Murphy replied. "It must have been some crabs or night birds you heard."

They both sat down again closer to the warmth of the dying fire.

"Ah, well, not to worry, Matty."

Slow listened to them talking for a while longer and smiled as their conversation faltered and eventually grew silent; he realized they were dozing.

Matthew heard the gurgling sound of Michael McDonald's windpipe being severed. He turned and looked into the grim countenance of the slayer. Before he could even gasp a warning, the razor-sharp blade had struck again, and as his head fell back, blood gushed from his throat.

Slow didn't even give a backward glance as he walked back to where his comrades lay in the sand. As he pulled back the cloth from each, he whispered a low shushing sound so as not to alarm them. In a low voice, he explained to them what had happened.

"Two fewer Irishmen for us to deal with," MacFetridge muttered.

They could see the glow of the fire in the southerly direction down the beach, but could only guess that the two objects silhouetted against it were two seated men.

"Perhaps it's best that you stay here while we sneak close to the water's edge and then come up behind those two and deal with them," Tommy MacFetridge said to Slow.

"I agree," Willy Mason whispered. "If someone from the main camp looks up here and cannot see a sentry, it could alarm them."

Slow nodded in agreement.

"If all goes to plan, as soon as the shooting starts, we make our move."

Again, Slow looked at them both and concurred.

As Slow made his way back to where the two bodies lay, he watched as the two Scots slowly faded out of sight. While he couldn't be certain, he thought he saw sudden movement at the other sentry fire, but there were no sounds that could have caused alarm.

So, he settled down to wait, making sure he could be seen from the main camp, but not recognised as someone different from either of the corpses that lay next to him.

## Chapter 53

Claire woke with a start. She knew.

The house was in complete silence. Perhaps it was the silence that alarmed her. Of course, she could hear the loud ticking of the big clock downstairs, but there were no other sounds.

Even the wind had died down, and then it dawned on her. There were no sounds of the night insects. Surely, a cricket or two should be sending out their little messages.

Something or someone had silenced them.

Claire knew then that they had come for her. "Please, dear God, whatever happens, please spare my children," she silently prayed.

Did she hear a creaking on the old floorboards downstairs?

"Padraig!" she said in a loud whisper as she shook her husband. "Padraig Joseph! Wake up, please wake up."

Her husband stirred. "What is it?"

"I think there is someone in the house."

They lay there together, listening for any sound.

"I don't hear anything," he finally said. He attempted to get up from the bed.

"No, no. Stay here. Don't go down there." Claire grabbed at her husband.

"Shoosh, woman! There is no one down there, and besides, I need to go outside to have a pee."

She listened as her husband walked out into the hall.

"Take the lamp," she called after him.

She listened as he descended the stairs. Her stomach dropped when she heard a crashing noise, then silence.

"Oh God, dear God," she whimpered.

Almost in a daze, she quietly rose from the bed, crept to the door, and peered out into the hallway.

Suddenly she remembered her father-in-law! Should she wake him? "Yes!" she answered herself in a terrified whisper.

As she made her way down the hall to the older man's room, she suddenly saw the darkness come toward her. She closed her eyes, and in that same instant, she felt no more.

*****

Bolton gave the signal. "Right men, let's go get them!"

The first rays of the new day appeared over the hills behind them as they commenced the run down to the water.

Hugo didn't need to hear them or see them. He knew they were on the way.

He had woken those who were asleep. Those that were already awake had risen before his calls.

Sean, as usual, had slept without any apprehension of what the day could bring.

Hugo smiled and shook his head. "You truly amaze me, my young friend."

Sean ran after some that were heading for distant trees along the shoreline.

"Hey, Sean, shit well now. We don't want you shitting yourself when Bolton gets here."

"You worry about yourself, Tommy Lynch!" Sean yelled back, and his hearty laugh trailed behind him.

Hugo looked out to where the sentries were posted.

In the early dawn, he could just see them standing by the embers of the dying fires. He called them in.

He gave the orders, and as all the men finished nature's calls, they picked up their weapons and assembled in a group.

"Bolton, if he comes, will be here soon." Hugo spoke quietly, but loud enough for all to hear. "You all know what you have to do. You have been well trained, and you have all responded to that training in a fine manner. I have only the fullest of confidence in your ability to overcome your enemy. No matter what happens this day, my friends, I want you to know I love you all, as I would love my own son. Now, let us go."

Hugo and his force of young men began to settle down in the fortifications that had been so carefully prepared.

★★★★★

Claire tried to open her eyes. Flashes of light and belts of pain hindered her efforts.

She could hear coarse laughter and cries for help, she thought from her husband.

Gradually, she became aware that she was lying on her back on their bed. She tried to raise herself, but she failed from the effort and fell back onto the bed.

Fighting back the feeling of nausea, she felt coldness and became conscious of her nakedness. Panicking, she searched around for her night attire.

"You look for these, perhaps?"

She tried to focus on where the voice came from. With the aid of the early morning light, the stark realization of terror hit her.

A man stood at the side of her bed, smiling down at her, mocking her. He held her shredded nightgown in his hand.

The awareness of pain in her groin and the sight of his half-naked figure sent convulsions of nausea through her, and she attempted to roll off the bed.

"Hey, Philippo, your turn to play games with the lady!"

She screamed, as from somewhere behind her, her hair was grabbed, and she was pulled back again.

Her legs were forced apart, and after an eternity, the terrible ordeal ceased, and she drifted into the welcoming bliss of darkness.

★★★★★

A cold finger of fear went through Hugo. He knew something was wrong, terribly wrong.

*No!* It hit him like a freezing shaft of ice through his heart.

Michael McDonald and Matthew Murphy and the two O'Halloran boys hadn't been with the assembled force when he was giving them his last instructions and good wishes.

The sound of gunfire temporarily diverted his attention, and he turned to face the threat that was still out of sight, but racing toward them down the hill.

Then the wild screams of fury from behind him confirmed his fatal error.

He saw the first go down. Tommy MacFetridge had split the head of Hugh McGovern wide open with a single blow from his highland axe.

A similar blow from Willy Mason felled the youngest of the Flaherty boys.

Sean had heard the highland war cries, and yelling at Danny, he turned and ran at the Scots. He saw Slow lumbering up with them and charged at him.

"You die, you bastard!"

The tip of his pikestaff entered Slow's belly, and the force of the thrust sent it clean through the body of his foe and out the back. Sean drove again, harder, then moving behind Slow, he pulled the pike completely free of his body, and with his right hand clenched around the staff, he cleansed the handle of the shaft, kicking the dying man in the head as he did so.

With Danny by his side, they confronted the Scots.

MacFetridge swung his axe to behead Sean, but the weeks of perfecting Hugo's training took over, and Sean responded like a well-oiled fighting machine.

As he ducked under the swinging blow, he glided past the huge man in a stoop. Almost in slow motion, as he stood erect, Sean, still with his back to the Scot, slammed his big right boot back into the middle of MacFetridge's leg.

With a screech, the Scot stumbled backward. Sean spun in an instant and smashed his boot down onto the face of the fallen man as he fell to the sand. He then stabbed the pike through the throat of MacFetridge.

Danny was in trouble.

Mason had also missed with his first swing, but had followed through with his elbow, slamming Danny in the jaw. Stunned, Danny had fallen, but twisted his body as he fell, to avoid the next blow from the axe, which threw sand into his eyes as it missed his head by inches.

Panicking, screeching, Danny scrambled crabwise on his back as Mason struck down again. This time, the axe sliced down the side of his head, cleanly slicing off his left ear and biting deep into his shoulder.

The shock of the blow and the grit in his eyes blinded him from the sight of Sean appearing behind the Scot, who was frantically attempting to free the axe to deliver the killing blow.

Sean had grabbed the dead MacFetridge's weapon, and bringing it high above from behind the stooped Mason, he swung it down with such force that it cut through the back of Mason's neck and wedged into the top of his spine.

He fell dead onto Danny.

Slinging him aside, Sean dropped to the side of his friend. "Oh, my God! Danny, Danny," he gasped.

He stared, numb, as blood gushed from the fallen man's horrific wound. His arm, almost cut through, lay limp on the sand, held in place to the shuddering Danny by slivers of bone and shards of skin.

Sean's feeble attempts to care for the stricken man were suddenly halted as screams echoed down from the road. Through the thin early morning mist came the riders and the running support force.

Hugo and his men lay motionless, watching and waiting as the enemy surged closer.

As Sean rushed forward from the beach to join them, Hugo yelled the call they were all waiting for.

"Stand! Attack and kill!"

As one, the young men of Ireland stood and charged, running at their enemy.

This time, however, before the pikes could draw blood, the guns were discharged, sending shot after shot into the faces and the bodies of the Irish.

Hugo felt a tug as a musket ball narrowly missed, whipping away his cap.

His killing knife then struck low, slicing through and up the first man he made contact with, disemboweling him.

Those that had survived the first blast of the firearms hit Bolton's mercenaries, and finally, the pikes found their mark.

Bolton sat in the saddle a short distance from the fighting, watching and smiling as he calmly fired and reloaded and fired again, each time the shot finding its mark, dropping the target dead.

He spied Sean Gallagher just as Sean drew back his blade from a mortal hit on one of Bolton's men.

As Sean looked up, Bolton pulled the trigger. "Die, Irish pig," he muttered.

*****

Padraig's faithful dog woke him. He watched the animal staring at him and then looking out toward the dawn, all the time growling low. "What is it, boy?"

And then slowly the realization that something was very, very wrong put a knot in his chest, and he rose and peered out the window.

The dog ran from the room and pawed at the back door.

Padraig followed and lifted the latch. The dog burst through, and barking madly, raced out into the yard.

"What's wrong, why all this barking, then?"

Kathleen stood at the door, looking out at him.

"I don't know . . ."

Suddenly, the dog wheeled around and raced in the direction of Padraig's parents' home.

A terrible feeling of dread engulfed him. "Stay here, please, Kathleen, do not move from here until I return."

His eyes stared at her, beseeching, a sense of uncontrollable terror descending on him. He could see it in her eyes, too, but she said nothing.

"I beg of you, my beloved, stay! Do not follow." With that, he turned and ran after his dog.

## Chapter 54

The old man stirred. The pain was agonizing. His hand swept his brow, and when it came into view, he saw that it was covered with blood. He looked around him and moaned, partly in pain, but mostly at the sight of his son.

Padraig Joseph Gallagher the Younger lay dead a few feet from him. Although the old man could not crawl over to him to verify the shocking sight, he just knew. His son was dead.

He tried to rise, but exhausted and weak, he fell back, returning to the unconscious state from which he had woken. Before he completely passed out, he thought he heard the sounds of a dog barking, then all went black.

"Hey, Mandino, listen! Barking. I think a dog comes."

The Gypsy stopped rummaging in one of the cupboards and went to the window.

"Ha, Philippo. It is the young Gallagher, and indeed, a dog. Come with me, quickly."

They had barely concealed themselves in a back room when Padraig burst through the back door.

"Mother! Da! Where are you?"

He raced up the stairs and stopped short at the hideous sight before him in the hallway. Unbelieving, he went first to his father. Sinking to his knees, he gently lifted his head and stared into sightless eyes.

"Da! Oh, dear God, my father!" Padraig could only shake his head in disbelief.

He looked over to the still shape of his grandfather.

Before he could move, he heard a faint sound from his parents' bedroom. Jumping to his feet, he ran to the door and looked in. "Mother! Dear God Almighty, what have they done?"

Somehow, he moved to his mother's side. Her broken, bloodied body lying naked on the bed shocked him beyond any feeling he had ever experienced. "Who did this?"

Sobbing, he attempted to place a blanket over her. A feeble hand raised and tried to pull his arm to her.

"My son, my son," she whispered. "They will come for you. Beware."

The quick bark of the dog suddenly alerted Padraig. The animal had followed him up the stairs and over to the bedside. Now it stood by his side growling, staring at the open bedroom door.

He eased over to the door and peered out.

Philippo stood there before him, his right arm out, poised to strike with the deadly dagger in his hand.

Padraig dived at the Spaniard. Frantically fending off the striking blow, he grabbed the wrist of his foe, driving him backward. Somehow, Philippo's foot struck the body of the dead man, and he stumbled. With one hand holding the knife hand and the other circling around and grabbing his belt behind him, Padraig shoulder-charged the assassin, rushing him back to the top of the stairs, where they hurtled down the steep flight.

The Spaniard hit the bottom first, his head striking the base with a thud. Padraig, cushioned by the man's body, was spared serious injury.

As Padraig lay at the foot of the stairs attempting to recover from the shock of all that was now about him, adrenalin began to kick in.

But before he could get to his feet, a boot struck him in his unprotected ribcage.

Screaming in pain, he turned in time to see a second kick aimed at his head.

He dropped his assailant's knife hand and raised his arm to protect his head. But before the blow connected, a furry shape of rage flashed past him and bit deeply into the attacker's thigh.

Clumsily, he stood and regained his balance. Instinct and certainly the weeks of training would now come to the fore.

In one motion, he bent and pulled free the dagger from Philippo's hand and stood to face Mandino.

The Spaniard had savagely chopped down, stunning and dropping the dog. He now stood and faced the young Irishman.

"Your mommy, she a good play thing. I have good time weeth her, yes?" He sneered.

Padraig's blood was cold. He heard, but he felt only a dull emotionless sensation.

The huge blade that had suddenly materialized in the Gypsy's hand plunged toward Padraig's belly. He dodged to his left, only to realize the move was a ruse to off balance him. Following through, the knife sliced into his right forearm, almost dislodging his own weapon.

"You leetle boy, eh, not so good at thees game. I play a leetle more, then I kill you."

Laughing at him, the Gypsy feinted, lunging at him, then pulling back, then coming at Padraig again.

Slowly the realization came to Padraig that he simply was not skilled enough to defeat this killer. As he edged back from the staircase with his back to the wall, he stood one final time.

"Then come and take me. That is, if you are as good as you say you are."

"Yes, I take you and slice you, just like I did with your stupid dogs. Then I hang your guts on the table, and then I play with your wife."

It appeared to the taunting Spaniard that his last words had destroyed all the fight in his opponent. The big Irishman just dropped his arms by his side. The knife slipped to the floor. He stood there, almost begging for the inevitable.

He glided forward, holding his knife down, ready to plunge it deep into Padraig's gut and slice it up open.

Then, just as the tip of the knife touched its mark, a huge fist struck, hitting the Gypsy full under his nose. The force of the blow drove the bone of the nose back into the skull, and if that blow alone did not kill, the cold merciless rage of the other blows did.

Philippo had regained consciousness and watched helpless and terrified as Padraig first destroyed his enemy's face, then holding him against the wall, smashed blow after powerful blow into the Spaniard's body, the sound of breaking ribs clearly audible.

With his left hand, Padraig held Mandino by his long, greasy hair, pulling his head back, exposing his neck. With savage ferocity, he slammed his fist full into the Spaniard's throat.

With a croaking groan, Mandino died.

Padraig then turned to Philippo and walked toward him.

★★★★★

Sean sensed rather than knew the shot would hit him. As he glimpsed the grim smile of Bolton, he hurled himself sideways. He heard the whisper of the ball as it passed by him.

He attempted to launch himself at the Englishman, but fighting bodies separated him from his goal.

Most of the guns had been fired, and the frantic hand-to-hand combat had prevented any further reloading. But the gun power had taken its toll, and now the Irish were hopelessly outnumbered.

Sean was suddenly hit on the side of the head by an empty musket. Stunned, he fell to the ground. Hugo was immediately by his side.

"Get up, Sean. We need you."

Hugo helped him to his feet, and then with newfound strength, Sean swung the highland axe he still held. Wading into the enemy, the weapon found its mark time and again, but gradually the Irish fell.

Finally, Hugo and Sean stood back to back, alone. All the Irish lads had fallen. Total silence descended; only the soft moaning of those awaiting death disturbed the stillness.

"Leave them be!" The order was shouted. Bolton, on horseback, sat watching as the din died down.

Hugo and Sean stood gasping for air as Bolton circled and then moved back, leaving them alone, but for the dead and the mortally wounded between them and Bolton's men.

"Normally I would salute the brave," Bolton said, his voice sardonic and mocking, "but I have only contempt for the stupid. And your brainless actions have brought this upon you. Any pity I might have for you has long been squashed by your disregard for my orders."

Bolton paused, looking down and gloating.

"But what do we do with you now—you, a despicable French Jew, and you, a worthless, useless pile of Irish dung. Speaking of the insignificant, pray tell, where is your brother? He was not with those fools that died up there." Bolton indicated back up the road.

"And I did not spot him here, or his head would now be home to one of my shots."

Bolton paused to give them a sneering smile.

"But back to the matter at hand, do I shoot you both in the head, or do I leave you to the pleasure of my men?"

"Don't reply," Hugo said to Sean, sensing the fire burning in his friend. "Give him no pleasure in his victory."

"What was that, Christ killer? Did I hear you whimper?" Bolton laughed. "Well, never mind. But tell me, have you heard the saying 'to the victor the spoils'?" Not waiting for a reply, he added, "Allow me to inform you of recent happenings this fine morning.

"You there, Irishman, by now your mother will have pleasured my Spanish friends, and your father and the old man, no doubt, will have felt some dissatisfaction before they died. And when I do find your brother, he will watch as I pleasure his pretty little bride. That is, before he dies, and slowly.

"And you, Jew, look around you. Your meddling ways caused all of this unnecessary violence. These fools have died in vain. Died, and all in vain, because you could not mind your own business. How do you feel now?"

"He is more a man than you will ever be, coward!" Sean shouted at Bolton. "Get down from your horse and show me how brave you really are. Come, face me."

"I think not," Bolton purred with an unsettling smile. "But now to sport! I understand you Irish have a fear of water; is this true? Well, we will soon find out.

"Here is how we will play the game. I once saw a running of the gauntlet. It was amusing. I wish to introduce it to my men. They will arrange themselves in two lines with a gap between them. You, Irishman, will run between them to escape to the sea. Should you fall, the men will cut you to pieces. If you reach the sea before I reach you, you can attempt to find solace in the deep water. That is, if my marksmanship fails me.

"The moment you break free of the last two men, that is, if you succeed, I will fire four shots. Two shots each from my pistols. You have the time it takes me to reload, and then I will chase you to the water."

At Bolton's command, his mercenaries formed two lines with six feet of space between them. Two hefty Englishmen dragged Sean to the head of the gauntlet, facing the first two grinning at him.

All held large pieces of driftwood in preparation.

Hugo was dumped in the sand close by.

"Now, should you succeed and escape, I will free him," Bolton announced, pointing at Hugo.

"Do not trust him, Sean. Go with God's speed and return and avenge the death of your family."

"Fear not, my friend," Sean said to Hugo, then he turned to the assembled line-up and snarled, "Now, damn you, do your best, but know this, I will return, and each of you will die."

"Your signal to commence will be the discharge of a musket," Bolton called out. "Remember, if and when you reach the end of the line, four shots will fire your enthusiasm; do not waste time dallying. Are you ready?" The musket fired.

Sean charged.

The first two aimed their cudgels, but they did little harm, such was Sean's speed. By the time he had reached the middle of the gauntlet, however, the English and Scots had perfected their aim, and each blow had more effect than the last. Sean could feel his strength fading, and he suspected that should he reach the end, he would never have the power to start the run to the tide. He began to stagger. Then suddenly he burst past the last pair.

As he nearly fell, drawing in huge gasps of air, he heard the shots and the screams!

He turned. "No!"

Bolton's first two shots had been fired into Hugo's right knee. Bolton aimed at the other leg.

"Run, Sean!" Hugo cried out. "RUN!"

Sean ran. The other two shots rang out. Then he hit the hard sand and gathered speed.

He heard the sound of a galloping horse, and he found himself in ankle-deep water.

The first shot fired, and a musket ball hit him in the shoulder. A wave came at him, and he dived into the safety of the breaking water. A second shot hit the water, but did no damage to him. But as the wave broke and flattened, he was without protection. The third ball smashed into his collarbone. The force of the shot and his determination to live drove him under the water again. Instinct took over, and he turned and swam under the water, parallel with the shore.

Bolton was obviously looking for his head to appear directly ahead as he prepared to aim for the fatal shot.

To his surprise, Sean appeared off to the right. A fist clenched in triumph rose from the water. Then he disappeared.

Bolton had his men search up and down the coastline to no avail. Sean's body never surfaced.

Bolton returned to the gravely hurt Hugo Cohen. "I won't kill you. Should you make your way back to safety, you will bear witness to all who challenge my authority in the future." Then, turning his horse's head to the shoreline, he grinned down at Hugo.

"Now I am off to attend to the other brother, and of course, to pleasure his wife!"

*****

The buggy pulled up outside the Bolton manor. Judge Throckmorton Squires alighted with much difficulty. He huffed and puffed his way to the top of the portico steps.

When no footmen hurried out to greet him, he called, "Anybody in? I say, anybody home?"

He was expecting to meet with the Lord and Lady Bolton.

Surely, they had arrived by now.

"Robert!" he called. "Conrad!" He pushed the door. It opened.

When he was halfway into the foyer, he was met by an ashen-faced maid.

"I didn't do it, sir. I swear I found him like that."

"Do what?" Squires asked gruffly. "Found who?" His voice rose in alarm.

"Him, sir . . . him." She pointed to a room down the hall.

The judge wobbled his way behind the maid. "Oh, my God. Who is this? Who did this?"

At first, he did not recognise Conrad Booth. Then he threw up. Staring in shock, he began backing his way to the door behind him. "Booth, is that you? Oh God, Conrad is that you?"

A horrible gurgle was all he could hear as he turned and ran for the door and his buggy.

Clambering aboard, he turned the horse's head, and whipping the animal frantically, he sped from the manor in the direction of the safety of Donegal Town.

## Chapter 55

Having dealt with Philippo and Mandino, Padraig walked up the stairs in a daze.

He went again to his father, hoping that his original findings were false, and his father would look up at him and smile, as if all were a great joke.

Shaking his head again in disbelief, he knelt by his grandfather. The old man had died while Padraig was fending off their attackers downstairs.

Padraig staggered to the room of his parents. As if in a hideous nightmare, he held his mother. She looked up him.

"My son, stay with me, let me hold you."

Tears gathered and ran down his face. "Shall I fetch you some water?" he pleaded.

"Yes . . . please."

He gently laid her back on the bed and raced down to pour the water into a mug and quickly returned. He seemed not to notice the devastation in the downstairs rooms.

Claire greedily swallowed the liquid and closed her eyes for a moment as if to gather inner strength. "Your father?" She shuddered and sobbed. She knew his fate without hearing the answer.

Padraig held his mother tighter until her grimace of pain made him lessen his hold.

"Do not worry, Mother. Please, just you get stronger, and we will take care of everything then."

She went silent and shrank back in his arms.

It seemed to Padraig an eternity passed before she opened her eyes and again looked up at him.

"My son, please pray with me. I am soon to leave this world to be with your father and grandfather. I am so afraid."

"Shh, Mother, I am with you."

"No, my son, I am not afraid for me. I am so afraid for you."

She again closed her eyes, only her lips moving as she reached out to those she knew were listening.

Then, she prayed aloud. "Oh, Holy Mother of God, please do not leave my son; always be by his side. There will be times when he will desert you as his faith declines. Please give him guidance to return to you and our Heavenly Father."

Claire lapsed into silence and then her eyes closed. After a while, she opened them again and looked up at her son.

"Mother, my faith is strong," Padraig said quietly. "You and my father both showed us the way. Do not worry. And besides, you and Kathleen will be there to make sure I do not stray."

"OH NO!" she screamed. "KATHLEEN!" Claire grabbed at him frantically. At that moment, the dog that had been by their side jumped up barking, leapt toward the door, and raced down the stairs.

Padraig, in a panic, looked first at his mother and then at the door. The ferocious barking reminded him that the door down below was closed.

"Oh, dear God, run, my son, run to Kathleen!" Claire gasped from the strain. "Go to her quickly, but I fear it will be too late."

"But, Mother . . ."

"Go, Padraig. Go, and please God, give him speed."

Padraig lowered his mother to the bed and ran to the door. He stopped and turned back.

"Go, my son; go to Kathleen."

Padraig turned and raced down the stairs. He never heard his mother's final words.

"But it is too late now. Please God, I beseech you, do not desert my son!"

★★★★★

"Hush now, hush, my little one," Kathleen whispered to her baby daughter. "Why can you not be like your brother?"

She was still quite disturbed by the sudden departure of her husband. However, as he had not returned, she presumed that he had decided to spend some time with his parents.

"When you have decided to be a good little girl, we will take a walk down to join them. Ah, now I understand, you think you are missing out on a wee bit of spoiling."

She giggled to the baby girl as she placed her back in her cot. "Oo, now, aren't you the clever one."

So engrossed was she that Kathleen never heard the sound of the horse and rider pulling up behind the barn.

The furtive actions of the rider dismounting also went unnoticed.

She did hear the door opening and movement in the other room, but naturally assumed it was Padraig returning.

"Such a pleasant sight!"

Kathleen whirled around at the sudden, unexpected words. "What! You! What are you doing in here? Who do you think you are coming into our home?"

"Your husband appears not to be here," Bolton replied laconically. "In his absence, perhaps you could show me some hospitality."

"I'll show you the door," came the fiery and indignant reply.

"Ah, Kathleen, sweet Kathleen—so much like your sister.

Whatever did happen to her? What would you give to know the true story of her last day?" Bolton smiled at her.

"Padraig," she shouted, moving to the bedroom window. "Padraig!"

The sudden outburst caused both babies to start crying.

As Kathleen turned to comfort the little ones, Bolton sprang behind her and smashed at her unprotected head with one of his pistols.

Kathleen dropped to the floor. Bolton bent over her, but as he struggled to pick her up and drag her from the room, he dropped the weapon.

He hoisted her over his shoulder and made for the door. He reached his mare and threw Kathleen over the neck of the horse, and in a bound, he was up in the saddle.

He spurred the animal viciously from behind the barn and turned to make his escape.

"Yes, my beautiful Bridget McGuire, we are all together again."

As they raced from the house, Bolton glanced down the fields. He saw Padraig running toward them, ashen faced, frantically trying to cut off their flight.

But he was too late. By the time Padraig reached his property, Bolton had turned into the lane. In a bizarre victory salute, he raised his arm and waved. "To the victor the spoils!" he shouted.

Padraig watched in horror, hardly believing the heinous events of this day.

Unable to do anything, but watch as Bolton disappeared into the distance, Padraig sank to his knees, sobbing. The image of his wife draped over the horse, screaming in terror, calling out his name, would stay with him forever.

"My children! My God, my children!"

He sprang to his feet and ran inside. Bursting into their

room, his daughter was still crying, but his son peered up at him almost bemused.

"What do I do? Oh God, give me wisdom. What do I do?"

Holding his daughter to him, comforting her, Padraig looked down at his dog. "Can you find them? Can you follow their track?"

The animal stared up him, his eyes full of trust and love for his master. To Padraig, it appeared that the dog nodded his head.

"All right then, let us go."

He gently placed the little baby back down again, and as her whimpering tore his heart apart, he whispered to her, "We are going to get your mommy; just be a good girl."

Together, man and dog prepared to leave.

"What is this?" Padraig spotted the pistol that Bolton had dropped in his haste to depart. He picked it up and thrust it into his belt.

Complete with pikestaff and dagger, he and dog took off after their quarry.

★★★★★

The Weasel had made his way back over the dunes and watched the decimation of his countrymen with very mixed feelings.

Looking down at the one-sided battle from the top of the sand hill, he had seen all but two fall.

"Ah, well now, will I be missin' dem? I tink not." He subconsciously shook his pocket and listened to the jingle of the silver.

"What's this then?" Fascinated, he watched Sean race the gauntlet.

He almost felt a feeling of relief as Sean succeeded in surviving the blows, but he jumped at the sound of shots. He couldn't believe his eyes when he saw Hugo Cohen stagger and then scream when he was hit in the legs.

But the Weasel's attention switched back to Sean as he ran into the surf ahead of the screaming mob.

"The cunning ol' divil!" he exclaimed.

From his vantage point high on the dunes, he could clearly see Sean rise from behind the breakers, take a breath, and go back under as the sea flattened.

Gradually, with the aid of the undertow and his weakening strokes, Sean moved down the coastline and away from his hunters.

The Weasel followed, watching from the top of the dunes, until he reached the rocky crags. Sean floated from view.

"Ah, well, time to go home!" The Weasel made his way toward Morag and the road that headed back inland.

## Chapter 56

"Well, not too far to go now. Letterkenny's only five miles away, and the manor is not too far from there," said the trap driver.

Lord Bolton and Lady Constance smiled.

"Yes, it has been quite a trip this time. I do believe I can taste the welcome brandy from here, my love."

"Yes, dear." She smiled.

A little tap from the whip brought a response from the two horses as they trotted on with a bit more purpose.

"What are your plans, now that we are almost there?" Lady Constance asked of her husband.

"After a truly wonderful dinner and a bottle of excellent wine and then a brandy or two, I will look forward to a good night's sleep so that I can greet the morrow refreshed. I don't intend to even consider looking at our financial statements until then.

"Late tomorrow morning, I have a meeting with our son and Conrad Booth. I understand that the rascally Judge Squires will be in attendance as well."

"Then perhaps I will wander around the shops of Donegal Town for the day," said Lady Constance. "I may be able to pick up some nice woollens for the winter and a new hat for you."

Patting her hands with affection, the Lord Bolton smiled and said, "Of course, my dear, of course."

The gulls wheeled and dived above the rocks at the base of Morag. Each had gathered a big fat juicy mussel, and from high above Morag, had dropped it and followed it down, pouncing on the smashed remains before a competing gull could claim it from the rocky crags. A feathery mix of beak and screech advised the other swooping gulls the ownership and outcome of the snack.

Oblivious to all of this, the horseman galloped down the rocky path to the grassy area overlooking the drop far below.

All that had occurred earlier that day was clouded over by the realization that all was now within his grasp yet again. This time Bridget McGuire would see sense. She would now surely understand his love for her.

Yes, his obsession was greater than her desire to live among those wretched Irish peasants.

Without doubt, she would graciously accept the offer to become the future lady of the manor.

Oh, yes, there would be concessions. He was not a man without understanding of the needs of others. Particularly, he was more than aware of the peculiarities of this strange, but very beautiful woman.

*Oh, yes,* he mused, and he smiled to himself. *She will gladly follow my lead, and all will be perfect.*

They would depart this sad and sorry place and be most happy living at one of their properties in the English countryside.

He would even consider a family.

He pulled to a halt and dismounted, then gently pulled her down from the mare, and laid her on the grass. He positioned her with her head resting on a mound.

She had moaned once or twice on the ride down, but had not yet recovered sufficiently to recognise him and all that he wished to tell her.

Suddenly remembering the water flask secured to the

pommel, he reached up and poured some water over her brow. She murmured a little, and he poured some onto her lips.

Greedily, she swallowed, and in a daze, she looked around her. In her concussed state, she could not grasp or understand where she was or how she came to be there.

"Bridget, my dear, how do you feel?"

"Bridget? Where is Bridget? Is my sister here?" Kathleen looked around her in confusion.

"There, there, Bridget, my love. All will become clear to you in a moment or two."

Kathleen lay back, giddy with nausea, as whirls of mist and red and black passed before her eyes. She forced herself to a sitting position, where she dry wretched and then helplessly fell back to the ground.

Bolton knelt beside her.

"Padraig, is that you?" she muttered.

"Of course not," Bolton answered. "He is no longer with us."

"Wh . . . what do you mean? Where is he? Where is my Padraig?" Shaking her head, trying unsuccessfully to clear the pain that consumed her, she looked at where the voice was coming from. "You! What are you doing to me?" Her eyes darted around, and she stuttered in panic, "Wh . . . where am I? Why are you here? Where is my husband?"

"You don't have a husband, Bridget," Robert Bolton replied.

"Of course I have a husband, and you know it. And why are you calling me by my sister's name? You know very well who I am, and what my husband will do to you if you harm me in any way!"

"Bridget, darling, I do not wish to harm you. I only wish that you become part of my life. Together, we can do so much, you and I."

"Are you mad? My name is Kathleen Gallagher. I am married to Padraig Gallagher." Kathleen was now quite angry, and her head had cleared. "And I will thank you to assist me back to my home. How on earth did I get here in the first place?"

Then gradually the memory of Bolton in her room came back to her. "Where are my children? Oh my God, did you harm them, you foul beast?"

Bolton smiled. "No harm came to any children, and I am not a foul man. I will choose to forgive you for that slip of the tongue. Now, let me offer you a little more water, Bridget."

"I am not Bridget, and I do not want any more water," she snapped. And then grabbing the flask from Bolton's hand, she attempted to scramble to her feet.

"Now, now, enough of that," Bolton warned. With a hand on her breast, he pushed her back down. "You should think very carefully about what you intend to do, my sweet. And understand that you must accept my kind offer."

Kathleen looked up at Bolton. Slowly, as the hopelessness of the situation dawned on her, she began to plan.

★★★★★

The collie loped on ahead of Padraig, stopping occasionally to sniff the ground and then moving on relentlessly, following the scent of the mare.

Suddenly, the dog stopped.

"What is it?" Padraig asked.

They had halted at the point where, as the road south cut back inland, another track headed down to the headland known as Morag.

Padraig was convinced that Bolton and his Kathleen were heading back to the manor house, which lay ten or more miles farther on.

"Good dog." He urged the animal forward, but to no avail. The dog refused to obey, but instead ran down the track, stopped, then looked back at Padraig, gave a little bark, and stood waiting, with an expectant look in his expressive eyes.

Padraig stood watching the antics of the dog, and then it all fell into place.

"It can't be, but my clever little friend, if you think so, then let's go find out."

As the Weasel topped the rise, he paused to gather his breath and recover from the steep climb from the rocks below.

The very narrow path that led down to the Morag Inlet was used by local fisherman to drop lobster pots when the winds came from the east, and the swells were at their lowest.

The Weasel looked down at the clear blue waters, the beauty of this spot not escaping him. "No, I still can't see him," he muttered to himself, looking in vain for Sean Gallagher. "Ah well, no loss."

He walked, following the path as it opened onto the grassy area, the high cliff edges still concealing him. As he emerged into the clearing, he saw Bolton, and what appeared to be a body lying in front of him.

Darting back quickly, before he was seen, he watched from behind the rocks. *I wonder what he's up to now?* he mused.

Then a dog bounded from the path above, followed by Padraig Gallagher. Fascinated, the Weasel watched as Bolton leapt to his feet.

Padraig looked down at the sight below him. His wife lay still, with Bolton kneeling beside her. He looked up at the sound of barking.

He saw the dog and then Padraig. He leapt to his feet to face the unexpected threat.

A pistol was in his hand.

Pointing the weapon down at Kathleen, Bolton called out, "Well, look at this. Who would have thought you would find us here? So, what do we do with you now?"

Kathleen made an effort to rise.

"Padraig! Be careful."

"Yes, Padraig, be careful." Bolton mimicked. "Be extremely careful, or this one dies."

He gestured with the pistol, holding it a hair away from her head.

"Why don't you come down and join us? But please, walk down slowly, or I will pull the trigger, and she dies. Oh, and I would kindly ask you to drop your pike."

Padraig moved toward Bolton, his weapon falling from his hands.

"Stop there!" Bolton demanded.

Padraig stood silently, watching his mortal enemy, ten feet separating him from his wife lying helpless at Bolton's feet.

"Why are you people so pig ignorant?" Bolton asked, looking at Padraig.

"Today, I have wiped out your friends and their weak attempt to defy me. And now, here you are, again trying my patience. Is it any wonder I have to use the ultimate punishment to make you understand and obey? So, I am left with this quandary." He gestured with the pistol to Kathleen.

"I can fire two bullets from this weapon—one to kill her and one to finally rid myself of you. But I am faced with a quandary: Do I kill you and allow her to live and maybe take her to a better place and a better life, or do I kill her and then you."

Bolton locked eyes with Padraig and waited. "Well? It's your decision, Gallagher; who goes first?"

*****

The Weasel watched, completely unaware of the figure behind him. It was only when the coldness touched him that he turned. He could hardly believe what he saw.

Standing motionless behind him was a woman. Her long, black hair disappeared into a cloud–like cloak draped around her. Her eyes looked deep down into his soul.

Finally, she spoke. "I cannot judge you nor can I save you. I can only offer you a chance to release you from the fate that awaits you, your life in exchange for the life of my son."

Astounded, the Weasel realized that the woman was suspended out over the cruel rocks below with no visible form of support, hovering in mid-air. The Weasel turned in terrified shock and ran from his hiding place.

"No, no!" he screamed. "Leave me alone, you ghostly witch. Leave me!"

Bolton and Padraig both turned at the sudden appearance of the man.

Seizing the opportunity, Kathleen grabbed the gun. The weapon fired, and the ball struck her with full force in the breast.

Padraig drew the weapon that Bolton had left in their room and levelled it at him.

But before he could fire, Bolton had lifted his pistol and aimed it at Padraig's head. "Too late, Irishman."

The Weasel, still terrified by the apparition, ran blindly toward the two men.

The charge hit him in his left ear, exploding into his brain as he went between them.

Padraig had cocked the pistol and pulled the trigger, not really knowing what would happen.

Miraculously it fired, hitting Bolton in the shoulder. He spun with the force of the ball hitting him. Not knowing whether there was another shot in the pistol, or even if Padraig was aware of the second charge, he ran for his horse.

He leapt into the saddle, and grabbing the reins with his left hand, he kicked the horse into action, his right arm hanging, bleeding profusely at his side.

As he sped off, he turned and yelled, "Another time, you bastard—another time!"

Padraig fell alongside Kathleen.

"Oh, no, my darling wife . . . not you . . . not you, too."

Kathleen lay dying, the gaping wound spurting blood from her chest with every beat of her heart.

Somehow, she opened her eyes and gazed at her husband.

"My darling man, I love you so much," she sighed.

"Kathleen, don't leave me, please stay with me. I cannot bear to be alive without you."

"Padraig, ah, my Padraig, I am going. I will be leaving you. You have the children to care for. They will be with you instead of me. I have to go now."

Her eyes left his, and she looked beyond him. "I am coming, Claire."

Padraig turned, expecting to see someone behind him.

He saw no one, but as he turned back to his wife, he heard the words. "Good-bye, my son. I love you."

"And Padraig, I love you, also. Good-bye my husband." Kathleen sighed for the final time.

## Chapter 57

It had been dark for some hours, but Padraig was not aware of the darkness or the late hour. He sat with the bloody body of his wife, her head in his lap. He told her of when they were younger, before they were married, when they sat just like this on the Brackey riverbank. He reminded her of the times they sat in newly mown hay fields, the field hands good–naturedly jesting them. He reminded her of their wedding day and their first night.

And he cried.

The faithful dog sat beside him, sensing his heartbreak and agony.

Finally, Padraig spoke to his canine friend. "There is no moon this night. I must take Kathleen home. You have to guide us."

Picking her up so gently and holding her tight to him, they set off together.

The night was pitch black, and Padraig stumbled many times. But he would not fall. He rested and then progressed on again. It was no surprise that the sun came over the hills to the east before he reached their home.

Eventually, with heavy heart, he looked down the road to where the little lane branched off and led to the house of his parents and to their . . . his home.

He couldn't bear to look over to the home of his parents as

he staggered past. He wondered if his parents were still lying in there. He only wanted to take Kathleen home and be with his children.

He saw them as he turned into the path that led to the back door.

He wondered why they were there. Of course, they were minding his little ones.

He could not understand what they meant.

"Padraig Gallagher, we arrest you for the murder of Conrad Booth."

The constable who spoke these words then turned to one of his colleagues. "Take her. I presume she is dead. She certainly appears so."

As Padraig struggled to hold his wife, he was hit from behind. He fell, but attempted to rise. "What is this? What are you talking about?"

He was clubbed on the head and face again and again.

He attempted to rise, struggling to hold his beloved wife's body.

"I warned you he was a big one. Hit him again to be on the safe side!"

Padraig finally collapsed, blood pouring from his nose, his face, and parts of his head. His dog attempted to protect his master, but was brutally smashed to the ground where, after several brief whimpers, he died.

Padraig never felt himself being dumped onto a horse and tied down. He never heard the sounds of the departing horses and constabulary. He never heard the cries of his little babies.

## Chapter 58

Bolton knew that his parents would be arriving sometime soon, but he was unsure when. He did, however, suspect that the traitorous behaviour of Conrad Booth and his liaison with Judge Squires would cast doubts over his ability to manage their Irish interests. It was most fortunate that he had discovered the proof of Booth's treachery.

So, it was no great surprise to find the welcoming party at the manor as he rode up. Obviously, someone had told of his imminent arrival. Although he was in pain and found it very difficult to stay in the saddle, he milked the situation as being greater than it appeared.

His parents, the Lord and Lady Constance, were standing in front of the manor, waiting for him, along with a number of the Donegal constabulary.

"Robert!" his mother exclaimed. "Good heavens! What has happened?"

"You and you," Lord Thomas Bolton ordered two of the men in uniform. "Help my son."

With care, they eased the injured man down from the mare.

"Take him in the house and directly to his room," Lady Constance said.

Calling for the maid, Lady Constance gave her the following orders when she scurried quickly and stood before her. "Fetch hot water—lots of it, and please bring dressing for that wound. Quickly, my son is bleeding very badly."

They eased Robert Bolton onto his bed.

Sometime later, Lord Bolton came to his son. "Right, my boy. There is a great deal of explaining to do. What a shock to arrive here today. Conrad Booth dead and what a death! I have never seen anything like it. He was hacked to pieces. Even his tongue was cut out. My God, I could hardly believe my eyes."

"Yes. I know," Robert Bolton groaned in pain. "I was the one who found him. When I arose this morning, that was the sight I had to endure. My best friend . . . perhaps the only true friend I have ever had. He actually died as I held him.

"But I found the identity of his killer before he left us—the same man who did this." He indicated his damaged shoulder. "He killed Conrad."

"How do you know who it was? Damnation, the poor wretch couldn't speak or write, or for that matter, even see."

"True, but these murderous Irish have been terrorizing us for months now. And when I asked Conrad if one of the leaders of that group did this to him, he nodded his head, poor chap. And then, it was confirmed.

"Father, it was the bastard who shot me—Padraig Gallagher. I went off my head in anger. When Conrad died, I called for my men, and we went directly to avenge his death. I left my friend as he was with the intention to bury him with dignity upon my return."

Bolton then went on to explain how he had defeated the rebel band and finally confronted Padraig Gallagher and his equally rebellious wife.

Lord Bolton stood and walked directly to the group of constables waiting outside.

"I demand that you go immediately to apprehend Padraig Gallagher. I will witness his execution before I return to England."

*****

Padraig Gallagher felt around in the dark.

He had no idea where he was. He heard other sounds, human sounds, but could not figure out who was making them or where the sounds came from.

As the dawn arrived, he looked around and realized he was behind bars. His head ached, and the memory of the dreadful happenings of the previous day returned. He had the horrible sick feeling that all was gone, his family, his wife, and oh, where, oh where, were his children?

Again hearing sounds, he called out. "Is anyone there? Is there someone who can help me?"

Finally, he heard footsteps.

"If you don't keep the noise down, you will receive more of the same you got yesterday."

"What am I doing here?"

"What are you doing here? Why, me hearty, you are a guest—our guest. And you will be for some time until we tire from looking after your sorry hide. Then the hangman can have you. And your hide will swing from the gallows."

"But why? What have I done to deserve this?"

"What have you done, me hearty? Murder, that is all. And a terrible murder it was, too, now wasn't it. A murder the likes of which we have never heard of or seen around here before."

"Murder? Who did I kill?" Padraig pleaded.

"Well, now, if you don't know that, then we do have a sorry case, truly a sad and sorry case." The jailer shook his head as he departed.

Padraig went to a bench. He pushed aside some sacking and soiled clothes that some other poor sap had left there and sat staring at the cold steel separating him from the world he once knew, a world that now seemed so strange, so very different to the life that he knew was gone forever.

***** 

"Try and swallow the milk. It will help you get better."

Sean Gallagher looked around him to see who had spoken. He was lying on a bed with a woman standing over him. "Is that you, Sarah?"

"Ah, yes now, indeed, indeed it is." Old Sarah smiled down at him. "And 'tis the lucky one you are, oh yes. Come, take a wee small drop of the milk."

"Where are they?"

"There's nobody here. Well, apart from them that is."

Sean could hear the squabbling of children in the background.

"How did I get here? And where are the Englishmen?"

"I tell you, there is no one else here. No Englishmen. No men of any description, to be sure." She said this almost wistfully.

"But then, how did I get here?" Sean asked again.

"I found you down at the water."

"Not true, I found him!" The small voice came from behind a curtain at the doorway.

"Yes, yes, young Tommy. You found him."

Sarah then went on to explain to Sean that her boys had been wandering along the shore when they saw a body. They ran to fetch her, and as they dragged the lifeless form from the receding tide, she recognised him.

"You were surely more dead than alive. And it has taken many days for you to wake as you have this day. You just lay there moaning and talking strange talk. I had to fix the cuts and wounds to your body, and I had to take all your clothes off you."

Sean suddenly realized he was completely naked, with only the blankets over him.

"Oh, don't be so shy with you now. You were shiverin' and

shakin' with the fever. It was a sorry shape of a man you were."

"Then how long have I been here?" Sean pleaded.

But before she could answer, he struggled to get up from the bed. "Get me my clothes, woman! I have to be gone from here." He wasn't as strong as he thought he was, and he fell back, helpless.

"Sean, you haven't eaten proper food for more than eight days. You will have to get your strength back. Now stay there, and I will get you a stew of mutton and potatoes. And then we will see."

Sean wolfed down the food, and his bowels, not used to so much food in such a long time, had an immediate reaction. Embarrassed, he suddenly said, "Oh no, let me get outside—quick, woman."

Together with the help of her eldest boy, they aided Sean out to where nature could take its course.

"Well now," Sarah said to him as she helped him back into the house and straight to bed. "It looks as though things are getting back to normal. Just you rest up a wee bit more, and we can talk about this tomorrow."

\*\*\*\*\*

Father and son sat in the back seat of the trap.

Not a lot had been said on the trip from the manor to Donegal Town.

In fact, tension had risen gradually from the day after the arrival of the lord and lady.

"How are things between you and Judge Squires?" Lord Bolton finally asked.

"What do you mean?"

"Exactly as I asked," Thomas Bolton replied. "Are you still on good terms?"

"Of course," Robert snapped.

"I say, old chap!" Lord Thomas Bolton spoke to the driver. "We have only a short way to go to the offices of the judge. Stop here; we will walk the rest of the way. Exercise, you know; does us all good."

"Of course, m' lord. Should I drive to the judge's offices and wait for you there?"

"Go and enjoy an ale or two at the tavern," Lord Bolton said magnanimously. "Here are some coins for your enjoyment. I will send a messenger to tell you when we are ready to return."

"Thank you, m' lord, that's very generous of you."

Father and son alighted and began the walk.

"You lied to me didn't you?" Lord Bolton looked directly at his son.

"What on earth are you talking about?" Robert replied.

"You said to me that you were with Booth when he died."

"Yes . . . I was. Of course I was," Thomas Bolton retorted.

"Then perhaps you can explain to me what the word was that he was attempting to write. Considering his hand had been removed from him and he was writing with the blood from his wrist."

"What word? What are you talking about?"

"This is all perfectly clear, actually. You told us that you left him after he had died, but that is impossible. You see, when I arrived, the body had still not been moved. But you expect me to believe that somehow Booth had woken from the dead and attempted to write a name before drawing his final breath."

"This is preposterous, Father!" Robert bluffed. "Why are you taunting me with such a story?"

"The name was Robert," Lord Bolton said, and then he was silent, waiting for a plausible reply from his errant son.

Not receiving one, he added, "Rather than let your mother see this sorry sight, I had the body cleaned up and the bloody mess mopped tidy. Now, you can give me your reply after our visit to Squires."

Judge Squires was obviously pleased to see Lord Bolton, and as he escorted them to his office, he noticed that the senior Bolton avoided eye contact with his son.

"It was quite a shock to find Conrad in that manner," Squires began. "I do hope you were not upset that I contacted the constabulary and sent them to the manor house."

"No, quite the contrary. We must be seen obeying the law no matter the consequences," Lord Bolton replied.

"Yes, of course. Shall we commence business then?"

The tedious matters of general bookkeeping were attended to, and finally Lord Bolton said to his son, "It is quite apparent that since your arrival, Robert, our business here has suffered dramatically.

"The Irish tenants' payment records, while not great, were certainly showing a growing increase. But then suddenly, about the time you took over, decline set in. Perhaps you'd care to explain."

Lord Bolton's request met with sullen silence.

"Robert, I have heard nothing but contemptuous comments from you regarding the Irish. Most of the other landlords agree that the Irish do not like paying the rents, but they do eventually pay them. Quite frankly, I don't blame them. I would probably react the same way were I in their position.

"But the fact is, they have been paying landlords all over Ireland except here, largely thanks to you and the blasted heavy-handed and extremely violent manner in which you've treated them.

"History may well record one day that the Irish finally overthrew the burden of the English; hopefully, not in my time. But if and when they do, it could be seen as a reaction to members of the aristocracy like you who, instead of understanding the responsibility of *noblesse oblige*, you take delight in tormenting those who are beneath your station in life."

Lord Bolton glared at his son, who drummed his fingers and looked everywhere, but in his father's eyes.

"Please go to the tavern and wait for me there."

Robert Bolton rose and left. As he did so, he turned and looked at Judge Squires. No words were spoken, but the judge felt his blood run cold. He had never known such a fear to come over him.

His attempt to follow the rest of the day's business went well until Lord Bolton left, but the moment that man had gone from the building, Judge Squires collapsed on the sofa in his comfortable library. He was a nervous wreck. He had to do something. He began to plan.

## Chapter 59

"I do not wish to discuss this afternoon's findings within earshot of others, particularly the Irish," Lord Thomas Bolton stated. "Good God, it's embarrassing enough to have lost face, let alone the profit on the investment of our Irish land purchases."

"What in hell are you talking about?" Robert Bolton argued, showing no respect for his father. "I put down an Irish rebellion."

"Don't take that tone with me, young man. I still have the power to disinherit you." Lord Bolton was not pleased. "You started that rebellion. You killed, nay murdered, a bunch of stick–wielding country hay gatherers. You, with your superior firepower!

"I have more admiration for them standing up to your pernicious bullying than I have for your weak business administration. But enough! We will discuss it when we return to the manor."

Robert Bolton fumed inwardly. *Someone will pay for this*, he vowed.

*****

Padraig Gallagher had fretted for two long days. He had absolutely no idea what was happening around him. Apart from drunken warbling and Gypsy dialects from itinerant wanderers arrested for a range of petty misdemeanors, no one, not even the jailers, had given a clue as to why he was in the Donegal jail.

But sometime during that second day he had a visitor.

"Father Sullivan!" he exclaimed.

"Would you be so kind as to open the door and allow me to talk to this man?" the good father enquired of the jailer.

A nod of approval. "But if there is any trouble, it will be the shackles I'll be showing him!"

The priest entered the dark and dingy cell.

"Father! Thank God you are here. Please, please tell me what is happening. Why am I locked in here?"

"Padraig, my son, there is no good news. Tomorrow we bury your wife, Kathleen, and sadly the bodies of your dear mother, father, and grandfather.

"The Requiem Mass will also be held to pray for the souls of the twenty-four killed by Bolton and his thugs."

"Holy God, no!" Padraig stared helplessly at the priest.

"You said twenty-four. That must mean there were survivors. My brother?"

"Sean has not been seen or heard from since that horrible day. Poor, poor Hugo cannot walk. He was shot many times by Bolton. He comes in and out of consciousness, and when he does speak, he is mostly incoherent. He did manage to tell me of Sean escaping into the sea, but Padraig, I can hold out little hope for his safe return."

"What about my children, Father Sullivan? Where are my son and daughter?"

"I am so sorry, Padraig—this is the worst news of all. When we came and discovered the bodies, our first thoughts were of the little ones. Padraig, there is no sign of them; absolutely no sign whatsoever. They have just vanished. Our prayers are continually pleading to Almighty God for some knowledge of their whereabouts. But there is nothing. It's a terrible, terrible mystery."

Padraig sat in stunned silence.

Father Sullivan felt so helpless. In all his life, he had never known such misery. "My son, would you like to share a prayer with me?"

After what seemed an eternity, Padraig spoke. "No, Father, I will not pray with you. I cannot pray with you. I cannot pray to a God who can allow such a happening to those who trusted in him. Why has he allowed evil to triumph over good?

"My mother, my lovely beautiful wife, and all those who believed in him, believed with all their heart that he would save them from harm. No, Father, I cannot pray to this God."

"My son, my son, you cannot say this. I beseech you, please place your trust in our Holy God. He has his reasons. And remember, those you love so much are with him as we speak. He has welcomed them to our heavenly home; they are with him now."

"Then, Father, let them tell me they are there. Let them give me a message."

"Padraig, the workings of God are not to be challenged. Your faith in him, your trust in him, all our beliefs and aspirations will give us the answers eventually. You must have confidence that his guidance and love will conquer all."

"Will it bring my wife and family back?"

"No, Padraig, what is done is done. But all for a reason."

"What damned reason?" Padraig stormed. "Is it reasonable to find my parents and grandfather murdered and my beautiful beloved wife? And what about my children? Who knows where they are? Is that the reasoning of your loving and guiding God?"

"Padraig, I know that this is hard for you. But faith will save you."

"Save me!" Padraig said, his voice rising in shock. "Save me?! Why weren't my loved ones saved? I'm sorry Father, there is no Saviour!"

"Padraig, you cannot talk like this. This goes against all that Rome and our teachings stand for."

"Father, I can and I will talk like this, and damn Rome and all those who can stand and state that what happened here is acceptable just because a God said it was acceptable. No, Father, I am sorry. Sorry that you came over here on a wasted journey, sorry that I cannot nor will not ever take the word of a man of the cloth ever again. I hold nothing against you, only all you stand for." Padraig buried his head in his hands and said no more.

The priest eventually broke the silence that followed. "Padraig, I must leave now. I will do all I can to help you."

"I suspect there is very little you can do. I do thank you for your visit. But please tell Hugo of my concern, and tell him I will do all I can to be with him soon."

As the shattered priest left, he heard the jailer laugh.

"The only place you are going to, me hearty, is to the gallows to be sure."

*****

Robert Bolton was livid. He could not remember a time when he was so angry. He and Lord Bolton had talked at length about the problems he had encountered with the Irish tenant farmers, and to his way of thinking, only a blasted old fool would have taken the stance his father had. And idiots such as that commanded no respect!

"Quite frankly, I have had enough of your pompous paradiddle," the younger Bolton finally snapped. "And as for bringing those screaming peasant brats back here to the manor, my home, what on earth for, may I ask?"

"I demand you show respect, you insubordinate ungrateful fool. Those children are now orphaned because of your actions.

Your mother has decided that they will need a home and support as they grow." He did not add that his wife and he had argued long and hard before he reluctantly agreed to her plans for the children.

Lord Bolton paused to take a sip of the strong coffee they had brought with them from England. "I do not wish to pursue these matters any further. The following are my decisions, and you will abide by them.

"Concerning the matter of Conrad Booth, the young Gallagher will stand trial for murder. You will return to England.

"Judge Squires will appoint an overseer to take your place, one who can mend the sorry situation between the Irish and us.

"That rabble you have collected will be dispersed—well, those who are capable of traveling will go now; the rest when they have suitably recovered.

"Now I suggest you go and commence packing your belongings. I want you away from here as soon as you can leave." Lord Bolton stood and stalked from the room.

★★★★★

Padraig did not know how long he had been locked up. As he was fed twice a day, he thought he could recall at least six or perhaps seven morning and evening pots of slops.

"You've got a visitor," the jailer announced in his usual surly tone. He unlocked the door and a portly figure stood at the entrance to the cell.

"Phew!" He snuffled, holding a lace-trimmed linen handkerchief to his nose. "I say, there's a dear thing," he spoke to the jailer. "Perhaps you could fetch me a chair. I don't feel as though I wish to sit there."

"Don't you move, or else," the jailer warned Padraig.

Quickly, a chair was found and positioned inside the cell.

"You may go!" the man announced to the jailer, who moved

off to a far corner where he could sit and keep an eye on them.

"Now, allow me to introduce myself. My name is Throckmorton Squires. You, of course, must be the unfortunate Padraig Gallagher.

"Regrettably, I will be the last person you will remember, albeit for a very brief time, who will have any bearing on your future. You see, I am the judge who will listen to those who will testify seeing you leave the scene of a particularly nasty murder."

"But I am innocent of any crime," Padraig protested.

"Yes, yes, of course. No one is ever guilty, are they?" Squires mused. "But sadly, for you, the respected Robert Bolton will testify seeing you with blood–soaked hands leaving the body of Conrad Booth. And of course, there is so much motive, considering the action of you and your rebellious bloodthirsty colleagues, not to mention a maid, two footmen, and a butler who witnessed your actions. No, it will be the gallows for you, my boy."

"But this is ridiculous . . . madness. I have never even been inside the manor."

"Young man, the testimonies of all the witnesses will be balanced, and eventually the scales will swing in favour of the truthful. As for the culpable, well, then I must decide the fate. But from what I have heard, I hold out little hope for you."

"But!" Padraig attempted to stand.

"Please stay as you are. Do not rise, or the jailer will take great delight in bashing you down and placing you in shackles."

Padraig settled back.

"Good. Now I want you to listen very closely to what I have to say." Squires lowered his voice so that Padraig could just hear him.

"I have every reason to believe you have little affection for Robert Bolton. Apart from you and your friend's problems with his demands, I understand you hold him responsible for the death of your dear wife and probably your parents. I have a written statement from him that will send you to your death.

"He has, however, returned to England. While this statement and the testimony of those that are still here will find you guilty, I can state that if he was no longer, shall we say, with us anymore, and I was to misplace the statement, there would be little evidence to convict you."

Padraig stared at the judge. "What do you mean? What are you saying?"

"I am saying that if you were to, perhaps, escape from here and follow him to England and do to him what he did to your family—indeed, you have more than enough cause. But before he dies, you get him to sign an oath that his statement was a pack of lies.

"Then, on your return, I would have little choice, but to exonerate you of all charges. You could then return to your community. Now, what do you have to say?"

Padraig looked stunned. "Why would you do this? How do I know I can trust you?"

"You don't know! But then, what choice do you have?"

Padraig sat silent, thinking.

"Oh, and if it helps you decide, I will be the one to arrange for the cell door to suddenly open. I will also arrange for a horse to be close by, and there will be a pouch of money to cover your costs and to enable you to find food and lodgings. There will also be directions as to where to find Bolton." Squires rose. "I will give you until this time tomorrow to decide."

## Chapter 60

Lady Constance could barely believe her good luck. When the chief constable told them of the two babies, she instantly dispatched the nursemaid and the housekeeper to collect them.

"After all this killing and no one to look after them, the least we can do is attend to their immediate needs. God knows they could be dying or even dead already!"

They had been under her care now for five days, and already she was captivated by the antics of the twins.

"My darling, we simply cannot pluck these infants from their home and just presume to take them back home to England with us!" Lord Bolton had argued.

"Our son murders their family, imprisons their father, probably to die, and you tell me not to feel some responsibility. I am now even more determined to provide for these little ones."

Knowing from many past and losing arguments with his wife, Lord Bolton did not disagree. "Yes, my love, whatever you say is best."

"Now, talking about our son." Heavily emphasizing the word *our*, Lady Constance continued. "What do you intend doing with him, and what will happen to that poor man in jail?"

"I have informed Robert of my absolute disgust regarding this whole sorry affair, as I have already told you. He will return to England after lodging a statement of all his actions with Judge Squires.

"I will accompany him during this matter and then send him packing. Quite frankly, if I never see him again, it will be too soon."

Lady Contance knit her brows in shocked concern, but remained quiet.

"It will be quite possible that I will be able to save the young Gallagher from the gallows, even arrange for a minimum jail sentence. As I have stated, I do have sympathy for the predicament the Irish find themselves in. But business is business, and we need to make an example of this fellow to show what will happen if these people overstep the mark."

"Well, then, that is perfect," his wife replied. "I can then be the children's guardian until such time as their father is free to look after them."

Staring defiantly at him, Lord Bolton declined to challenge his wife. "The Dutch!" he muttered.

"What did you say?"

"Nothing, my dear, just agreeing with you. Well, now, time for a snorter, what?"

*****

The meeting had gone quite well, very well, in fact.

"Yes, the cards have fallen very much in my favour," Squires smiled, as he poured a celebratory brandy.

He had agreed with Lord Bolton that Padraig Gallagher should not have to face the hangman. He also agreed that a small jail sentence was probably the correct action.

"A month or two? Maybe six months would be quite adequate," he had concurred. And he had quickly agreed that such kindness and understanding would bring the Irish back into line to recommence their land rental payments. "Just leave everything to me. I will take care of it," he had stated as he said good-bye to Lord Bolton and his son.

He had even smiled, staring boldly into the cold hateful eyes of Robert Bolton.

*Not so bloody likely*, he thought to himself.

★★★★★

"Oh, no. Lose my trump card, not a chance. Just you wait, young Bolton, keep looking behind you!"

Padraig Gallagher looked up as the jailer called to him.

"A visitor. Look lively there!"

"Ah, so there you are." The judge beamed.

"Well, come on now. Open the door," he ordered the jailer.

"And, pray tell, how are you?" Squires asked of the younger man.

Just as Padraig began to reply, the judge touched his lips in a warning sign. "I wonder if we could have some privacy," he said to the jailer. "I wish to inform this young fellow of his situation. We do not need ears others than ours involved."

The jailer scuttled off.

"Now, then, bad news I am sorry to have to inform you."

Padraig waited to hear more.

"It was as I feared. The English aristocracy, which at times, I confess, I'd prefer not to belong to, must always be seen to be in power. In this case, they intend to show no mercy because they clearly see you and your colleagues as the villains in this sad and sorry saga. Perhaps if it were not for Robert Bolton's damning testimony of your actions, things may have gone better for you."

"But!" Padraig protested.

"I know," Squires interrupted. "I spoke long and hard on your behalf." Squires paused to gather his thoughts. The plain truth is Bolton wants you dead, as it clearly indicates in this statement." He held up an impressive sheaf of papers.

Judge Squires sat back, watching quietly as the young Irishman absorbed the disheartening news. "But I did tell you there is another way," the judge continued. "Your guilt rests on the words of Robert Bolton in these papers. So, in fact, does your future. Now if Bolton was not, shall we suggest, around to confirm this testimony, then I would have little choice other than to dismiss the actions.

"If you have disappeared by the time you are to appear before me in a day or so, and Mr. Bolton is not around to testify, then the case will be scrapped, and you will be free to live the rest of your life as you wish." Squires talked quietly to Padraig Gallagher, reinforcing the lies he had already told.

Gradually the picture began to come clear in Padraig's mind. He had to kill Bolton.

Hatred began to simmer and burn deeper and deeper as the judge highlighted the atrocities already committed by Bolton and his English and Scot murderers. The deception concocted by him fueled the intensity of outrage boiling within Padraig's heart.

"When Bolton is dead, you may return to your community and be with your people. I will not bother you. I will have no need to."

"And my children—have you any news of them?" Padraig pleaded.

Squires peered over his glasses as he made his last play. "You will be most unhappy to hear. While all were unaware, he returned and murdered your little ones. Cut them to pieces."

"NO!" Padraig screamed. "NO!"

At this sudden commotion, the jailer appeared.

"Go away. Please leave this poor young man to grieve in dignity." Squires dismissed the jailer.

Padraig Gallagher sat, his head buried in his big hands. Long,

long minutes passed. He finally looked up. Staring with haunted aching eyes into the judge's, he whispered, "When can you get me out of here?"

# Part 2

## New South Wales

## Chapter 61

Padraig Gallagher did not like England. He had been here for three days now, and already he longed to return to his homeland.

The escape had gone without incident. From the darkness of his cell bed, he had heard noises, at first a clinking sound from the area of the cell door, and then the familiar squeaking of the door opening little by little.

As he rose and pushed the door fully open, a man stood waiting.

"Come," was all he uttered.

Outside, two horses were tied to a post. He was told to mount up, and the two of them rode quietly from the sleeping Donegal Town. They rode until daybreak with Padraig having no idea where he was or where they were heading.

With each village they reached, the unknown man indicated caution as they rode through it or around it. The only time he spoke was to tell Padraig to halt his horse and dismount to eat the meager rations he had brought for them to share. They also stopped to rest and water the horses from time to time.

The two nights after the escape were spent in silence, and as Padraig waited for sleep to overcome him, he didn't much care to talk anyway. The pain and anguish he was feeling was too deep for anything other than to meet the man responsible as speedily as possible.

Finally, they reached the outskirts of what Padraig presumed to be Dublin.

They made their way to the dock area where Padraig gaped at the large ships tied up. The other rider showed no interest at all in the frantic activity of the loading and unloading.

"Wait here," he ordered.

Padraig watched as the man went over to some dockworkers and began talking in animated fashion, turning and pointing to him before resuming conversation. He saw money change hands, and then he was beckoned over.

"You and your horse are to be loaded onto that boat there. You will be taken to Portsmouth. From there, you will travel to London. It may be difficult to find your way around, but that is your problem. The man you want is at this address."

He handed Padraig a package. "The details you want are all inside. There is also enough money to enable you to complete your task." With that, the stranger mounted his horse and rode away.

Padraig had finally reached the outskirts of London. The trip had been easier than he had expected. In the country regions his request for directions had been given in friendly but difficult to understand local dialect.

But now, closer to his destination, he was treated with surly suspicion.

The address he had been given was north of the Thames, but not far from London Bridge. He could not believe the hustle and bustle of the city.

He had been told of an inn close to the vicinity where Bolton was supposed to be living. The final page of the instructions showed a reasonably clear map of the street where the inn was located, as well as the street and house number of his enemy.

"So, you have traveled far then?" was the question asked as

he negotiated with the innkeeper.

"Quite far," Padraig replied. "Far enough for my horse and me to enjoy a welcome rest. Indeed so."

"Fine, fine. Now there is the stable."

"When you have tended to the 'orse, come inside where a fine ale and a fine supper are waiting for you . . . and the attention of a buxom wench or two should the need arise." The innkeeper chuckled and gave a knowing wink. "But a word of advice," he added. "Don't be wandering far. There are many a bad lot 'round 'ere what are ready and able to separate you from any wealth thee might 'ave."

"That won't happen," Padraig replied. "I intend to sleep, and then see what the new day brings."

Later that evening, Padraig sat alone at a table by a window, watching the comings and goings of London's nightlife. He had eaten a huge plate of food, wolfed it down, as he was thoroughly famished.

"Another ale then?" a barmaid enquired.

Startled, Padraig looked up. "Oh, yes, one more if I may."

"Oh, my poor lovely, did I disturb you? You looked miles away."

Padraig attempted to smile at the young lady. "I am sorry, I am tired, and yes, my thoughts were of other matters."

"Well, never mind then, I'll fetch you your drink, and maybe a little later I can bring your thoughts back to these." She giggled as she shook her very ample bosom.

"With regret, I must decline," Padraig replied politely. After the barmaid left, Padraig cast his eyes about the room and was amazed at the mix of people gathered there.

A dark man, black almost, with curly hair and a large earring through each ear stood at the bar, laughing loudly. The men with him were also strangely attired and had peculiar eyes. They seemed to Padraig that they were mere slits on either side of their noses.

At times, he heard the unmistakable brogue of his countrymen mixed in with the peculiar accents of the local people. He listened to smatterings of other tongues, some of which were familiar, which he recognised from the teachings of Hugo Cohen.

Sadly, thoughts of his friend interrupted his mood. Rage began to simmer as the memories of the atrocities committed by Bolton returned. His fists clenched as he tried to control the killing urge within him.

"Well, here we are then, deary!" A large pot of creamy topped ale was plunked down on his table.

"Thank you," was all Padraig could utter.

"Will that be all then?" She smiled.

"Yes, what do I owe you?" Padraig paid the woman and thanked her as she walked away.

She did not see the tears that dropped from Padraig's eyes and disappeared into the brew as he sat staring down with his head in his hands.

"I am coming," he muttered. "Oh yes, I am coming."

Sometime later, he walked to his room. Not taking the slightest notice of the odours or the clamour outside, he fell onto the bed and into a deep sleep.

## Chapter 62

Robert Bolton was now a happy man. His return to London, while in circumstances not at all to his liking, was quickly forgotten as he found his old cronies and went back to his old haunts. It seemed like he had been away for only a day or two.

"Quite frankly, my father is a fiddly dud, silly old bastard," he wisecracked to his mates.

"Well then, what does that make you?" was the laughing reply.

The four men sat together, drinking in a tavern overlooking the Thames.

"Truly, I couldn't care less. It's what I make of me that I care about," Bolton replied. He had summarized the story of his actions over the past year in Ireland, taking care to skim over the parts that he felt would discredit him.

"I would have done exactly the same, but then all know of my personal feelings toward those people," one of them agreed with haughty laughter. "The Irish should have been wiped out years ago."

"But more to the point, what do you intend doing now?" asked another.

Bolton raised his pot and drained the ale. "A very interesting question. As you all are aware, there is much fortune to be made in the new colonies. Huge amounts of gold are being discovered every day in America, and it could be ours for the taking. Just look at the opportunity being talked about in the lands recently discovered by Cook. Who knows what is there for the taking in the place they are sending that rabble!" Bolton pointed to a rotting hulk at anchor in the Thames.

"Yes!" replied another of the four. "And the sooner they clear the streets of that vermin, the better. I hear tell that as many as forty shiploads of convicts are to be sent from here."

"Maybe not that many, but certainly a fair number will be leaving by the shipload. And bloody good riddance I say," another commented.

"Indeed. Well, I intend to get my share of the takings before the word gets out," Bolton concurred. "And I leave in two weeks for New York. My family has investments there that need my attention, and from there, well, who knows where I might end up. But one thing is certain, if a pound is to be made, it will have my name on it." He clinked their glasses to seal his confident boast.

He did not add that he had little in the way of choice. His father's instructions were perfectly clear. Lord Bolton did not want him dirtying the family name any more than he already had done.

\*\*\*\*\*

Padraig woke on his second day in London. He had slept soundly until around three a.m. and then awoke to the strange sounds of London's nightlife. He tossed and turned until the first rays of light broke the gloom of the night's darkness. When he finally did open his eyes, he was drained. He staggered from his bed and splashed cold water over his face from the basin by his bed.

Looking out the window and seeing no one in the street

below, he threw the smelly contents from the chamber pot.

He smiled grimly and muttered, "Take that, England, the shit you served me is being returned."

After finishing dressing, he made his way out to the stable. "Well, my beauty, maybe today we can finish what we came here for. And then we can go back home." After tending to the horse, he walked out into a bleak late autumn morning.

He knew, or at least had a fair idea, where Bolton was residing. His plan was to conceal himself until his enemy came out into the street, and then he would follow him until he could corner him and kill him. He ached for the moment when he could look Bolton in the eye as he plunged his knife deep into his belly.

He followed the route he had taken the previous day, knowing that Lord Bolton's properties were not far from the markets. Feeling hungry, he wanted to sample some of the freshly baked bread and perhaps another one of the coffees that he had tasted for the first time the day before.

He walked faster to outpace the street urchins that approached him, but to no avail. Soon they were alongside him, chattering to him, offering him assistance he neither wanted nor needed.

"Please leave me be, I wish to be alone," Padraig snapped to them.

Suddenly, as one of them took his attention, he felt another slip his purse from his side pocket.

"Hey!" he yelled and started after the fleet–footed little thief. The boy's friends impeded Padraig's progress by running in and out of his way, laughing at him the entire time.

"We'll help you, Guv."

The young urchin darted down a dingy alleyway. Padraig followed. But the youngster had quite simply disappeared. Padraig looked around him in all directions. Seemingly out of nowhere, he was surrounded by three men, who blocked his exit to the narrow street.

"What's up then, Guv? Got some bovver, have we?" The voice came from a nasty-looking man with a badly scarred face. His two comrades looked equally threatening.

"Now, let's tell you 'ow it is. It's quite simple, really. You give us any money you 'ave left and anyfing else that might do, and we'll let you go."

"Maybe!" one of his grimy cohorts muttered.

A cold blue sensation came over Padraig. He did not know how it happened. All he could remember later was leaping at the three men with his knife levelled at them.

The man who had first challenged him stood a foot or so in front of the other two with a knife in his right hand.

Padraig was suddenly inside his guard. At the same time as his head smashed into the man's nose, his knife slashed down under his face, slicing into the assailant's wrist. Padraig then turned and stooped, and with his back now into the man's belly, pushed his body up with such force he drove the scoundrel back and behind the other two very startled fellow thieves.

Screaming and snorting blood, he fell to the ground on his back.

Padraig's heel crushed into his groin.

Lifting his knife hand high, Padraig then smashed the hilt down on the second man's head, who immediately slumped to the ground.

The third man turned and ran.

Padraig jumped over the body of the first would–be robber and chased after him. Padraig's speed overtook the badly frightened rogue, and he grabbed him and slammed him against the wall of a house.

"Where are those children who stole from me!" He smashed his fist, still holding the knife, into the face of the robber.

The strange sound of the whistles meant nothing to Padraig, even if he had heard them. And he certainly did not feel the baton as it smashed into the back of his head. As he lay on the dirty London street, he vaguely heard the order.

"Lock the both of them up!"

The horse-drawn wagon made its way over the cobbled streets, carrying Bolton and one of his friends to a coffee shop. They both stood and watched somewhat bemused as the barred police wagon went past.

Bolton's face then suddenly turned ashen.

"What's up then?" His friend enquired. "You look as though you have seen a ghost!"

He could not understand why the man in the wagon was screaming "NO, NO, NO!" at them or why Robert Bolton stood rooted to the pavement, staring in shock.

# Chapter 63

Judge Throckmorton Squires lay cuddled up under a pile of blankets pulled to his chin. He gazed up at the ceiling contented, with a very full belly of mutton and potato. The roasted onions that he loved, however, kept reminding him of his lack of restraint.

Two empty wine bottles were also evidence of a most delightful evening meal. He burped and grinned happily. "Time for sleep," he said aloud. "Ah, yes, this is the life."

He then turned and blew out first the lamp on the small table to his right, and then stretching across the bed, snuffed out the two candles waxed onto a dinner plate. Within moments, he was snoring, dead to the world.

Three figures quietly snuck up the stairs and then along the corridor and peered into the darkened room. They could just make out the portly figure of the judge, his prodigious belly rising and falling in rhythm with his snoring.

Softly feeling under the blankets, first one fat ankle and then the second, the intruders roped the judge to the bedposts at the foot of the bed. They gently lifted each arm, both of which lay across his chest, and secured them to the posts at the head of the bed. They pulled off the blankets and left them in a heap on the floor.

And the judge snored on.

He didn't stir when the two candles were lit, showing his

huge shape lying on the bed. With his nightshirt and woollen hat, complete with large woolly ball lying alongside his ear, he amused the three figures standing by his bed.

"Well, now, 'tis a sight to see, surely is it not?"

Still the judge didn't stir.

But the sudden shot of pain to the lower part of his body did wake him. "What the—who are you? What are you doing?"

He watched, terrified, as the candle was tipped to the side, spilling another large dribble of hot wax onto his exposed testicles.

"Phew! They smell a bit, don't they?"

Trying to fight against the rope restraints, he farted, partly in fear, but mostly through necessity.

"Oh, shit! What is that? You stinking fat pig."

"Careful with that flame! It might set him on fire," one of them wisecracked, and they all laughed.

The now petrified judge started begging. "Please let me go. What is it you want? Who are you, for God's sake?"

"It matters little who we are. But it should matter a great deal to you and whether you wake to greet the new day. Now think very carefully, and do not lie when you answer this question. Where is Padraig Gallagher?"

"Who? Padraig who?"

A sock was thrust into Squires's mouth.

"Wrong answer!"

A vicious blow to his testicles scattered cooled wax and caused the judge to almost faint with the pain. He tried to cry out, but the woolly sock halted the scream.

"Now, let's try again, shall we? Where is Padraig Gallagher, and why is he not still in your stinkin' jail? Careful now when you answer; you don't want another dose."

A nod from his head, and a bigger collection of hot wax found the target.

The big belly thrust up in agony. His head shook from side to side in a vain attempt to spit out the sock.

"Take this out then, should I? Now tell us what we want to hear."

With tears of pain spilling down his face, Judge Squires told everything that the three men needed to hear.

After standing there listening silently, the largest of the three said, "Put the sock back. Now listen to me, my good judge. If you lie still and breathe carefully, you might live till the morn. I care neither way. You are an extremely lucky man. Fortunately, you did not harm Padraig; you may have lied to him, but you did not injure him. For that reason alone, I will not kill you. But if you attempt to make any enquiries as to who my two friends and I are, then we will return and give you more of our special treatment, and this time you will die." Quietly they left the room.

"Oh, by the way, I lied." The voice came from the doorway, and the two lit candles landed on the bed.

They quickly started to smolder, and the smell of burning cloth hit the nostrils of Throckmorton Squires. His belly emptied in fear, as suddenly a flicker lit up the room, and larger flames caught and then the whole bed was alight.

From the street below, the three men watched and then turned and strode away as the glow from the window indicated the house was truly doomed.

"Do you think he went to England then, Sean?"

"Aye, I do! My brother probably thought that we were all dead. The bloody judge filled him with just enough knowledge to hunt down Robert Bolton and little else. Who knows where he is now. But my feelings are that Padraig will not rest until he has destroyed Bolton, and then he will come back home and attempt to find what is left."

"What are you going to do then?"

"I will leave for London as soon as I can, and with luck, I'll find him and bring him back with me."

The night swallowed up the three men as shouts from behind them indicated that the burning house had been discovered.

## Chapter 64

The despair of being an inmate in a second prison in less than a week was almost overpowering. But being incarcerated in Newgate Prison was a vastly different experience to that of being held in the Donegal holding cells.

Padraig found it very hard to come to terms with his fellow inmates. They ranged from young boys arrested for street misdemeanors to hardened criminals, all who would face the judges at the Old Bailey. Most were openly friendly toward him, although there were others that he did not expose his back to.

As Padraig prepared to settle down for the night, one he was particularly unwary of approached him.

"Hey, Irish! What'd you give me to pleasure this pretty boy then?" The man standing in front of him had one of the young children by the collar of a dirty tunic.

Padraig looked up for only a moment. In a fit of rage, he was on his feet, and with only one blow to the head, he felled the man.

He grabbed the startled child and pushed him over to where another couple of youngsters sat.

"Stay there," Padraig said. "He won't trouble you further!"

"I'd be watchin' out for 'im, mister."

Padraig nodded, and as he sat back down, another man came and sat by him, a man as black as charcoal and unlike no other that Padraig had seen. His first reaction of fear, however, was quickly dispelled when the man smiled as though a lamp in the night had shone. Pure white teeth flashed as he spoke.

Although he had trouble understanding the thick accent, he soon began to follow the words of the black man.

"That was a good thing you did, but he won't forget you. He will want to kill you and will do so if you are not ready for him."

"Perhaps," Padraig replied.

"They call me John Caesar." The dark man offered his hand.

"Padraig Gallagher is my name."

"You are not from here, Padraig?"

"No. I am here from my homeland, Ireland. And you?"

"I am from far away. I came here to find work and earn enough money to return to my island and sit in the sun and grow old," Caesar replied.

He told Padraig of how the English had followed other nationalities to profit from his island known as Madagascar. He told stories of slavery, and how his people were captured from their homeland, placed in shackles, and put on ships, after which they were sold in markets in strange and unfriendly parts of the world.

"We were taken many years ago and sold to work in chains for the white man. I managed to escape and worked my way here. I was caught in a town called Maidstone, and now I await what fate will deal to me here in this white man's hell."

Padraig smiled. He felt much in common with his new comrade. He told the story of how he had come to be in his predicament and of his hatred of the English. "From what you tell me, John, they seem to think they can steal from whoever and wherever they wish."

"Oh, indeed, but they don't have that all to themselves. There are others, the Spanish, and of course, the French; one day, maybe me." That big grin returned. "But for now, time to sleep. I will watch he doesn't come uninvited in the night." Caesar nodded in the direction of the man who nursed a huge cut over his eye.

*****

Padraig understood that he had to appear at the Justice Hall for his case to be heard.

John Caesar held out no hope for him. "There is no justice here! Not for us. When I appeared at the Old Bailey, I tried to explain, but I was laughed at. I am to be sent to a place for us convicts. I have no idea where and when. All I know is I'm to wait here until the day they call for me. All of us here in Newgate Prison are to go. But anywhere is better than this stinkin' hole."

Three uneventful days passed, and then on the fourth morning, Padraig was called for.

He was led in shackles with several others, and on a misty cold morning, they shuffled their way from Newgate Prison to the Sessions House.

"There she be!" a prisoner alongside Padraig said.

"The Old Bailey—naught in the way o' good luck for us in there, I tell ee. After this day, there be our new homes." He nodded his head down toward the Thames where the dreaded hulks lay in the cold and forbidding river.

Padraig and the others filed into the courthouse.

There was a general hustle of activity as clerks, lawyers, and court writers busied themselves prior to the judges' arrival.

While each of his fellow prisoners stood and faced the charge read out to them, Padraig watched and listened, fascinated.

And then it was his turn to be called.

He was told to stand at the bar and so shuffled forward to where he stood facing the witness box. He looked to the judges seated on the other side of the room. The light from a reflector gave a sad sight to those who were to try him.

Unshaven with unruly and unkempt hair, Padraig, in disheveled and torn clothing, listened to the charges leveled against him.

"He attacked us, nearly killed me 'e did. Tried to take me money from me!"

Padraig listened, attempting at times to interrupt and tell what really happened, but each time, one of the judges barked, "Silence! You will have your say."

Eventually, he was allowed to state his case. As he spoke to the jurors seated in stalls to his right, Padraig knew he had no chance. The contempt in their eyes was even more evident as his brogue told of his Irish heritage. Finally, it was over, and standing alone and in shock, he heard the worst.

"Padraig Gallagher, if indeed that is your name, you will be taken from here to await the time you are called to the prison ship *Sirius*, where you and the rest of those that are unwelcome here will be transported to the convict settlements in New Holland."

## Chapter 65

Lord Bolton was truly excited. As he listened to the plans being outlined for the transportation of the prisoners to the vast land and the islands that Cook had spoken so positively about, he wished he was years younger.

"What a challenge! You know, my friend, I feel somewhat envious of this Commander Philip."

His colleague, Lord Franshome laughed. "Send your son instead. I'm sure young Robert would cherish the chance."

Lord Bolton snorted and turned his attention to the speaker.

"Eleven ships will make up the fleet. Five ships will carry the convicts. There will be three store ships and accompanying these will be the two escort vessels HMS *Supply* and HMS *Sirius*. Commander Arthur Philip will head the fleet.

"Commander Philip is with us today. Let us welcome him and listen as he shares with us his thoughts as the time for departure draws near.

"My lords, I introduce to you Commander Philip."

The impeccably dressed man that stood before the lords was a person who inspired confidence. He spoke briefly about his time as a Merchant Navy apprentice before transferring to the Royal Navy where he was promoted to lieutenant in 1762.

After retiring at the end of the Seven Years War, he spent fifteen years as a farmer in Hampshire, but the call of the sea was too strong, and he served with the Portuguese navy an additional four years. He then returned to the English navy to become a post captain during the American War of Independence.

"And one must presume that with all that experience, I have been chosen with very fine precision to take good care of your more dubious folk that currently live at our Royal Majesty's disposal." A murmur of polite amusement rippled throughout the room.

"But on a more serious note, it is quite apparent that the situation with our prison systems can no longer be tolerated. You are more than aware that some of our older vessels are now almost bursting apart with the excess of those convicted for their crimes. These vessels—hulks, as it were—crowd the Thames at Woolwich, Portsmouth, and Plymouth.

"For that reason, Lord Sydney has forwarded to the Lord's Commission of the Treasury the king's instructions to formulate a new penal colony on the eastern coast of New Holland. It was at first suggested that we settle farther out into the Pacific in New Zealand, but as I understand it, the inhabitants of that land would gladly have welcomed our convicts as dinner."

Commander Philip paused to allow the laughter to die down.

"And so I will join Captain John Hunter on HMS *Sirius*, formally known to some of you as the *Berwick*. She has been completely refitted, and I shall take formal command of the fleet with my fellow officers, surgeons, and crew. We will depart with seven hundred and fifty of our less salubrious citizens and set sail for Botany Bay in the new year."

Commander Philip stood to the thunderous applause of the assembled lords.

As question after question was fired at Philip, Lord Bolton stated firmly to Lord Franshome, "Now more than ever, I believe that opportunity abounds in these new lands. It is all there for the taker, and no one can stop us. A few uncivilized natives in New Holland and these cannibal types in New Zealand—well, they can hardly pose a threat with our far superior forces now, can they?"

"You could always send Robert to tend to them!" Franshome said with a smile.

"Actually, that's not a bad suggestion," Lord Bolton mused. Then, with the crook of one eyebrow, he added, "I care not what devilment he may get up to. At least I wouldn't have my ear continually assaulted by his mother—as if it were my fault he turned out to be such a sorry excuse for a man."

*****

As the new year of 1787 began, so also did the serious preparations of the First Fleet.

HMS *Sirius,* the flagship, and HMS *Supply* would escort *Alexander, Scarborough, Prince of Wales, Lady Penrhyn, Charlotte,* and *Friendship,* the convict carriers.

Three supply ships, *Borderdale, Golden Grove,* and *Fishburn,* would transport the stores and all the necessary supplies for building the colony in New South Wales. The supply vessels were designed to carry horses, calves, sheep, geese, pigs, chickens, ducks, and rabbits—enough to enable all to live for two years before additional stores would be landed.

The ships would call at other ports on their voyage to bring onboard stores that were not available in England, along with fresh water, plants, and other provisions that would be needed to establish the colony.

As spring and better weather replaced the cold and wintry conditions in March, the strategy was to assemble on the Thames. The prisoners would be taken from the hulks and prisons and put onboard ship and from there would set sail for Portsmouth and then Plymouth. The First Fleet would then depart for the long journey south to the Cape and then across the Indian Ocean for the birth of the colony of New Holland.

## Chapter 66

John Caesar had forewarned Padraig of the dreaded hulks. He was already aware that fellow Irishmen, along with English convicts, had been transported to America to assist in the claim for American land. But when the War of American Independence ended in 1775, the practice of sending unwanted offenders to the colonies also came to an end.

The colonists were adamant that they wanted no part of the exportation of convicts from Britain to their country, and because there was nowhere for them to go, the build-up of convicted men, women, and children had reached unacceptable levels. Each county that had a prison soon had a major crisis of overcrowding.

The Home Office secretary, William Eden, needed to find accommodation for at least a thousand or more and ever increasing numbers of convicted criminals each year.

A decision was reached, very much against the wishes of the Liberal Parliamentarians, to utilize the now useless convict transportation vessels. They would be moored on the desolate and bleak Essex marshes along the northern shores of the Thames.

A controversial decision was made to entrust the overseeing of the Thames River Hulks to one Duncan Campbell.

As the number of hulks increased, so also did the grim tales of grief and despair as disease, death, and hopelessness descended on those who were forced into the appalling conditions onboard the vessels.

As Padraig stared in horror at the sight before him, he realized that Caesar's words had been thoroughly understated.

"Guests of Mr. Campbell, that's what we be. Hee, hee, guests on his pleasure barge!"

Padraig turned his back as the caustic comments were interrupted by a bout of coughing. A spray of spit and phlegm hit his shoulder.

The sight of the prison ship sitting in the Thames mist at Woolwich sent a shiver right through Padraig. The hulks were old and now disused war ships that had been turned into floating prisons.

Between coughing spells, he was told of the plight that awaited them all as they stepped onboard. "Aye, the devil take him! He what takes the king's shilling for keeping us on these floating hell vessels, a pox be upon him—our new landlord, Mr. Campbell."

As Padraig stepped onto the deck of *Sirius*, the sight was all that a vision of hell could conjure.

Each deck was divided longitudinally with crudely constructed rooms on either side, which were barely capable of housing four people in comfort. However, ten, and as many as twenty, hammocks gave ample proof to the terrible conditions he would now face.

As mid-afternoon came and the cold damp darkness began to fall around them, he and his fellow prisoners were ordered by the guards to find and secure a sleeping hammock. Gaslights and other lamps revealed the filth and squalor.

Squeaks and rustling were only a warning, and then the sight of enormous rats confirmed the worst. As a meager supper was served, Padraig dropped his hand, holding a piece of bread to his side, and then to howls of laughter, he felt the crust grabbed, and the victorious rodent ran only a few feet away, before sitting on two back feet and devouring the prize.

Padraig suddenly ached for the company of his new friend, John Caesar.

Although not a month had passed since leaving Donegal, the memories of Kathleen, his beloved twins, his parents and grandfather and his brother, Sean, all seemed as if they had been part of a dream. The pain in his head, the terrible longing in his heart—all that was real, but the memories of his life in Ireland were from another time. He now knew. He was overcome by the horrible dreadful realization that he would never see his beloved homeland again.

He would never again smell the fragrance of new cut hay. He would never again watch and listen to the diving and swooping joy of the welcome swallow in spring. He would never watch the summer sun sink over the Atlantic horizon ever again.

He would never see, hold, or love Kathleen and his children ever again.

But most of all, he knew he would never again be the Padraig Gallagher who left his Irish innocence behind him that night he escaped from Donegal.

He, like his beloved wife and children, were now lost in the ashes of his past.

The next day came, cold and miserable, and other days like it came and went. Food and eating became a necessary habit.

Sickness and disease was rife. Death was all around them.

Padraig would wake to the sound of a dying man, and scarcely before the death rattle indicated his last breaths, his fellow prisoners would turf him from his hammock and fight for any possessions he might have hidden beneath him.

The boredom of the following day was interrupted by the sight of the luckless soul being boated ashore and then wheelbarrowed to the dead house.

When conditions allowed, he and others were transported to do dredging work on the Thames. As gaol fever hit and took lives, more and more convicts replaced these.

But strangely, while others weakened, Padraig grew stronger. At first, his hatred for the accursed English accent was almost overpowering, but gradually he realized that these poor wretches were caught in the same situation he was in.

They all, in fact, shared the same hatred, but aimed it at the British aristocracy.

He had been sentenced for fourteen long years for a crime he had not committed. But others had been sentenced for seven years, and indeed, fourteen, for crimes as simple as taking a piece of bread or pie because they were starving.

And then came the final day, the day he would say farewell to the hell on the hulks.

On that day in late February, he and many others were transported from Woolwich and Gravesend to Portsmouth. There the ships lay, the ships that would take them into the unknown.

Strangely, Padraig was not unhappy. The life that lay in front of him could certainly not be as bad as the life he was about to leave.

There was, however, the memory of who had created this hell. That beastly man was still alive and well. Padraig knew that he could now never face Robert Bolton and exact retribution for all he had done to the Gallaghers and so many innocent others. However, deep inside him, some nagging doubts suggested otherwise.

## Chapter 67

MS *Alexander* was the largest of the convict vessels.

Barque-built in Hull in 1783, not quite 115 feet in length and with a breadth of thirty-one feet, without galleries or figurehead, but with a quarterdeck, she was a vessel that would normally be an inspiration to her master, Duncan Sinclair.

But carrying the greatest number of convicts, 190 no less, she would pose a continuing challenge.

She had been cleansed a number of times during her stay in port, while waiting for her human cargo of misery to be loaded, but despite the cleansing and smoking, she was still considered the unhealthiest.

Duncan Sinclair had been relieved to receive the order to strike off the irons a week out from Spithead, but despite the fact that the convicts were free to roam the decks at will, disease was still a major concern. Twenty-one had already died and twenty-one were seriously ill.

The vessel was infested with rats, cockroaches, and a variety of other disease-carrying vermin, and the atmosphere below both decks was foul with the stinking bilge water and ongoing collection of putrid human waste.

So, it was a relief to see the islands appear on the horizon ahead, and the almost overpowering desire to be ashore came over the crew, who were eager to taste whatever delights Teneriffe would offer.

For the convicts, however, this would not be the case.

"What say you, Black Caesar, and you there, Irish Padraig. Jump ship, shall we?"

The tall black man smiled down at the man. "Aye, Will Hatfield, and they . . ." he nodded to the soldiers on the ships close by, "would love nothing more than the excuse to stretch your neck on the yardarm."

Padraig smiled at his tall Caribbean friend and the other two men standing on the deck with him. "Indeed, and it would take only an hour or two to find us, and then what?" He ran his finger across his throat. "Time will offer the opportunity to flee, and when it comes, I will be long gone," Padraig said.

He was silent before adding quietly to himself, *And then I will find you, Robert Bolton. As God is my judge, oh yes I will find you.* Padraig Gallagher had decided many years before that he hated the English with just cause. During and since the unsuccessful attempt to overthrow the English theft of his homeland, little had been done to alter his stance.

But sharing the horrific conditions in prison and onboard the convict ship with Englishmen who had suffered also at the hands of their upper class aristocracy, he had come to the realization that apart from accent, there was little to separate them with the common atrocities that were now their lot.

While James Bradley had been incarcerated for simply stealing a single handkerchief, William Hatfield had been jailed for the more serious offence of armed robbery. And John Caesar for theft, necessary simply to live.

Certainly, conditions onboard the convict ship indicated that many had not left their history behind them, but Padraig still felt a growing bond between many of his new shipmates.

Each new hardship thrown at John Caesar only produced another burst of laughter and a, "Hey, mon, the sun is still shinin' somewhere!" It seemed nothing could diminish his spirit and good humour.

John Caesar was born in the West Indies, and as he grew older, he lived a life of slavery on the sugar plantations. He developed a huge muscular body, and while some dismissed him as a common black oaf, others such as Padraig recognised a deep intellect, which he used to great effect when required.

Possessing a huge appetite, it sometimes required guile to fill his muscular frame, and he accomplished much through his great sense of humour and a sneaky sense of craftiness, both of which were a constant source of amusement.

With absolutely no fear of death, he had escaped slavery and other dangerous circumstances on his travels and had eventually arrived in London where he had been arrested for the theft of two hundred and forty shillings. In due course, he was sentenced to be transported to the new colonies to serve seven years.

His lack of fear of dying or the threat of the hangman's noose continually gave him the chance to joke about creating a laugh at the executioner's expense should those circumstances prevail.

Gradually, the fleet drew closer to the port of Teneriffe, and in due course, all were at anchor. Those who were free to go ashore did so and were greeted heartily by the town officials.

As the working seamen who were allowed to go ashore returned, much hilarity and envy ensued as the news of the travel from England to the Canaries was relayed to the prisoners.

"'Ere, you lot, 'tis a great shame we are to be looking after your miserable hides. Now on the *Friendship*, the ladies are servicin' the crew right proper, they are!"

While most of the male prisoners were relatively well behaved, the same could not be said of their female counterparts on the other vessels.

The fear of flogging or other punishments could not deter the women from finding their way into the bulkheads to be with the mariners or soldiers, and certainly, no refusals were offered in return.

Thieving and quarreling were most prevalent among the womenfolk, and consistent abuse between them and the officers and surgeons only encouraged journeying to the crews' quarters.

"Bitches is what they are; these damned troublesome whores should not be allowed on the ships, should they?"

"No, damn bloody right, they shouldn't be. They should all be put on 'ere wiv us, they should, and get rid of this scurvy lot!" This coarse reply was met with howls of crude laughter.

Eventually, after loading fresh provisions, which were also given to the prisoners, the fleet weighed anchor to continue on to Rio de Janeiro via the Cape Verde Islands. But indifferent weather and heavy swells compelled Commander Phillip to alter his plan to pick up additional supplies at Port Praya.

Instead, as the northeast trade wind was lost, and then heavy rain, thunder, and lightning produced variable winds, Phillip was compelled to push eastward.

However, some days later, the fleet picked up the southeast trade wind and was able to get to the westward side with ease. The equator was crossed, and much better advancement was made after that. Certainly, the better progress allowed the rations that been limited to then be increased.

The mood was even jolly as King Neptune received his traditional recognition as the fleet crossed the equator, so much so that due to the good humour, the crew of the *Lady Penryhn* was so engrossed with the tribute to Neptune that they nearly collided with the *Charlotte*.

Despite the heat and rain of the tropics, the members of

the fleet were remarkably healthy, despite all the negative forecasting, although five men and one woman had died since leaving Teneriffe. This brought the total dead since leaving England to twenty-nine male and three female prisoners, a small number considering the number of sick seamen, mariners, and convicts.

With Phillip's order to acquire fresh provisions, the health of all was continually improving.

Overall, the weather had not been too bad; some said it was extremely favourable, and the fleet had been able to keep close company with the exception of the *Lady Penrhyn*, which had proved not to be the best sailing vessel and at times languished some miles astern. This could have been due to the problems caused by the prisoners to Captain Sever and his officers.

But again, due in main to the unique skills of Commander Phillip, the overall progress was steady. And of course, the deeply laden transports and store ships were always of utmost consideration, and no matter what state the weather or conditions, the fleet ships stayed in communication with each other. It was noted that on one day an excellent run was recorded. No less than one hundred and seventy miles had been covered from noon that day until noon the next.

## Chapter 68

"Move! Come on, you lot. Look lively!"

The orders to climb onboard the ship were met with grumbles and coarse comments.

When Padraig finally reached the deck, he paused and looked around him. It seemed to him that Portsmouth harbour was full of vessels of all shapes and sizes. He was pushed and shoved with others until they were all standing and awaiting further instructions.

Eventually they were led to the decks that would be their living quarters. Strong hatch bars were fitted out between the decks, with bulkheads to separate the convicts from the crew.

Padraig was most surprised and pleased to find his new home to be relatively clean and tidy.

"What about this then, mate? This a right little change for the better."

Padraig smiled and nodded in agreement. "To be sure!"

General conversation broke out all around as the convicts began to settle down.

Sometime later, the murmurs of conversation increased with considerable enthusiasm as food was brought 'round.

"Beef! Here lads, we must be getting the Old Man's dinner."

Padraig could hardly believe it. He could not recall when he had eaten so well since leaving Ireland. "Should that be the case,

# SAVAGE Sympathy

then thanks be to the captain," he replied between mouthfuls.

That night there was none of the usual dissension among the men. The huge change from the horrific hulks to the new prison ship and a full belly of food had done wonders for the morale of the convicts, and all slept soundly.

The following morning, the master of the vessel, addressed the assembled convicts. "Until we set sail, you will obey all the following instructions.

"Any attempt to disobey or to contest my command or to escape will result in the instant death of any who are foolish enough to do so.

"I demand that the safety of my officers and the soldiers appointed to guard you is to be of constant concern, and any attempt to disobey any order from them, or any display of insubordination of any kind will result in immediate execution.

"You will be treated well otherwise. Along with your normal rations, you will be allocated a daily quantity of beer. And finally, so long as all my orders are obeyed without any exceptions, you will be treated fairly. If just one of you causes any problems, however, that will quickly change. Good day to you all."

"Well, Irishman, what do you think of all that?"

Padraig turned as he heard the familiar accent. "John Caesar! The day is getting better by the moment. Dare I say, it is good to see you again."

"It is certainly good to see you again, my friend," the tall dark-skinned man replied. "And I am happy to add that I will be most pleased to bid farewell to that." He nodded toward the shore. "Who knows what this new land will offer, but it is certain to be better than where we have just been."

"For you, maybe," said Padraig. "But just out from here and taking a starboard coarse is where I belong—bonny Ireland. Who knows if I will ever see those shores again?"

John Caesar placed his hand on Padraig Gallagher's shoulder. "I know how you feel. Remember, I was stolen from my home, also. Maybe one day we will return. The white man's chains will not hold me down forever. I will claim my freedom, as you will fight for yours. That, my friend, is my promise to you."

Padraig looked into the eyes of his new companion. "Thank you, John Caesar. Thank you."

★★★★★

During the following weeks, Padraig, John Caesar, and the other convicts watched fascinated as the stores for the journey were loaded onto the store ships and the growing fleet.

Wagons were loaded with tents, wheelbarrows, furniture, crockery, and cooking equipment. Panes of glass, tools, agricultural implements, and seeds were also included along with spirits, medical supplies, bandages, and surgical instruments. Bricks, as well as other construction materials and nails, along with a prefabricated house for the governor, went into the holds.

Handcuffs and chains and leg irons, reminders of their status, did not go unheeded.

And then, closer to the fleet weighing anchor, the livestock were led onboard. Horses, cattle, pigs, sheep, goats, and all manner of poultry were housed below with enough fodder for all.

As more and more convicts were brought onto the prison ships, disease became prevalent, with some of the marine guards dying from contact with those prisoners.

But closer to the time of departure, the chief surgeon, John White, considered by many to be a highly professional and enlightened medical officer, demanded more appropriate clothing for the prisoners and their quarters to be thoroughly cleaned and disinfected.

They were also allowed more time on deck for fresh air

and exercise.

From March through early May of 1787, the preparations for the expedition ran smoothly. And on the morning of the thirteenth day of May, the commanding officer of the *Sirius* gave the signal to weigh anchor. With the weather fine and a mild, favourable easterly breeze blowing, the fleet under full sail proceeded through the Needles.

The fleet of eleven plus the frigate *Hyena* headed westward.

His Majesty's ships, *Sirius* and *Supply,* had enough stores and provisions onboard to last for two years at the new settlements.

The six transport vessels *Alexander*, *Charlotte*, *Friendship*, *Lady Penrhyn*, *Prince of Wales*, and *Scarborough* were now home to the convicts and troops.

Onboard the transports *Borderdale*, *Fishburn*, and *Golden Grove* were embarked 4 captains, twelve subalterns, 24 sergeants and corporals, 8 drummers, and 160 private marines.

Also onboard *Sirius* were the major commandant and staff. Of the overall staff of 212, only 2 were not volunteers.

The total number of convicts numbered 565 men, 192 women, and 18 children, the major part of whom were mechanics and husbandmen, purposely selected by the government for the settlement of the land that lay many weeks' sailing ahead.

By mid-morning, the fleet had passed the Isle of Wight, but to Padraig, in the confinement of the fetters, it was just one more piece of land that would now be only a memory. A terrible pain came over him as the recollection of the events that had created this nightmare came over him.

His mother, father, and grandfather slayed by Bolton, his beloved wife and twin children taken from him, and with the probable death of his brother, also at the hands of Bolton and his murderous gang of cutthroats, the unbearable anguish was all too much for him. His head dropped, and with his heart breaking, he sobbed uncontrollably.

His new shipmates could only wonder at the cause of such grief. Some felt the pangs of severance from their land of birth, while in large part, most were happy to be free of the hardships now behind them. Certainly, the women prisoners were in relatively high spirits.

Later that day, approaching evening, the *Hyena* turned and headed back to England.

As the days progressed, orders came from the *Sirius* to release all from the fetters. This decision was due to the now favourable dispositions among all, convicts and crewmen alike, although the threat of ironing, particularly to the men, was a constant reminder not to squander this newfound freedom to roam about.

The Madeiras were passed, and the fleet then headed for Teneriffe.

## Chapter 69

On the morning of November 11, the fleet prepared to depart Table Bay, but it was not until November 13 that the weather cleared enough to enable the expedition to continue on its way.

For nearly a week, southerlies and sou'easterlies drove the fleet westward.

It was Commander Phillip's intention to go ahead of the fleet to prepare for the landing, but on account of the weather, he was unable to transfer to the *Supply*.

However, on November 25, with more favourable weather conditions, Phillip transferred to the supply vessel, and with the *Alexander*, the *Friendship*, and the *Scarborough* in close company, the four ships were soon making excellent progress.

But by the following day, the *Supply* was a long way ahead of the three transport vessels, with the *Sirius* and the rest of the fleet even farther back.

The situation worsened with strong gales, heavy seas, and bitterly cold conditions below deck, so cold that even those prisoners that had become accustomed to sea travel become very seasick. With only regulation dress and a single blanket to cover them, all the prisoners were freezing cold all the time.

The convict women were terrified of the storms, and most were on their knees praying, but an hour after the weather had abated, they were back to uttering the most horrid oaths and imprecations.

The male prisoners were so weakened that the constant petty thievery, quarrelling, and fighting among them was halted.

The mortality rate of the livestock in each of the ships was also very high. The heavy weather and the failure of fodder supply took a huge toll on the sheep.

There was damage to the vessels with the main topsail of the *Prince of Wales* being split and major damage to her top staysail. The *Golden Grove* also split her topsails.

On January 5, the coast of Van Diemen's Land was sighted. A gale was blowing, and the three transporters were constantly losing sail as they wallowed in heavy seas. The *Sirius* and the main body of the fleet were following a day's sail behind.

Against all the odds and the appalling conditions, the *Supply* reached Botany Bay on January 18, 1788. The three fastest transports arrived on January 19, and the slower ships, including the *Sirius*, arrived the following day.

Arguably, forever to be known as the greatest of all sea voyages, these eleven vessels, carrying close to fourteen thousand people, stores, and livestock that had traveled for 252 days over a distance of fifteen thousand miles without losing one vessel arrived in Botany Bay all within forty-eight hours of each other.

The thirty-six-week journey from Portsmouth was surely a most arduous undertaking. Of the 212 marines, only one had died. Of the 775 convicts, 24 were buried at sea—all a testimony indeed to the outstanding skills of Commander Phillip.

*****

"Just look at yon shore, Padraig. What land is that that awaits us?" asked John Caesar of his friend.

"A land that gives somewhat more warmth than that of the days behind us," Padraig said with more hope than he had felt in a long time.

They stared in disbelief at the sight before them. Paperbark scrub and greenish-gray eucalyptus stretched along the shoreline. A glare of almost blinding light, contrasting with the gloom of belowdecks, insisted they shielded their eyes as they watched boats being launched to go ashore to search for water.

"Where is the lush green grass that Cook spoke about?" one of the officers asked of a fellow officer.

"The good captain also told of deep black soils. Where these may be is of conjecture. I suspect he never landed here, although, his log books tell otherwise," the officer stated.

Later that day, they could see figures moving along the shoreline and assembling on the rocky spits and the white sand beaches.

"Hey, Caesar, look yonder on shore. They be relatives of yours?"

The prisoners watched as black figures carrying what appeared to be spears stood watching the strange sights before them.

"Where's their bleedin' clobber, then? Buggers are stark naked!"

"That they be," John Caesar said with a chuckle, "but I know of no people where I am from who look like these."

As the scarlet tunics of the first landing parties moved toward the aboriginals, one of them brandished a spear and cried out, "Warra warra!"

Unbeknown to Captain John Hunter, head of the landing party, those first words spoken by the indigenous leader were, "Go away! Go away!"

The intruders did not go away. Trampling the scrub and pushing through bushes and entangling themselves in their search for water only served to infuriate the warriors.

One tribesman threw a spear, but it deliberately made a wide arc, almost as a warning. This was followed by other spears, which prompted a reply of a blast from the rifle of one of the marines.

The tribesmen ran beyond the beach and disappeared into the jungle-like vegetation.

Caesar gave a cynical grin and commented to Padraig, "I warrant two sovereigns they will break out the beads, buttons, and ribbons, and that mob of savages will be swarming all over us by sunset."

"Perhaps, but where will you find the two sovereigns if you are wrong!" his Irish friend replied.

And later in the day, to confirm Caesar's prediction, the islanders indeed accepted the gifts handed out by Phillip and the crewmen and were soon swarming around the boats with arms and hands extended to grab whatever they could.

At first, from the European perspective, the complete nakedness of the natives created the most interest, obviously as far as the women prisoners were concerned, with many a lewd comment or agitated pointing to the item of interest.

By contrast, there was much amusement among the islanders concerning these bizarre newcomers; whenever able, they would touch or pull at the white visitors' clothing. There were grunts of laughter and looks of amazement whenever a hat was taken from the head of one of the men.

Two of the islanders were given a taste of wine, which they promptly spat out.

Padraig, with his ability of being able to understand or follow languages and dialects, took note of the names the black natives gave to the objects handed to them.

The breeches of the marines created perhaps the most intrigue, and an order was given to a very embarrassed marine to expose all. The islanders, or aboriginals, as they were later named, gave great shouts of admiration as the first white cock was shown to the new land.

As the suspicions of the natives diminished, several women and girls appeared on the beaches in full sight of the visitors. Many had infants sitting on their shoulders, and like the menfolk, they were completely naked.

More and more boats were lowered as the crewmen and mariners went ashore. However, the convicts still remained under constraint on the ships.

To the relief of Phillip, there were no further hints of violence toward his men or from his men to the aboriginals, and the development of mutual acceptance began.

In his first statement as governor of the colony, Phillip made it clear that his order not to molest or harm the natives was to be adhered to strictly.

It was observed, however, that many of the English turned their noses up at the living conditions of the blacks and were openly contemptuous of the dirty wigwams they slept in and their overpowering fishy smells.

But as further inspection revealed that Botany Bay gave no hint of water or sustenance of any kind, the order to lift anchor and locate more bountiful land was given.

Governor Phillip decided to take selected crewmembers and proceed to Port Jackson some miles north. Captain Cook, in an earlier voyage, had indicated on his maps that good shelter could be found there, as well as fresh drinking water.

And certainly this was confirmed, so Phillip then gave the order to return to Botany Bay to bring the fleet to the more favourable harbour to set up the landing of the fleet.

This order had also inspired urgency as two large vessels of European appearance had been spotted many miles out to sea.

The possibility of them being Dutch men o' war or unfriendly French who could make a claim on the new harbour created major anxiety among the officers, who feared that the convicts would take advantage of any opportunity to escape.

The two ships were French. The *Boussole* and the *Astrolabe* under the leadership of Commander Jean-Francois de la Perrouse had been sent by the king of France to explore the Pacific, and the French were most amazed to find that the English already had landed.

The English were most perplexed to find the French in such close proximity.

As the French dropped anchor at the mouth of Botany Bay, the fleet weighed and only salutations were passed as Governor Phillip gave the order to move to Port Jackson.

But to the amusement of the French, all did not run smoothly for the English.

The *Prince of Wales* was rammed by *Friendship,* causing the former to lose her jib boom. The *Charlotte* almost hit the rocks, and in correcting course, she cannoned into *Friendship. Lady Penrhyn* only just avoided colliding into her, also.

By late afternoon and in total contrast to the earlier excellent nautical achievements, the whole fleet had cleared Botany Bay and steered course north.

By evening, the setting sun was witness to the First Fleet's arrival to Port Jackson. The settlement of New South Wales would begin now in earnest.

## Chapter 70

Father Sullivan watched Hugo Cohen attempt to sit at the table unaided. He knew that his friend would not appreciate his help. Finally, Hugo smiled at the priest.

"So, now then, let's see what the Catholics can do to the Jews this evening!"

Father Sullivan smiled and began to open the pages and read from the scriptures.

Much had happened in the village of Bandara since that time some months back. They had brought Hugo Cohen back from the coast. Although Jewish, the priest had still given Cohen the last blessings normally reserved for Catholics only. He had looked down at the gray body and feared the worst; it was almost totally drained of blood from the wounds inflicted by Thomas Bolton.

Contrary to the instructions from Rome, he felt that loyalty to his friend overruled all else, and besides, maybe it was a miracle that God's blessing had returned life to Cohen.

The Donegal constabulary had scoured Bandara and all the northern coastal regions around Killybegs and down to Sligo. They had traveled deep inland and still could not locate the rebels, Padraig and brother, Sean Gallagher.

They had searched the corpses down on the Atlantic sands, and none was recognizable as Sean Gallagher or the rebel leader Cohen. Cohen, they were told, had been swept out to sea with

Sean Gallagher, after being blown to pieces by the guns of Bolton and his men.

Nothing had been seen or heard of Padraig Gallagher since his mysterious escape from Donegal jail and the murder of Judge Squires. There were rumours that he had fled to England to find the killer of his family and babies, but this was pure speculation.

Lord Bolton was still very much alive, as was his son, Thomas Bolton. The landlord that had replaced the younger Bolton, while considerably fairer than his predecessor, had imparted the news to the family now residing in Suffolk. It was rumoured that Thomas Bolton had sailed to find fortunes in the lands being discovered west of New York in the new American territories.

The local Irish farming families were now very quiet and somehow finding monies to pay the rents, and there was no more talk of rebellious behaviour or of retaliation for the deaths of their sons by English hands.

Father Sullivan had been torn apart by the murders of his friends and parishioners, and had it not been for the spirit of Hugo Cohen, the good father quite easily could have lost his faith.

He was shaking his head in disbelief at the strength of his friend Cohen, who was teasing him.

"Come on, priest, Jesus was a Jew. How could he possibly have formed the Catholic Church and turned his back on tradition and family?"

"If you are not careful, blasphemer, I will turn you over to the constables," Father Sullivan smiled. "And besides, it is us Catholics who are hiding you—remember that!"

"Oh yes, oh yes! But one day I will walk again, upright and strong! And then you had best take care with your cruel banter."

Both nodded, both knowing that this would never be possible. Cohen could possibly walk again, but only with the aid of walking sticks.

"But away with that, I want your opinion on the Vatican's rigid stance on the domination of women by their husbands and fathers."

The two friends were still arguing, both fortified by sips of locally brewed poteen.

Neither heard nor saw the stealthy approach of the tall red-haired man until disturbed by a quiet tapping at the door.

"What's that?" Hugo asked. "I wonder who that could be at this time of night. Surely not trouble."

"Quiet," warned the priest in a subdued voice. "Let me go check."

Hugo heard the front door open and then a gasp.

"Sean, my good God, come in lad. You must be freezing. Come in by the fire. Hugo, look who is here! By the grace of God, it's Sean Gallagher. Come in lad. Come quick before someone sees you."

Sean stood by the fire warming himself. "Ah, now, that's better. And I can say and surely, it's bitter out there!"

"Sean, Sean, it's so good to see you. Where have you been? Quick, man, tell us the news. Is it good or bad?" Hugo could hardly contain his excitement.

"But first, look at you!" Sean smiled at the Frenchman. "I'd best take care and be polite to you, or perhaps it's the blackthorn stick you'll be hitting me with."

"Not so likely now," came the reply. "Not in this pitiful state I am in."

"Hugo Cohen, in a day, or maybe a month or two, you will be back fighting fitter than ever." Sean laughed good-naturedly, though he knew this could never be. "Now don't tell me I have come all this way and still not a drink in my hand."

Father Sullivan stood quickly. "Oh, in the name of God! Where are my manners? It is such a surprise to see you!" He rushed out and returned with a glass. "A brandy for you and the potatoes for us." He laughed, as they raised their glasses and drank.

"Ah, now that's grand." Sean sighed, as he drained his glass. "And talking of the potatoes, may I have a glass of the good stuff. There is not a drop of poteen to be had in that hellhole over the Irish Sea."

"Please lad, please tell us," Father Sullivan eagerly enquired. "Have you news of your brother? And what of that devil himself, Bolton? Did you find out anything?"

Sean Gallagher told them of the happenings since the torching of the home of Judge Squires.

"I traveled to London and from there to Sudbury in Suffolk. The good judge provided me with the purse for my traveling funds." This he stated with a conspiratorial nod to both men who chuckled. "That is, before he departed this world."

"Yes!" Cohen agreed. "The flames you left him in were just the start of the flames he now finds himself in!"

"The information the judge gave me confirmed Padraig had left to find Bolton in England. But sadly, as you no doubt know, London is not small. I spoke to the thieves and robbers who roam those streets, but it was some time before I discovered someone who could help me.

"I found the inn he had been staying at, and the innkeeper informed me that to the best of his knowledge, Padraig had been imprisoned."

"For what crime?" Hugo almost shouted. "Hopefully the dispatching to hell of Bolton himself."

"Sadly, not so, and there's worse news to come."

Sean went on, and in as much detail as he could, he told of how he had paid a clerk of the courts to give him the information he required. He learned that Padraig was jailed on one of the prison hulks and transported to a foreign land.

"As there was little I could do, I then traveled up to

Suffolk. Posing as a farmhand, searching for work, I found the home of Lord Bolton in Sudbury. There, to my amazement, I saw both Lord Bolton and his wife, Lady Constance, and who else but . . ."

He looked at both men and waited for them to guess.

"The scoundrel Thomas Bolton and you killed him!"

"No, no, not so. But I did see the twins."

"The twins?" both men said simultaneously. "Surely not!"

"Yes, the children of Padraig and Kathleen. The lord and lady were in their carriage outside the Sudbury market, and there with them both were the little ones."

"What did you do? Did you bring them back with you?"

"No," Sean replied. "In truth, I never would have made it back here without being arrested myself. I am certain they are safe; the Lady Constance seemed very protective of them, and my task was to obtain the information I needed to find my brother and then reunite him and his children."

"Yes," mused Cohen. "You were right to do this. Your actions were correct, but what of now? Where do we go from here?"

"This is my plan." Sean then went on to explain that, as a seaman himself, he could quite easily obtain work as a crewman on any one of a hundred or more vessels plying the seas. "But to find a ship going to where Padraig is now? That is not so easy."

He explained that to the best of his knowledge, there were many more convict ships headed to Van Diemens Land, as well as the huge continent. But none were leaving in the foreseeable future.

He had discovered that whalers were operating from America around another new land off to the east of the prison colonies, a strange land inhabited by savages, possibly cannibals, and maybe he could find transport from there to the colonies where he could find and rescue his brother.

"I have to get to the Pacific. Once there I will find Padraig.

Oh yes, in God's name and with his help, I will find him. And then Bolton. Together we will find Thomas Bolton, and as sure as God is my judge, Padraig will finally settle matters."

The three men sat and talked until the dawn slowly announced a new day.

"And now it time for you to get some rest," Father Sullivan concluded. "I will prepare a bed for you, and when you awake, we can plan our next move."

★★★★★

Maloney's Tavern was quiet. A couple of the local farmers were enjoying a mid-afternoon ale as Sean walked in. All heads turned as the door opened.

"Sean Gallagher, surely to God, and it's you!"

Paddy the barman looked stunned. "Sean! The bastards are after you. What are you doing here?"

The questions fairly flew.

"I know, I am aware of all that," Sean replied. "But to be sure, if it's a drink I'm after, then surely you can pour me one!"

"Oh, indeed, indeed, and it will be on me, so put that money away. We all thought you were over there." The barkeep nodded his head, as if pointing to England. "When did you get back? And you know they are looking for you. That is, those that don't believe you drowned. And a bloody good job you did on the judge and all!"

Sean watched as his ale was being poured and listened to the excited barrage of questions. Finally, he tipped back a hearty swallow and began to talk. He told of his visit to his old home, and how he sat and imagined the atrocities committed on his parents and grandfather. He then walked to the home of his brother and sister-in-law.

"I cannot tell you how it was," Sean began. "I simply cannot hold any feelings other than hatred for those that did what they did to Kathleen and my family."

"But of now? Where will you go? You know you are safe here, but there are informers."

"I know. But they will not get me."

He gave little information of his plans other than to say, "I am going to find my brother. Wherever he may be, I WILL find him. And then we will return to destroy all those who did this to us."

The look in Sean Gallagher's eyes brought an involuntary shudder to the bartender. "Indeed, Sean, indeed."

"All over Ireland there are those who will not stand for this occupation of our land," said Sean. "Since the time of Henry the King and his bitch daughter, Elizabeth, who both claimed Ireland as theirs, and then the Dutchman, William of Orange, King Billy himself, who also claimed our land as his—all over our country, Irishmen are now coming forward to follow our actions here. They will make a stand, and one day—maybe not tomorrow, maybe not even this year or indeed the next—we will send the English back to their stinkin' country, or they will die!" Sean drained his mug and set it down on the bar.

"Another one, Sean? Have another. It's on us."

"No, my friends, but thank you. Thank you with all my heart and soul. I will treasure that last one with you. I will remember until one day I return, and then we will drink in triumph, my brother Padraig and I." Sean nodded to each and walked to the door.

There was silence in the bar until finally one of the farmers spoke. "He will never return. We will never see him or Padraig again."

## Chapter 71

"Right, lads. This is our chance to scarper. I say we clear out from 'ere and make our way back to the Frenchies! What say ee all?"

James Bradley spoke to some of the convicts seated close to him. They included John Caesar and Padraig Gallagher. Others were William Hatfield and fellow convicts from the *Alexander*.

"The desire to be long gone from here is strong, I agree, James. But the French! Surely they will only return us back to them." Padraig nodded to the armed soldiers supervising the erection of tents and living quarters.

"To Hades with them, Irishman. I'm gone for dear life either with the French or finding my way miles from here and in the hope of searching for another vessel." John Caesar's words were cut short as a bellow from one of the soldiers disturbed their conversation.

"'Ere, you scurvy bunch of scum rats! Get your shoulders round these 'ere crates and do some work, or it's the kiss of this you'll be tastin'!" He waved a rod of eucalyptus in his hand and pointed in the direction of cargo that had been landed.

The fleet lay at anchor in a sheltered bay close to a stream from which clean running water flowed. Eucalyptus trees grew thickly along the rocky shores, while some actually grew from cracks in the rocks.

Governor Phillip had marveled at this, amazed that with such small amounts of soil these plants could flourish.

But all this was lost on the work gangs goaded into moving the cargo from ships to positions on shore. Convicts cursed with great vigor as they stumbled and beat down fernery and other foliage as gradually the settlement began to take shape.

Certainly, there were runaways, and Padraig's warnings to his convict friends were proven correct as they were caught by the French themselves and sent back to a fearful flogging.

Steadily, the camp progressed from disarray into a semblance of order.

The blacksmith's forge was set up, while elsewhere, parties of convicts dragged loads of foundation stones, and others felled timber and hauled the logs to be cut into planks for building purposes. Some of these trees were giant red gums with trunk girths of twenty feet and more. The root systems also had to be dug out from the stony soils, all which took a toll on the convicts who had lost muscle and their usual fitness while at sea.

The female convicts were finally allowed ashore. They had been held on the ships until decent living quarters had been established for them.

As the women were ferried from ship to shore, the males noticed that those who had reasonable or better clothing had dressed for the occasion.

"Just look at the sight of 'em, lads; a sight for my eyes as I have not seen before!"

"Aye, and that and more trouble if you look over there." Padraig pointed to the gathering thunderheads.

"I doubt if those tents will be able to stand up to the storm that will hit tonight, if I'm not mistaken."

"And if it does, if the storm does hit?"

"Then those who have not tasted the pleasure of a woman

for ages will find a way this night," Padraig said with a conspiratorial grin.

The impending stormy weather lit the lustful desires of not only the convicts, but also the crewmen and marines. As the day faded into early darkness, many of the sailors took advantage of the liquor and the opportunity. While the convicts eyed the quarters of the female convicts, so also did the sailors.

Later that night the weather did just as Padraig predicted, and as the rains lashed down, the camp quickly became a bog. The wind howled and the rain poured down. The thunder and lightning produced a display that differed dramatically from anything the English convicts had ever witnessed.

While the majority of the tents were flattened like corn in the heavy downpour, Padraig had secured his and the tents of fellow convicts with pieces of timber and extra roping. He and John Caesar were checking the ropes when, above the noise of the storm, he thought he heard the sounds of distress.

"Did you hear that?" he asked of his friend.

"It came from over there, the women's quarters."

"Damn them to hell! Those scum are after them. Come, John Caesar!"

Mary Watkins screamed as the tent around her collapsed. Elizabeth Dudgens tried to lift the canvas to free them and two other female convicts.

As they released themselves and attempted to find cover, Mary felt cold hands on her body, and before she could defend herself, she was hit around the head and dragged through the mud.

Her friend, Elizabeth, while attempting to save her, was also hit from behind.

Between them, six male convicts dragged the struggling women from the campsite farther back to where the tree felling had taken place. Their cries for help largely went unheeded, and as they were flung to the earth, the convicts towered over them. Their clothing was ripped from them.

"Hold 'er down, me 'earties. Keep them legs apart, let 'er feel the throbbin' of old John 'ere !"

"Release her, Richardson!"

Two of the convicts turned as Padraig crashed a length of hardwood full into the face of one and then the other. A third looked up and took the brunt of the end of the timber in his mouth, smashing teeth and nose, spraying blood and gore before falling to the ground.

John Caesar bashed another, and then in panic, the remaining two ran.

Neither John nor Padraig felt the blows that felled them.

Sometime later, Padraig stirred to find he was in irons. John Caesar lay in irons next to him, as did the injured convicts.

With aching head, he was told somewhat begrudgingly that the soldiers had come at them with clubs and batons.

Meanwhile, chaos reigned in other parts of the settlement. Drunken sailors joined the search for scattering females, many of whom were quite happy to be part of the debauchery. Rutting couples were disturbed by others quarreling or physically fighting to be next.

But for John Caesar and Padraig, little of this was obvious to them. They lay in the mud with the rain pouring over them until dawn. As the camp came to order and calm was restored, soldiers approached them.

"Right, you lot, move it!"

They were pulled roughly to their feet and dragged to a standing marquee where three men sat a table.

"Your names?"

Each replied.

"I will not have this behaviour from you or any other,"

Phillip stated to the six men.

"No woman, whatever her past, deserves what you intended for them. I warned you that this conduct would not be tolerated. You will each be flogged as a lesson to you and all who flout my orders."

"But, sir, it weren't us, me and Padraig," John Caesar protested, nodding to the other convicts next to them. "We were trying to save the women from them!"

"Silence!" roared one of the officers.

"What else can we expect from the wretched likes of you, a black and him Irish and all. We have enough problems with our own rogues and vagabonds without you dregs coming to our shore to commit more felony."

"Correct!" the third officer added. "If I had my way, I would hang the lot of you."

"No more, John," Padraig sighed. "Nothing you say will change their minds."

Phillip then called the remainder of the camp to a meeting. Standing with his senior colonial officers, clergymen, and surgeons, he faced the assembled convicts, men and women, who were herded into a ring and ordered to squat. The soldiers stood behind all watching carefully.

The royal instructions were read confirming Phillip as governor. This gave him power to appoint officers, convene criminal and civil court, and emancipate prisoners. Among other powers, he could raise armies, execute martial law, and build the boroughs, towns, and fortifications as he saw fit.

Phillip then turned his attention to the convicts. He stated that any repeat of the behaviour of the previous night would result in the prisoners being shot. Those convicted of theft of livestock and chickens would be hanged, without exception of gender.

Those that did not work would not eat.

Total discipline would determine that all would be involved in the hoeing of gardens, clearing of brush, or building the houses of the officers first and then the marines and finally premises for themselves.

The six men found guilty of the offences the night before were then led out into the mid-morning sunlight.

Six timber T-shaped frames had been erected and stood waiting for them to which each had his hands tied.

"Commence!"

Padraig cried out involuntarily as the first of the lashes of the cat o' nine tails struck his naked back. Fourteen more followed, causing blood to flow. But as the pain of each lash increased, Padraig's determination to remain silent grew in intensity, as did his hatred of the English authority and their lack of compassion and ability to show true justice.

Through the mist of clouded anguish, he thought he saw the image of his beloved Kathleen. "Stay strong, my beloved! Stay strong!" Padraig thought he heard her whisper as he fell into an unconscious state. He didn't feel his bonds being cut or hear the order to cut him down. Only darkness, merciful darkness, surrounded him.

The tents and marquees that had been set up for the troops and the officers now stood strong and erect, proud almost, now that all that the tempest had thrown at them had abated.

And throughout, Governor Phillip had placed those chosen to head each section with responsibility who would respond accordingly. Thus, confusion gave way to orderliness.

The convicts, after seeing the result of any disorder, had fallen into line very quickly, and early Sydney began to take shape.

Phillip had decided to name the port after his friend, Lord Sydney, and he was most satisfied with the progress of the colony since leaving the ships. Those back in England would also be happy that the plan was falling shape.

Administrative meetings continuously monitored improvements. It was at one of those meetings that the group of women convicts came to discuss an important matter with Governor Phillip.

"Convicts Watkins and Dudgens, what brings you to us this morn?" Phillip addressed the women.

"Governor, your honour . . ." Mary Watkins began.

Governor Phillip smiled.

"You punished the wrong men! Both the Irish man and the black man were helpin' us. It were them other bastards what were about doin' us."

"What do you mean?" Phillip enquired.

"It were those Richardsons what done it. Well, they would 'ave 'ad their way 'ad it not been for those other two," Elizabeth Dudgen confirmed.

"The bleedin' cowards run for it!"

Phillip and his officers listened as the story was told. These women were known to be tough, but it was also understood that they stood firm when they felt they were in the right.

"Bring Caesar and Gallagher to me," Phillip ordered.

Sometime later, both men were brought into the marquee. Both were still in considerable discomfort, and the scars were very apparent under the scanty upper garments they wore.

"Gor blimey! Look at that, what you did!" exclaimed Mary.

"You poor blighters," Elizabeth added.

"What do you have to say for yourselves?" enquired Governor Phillip, as the women related their tale again.

Padraig stared at the English officers seated before him. "What you did has been done. The women are safe, as safe as this miserable place will allow. I have nothing more to say."

"No, no, Irishman!" Mary urged. "Tell 'em what happened.

Tell how you saved the women."

While waving his hands, John Caesar excitedly told of how he and Padraig had intervened before being apprehended.

"Is this so?" Phillip asked.

Padraig simply shrugged.

"It is my intention to be fair. It would appear that more investigation should have taken place before punishment was given. I can only apologize for this wrongdoing.

"Bring those to me who were responsible for this error and also, " He paused, then thundered, "And I want to talk to these Richardsons and any other convicts involved. And you ladies can identify them for me."

He turned to John Caesar and Padraig. "You men will be released from your duties until your backs have healed. Go and speak to the surgeons. And again, I am sorry that this happened to you."

"Thank you, sir, thank you," John Caesar said with a big smile on his face.

Padraig Gallagher merely looked at each of the Englishmen, then in silence, he turned and walked away.

Five days later, he escaped from Port Jackson.

## Chapter 72

Padraig had no idea at all what would lie ahead of him as left the convict camp. He had managed to conceal a filled water bag and whispering good-bye to John Caesar, he departed.

Caesar at first attempted to come with him.

"No!' Padraig whispered. "If I am captured, then we will have some information of where we are and where to go in a future escape; besides, if there is no food out there, I may be able to live on the fringes, and you can maybe leave some food out for me."

Guided by the rising sun, he struck out westward. At first, he followed close to the shoreline, but then he decided to go inland as the inlets and bays would help to create diversions.

Also, he observed the black-skinned savages poking life back into their morning campfires close to the water, and while they saw him and stared at the stranger in their midst, they made no hostile moves.

Strange birds flew around him. The noises they made were so different to the songbirds he remembered back in his homeland. The colors of some and the screeching of others amused and startled Padraig as he traveled farther from the convict camp.

Huge white birds with yellow plumes shrieked at him now and then while others looked at him with their heads cocked to one side and then skipped or flew away as he walked closer. Smaller multi-colored birds flittered from tree to tree chittering as they gathered food.

He was most surprised at the unchanging landscape surrounding him. At times, when higher up on a hilltop, he could see nothing, but the same familiar sight stretching away to what appeared to be a bluish-colored mountain range way out on the far horizon. There seemed to be a series of tracks, some making their way down to the sea, others heading in the direction he wanted to head in.

So, whistling a tuneful air in harmony with the birds, Padraig set out for the distant mountains, feeling much happier than he could recall since leaving Ireland.

As the warmth of the morning sun intensified and his pace increased, he began to sweat, but he needed to put a lot of space between him and those who were sure to follow, and so he did not let up.

His water was running lower as he drank and then drank more. Finally, when the sun was directly overhead, he sat on a fallen log to rest.

A movement to his right caught his attention. As he stared at the strange sight, the object, a long eel-like creature, reared up. Startled, Padraig leapt away from the lightning speed of the attack. Very frightened and gasping for breath, he stood across the clearing as it slithered into the bushes and disappeared.

"What was that?" he spoke aloud. "What place is this that has such unfriendly beings?"

Still shaking, he continued, but this time his eyes were glued to the terrain.

Eventually, he could see a bay down below him surrounded by a thick stand of trees. It appeared to stretch away to his left, and he could see that it narrowed into what he thought could be a river flowing into it. "Fresh water, I wonder," he mused.

Around mid-afternoon, he stood and looked down on water flowing over rocks and then into a pool. He saw strange naked men and younger children seated by the water.

The noise of his arrival alerted them, and they looked up. They gave no indication of either hostility or fear, so he made his way down the track to the waterside. He knelt and tasted the water. When he found it fresh and not salty, he drank thirstily.

"Ah, good!" He rested a moment and then drank again. His thirst quenched, Padraig looked around him.

The strange, almost musical, uttering sounds the aboriginal people made intrigued him.

He sat on a rock and smiled at them. "Hello to you all!" He laughed good-naturedly as a friendly greeting. "My name is Padraig. I come from a land far from here."

The mutterings continued.

He watched as the naked men listened to him. Some of the younger men laughed back at him and pointed to him. One of them approached him with what appeared to be a burnt longish piece of flesh.

He nodded to the man and took it from him. At first Padraig wondered, and then he pulled a piece of meat from it and tasted it. "Mmm, good!" he stated and hungrily chewed and swallowed the whole piece.

The young man who had given it to him pointed to the water and rocks and jabbered a strange sound.

"What was that you said?" Padraig asked.

The aboriginal spoke again, and this time took Padraig by the arm and led him to a hollow in the sand.

"Ah, now I understand." He looked down at some rather large eels.

Remembering the fright earlier in the day, he joined his

hands together and opened and closed them in a biting motion and then wriggled his hand and arm in a slithering motion.

Jabbering and nodding in agreement, the men laughed and pointed to the water again.

"No, no!" he said and pointed up the hill toward the trees.

Shaking their heads and looking at each other, not understanding, they chattered, still pointing to the eels.

Suddenly one of them, a young lad, shouted out and ran to Padraig. He took him to some bushes and grabbed a sapling. Excitedly, he wriggled it and then jabbed the point to Padraig's leg. He then knelt on the ground, and still wriggling the sapling, he poked it into the undergrowth.

"Milyura! Milyura!"

"Yes, yes. That's it. That's it," Padraig nodded hopefully and laughed in agreement.

The young man feigned fright and then very ceremoniously stepped back and back away from the bush, still looking at Padraig in mock fear.

He then took Padraig by the arm and slowly pulled him away from the bush with him.

"Danger! Is that thing dangerous? Is that what you mean?"

Whether he understood or not, the young man nodded his head. "Milyura, milyura."

"I'll take that as a yes," Padraig said, and he chuckled, still not quite understanding, but having a fairly good idea. "I'll be much more careful in future."

The young lad brought some more of the burnt black eel to him, and Padraig munched on it most happily and took more notice of his surroundings.

From the trees above, he heard the laughter of women, and soon they were too curious to stay away; they surrounded him, totally naked, young and old.

"Well, hello to you." He laughed.

Like the scraggily haired and whiskered men, the women had almost shining black skin. They also showed absolutely no emotion or shame at their nakedness. Some carried babies who fed from time to time from ample breasts.

Occasionally one of the women would come forward and tug at his trouser legs and giggle.

Padraig stood and walked to the water's edge and looked upstream and then down to where the water ran through trees that seemed to grow out of the water and then disappeared around a corner and away.

The young man who had brought him food reappeared and beckoned Padraig to follow. Together, they walked up the side of the strong flowing stream and onto the flat. There ahead of them was the aboriginal camp.

Padraig observed mostly women and children as they approached the camp. All appeared busy preparing for the evening. Open fires were being stoked up as the women used wooden bowls and other cooking utensils to heat up food.

With great interest, Padraig watched as some ground seeds and other items were mixed and pounded, and at times water was added as the meal was prepared.

Padraig was led to a fallen log, and with beaming smile, his new companion indicated he should sit. He did so and continued watching with great interest.

A little later, the men arrived, some carrying eels and others an assortment of furry and scaly objects, either over their shoulders or by their sides. They then began to use sharp wooden objects to arrange the animals either on or above the flames and stones close to the fires. None seemed to take too much notice of him apart from sideward glances from time to time.

As the evening drew to a close and a beautiful sunset lit up the western skies, the young aboriginal lad approached him, and with obvious signs, he beckoned Padraig should follow.

It was then the aromas of cooking food reminded Padraig of how hungry he was.

With sign language, he was told to sit and soon was handed an assortment of foods. With absolutely no idea what he was eating, nor did he care, he wolfed the lot down.

Padraig couldn't recall when he had last felt so content; he had a full belly and was with good people, very strange people, but people, nonetheless, who meant no harm to him.

Gradually, as the work for the evening was completed, they all sat around talking and listening and watching as words and signs were exchanged. Occasionally a male would stand and speak, and the others would listen most intently.

His young companion looked at Padraig as if asking whether he understood.

Finally, Padraig pointed to the camp and down to where he had first met these people, and with a circling motion of his arm, he asked, "Where is this place? What is it called? What name?"

Then, most excitedly, the young man stood and copied Padraig's actions.

"Baramada! Baramada!"

"Baramada? This place is Baramada?"

Very proudly, the young lad nodded his head.

"Baramada." He laughed.

Then two of the older men firmly stated, "Baramada."

"Well, at least I know now where I am." Padraig smiled at the people around him.

"Your name, what is your name?" Padraig pointed to the youngest of the three.

He nodded, understanding the puzzled expressions that followed this question.

Pointing to his upper chest, he stated, "Padraig! My name is Padraig. Me, Padraig."

The youngest suddenly laughed. "Pard . . . Pard . . . Pard . . . Pardraig!"

Joining in the laughter, Padraig nodded in agreement. "Padraig!"

"Ah, Padraig!" Then almost in triumph, the young man pointed at his naked chest, and he firmly stated, "Burabura," followed by further words that Padraig could not understand. He finished by tapping his finger on Padraig's chest. "Padraig." Then he tapped his own chest. "Burabura."

He then pointed to the other two men, and to the first he said, "Murawa," and the second, "Dunguti."

They motioned for him to sit with them, and he watched in fascination at these people the English called Indians.

Padraig had no idea when he fell asleep, but when he awoke the next morning, he noticed that someone had placed a skin covering over him.

In the days that followed, he observed closely the ways of these people, his friends.

If the children appeared to break the family rules, the family group would discipline them. He watched as the children were taught stories in a dramatic fashion or by way of song or strange dance.

From time to time, the men he took to be elders would take him to one side and indicate to him by various signs and actions what they felt Padraig should know.

They took him hunting *karlaya*, the big flightless two-legged bird that ran so fast from them as they approached. They hunted the *yawarda*, the gray animal that bounded away from them on its two legs aided by its long tail.

The hunting weapons astounded him; spears, which of course

he was familiar with, but he was amazed at the curved wooden object that felled prey with astounding accuracy and amazingly returned to the thrower when flung correctly.

How his friends laughed when, on his first throw, the object returned and could well have hit him on the head. Padraig learned to either catch it or get hurt.

As the days progressed, the weather got cooler, but certainly not as cold as he could remember back home, and then the days got longer and hotter again. Padraig realized that the winter of this strange new land had come and gone.

A strange feeling of contentment had also become very apparent.

Then one day, he and five of the men went out on an extended hunting journey. They had excellent luck, and when returning to the camp, the women began preparations for the cooking of the day's catch.

Later, when the sun slid behind the blue-hued mountains in the distance, Padraig was approached by his new young friend and a younger female.

She was naked and did little to cover her private parts. Her breasts, largish, but firm swayed invitingly as she moved toward him. She sat by him, and giggling, she began to touch him on his stomach. Padraig smiled and nodded his contentment at the obvious bulge of the food he had consumed.

Then slowly her hand progressed farther down to where the sudden realization of what was happening caused a swelling and a longing in those parts of his body that had not been apparent since the murder of his beloved Kathleen.

A sudden cold and emotionally dead feeling engulfed Padraig, and he abruptly stood and stumbled and fled to the riverbank.

Falling to the water's edge, he lay staring at the movements of the small fish searching for food as the darkness descended. Memories, sad, bad recollections of those years now behind him, came flooding back, smothering him in the deep dark depths of depression.

Sometime later, he stood and slowly made his way back to where a group of the tribesmen sat staring at him in curious wonderment. Somewhat in a daze, he walked to where the village elder sat among a group of male tribesmen.

In his first days at the village, Padraig had been most intrigued by the bearded and curly gray-haired man of an age he could only guess at, but would not have been surprised to learn he had lived beyond eighty years.

Staring at the elder, he sat, and in a mixture of Gaelic and English, the words tumbled from his mouth. Caring little whether there was any understanding, Padraig wanted only to empty the pain, the hatred of his enemies, the indescribable loss of his wife and family, and the total emptiness of his life.

His words told of his youth and of his meeting his beloved Kathleen. He spoke of the birth of his twins and subsequent loss. There could be little doubt to his listeners of the agony he'd endured; they watched in silence as his pained body illustrated the utter hatred of the one who had destroyed all that he had loved. Finally, his words faded into mutterings and then silence.

One of the tribesmen handed Padraig a wooden bowl of liquid that Padraig gulped greedily. Nodding his gratitude, he gazed at each of the tribesmen and then finally the elder.

Padraig felt a slow release of peace surrounding him and engulfing him. In total amazement, he watched as the elder stirred the ashes of the fire and then threw in a collection of powder and leaves. The elder's lips stayed closed, but silent unspoken words began to infiltrate Padraig's mind as the odor of the mixture's smoke wafted around them.

Padraig began to understand the thoughts of the elder, and in bewilderment, he understood clearly as those words spoke of his two beloved children being alive, not dead, as he believed, but alive!

His mind drifted back and forth from his time in the past to now in the present, and as the wind around them stirred the trees and bushes, there, standing smiling at him, was his beautiful Kathleen.

Gasping and staring in amazement, Padraig watched the figure before him smile and then slowly disappear.

He fell into a beckoning state of dreamless sleep.

The following morning, Padraig awoke. Noise and confusion were all around. At first, he stood there confused, and then with a sudden cold realization, he understood.

"There's the bloody Irishman. Catch him. Don't let him get away."

Surrounded and fighting furiously, Padraig was finally clubbed to the ground.

He gradually regained consciousness, and with aching head and body, he found himself tied securely. He was pulled to his feet, and to howls of derision, he fell to the ground again.

"Get up and start walkin'. Your days of freedom are over."

As he was taken away, he looked back at his friends, and in particular his young companion, he who had taken so much time to help him and assist in the ways of learning to understand and come to love these people that the English called savages, but who were more civilized than any Englishmen he'd ever met.

They looked so shocked and deeply hurt that this was happening. The white man had intruded into their world. It would never be the same again.

## Chapter 73

Padraig peered over the side of the longboat. Hogtied, he could only shuffle his body to watch as the boat approached the landing. He could hardly believe the changes to the confusion he had escaped from those weeks or so back.

Port Jackson now consisted of wooden storehouses covered with thatch or shingles in which the cargo from the ships had been stored.

As he was dragged off the longboat, Padraig walked unaided, but bound with his hands behind his back. As he walked up from the landing, he saw barracks that had been built for the military with collections of huts scattered around. Farther along, two stone houses stood, which he presumed were the homes of the commander and his lieutenants and captains.

Shouts from convicts turned his attention to a work party yelling out at him. But sharp shoves from his handlers and bellowed orders allowed him little understanding of their support.

They finally reached a shabby hut with an open door that he was shoved into, and then he was thrown to the floor.

"This 'ere's ya new home! Welcome back." The handler sniggered as he slammed the door closed.

Padraig fell back on the sandy base of the cell, hurt and broken, as he remembered the days prior to his recapture. With only memories of his youth, the horror of the deaths of his family, then the subsequent journey to London followed by his arrest and sea journey to this strange land, his mind and spirit were so broken that he could only lie there and wish for an end to his miserable life.

"Lord in heaven, God our Father, if you are there and you can hear me, please take me to be with my mother and my father. Please let me be with my Kathleen and my little ones and my brother and my grandda . . ." His voice trailed off into silent inner sobbing.

The chortling chuckle of one of the strange birds of this strange land was the only sound he heard in reply.

★★★★★

Young William Hubbard was eight years of age when convicted in London of theft. He was twelve years of age when taken from the hulks and placed on *Friendship* and shipped to the colonies. Bastardry was just some of the humiliation the young lad had endured, but he had maintained his sense of humour, and many of the convicts saw in young Billy a spirit they jealously envied for themselves.

The guard opened the door to Padraig's cell and entered with a dish of food.

"Watcha Irish!" He grinned. "Gotta dish of slops 'ere for ya."

Padraig looked up and shook his head.

"Nah! Don't go doin' that to me. Those bags of shit might think I ain't doin' me job."

Padraig looked at the young man in dirty raggedy convict clothing. Long, straggly unkempt hair with a trace of whiskers beginning to show on his chin did little to hide the obvious concern in his face.

A sudden hunger and urge to eat awoke in Padraig. He

grabbed the bowl and began to shove the food in his mouth.

"There ya go! Not so bad after all, in it?"

Leaning closer to Padraig, he spoke quietly so the guard couldn't hear him. "John Caesar said to tell you he is lookin' out for ya. Keep up the spirits tho', eh?" Young Billy then left the cell. Turning, he gave Padraig a cheeky grin and a wink of his right eye.

The cell door slammed as the guard laughed and called out, "You'll get yours on the morn, ya Irish bastard."

Padraig slept little through the night, and the dawn brought a feeling of dread as he heard the doors slamming and the sounds of soldiers and guards rousing what he suspected were other prisoners.

The door of his cell was pushed open. He was roughly dragged and pushed toward one of the newer huts where male and female prisoners watched as he was thrown inside. It was the twenty-eighth of that month, little more than seven weeks in the land of New South Wales, and today he would face more injustices by the power of the British monarchy.

He and five others were made to sit on wooden benches.

"Keep ya mouths shut and speak when told to!" The soldier then stood behind them.

Sometime later, Governor Phillip and three of his ranking officers arrived and sat before them.

Charges were laid, and finally his Excellency spoke.

"James Bailey, John Power, Thomas Glenton, Walter Batley, and Thomas Barrett, you each have been found guilty of violations of public security and the theft of provisions.

"Bailey, Power, Glenton, and Barrett, you are condemned to die. Your execution will take place at dawn tomorrow. Walter Bartley, you will receive one hundred and fifty lashes.

"Padraig Gallagher, it seems that you have learnt little after your last offence. You also will be executed at dawn tomorrow.

Take them away!"

It was later that afternoon when Governor Phillip, Watkin Tench, and a group of officers sat and reviewed the actions of that day.

"It could be suggested that a drop or two of fine brandy be considered inappropriate on the eve of the deaths of scum such as convicted today," one commented.

"I certainly do agree," Tench stated. "I will decline."

"Come now, Watkin," Phillip replied. "One will do thee no harm."

"The mood is far from conducive. May I make some suggestions?"

"Of course." Phillip nodded agreement.

"These men convicted of theft of provisions—may I ask, what would each of us have done in the same circumstances? What if that was the only way we had of feeding our families? And does their crime truly warrant execution?"

Tench did not wait for an answer.

"And the Irishman, Gallagher: his statement regarding his arrest in London. If he truly was attempting to protect his property, does he not have the right to believe his innocence? And on that subject, have you not noticed his accent? He speaks as one who has been well educated and is certainly not a lowlife Irish vagabond. And as you each are very well aware of my interest in these strange natives of this strange land, would it not be an idea to question Gallagher regarding his interaction with them prior to his recapture?"

"Most interesting," Phillip mused. "Who else agrees that perhaps a conversation with the Irishman could offer some valuable information regarding our future objectives here?"

All gave comments of approval.

"Agreed then! I will have a guard bring him in for questioning before nightfall."

Padraig heard the guard approach the crude hut that represented his legal holding cell in New South Wales.

Instead of the rough treatment he expected, he was mildly intrigued at the simple request of, "Come! The governor wants ta' talk wi' ya!"

With his hands still bound in chains, he stood and followed. They walked to one of the new buildings that Padraig presumed was for administration or homes of the executive officers.

They were beckoned inside to a largish room where Governor Phillip, Captain Tench, and other officers whose names he could not recall were seated.

They saw a well-built man, now suntanned dark bronze. While most in the community were skinny and undernourished, Gallagher appeared well fed and certainly fit and healthy. His demeanor showed curiosity and not animosity as would be expected.

Phillip arose and pointed to a wooden seat and asked Padraig to sit.

"Guard! Please remove the prisoner's manacles!"

After some rustling and searching, a key was produced and Padraig's hands were set free.

"Thank you, that is all." And the guard was dismissed.

"Gallagher, we have asked you here to give an account of your actions and to provide information that may be of benefit to us as well as to your future here."

Commander Phillip gestured toward Tench and the officers present. "You, of course, know Captain Tench and the other officers here with us today. I do confess, Gallagher, you offer us a complex mix of curiosity and concern. Your demeanor, as you sit before us, suggests that you have little or no fear of what the morrow may bring as to your death by hanging.

"Captain Tench is most intrigued by your manner of speech. You suggest either an educated past or a background of some worldly understanding. Perhaps an explanation may, I repeat *may* decide a stay of execution. What have you to say?"

Padraig stared at Phillip then Tench. "Truly, I have nothing to say, other than I was wrongly tried and punished for a crime I did not commit in London. I have been sent here as a wrongdoer, which I should resent.

"I am about to die, which in truth will reunite me with my wife, my parents, my brother, and my children, who in my country were murdered by no less than one of your aristocratic people of supposed excellence. And if God is as I have been led to believe, then I shall be with those I love some moments after you send me to my death."

Somewhat stunned Phillip and Tench glanced at each other, and then Watkin Tench spoke. "Gallagher, or may I call you Padraig, I believe?"

Padraig nodded assent.

"Padraig, may we ask you to give a full account of what you are referring to?"

Padraig thought for some moments, and believing he had nothing but his life to lose, he began to tell of his life and loves of his country Ireland and his past.

On completion, one of the officers spoke.

"You expect us to believe a ridiculous tale of rubbish such as you describe? England is only too aware of your rabble and ignorance. And you speak of truth. I suspect you know nothing of the meaning of the word."

Tench suddenly interrupted. "Lieutenant, please! Padraig, the manner in which you speak—tell us where you obtained your educated accent and excellent vocabulary."

Padraig glared at the lieutenant. "A very close friend, a

Frenchman with a Jewish background and a man of great honour, discovered that I have a gift for language and the understanding of cultures, which allows me to grasp the meanings of words in other languages and to learn to speak those languages with ease. And while I have a problem with the people of England, I have no problems with their language. Indeed, whenever possible, I enjoy reading your literature and am able to learn more."

"And so," Tench continued, "this enabled you to converse with the savages and live with them in mutual understanding?"

"Savage is a word I find insulting and not the least bit descriptive of these people who I am proud to call friends. They were most kind to me and are civilised in their own way, and I was and am still sad to know that I will never see them again."

Tench suddenly said, "Commander Phillip, may I speak to you in the other room?"

Both Phillip and Tench left the room, leaving a bemused Padraig and assorted officers in silence. Ten minutes or so passed, and they returned.

"Padraig Gallagher," Phillip began, "after considerable discussion, Captain Tench and I have decided to drop the charges and dismiss completely your execution tomorrow.

"However, we will spend some time with you to determine how you can be of considerable assistance to us for our generosity in commuting your sentence. What have you to say?"

Again, Padraig stared at each in silence, then smiled. "I am confused to say the least. But while we are in a bargaining mood, may I also ask for leniency in the death of those other four who also face the hangman tomorrow?"

Phillip stated firmly, "I cannot promise, but I will look into their charges once more. You are free to leave."

## Chapter 74

It was widely believed that Captain Cook had offended the aboriginals that he had encountered in his earlier landings, and while the engagements to date with the aboriginals in New South Wales had been reasonably amicable, Watkin Tench had reason to believe that all must be done to avoid serious confrontation.

Tench found them to be of stout appearance and nimble of body, sprightly and vigorous.

Captain Cook had classified them as deep chocolate in color rather than black, but a cleanliness marred by greasy filth. Tench's opinion was two degrees less black than an African Negro.

Padraig had mentioned that he found no problem with the scars they adorned themselves with, which in the view of the English officers, only made their appearance more hideous.

Tench, however, did find the act of sticking a fishbone through the nose somewhat disturbing.

The white clay that both sexes daubed themselves with was a practice unlike other inhabitants of the Pacific Islands who used bird feathers for adornment.

Tench sat and reflected on the day. After considerable discussion, it was decided that only one execution would take place, and Thomas Barrett died a little before sunset.

Padraig was quiet on that issue, and as Barrett was much older and becoming more and more feeble, he had offered Tench the opinion that four saved and one dead was indeed better than all five facing the hangman. Tench observed the immediate gratification to Gallagher by the convicts whose lives were spared.

The aboriginals that lived local to New South Wales had obviously heard of Gallagher's meeting and subsequent living with their people much farther up the harbour and thus showed him warmth instead of the cool reception they gave the rest of the convicts and the English officers.

He found little issue with their rudely constructed huts or their complete lack of clothing, and when questioned as to how they adapted when the weather turned colder, he commented that they simply huddled closer to their campfire.

Gallagher was amused by their methods of fishing, and coming from fishing stock in Ireland, he had made some very helpful suggestions as to how they could improve their fishhooks. However, he found their netting methods more than adequate.

So, all considered, Tench was most happy with the new arrangements made with Padraig Gallagher, and indeed, he found a warmth developing between the two men that did find him wondering more and more about the truth of Padraig's life in Ireland.

Padraig quickly fell back into convict life at Port Jackson. John Caesar was most pleased to have his friend back in the fold, and Young Billy Hubberd, as most called him, let his feelings be known.

"Watcha ol' cocky! Did the bleedin' 'angman not stretch ya neck? Bleedin' good job. We needs ya 'ere wiv us!" His big wide grin had everyone smiling.

The following day, Padraig and John Caesar had finished their assigned tasks somewhat earlier than planned. Caesar pulled him aside, and they both sat on a fallen gum tree to talk.

"Padraig, I intend to do a runner. Please tell me about the

country you saw and traveled through, and how far do I go before I am well clear of this lot?"

"John, it is a far different country than I could ever imagine. You will only survive with the help of the natives, and even then, the way some of the convicts and English officers treat them, I can only see trouble ahead. There is already talk of shooting some of them to keep the rest in line."

"Yes!" John Caesar replied. "Their canoes for sea and river fishing are nothing but large pieces of bark tied at each end, and I have watched them helping themselves to our fishing nets. A musket was fired at one canoe, and as they were chased away, I saw much anger in their faces."

"Have you seen their dogs?" Padraig asked. "They are much like our foxes. They stay close to the natives and are wary of us, but I did make friends with a young puppy while I was with them. They call them dingo."

"Yes, Padraig, one of the bloody English bastards shot one here a week back, causing much anger among the natives."

"What do you think of the aboriginal people, John?"

"The men talk very guttural, while the women are more soft-spoken, though the men do tend to keep them well back from the obvious intent of some of the convicts and the soldiers and sailors, also. Some of the women in their nakedness do suggest much more to offer than what the female prisoners care to show."

Both laughed, and then Padraig spotted Tench walking toward them.

"Hush of escape talk, John. Here comes danger."

"A pleasant day to you both, Gallagher and Caesar! Padraig, would it be possible for us to talk about some thoughts I have. I need any suggestions that may help."

"I shall leave you two," John Caesar said. "Please sit here, captain," he added, offering his seat.

As Caesar left, Watkin Tench suggested they walk up to the top of higher ground to survey the settlement below them. "What do you think of all we have achieved since our landing, Padraig?"

Padraig looked down. The ships were anchored securely in deep water some distance from the shore, while the occasional longboat scurried back and forth, bringing provisions or building equipment to the wooden structure soon to be the first fully completed wharf.

Convict labor combined with skilled craftsmen had achieved much in the short time since the fleet's arrival. Already streets had been laid out, albeit with cruder temporary structures mixed with grander, more permanent buildings for housing officers, as well as safer and more secure premises for food, water, and general cargo.

Padraig nodded approval and agreed that much had been done in his absence.

"The reason I need to talk with you, Padraig, is that I need your help in a number of concerns of mine.

"First, allow me to explain my love of fertile soil, grasses, and plants and vegetables, which we will have to harvest soon. I know nought of the growing seasons other than what Captain Cook described, and in truth, I have gained scant knowledge, so as a farmer and crop grower yourself, any help you may offer will be to the advantage of all. Also, I am curious to know whether you saw much in the way of better growing ground on your rather illustrious journey up harbour compared to that which we see before us here in Sydney.

"Another concern is the disappearance of twelve or so convicts employed as grass cutters farther up the harbour. We found two who had been very badly butchered by spears, and two others had been speared, with one escaping and the fate of his friend still unknown.

"Their skill with these spears is remarkable. I personally witnessed only one spear bringing down a very large kangaroo by one of these natives. I have no doubt that should we come to unfriendly terms with a tribe, we could be in serious danger."

"The solution is simple, Captain Tench," Padraig stated firmly. "Treat them with respect and dignity, and you may not need to be troubled. I found those I was with extremely agreeable and possessing both humour and curiosity to know more about us."

"How are you with their language?" Tench asked. "Do you fully understand what they talk about, and do they understand you?"

Padraig smiled. "I did have great trouble at first, but with a combination of signs, gestures, and patience, we eventually managed a form of conversation that was understood by us both. In particular, a young lad and I achieved an excellent understanding of each of our ways. That was before I was captured and beaten by your men."

"Indeed, Gallagher, indeed. But let us move forward and find solutions to present matters in hand."

Padraig stood in silence, watching as a group of female convicts tended to some cattle and horses by offering them bunches of grass.

"Yes," Tench began again, also observing. "We will need to have ample hay if the weather turns unseasonable. We cannot afford to let the animals die for lack of grass."

"So, then, Captain Tench, what do you require of me?" Padraig finally asked.

"I would like to think that you would serve as a translator in whatever conversation we have with the natives. We will also need you to journey farther inland to find suitable farming ground that we can use for growing crops and vegetables. And more importantly, can we trust you to return, or do we need to send soldiers with you to insist on your returning to Port Jackson?"

Padraig looked toward the hazy blue mountains on the inland horizon. He watched as the sun and skies turned golden as the sun moved closer to the western horizon to signal the end of yet another day in this very strange land.

He was reminded very vividly of the sunsets over the Atlantic in Donegal, and thoughts of home suffused him with sorrow and pain as the faces of Kathleen and his children appeared before him.

"We will see," he replied. "We will wait and see."

Tench sensed rather than saw Padraig's emotional pain. Not wanting to press the matter further, he said, "Come, let us see what food awaits us below."

*****

The French had departed from Botany Bay back in mid-March. There had been a general feeling of comradeship between both the French and the British. However, the commander of the French fleet had scant respect for the former Captain James Cook, because in his opinion, Cook had done little to earn the respect of the aboriginals or indeed many of the islanders of the Pacific.

The French had had some confrontation with some of the natives in the Botany Bay region, but had sent musket blasts of warning, and the natives had run off.

His final comments before sailing were that while the First Fleet was more than adequately armed and capable of beating off any attacks or danger from the natives, there would be long-term risks of reprisals or other forms of retaliation.

Not long after the French departed, the *Supply* returned from Norfolk Island.

The captain, a Lieutenant Ball, told his fellow officers at the new colony that giant pines grew to great heights on the island, but because of their size, and because they grew right up to the shoreline, it was very difficult for the ships to come ashore so that the trees could be felled and thus utilized for construction.

However, he had no trouble landing at another island he had discovered, which he named Lord Howe Island. The island was uninhabited, but was home to many types of birdlife, some so tame and large they were killed with ease with fallen tree branches.

The island was also home to large green turtles, some of which Lieutenant Ball brought back with him, much to the satisfaction of the officers and chosen members of the colony who then delighted in partaking of their flesh.

Since the landing, the pleasant summer months had been replaced by the beginnings of winter, and with the warnings of such a low latitude bringing in much colder weather, the colony had not a great deal of time to build the shelters they would have much preferred.

The need for eight large buildings for soldiers' barracks became four in number due to the lack of good quality timber and other impediments.

The married couples had, however, been granted more appropriate quarters.

But all in all, Governor Phillip felt that good progress had been made.

He had travelled to other bays and landings north of Port Jackson, but apart from good water, the land was too rocky and bare to prove of any use to the colony.

As Padraig listened to John Caesar relaying all the news, he began to understand why Watkin Tench had spent so much persuasive banter in an attempt to have Padraig work with him.

Would he? Could he help those that been part of a nation and so-called legal system that had caused him so much pain and grief? Padraig Gallagher had yet to decide.

## Chapter 75

The weather had indeed begun to cool off so much that the acquisition of food was now becoming a serious problem. The *Supply* sailed to Lord Howe Island in late May to gather more turtles, but returned with little reward for the journey.

Padraig agreed to lead a party of eleven to the mountains, where Governor Phillip believed food relief could be found. He did this out of boredom more than any other reason.

From Port Jackson, the mountains inland did not appear to be too far away, but it was several days' journey. They had seen little in the way of gatherable food and very few animals. A few average-sized kangaroo were the only quadrupeds seen.

On the fourth day, Phillip spoke to Padraig. "We do not seem to have achieved too much, Gallagher. Did you come this far on your previous journey?"

"This is much farther inland than I travelled," Padraig replied. "And I am most surprised that there appears to be very little in the way of streams or rivers other than these small pools here and there."

Padraig did not mention the figures he had observed appearing from time to time through the trees in the distance. He was most bemused that the others in the party had failed to see the natives.

They returned to Port Jackson with nothing to show for their journey. Soon the colony faced the worsening situation of decreasing food and supplies.

Even the fish, so abundant in warmer months, became harder to locate and catch.

Morale was now also a major concern to Phillip and his officers, but strangely, very few offences were committed except for one burglary.

Padraig, John Caesar, and other convicts that were now friends of Padraig watched in silence as the young man's bowels emptied, signalling his demise at the end of the swinging hangman's rope, and this for the crime of petty theft.

Two days later, John Caesar's mood changed. "Padraig!" he whispered. "I am sick to death of this bloody country and the English. It is time for me to go. Come with me."

For some strange reason, Padraig felt uneasy about leaving. "Let us wait for better weather," he said to his friend.

"Look at those regal bastards," John snarled.

It was the anniversary of the King of England's birthday. Governor Phillip had invited all officers not on duty to wine and dine in honour of His Royal Majesty. Padraig had watched as officers arrived and left to return to duty, most happy under the influence of the wines, but also content with a full belly.

Port Jackson had been renamed Sydney Cove of Cumberland County, and earlier that day, the ships of war had fired twenty-one guns each. At noon, this was repeated. As the battalions of marines responded, the sound of the guns echoed throughout the newly founded land. Natives close by looked startled and concerned as the sounds reached their ears.

Even when the convicts were allocated their shares of grog and rum, and as the evening brought the warm glow of wood fires where more pots of porter were handed out, little was done to fire up the moods of both Caesar and Padraig.

"I agree with you, Padraig. I wish I was with you back in your land of the Irish, or you were with me in my land of Madagascar or the Caribbean—it doesn't matter where we go, as long as we are far away from the pomp and grandeur of these bloody English!"

It was only weeks later that Caesar reminded Padraig of his comments as again they witnessed the execution of two of their friends. One was convict Samuel Peyton, who on the night of the king's anniversary, had interfered with an officer's musket. Another convict had run for freedom, and on his recapture was falsely accused of cattle rustling.

Their executions did nothing to alter the moods of both Padraig and John Caesar.

The next morning, Padraig awoke to find John Caesar gone. It did not take long for his disappearance to be noted, and Padraig was ordered to face Major Robert Ross, Commandant of the Marines.

"Gallagher!" The man of rather large build dressed in uniform fairly barked his name. "Your troublesome wretch of a friend has decided our company is not fit for one such as he. Have you any idea as to where we may locate Caesar?"

"No," Padraig answered.

"Is that all you have to say, or may I presume that you also have intentions of joining him?"

"No."

"No what?" snarled the commandant.

"No, I have no intentions of joining him, and no, that is not all I have to say. But I would prefer to speak to Mr. Tench on the matter."

"Indeed. So be it. Lieutenant Long, please have a marine escort this Irish tramp to Captain Tench. May he find pleasure in the company of this scum, as I surely do not. Take him away!"

Padraig followed a marine to Tench's quarters.

"There ya Irish shit bucket, wait here!" The marine knocked at the crude wooden door.

An orderly opened the door. "Who do you wish to see?"

"I been ordered to bring 'im 'ere to see Captain Tench," the marine grunted.

Captain Tench appeared. "Gallagher, a pleasant surprise! Please enter."

Padraig smiled at the departing marine, but declined to offer any comment.

"Some water perhaps?" Tench offered Padraig a jug and a glass. Padraig declined.

"Padraig, we are about to send a party of one hundred convicts up to the head of the harbour. A captain plus two subalterns and twenty marines will accompany them to protect them from harm and to ensure no sudden departures. Our intention is to take advantage of what appears to be better land for cultivation and to establish a settlement there. I am of the opinion that your experience of farming in your native land could be of benefit to us. Should you see merit in this statement, I would entrust to your care some valuable, high-quality seed for cultivation. What do you say?"

"Certainly a change of scenery has merit, and my sleeping quarters of late leave much to be desired," said Padraig. "So, yes, I accept your offer."

"Excellent. We plan on the party leaving tomorrow or the following day. I will call for you and have you sit with us while we put our final plans in place. For now I bid thee good day, Padraig."

On the second day after Tench had spoken with Padraig, the sun rose in a cloudless blue sky. The party soon gathered, and with good humour and ribald comments from those at the settlement, the convicts and the captain and marines departed on their journey.

Padraig knew some of the convicts, and he soon felt that he had made a good decision. However, he did miss the companionship of his friend John Caesar.

It didn't take too long before they were looking out to the open sea. Padraig wandered down to some rocky crags that jutted out into the water. He could see the flash of small fish glistening in the water and knew that a good catch was to be had. He went back to the captain and asked if fishing lines had been included in their stock of work items.

"Indeed, we do have lines and hooks," the captain replied, and with a wide grin suggested, "Is it fishing you wish to do to avoid work, or is it for our evening supper?"

Padraig laughingly replied, "I shall let you be the judge."

"First we must make camp," the captain said. "However, the weather being agreeable, you and some others can see what you can catch us first thing in the morning."

The sounds of early chortling of the birds the natives called kookaburras woke Padraig from a sound night's sleep. He pulled back his blankets and stepped into a sunlit clear sky. He watched as the birds flew from gum tree to gum tree down to the sandy foreshore. He heard the others waking behind him and turned his attention to the one chosen to cook that morning. He was shaking up the ashes of the previous night's campfires to stoke a new fire.

"Watcha, Irish!" he said. "How about fetching me some water from that stream yonder? I'll boil up some tea for us."

Padraig duly obliged, and soon cups of tea were passed around.

"Well now, Gallagher, it's a fisherman ya claim to be, uh?"

The captain grinned broadly. "Here, take some of these lines, and you and these other wasters take off down and see what you can get for us."

Padraig and four other convicts walked from the sandy beach area some distance away to where the rocky foreshore began. There was little wind that day, and the currents were causing swells, but nothing Padraig considered to be of risk to the fishermen. Two of his comrades were Londoners, but the other two were from Devon and Bristol. John Wisehammer and Samuel Barsby were both experienced fishermen and joked about Londoners knowing nothing about the 'ook and sinker. And so the mood was set for the morning.

Padraig walked to the farthest point of the rocky outcrops and cast his line out. The other four took up similar positions, and soon the banter began.

Wisehammer received the first tug, and soon he had landed the first fish of the day.

"Ha, ya lazy good for nothin's!" He laughed out at the other four.

This caused a frenzy of casting and reeling among them as the competitive spirit took hold. Soon there were small piles of shaking and jumping fish beside each of the fishermen, and their good-humoured taunts kept them laughing as even more fish were landed.

Padraig then saw a large dark shape merge with the seaweeds out where he threw his line and hook.

Wisehammer laughed and called out for all to hear, "I got a big 'un 'ere. None of ya will do better than me and this one."

His line was taut. Padraig felt a thrill of alarm. "Be careful!" he shouted to Wisehammer.

"Ha, jealous is ya, Irish? I got the better of ya this day!"

Suddenly, as he tried to pull a large struggling fish, which had appeared at the top of the waves, a great shape hurled its head from the water, grabbing the fish in its huge jaws. It pulled the fish back underwater and jerked Wisehammer from the rocks into the sea below him. Padraig watched in fright as the line wrapped around Wisehammer's wrist.

Screaming, Wisehammer was dragged farther out from the safety of the rocky shoreline.

The other three watched in disbelief as Padraig grabbed a gutting knife and dived in after him. He swam out to where Wisehammer's body was appearing and disappearing in the waves; he grabbed him under his arms and pulled him to the surface.

"Stop fighting me!" he shouted into the terrified man's ear. "Let me carry your weight!"

Padraig slashed at the line, which suddenly went slack. He realized that the fish was probably in the jaws of the monster.

He dragged Wisehammer to where the waters were shallower. Samuel Barsby stood above them with arms outstretched.

As Padraig pushed and shoved Wisehammer toward safety, a great shape launched itself out of the waters, aiming a huge jawed mouth at the trailing legs of Wisehammer.

Somehow between them, Barsby and Padraig pulled their comrade to safety, but not before the teeth had snared the heel of Wisehammer's boot, biting through and taking a chunk of leather.

The two men lay on the rocks, exhausted, caring little for the sharp shellfish and rock cutting into their exposed bodies.

The three other men stood staring at them in total disbelief of what they had witnessed.

"What was that bleedin' thing?" the Londoner Walter Bately whimpered.

"It was a shark," Padraig replied. "We have them in the North Atlantic, but nothing like the size of that one. I have never seen or heard of the likes of that brute. My brother, who is a boat fisherman . . ." Padraig's voice trailed off. The shock of the past few moments and the painful remembrance of his past stopped him from continuing.

When they were all fully recovered and rested, the five men gathered up the fish in sacks and made their way back to the camp.

It was only when they had reached the safety of the sandy foreshore that John Wisehammer suddenly dropped his sack, turned to Padraig, and put his arms around him. He hugged Padraig close for several moments before bursting into uncontrollable weeping.

Barsby and the two Londoners watched in silence, and as Padraig released the distraught man, they each moved to Padraig and held him between them.

"Ya bleedin' Irishman!" Walter Bately finally spoke. "What do ya tink ya were doin'? I nearly shit in me trousers!"

Suddenly, all five men looked at each other and burst into uncontrolled laughter.

"Come on. Let's get these fish back to camp. I need a cuppa tea."

## Chapter 76

Gabriella Borthwick studied herself in the full-length mirror in her bedroom. She combed her ebony-black wavy hair that reached down to her slim elegant waist. Piercing blue eyes sparkled as she adjusted her beautiful new ball gown to show a hint of her ankles. A radiant smile showed approval as she slipped on her new shoes that would dance the night away at that evening's ball to mark the end of summer and the beginning of autumn.

"Robert Bolton!" she murmured to herself then giggled. "You know not what a lady should be until you know me."

In five days' time, she would be the centre of attention on the night of her nineteenth birthday, a night her father intended all to remember at the gala evening he had prepared for her.

Her father, Barnstable Herbert Borthwick, known by his friends as BHB sat sipping a glass of French brandy in his study on the ground floor of his vast four-story mansion. His friends, or rather those that he conceded were not enemies, were, on the whole, treated with contempt. This had earned him the nickname Bloody Haughty Bastard to match his initials.

He had arrived in America in 1760, soon after the French had been defeated and the English had seized its colonies. Wealth that he had brought from England enabled him to set up a banking business that soon blossomed into one of the leading banking groups in New York. He then extended his business into Virginia where he and his wife and daughter now resided.

His daughter was, in fact, the only person he treated with any form of affection, and on this special day, he waited for her to descend from her third-floor bedroom to greet the gentleman Robert Bolton, soon to arrive, who would escort her to the evening's ball.

Bolton's attitude had angered Borthwick on more than one occasion. He was the son of one of England's leading aristocratic families, and indeed Borthwick's wife had been very friendly with Lady Constance, wife of Lord Thomas Bolton, during their trips to England.

Borthwick was aware that his feelings should not show as his daughter was most taken by the young Bolton, and he wanted a successful marriage for her.

He looked to the door of his study as the sounds of laughter and giggling announced the arrival of his wife and daughter.

"Hello, Father! Do I not look the most beautiful sight you have ever seen?" His daughter curtsied before him.

"Indeed, my daughter, you do." He glanced at his wife and muttered, "Unlike your mother."

If his wife heard, she gave no indication. Their marriage had been strained for many years, and she knew that a great deal of his time and energies and money went into the hands of the countless harlots that pranced the floors of the many brothels her husband owned. This side of his business dealings was not a known fact, however, as it was concealed very cleverly in the bookkeeping of his banking business.

He poured another fine brandy, and as he raised the glass to toast the beauty of his daughter, the sound of a horse-drawn carriage crunching on the gravel drive of his mansion reached his ears.

Some moments later, his butler stood at the door of the study.

"Robert Bolton, sir! May I allow him to enter?"

"Bring him in, bring him in!" Gabriella giggled.

Robert Bolton then appeared.

Dressed in an uniquely tailored suit, with hair barbered to perfection, he stood before them. "Good evening, sir, madam, and who may I ask is this?" He smiled at their daughter. "Surely an angel of much magical beauty could never match the beauty of this remarkable young woman standing before me."

He went over, and holding her hand, he placed his lips on her fingertips.

Blushing as a young lady should, she again curtsied and replied. "Oh, come now, I am certain you have known many ladies far more beautiful than me."

For a brief moment, Bolton stood staring at her. "In truth, I have known only one who could stand as a match to yourself, but she is no longer of this world."

He then smiled and continued. "But come, may I have your parents' approval to escort you to the ball?"

Both parents nodded, he staring at Bolton and she glancing from daughter to Bolton as a mother with concerns.

They all walked out to the waiting carriage. A beautiful black stallion kicked his heels impatiently in anticipation of leading the gleaming scarlet-red open carriage from the country estate of the Borthwicks to the township and the venue of the annual autumn ball.

Bolton politely assisted Gabriella to her seat, and he climbed up after her. The driver flicked his whip, and the stallion bounded forward and trotted head held high to the township.

Both Bolton and Gabriella chatted amiably about their day and the expectancy of a magnificent night ahead of them.

Changing the subject, Bolton said, "Gabriella, I understand it is your nineteenth birthday in five days' time. May I ask if you have ever had the company of another man prior to myself?"

"Robert, pray tell. What are you asking of me?"

"I am enquiring as to whether you are still a virgin. Does that offend you?"

More in anger than embarrassment, she replied, "A gentleman asketh not that question!"

Bolton smiled as the silence was broken only by the sounds of the trotting hooves. He thought of the saying, *those who speak first lose*, and he remained quiet.

"And besides, are you so sure of yourself that you presume to be the one to whom I will give my virginity?" Gabriella snorted. "You're assuming that part of my body is still intact!"

"Touché!" Bolton exclaimed, and he grinned in anticipation of all that he was certain would eventuate.

The coach came to a halt outside the venue of the ball. Men and women dressed in an amazing array of finery were gathering outside, waiting to enter. Bolton ran his eyes over those whom he felt were worthy of his assessment, whilst Gabriella looked for those who might upstage her on the ballroom floor.

"Come, my dear." Bolton assisted her from the coach.

Then turning to the driver, Hat Wong, he stated, "Wait for us until I call for you, and Wong, do you have what I asked for?"

The driver of obvious Chinese birth nodded. "Yes, master. Yes."

The couple entered the ballroom and made their way to one of the tables where large bowls of punch were available for those who wished to partake.

A number of young ladies with escorts spoke excitedly to Gabriella, who introduced them to Bolton.

"Gentlemen, please take your partners for the next dance." The leader of the twelve-piece group of musicians announced the next dance.

Robert Bolton smiled down at Gabriella. "May I?"

"You dance divinely, Robert!" She laughed as Bolton twirled her in a circle.

"As do you, my dear." He smiled back at her.

An hour or so later, her parents appeared. Barnstable stayed at the back of the room with an assortment of fellow businessmen, and her mother sat with other wives showing equal dissatisfaction toward the behaviour of their spouses.

It was 1:00 a.m. when the orchestra played the final musical selection, and shortly afterward, Bolton led Gabriella to his waiting coach.

Wong nodded as Bolton again helped Gabriella onto the seats. A warm breeze greeted them as the coach began the journey to the Borthwick home. It was when they had reached the top of a small wooded hill that Bolton suggested a walk in the moonlight.

"Why not?" Gabriella agreed with a smile. "It is a beautiful evening, and soon it will be much too cold for a late-night stroll."

Bolton said quietly to Wong, "Give it to me, and take the carriage off the road."

When they sat on the rise looking down the valley, Bolton produced a flask.

"I have brought some of the punch from the ball and two glasses; may I pour for you?"

With a slight hint of hesitation, the young lady nodded in agreement.

Some moments passed as they listened to the sounds of night birds enjoying the light of the moon as they scurried for food.

Bolton placed his arm around Gabriella, who looked at him with slight rebuke.

"Robert, we barely know each other. I cannot allow you to go too far."

"Too far? What do you mean?"

Then a sudden shudder and a groan from Gabriella's lips indicated that all was not well with her.

She looked up at Bolton and asked, "What is wrong with me?" Slowly, she slumped down onto the grassy edge of the hillside.

Bolton stood and stared down at her, then knelt, and began to unfasten her shawl. Alarm flashed in her eyes, and then panic hit as she was unable to defend herself. Silent screams stayed within her as Bolton opened her bodice to expose her ample bosom. He bent over and gently kissed each nipple.

"Now, my dear! Is that not wonderful? Now, let us investigate as to whether you are still a virgin, and if you are, let me remedy that for you."

As she slowly passed out, she was vaguely aware of the searing pain in her lower body as Bolton entered her time and time again.

Sometime before dawn, Bolton carried her senseless body to the carriage where Wong lay sleeping. "Wake, man, and drive to the Borthwick place."

They drove onto the long driveway leading to the mansion. "Wait here!"

He picked up a bag from under the seat and walked to the door; he found it unlocked and was relieved that he wouldn't have to resort to forced entry.

"Waiting for your daughter, I wonder?" he murmured in sarcasm as if he were speaking to Borthwick.

The moonlight allowed him to investigate each of the downstairs rooms until he reached the lamplit study where Borthwick lay asleep in his chair. Bolton opened the bag and produced a handgun. He shook Borthwick awake and placed the cold steel onto the skin under the left eye of the now frightened man.

"Take me to where you hide your money. You have ten

seconds to respond, or I will pull the trigger." He jabbed the gun twice into the face of Borthwick to emphasize his demand.

"Don't shoot!" Borthwick stammered. "I will give you the money. Follow me."

With lamp in hand, the two men walked to a large library, where Borthwick lit another lamp.

The light allowed Bolton to watch as Borthwick opened a hidden wall safe. As Bolton walked to peer inside, he slammed the gun against Bothwick's head behind his right ear, dropping the man to the floor. With a broad smile, he helped himself to the folded wads of money in the safe.

"My goodness, you are a greedy man, hiding all this for none to see."

It took him some time to count the notes and then locate a messenger bag large enough to pack the money without raising suspicion.

Borthwick slowly awakened, muttering to himself, and when he focused his eyes, he saw Bolton stuffing his money into a bag, and all came clear to him. He tried to stagger to his feet, but Bolton pushed him to the floor.

"I don't know if you remember me from the past, Borthwick, but many years ago, when I was only five years of age, you were a guest at our family home outside London. I approached you as a young and curious child and attempted to be friendly. You deduced that my parents were not taking too much notice, and so you hit me. Later, when we were alone, you fondled me, attempting to play with a certain part of my lower body—that which has just completed its entry many times into your daughter. Does this sound familiar, or do I need to help you remember?" Bolton wagged his gun in Borthwick's face.

Slowly, recognition and then fear caused Borthwick to shiver. "No, no, that is not true!" he stammered. "You must be remembering some other man. I would never do such a . . ."

"Liar!" Bolton slapped him across the face, then he planted the gun muzzle at Borthwick's temple.

"I have enjoyed the last hours of this night doing incredible things to your daughter," he said with a smarmy grin. He then went into full detail, describing the assault of Gabriella Borthwick. Her father whimpered at first, and then he sat, blood streaming from his face, sobbing uncontrollably.

"She is outside in my carriage, albeit a bit senseless right now, and I intend to bring her into this room and do so again with you watching. And then I am going up to your room to do likewise with your wife."

"No, oh no . . . no," Borthwick cried softly into his hands, tears dripping through his fingers. "May you go to hell to be with your master the devil!"

"Maybe I will; perhaps you may be correct in your assumptions. Will I meet you there? One never knows, does one? But first, we must ensure you do not run away. Wouldn't you agree?" Bolton laughed.

Ripping a large curtain from the study window, he wrapped the gun, and pointing it at Borthwick's right knee, he pulled the trigger.

A muffled explosive sound emanated from the concealed weapon. Borthwick screamed as his knee burst into a mush of blood, bone, and skin.

"And now for your daughter." Smiling, Bolton walked from the room, leaving the wounded man rolling in agony.

Some moments later, he returned with the still unconscious Gabriella in his arms.

A sound from the door caused Bolton to turn. There stood the butler. In a flash, Bolton was by his side. He produced a large hunting knife and in seconds had slashed the startled man's throat. The butler dropped to the ground with his hands attempting in vain to stifle the gushing blood flow.

With the same knife, he went back to Gabriella and held it against her throat.

"Borthwick, I am bored, and I am tired. It is time to end this now."

Sometime later, he returned to the carriage. "Come now, Wong, drive us home."

The following morning, Robert Bolton burst into the office of the town sheriff. In shock, he pleaded to the man.

"Sheriff, I have just returned from the Borthwick home where I was invited for an after-ball breakfast. A terrible sight awaited me there. A terrible scoundrel or possibly several have murdered some or maybe all of the family. Please come quickly!"

Two weeks later, Bolton sat with the sheriff.

"Mr. Bolton!" he began, "I must thank you for all you have done to help us with the murder of the Borthwick family and their butler. I am well aware how much the young lady meant to you, and I can fully understand your grief and your reasons to return to England. We will continue to search for those responsible and will do our best to notify you when we have succeeded. And succeed we will, as we believe a gang of murderous bank robbers, who have been active in this county for some time, are responsible. I do, however, wish you luck in your travels."

Robert Bolton walked out into the street. As he strolled to where he would wait for the midday trolley to take him to New York City, a few of the townsfolk came up to wish him well and express their sorrow.

Finally, he reached the rendezvous point. His faithful driver Wong stood by the carriage.

"Wong, the carriage is yours, and so is this." He handed the man a package that Wong opened. He nodded thanks with no expression other than a brief hint of a smile.

"This is between you and me, Wong, just between you and me."

The train departed on time, and Bolton sat watching the countryside passing by and then turned to read the latest in the town's local newspaper. It summarized the horrific details surrounding the murder of esteemed banker Barnstable Borthwick and the rape and subsequent murder of his wife and daughter. It went into some detail explaining the loss of a large sum of money stolen from Borthwick's safe and the murder of the household butler.

"Simply shocking!" Bolton smiled to the image in the train's window smiling back at him. "Who could believe anyone could commit such a ghastly crime?"

## Chapter 77

Shortly after nine in the morning, the horse-drawn carriage drew to a halt outside the home of Lord Thomas Bolton near Lavenham in Suffolk. Six men descended and walked to the door where they were welcomed by the butler. They entered and were met by Lady Constance and two bright and cheery toddlers tugging at the dress of the lady of the house. Nearly three years of age and with the promise of lots of presents from London, they were eagerly awaiting the delights that could soon be theirs, subject to their good behaviour. Naturally, any newcomers were possible donors to their expectations.

"I see the twins are as they should be, delightful and full of mischief," Lord Bryant commented.

"Hmph!" Lord Squires muttered. "They should be upstairs in the nursery where children belong."

Lady Constance smiled politely. "Of course, of course. Come, children, upstairs to where Nurse Martha is waiting for you."

To the men, Lady Constance said, "Gentleman, the butler will show you to my husband, who awaits you in the library."

The group of well-suited gentlemen entered the large room where Lord Thomas Bolton sat at a table studying some documents. He stood to welcome his fellow members of England's House of Lords.

"Gentlemen, please be seated." To the butler he added,

"Please ensure we are not interrupted until food is prepared for the midday meal."

"Yes, m'lord." The butler quietly left the room and closed the solid wooden double doors behind him.

After commenting on the arrival of cooler weather and general conversation about the daily goings-on of London life, Lord Bolton stated, "Gentlemen, let us get down to business. I have prepared an agenda of this day's meeting. The papers are in front of you. Let us address each item and make our decisions."

Silence prevailed, broken only by the rustling of paper, as the men glanced through the documents.

"Right, then," Lord Bolton began. "For the first item of business, as you are each aware, we have agreed that there is huge financial potential in the new fields of medicine. The raw materials are not readily available in England or the colonies, so we need to evaluate options in recently discovered lands."

"Invaded lands, I suspect is the correct description," Lord Bryant interjected with a smug chuckle.

Lord Bolton peered over the top of his reading spectacles at the speaker. "I do not think His Majesty would approve of that comment, but it does bring us to another point of discussion: the issue of the convict problem. The new convict settlements in New South Wales appear to be a perfect solution to the ever-increasing problems we have here with the robbers and rapscallions, rogues and vagabonds. Our prisons and shipping hulks are hugely overcrowded, and we are planning to send at least three more fleets of these scum to those shores. We may then utilize them to venture forth to find all that this new country may offer in the way of new medicine components. We can then force them into mining or laboring at absolutely no cost to us. The neighbouring country of New Zealand is already proving most profitable with flax and many other forms of agriculture."

"But what of the problem with the savages that we are led to believe reside there?" one of the lords enquired.

"Simple solution!" Lord Bolton replied quickly. "We have more than adequate arms and ammunition from the factories we own. We create some activities to allow those that enjoy killing to wipe these black and brown ignorant savages to extinction."

A murmur of agreed satisfaction swept around the table.

The meeting was adjourned some time later for lunch, and at 4:00 p.m., Lord Bolton called an end to the business of the day.

"Gentlemen, brandy and ales will be served in the adjoining room."

"I say, Thomas, old chap," Lord Humphries posited, "I understand young Robert was involved in a nasty set of circumstances over in New York or was it Virginia? I understand there was a murder or two."

Lord Bolton peered over his glass of brandy at Lord Humphries for several long moments before he replied. "Yes, you are somewhat correct in your assumption. The facts, as I understand them, indicate that my son was most helpful in assisting the local law enforcers to ascertain that the robbery and murder were committed by a ruthless gang of outlaws.

"Moreover, since his forays into searching for business opportunities in the new lands of New South Wales and possibly New Zealand, I am proud to state that he has more than proved his worth as my son and successor to our business interests. In fact, you may recall earlier today that I spoke of the third, fourth, and fifth fleet soon to be finalized for departure. The second fleet should have landed some weeks back. Those plans will be discussed with my son when he returns from New South Wales later this year."

Lady Constance, who had quietly opened the door, listened to the statement from her husband, and without comment, she left the room again. Her husband looked up just as she left the room. Lord Humphries could not help noticing the tension between them.

*****

"My dear, you looked somewhat troubled earlier today," Lord Bolton said to his wife. "What bothers you so?"

Lady Constance stared at her husband. "It's about our son. Why do you talk about him as if he were some man of great distinction?

"You are more than aware of the evil he creates wherever he travels. Why do you cover up all the trouble that always emerges from his activities wherever he may be? The deaths of many over in Ireland . . . and now more deaths during his travels in America. These horrendous events always occur in the closest of proximities to our son, who somehow manages to be totally innocent of all wrongdoing, in every case."

"My dear Constance, Robert is our son, and I have great trust in him and his ability to do well for us. Now please, run off and look after those little ones, those twins you love so dearly. And do not forget, it was our son who made their presence here so very possible for you."

"How could I forget, Thomas? How in heaven's name could I forget?"

## Chapter 78

Sydney was now very much established. From the first tents erected by the Tank Stream, named and described by Governor Phillip as a fine stream of fresh water, and the ensuing buildings that had been built, all agreed that the commander had indeed planned well and achieved much.

The marines and the convicts had begun their new lives on the eastern side of the stream, and the governor, the civil department, and selected convicts resided on the west side.

Landing wharves had been built on the clean white sandy shores that had greeted the first boats from the First Fleet. The swamp mahoganies, the salt-water swamp oaks, and the blueberry undergrowth had been cleared, and buildings erected in their place.

The settlement initially boasted a hospital, the governor's house, a church, and the storehouse, all built in line with Phillip's plan to have the first main street run in a southwesterly direction, and the new streets were built accordingly.

The early primitive Sydney was no more than a collection of squalid huts built from cabbage tree stems with others a mix of wattle and daub. The wretched view from the filthy reeking ships in the cove showed tents that sagged in the downpours and night fires in the region that would eventually be known as The Rocks. In truth, early Sydney looked more like a sad, sorry Gypsy encampment.

As buildings became more in line with the governor's far-sighted ambitions, the provisions store and granary had been added to those that once stood alone on a track in the bush.

The stream that proved a barrier between the convict side and the more elitist governor's side and the problems that grew accordingly were solved when a bridge was erected over the stream.

Wild fruits were not overly abundant, and those that did provide sustenance appealed to some people, but not most who called this new land home.

The land now belonged to the crown, which made no sense whatever to Padraig Gallagher.

He stared down at the activities below him. Carpenters, stonemasons, laborers, and marines scurried to and fro, working to ensure that Governor Phillip's plans and ambitions would succeed.

Padraig respected Phillip, and he had no feeling of dislike toward Captain Tench. In truth, he admired both men for what they and their colleagues had achieved.

However, he did have an immense sorrow as to the manner in which the natives of the land now called New South Wales were being treated. And that sadness was magnified when he realized that colonialism took no prisoners.

The settled land belonged to those who settled it or to the King who claimed title through those he sent to steal it.

He was more than aware that claims were being made in England by the rich and those with aristocratic backgrounds, who wished to gain wealth from claiming title to acreage in a land that they had little or no knowledge of, other than that it was theirs, simply for the asking—just as they had done to his own homeland.

Padraig closed his eyes and reached out to his wife, Kathleen, and his two little children. He stood there alone, praying that they would be there to greet him when he opened his eyes again. His prayers were not answered.

## Chapter 79

The four convicts watched the soldier turn his back to them and proceed to urinate onto a gum tree.

They had left early that morning to walk up harbour to a sandy cove that had produced good fishing two days prior.

"Get 'im now, John boy!" one of the convicts whispered.

Convict John picked up a lump of wood, and quietly creeping up behind the soldier, he smashed it down on the soldier's head. The other three convicts began kicking and hitting him with rocks they found lying around.

"Take that and that and that, ya shit lump!"

They dragged the now unrecognisable lump of bleeding, broken body farther into the bush, away from the track they had taken to the cove.

"Leave ya for the beasts to feast on. Ya won't bovver us no more," one of the convicts said, and then he laughed in derision. "Let's go, me boyos. We'll put plenty of distance between them back there and where we bed down tonight."

They walked on, laughing and joking about the dead soldier, until the convict who was leading the trek stopped in his tracks.

"Bleedin' 'ell. Look at that one, will ya!" He pointed to the sandy cove ahead of them. "Ain't seen nipples like that in years."

They sat quietly, peering through the trees down to where an aboriginal woman and a younger female stood by the water's edge.

A young male was standing knee deep with a line in his hand.

"What about them. What an arse on that black 'un. What say we help ourselves, lads?" They crept down onto the sand.

Suddenly the young female turned and saw them. She spoke, shoving the older woman and indicating what she perceived as danger coming toward them.

The fisherman walked from the water, waving his right hand in an attempt to calm the women.

Mistaking this as a threat, John yelled, "Get the bastard, Henry!"

Henry rushed up to the younger thinly built aboriginal and swung the length of branch against his head with such force that he dropped instantly.

"I fink ya killed the bleeder, Henry!"

"Bleedin' good job is wot I say, John. Let's get those wimmin."

The two females stood petrified at the sudden violence and gave little retaliation as they were flung to the ground.

Two of the convicts ripped down their trousers and immediately entered the two women, the younger child screaming in pain as the violation ended her virginity.

"I'm gonna go round the back door, so dontcha worry too much 'bout that blood there, John boy." Another of the convicts laughed uproariously.

It was late afternoon before the convicts' sexual desires were finally satisfied.

"Time we went, lads," Henry said to his friends.

"What we gonna do wiv 'em then?"

"Ah, leave 'em be. We 'ad our fun. Let's hit the trail and get the 'ell outa 'ere before they come after us."

The sun was just setting when the convicts decided that they had traveled far enough for the day. They made a rough camp and lay down to prepare for sleep.

The first to die did not feel the spear drive through his heart.

As the others jumped to their feet to fight back against the sudden arrival of ten or so aboriginal males, they were speared mercilessly one by one until all lay around the clearing dead.

They were then dragged off to where the natives knew animals would be, to quickly dispose of the now hated invaders of their land.

The dingos would have a feast tonight.

*****

"Hey, wotcha think about Daly? They 'ung 'im! Won't 'e a mate o' your'n, Padraig?" The agitated enquiry came from a convict who had just returned from Port Jackson. He went on to explain that the convict had been found guilty of a plan to foil the authorities by the pretence of a gold mine that he had discovered.

After it was found that he had lied, he had been dutifully hanged.

"Sure and to be certain, it takes very little for your English heads of this new country to do to those they find dislike for," Padraig replied with a tone of distaste.

"Bleedin' 'eck, Irish, we ain't all like that!" prisoner Jimmy Burne replied in his thick Cockney accent. "But we still luvs ya."

The convict that had just joined the group from Port Jackson went on to add, "They got ya mate Caesar and all."

"What!" exclaimed Padraig.

"Yep, he was brought in beaten and bound a few days back. That bastard cat o' nine tails whipper cut 'im to ribbons wiv 'is whip. Nearly killed the black bleeder. He told me to give you a message. 'Tell Padraig I am well. They can't kill me!'"

Padraig looked up to the cloudless sky. "They can't kill me!"

Memories of other friends and family that "they" did kill flooded back and sent a chill through him.

*Time to move on*, he thought. But move on to where?

Certainly, the mix of those English he had learned to like and get on with were now tangled with those English who had caused him so much heartache and pain.

He walked from the camp down to the water's edge. The tide was out and about to turn. Without any wind or breeze, the sea lay smooth and peaceful. As he walked along the shoreline, he remembered so vividly the first time he had ventured into the sea. He could visualize the face of Hugo ordering him and Sean into the Donegal Atlantic. He clearly remembered the fear of his friends as they also jumped into the waves, and then the satisfaction as they lay on the sand with the knowledge that they had conquered the sea, and then on to conquer the British who had stolen their land.

Now all he had was the knowledge that they and he had lost—lost his family, his brother, his beloved wife and children, his friends—all lost, gone!

His thoughts suddenly halted when he saw three natives walking toward him. As they came closer, he recognised one as his young friend from farther up the harbour. It was Burabura!

Delighted to meet him again, Padraig put out his arms in greeting.

Soon they were together and chattering in a manner that gradually Padraig began to understand.

With sickening realization, he finally grasped the meanings of their hand motions and some of their words as they described the rape and brutality of the two aboriginal women at the hands of the convicts. He was most horrified to discover that the young woman who had been raped was she who had befriended him before he was carted off by the British that morning those weeks back.

Somewhat relieved to learn that she had recovered, Padraig smiled as they described the violent ending of the lives of the convicts. Padraig spent some time with them and returned to camp, waving good-bye as he left.

## Chapter 80

The boat landed on the sand below the camp where Padraig and the others had now established their base at the head of the harbour. It was three hours after the sun had dawned on yet another cloudless morning.

One of the three sailors adjusted the sails as a marine stepped out onto the sand. Looking up to where Padraig and three others stood watching, he yelled out, "Hey, convict Gallagher! Get ya Irish arse o'er 'ere!"

Padraig shrugged and grinned at his comrades. "Sure and now a gentleman, would you not agree?" And he began to walk down to where the boat rode in the gentle swell.

"Top of the mornin' to ya and to yaself," Padraig said, good-naturedly mimicking the marine's cockney accent. "And what can I be doin' for ya an' all?"

"Get in the boat. Governor wants a word wi' ya."

Sometime later, they landed up harbour, and the marine escorted Padraig to where some officers stood talking outside one of the main new wooden premises where Phillip and his head officers conducted the day-to-day business of building Port Jackson.

"The Irishman for the governor," he stated.

Padraig was taken into the room where Governor Phillip, Lieutenant Ball of the *Supply*, and Lieutenant George Johnston of the marines sat talking.

"Oh, good morning, Gallagher," Phillip said as Padraig walked in. "You do know my two officers here. We have a problem, and we all agree you could be just the man to help us."

Padraig stood listening.

Lieutenant Ball stood up and addressed Padraig. "Gallagher, we are having a major problem with these beastly natives. It was always our intention to wipe these troublesome savages out should they pose a problem. Well, it now seems they are more than causing us concern. Some of our marines and convicts have disappeared. We have reason to believe they have been murdered by those black scum, and we wish to give them a lesson they will not soon forget. We are ordering you to come with us so that you can locate them for us, and we can deal with them."

"And if I refuse?"

"You will not refuse," Lieutenant Ball interjected. "Not if you know what is good for you."

"I understand my friend, John Caesar, has returned. Perhaps if I could spend some time with him, I may find your orders more palatable." Padraig smiled back at him.

Governor Phillip spoke. "Gentlemen, I am sure we can allow Gallagher a visit to the cells where Caesar is confined; a half hour or so while you finish rigging your boats, and then we can begin. Padraig, do you agree?"

Padraig smiled at the subtle use of his Christian name. "Thank you, Governor Phillip, and perhaps, may I suggest he could join us."

"Enough for one morning. I think we may all agree. Lieutenant Johnston, arrange for one of the men to take Gallagher up to the cells."

Padraig gaped in shock at the beaten and bloody body of his friend asleep on the dirt floor of the cell. The open door had allowed enough sunlight for him to see the sleeping man.

Moving to his side, he held his friend's hand.

He called out to the guard. "Hey, give me a jug of water!"

Caesar stirred as the words aroused him. Padraig gently eased some water into his open mouth. "Take it easy," he whispered. "Plenty more here, John."

Gradually, Caesar began to gather his senses. "Padraig!" he stammered. "Where did you come from? What are you doing here?"

Slowly Padraig explained. "Tell me about yourself, John. Where did you get to, and how did they capture you?"

Caesar told of how he made his way south of Port Jackson where he met and joined a small group of natives who offered him food and allowed him to stay at their campsite. He had been most intrigued by their dances each evening and their use of facial and body paintings. He had presumed that because of the noticeable absence of females, he had been witness to a tribal gathering. They had left him in peace to watch and enjoy the relative safety of their camp until late one afternoon they were attacked by the English marines. Some were killed and others disappeared into the bush. Caesar had been recaptured.

"Padraig, I fully understand your hatred of these bastards. What will they do next?"

Padraig was just about to tell him of the governor's demands, but was interrupted by the guard.

"Irishman! Go to the governor now!"

"Go, Padraig. I will be here when you return."

Governor Phillip sat watching him as he entered the room. "Punishment and discipline are the ultimate conditions of convict life, I am sad to say, Gallagher. You will no doubt be concerned regarding the state of your friend Caesar. It is quite simple. If he stays out of trouble and obeys all orders, he does not receive the lashes. Now allow us to return to our business.

"Are you willing to accompany us as we seek these native

troublemakers?"

"Yes, but on the condition that you release Caesar from that cell he is in."

Phillip stared in silence at Padraig before replying. "Gallagher! You do not give orders here. However, I will agree to your request, but on the conditions that we have no more trouble from him, yourself, or any other of your convict friends. Agreed?"

Padraig looked at Phillip and nodded his head. "Agreed. But I ask of you this one request. There has been enough death and injury to the convicts and the natives. Can we perhaps approach these people with respect and an offer friendship instead of hatred and a musket?"

Phillip glanced over at the other officers. "I do not totally agree with the wording of your statement, Gallagher; however, I do concede that perhaps caution may be more appropriate.

"Before they embark, I will discuss with my men some options that may well offer more peaceful resolutions to these concerns."

Later that morning, two boats set out with orders to seize and bring back any of the natives they found.

*****

Padraig watched as the two boats drew nearer to a beach where several black-skinned naked natives stood waiting. After landing, they were approached by two marines who handed out items to entice them into greetings with them. While their attention was on the items, the rest of the marines rushed over and manhandled two of them onto the sand. The rest, who had been watching, immediately ran for the safety of the bushland.

However, as the two on the sand began crying out in panic, those who had fled returned with additional members of their tribe. Padraig was shocked to see them clubbed ferociously until they also ran back to the safety of the forest, leaving one of their fellow tribesmen lying face down in the sand.

*So much for the sympathy that Phillip spoke of,* Padraig grimly pondered. Sympathy, indeed—savage sympathy!

The bruised and battered black man was bundled into one of the boats, and as the two boats departed from the beach, the natives threw stones, lumps of wood, and spears at the marines.

Lieutenant Ball and Lieutenant Johnston both ordered the muskets to be loaded and fired.

Padraig watched as the shoreline and the angry natives faded from sight. He also wondered why he had been needed, as neither Ball nor Johnston had shown any interest in him, or how he may have intervened to prevent any violence toward the natives.

## Chapter 81

The free sound of the breezes misting through the sails of the boats nearing the newly named town of Sydney was in complete contrast to the mournful and lamenting cries of the native prisoner lashed to the side of the boat. On landing, however, he gratefully swallowed some boiled fish and seemed to accept his fate as he gazed around at his new surroundings.

Standing with a mixture of angry and curious eyes upon him, he appeared to be in his early thirties. He was black, of medium height, bearded, and hairy, and showing an excess of black hair not concealing a very healthy manhood, which had the female convicts mouthing vulgar, but humorous expressions of ambitious nightly behaviour. This, coupled with a most musical voice, as he uttered words from his native dialect, begged an answer from Padraig as to what he might be saying.

"What say you, Gallagher? What is the black beggar yabbing on about?"

"Words I cannot understand, Governor Phillip, but words of polite anger at being taken from the safety of his home region, I would suggest," Padraig ventured.

"Please sit with him, Gallagher, and work your way through the words you understand to determine whether he understands those, or any he may relate back to you."

Together the two men sat, the black man cross-legged while

Padraig squatted.

Gradually, as Padraig worked his way through the words he had used before his capture, the eyes of the black man lit up.

"Ah, Burabura!" He gestured wildly, pointing to the rope handcuff around his wrist. "Ben-gad-ee. Ben-gad-ee!"

"You are Ben-gad-ee?" asked Padraig, pointing to the man's chest.

Vigorous shaking of the black man's head and waving his tied hands in a circular movement gave Padraig the answer.

"I think he wants his hands untied, Governor Phillip."

"Do so!" Phillip ordered a marine.

Free from the rope binding the man's hands, his mood changed dramatically.

Giggling and with eyes gleaming, again he pointed to some of the women watching with keen interest.

"You man," Padraig explained. Then pointing to the ladies, he explained. "Woman!"

"Ah, woo-man . . . woo-man." He laughed.

At that stage, Phillip suggested Padraig lead the aboriginal up to the governor's building.

Together, as they walked toward the officers' buildings, the prisoner began pointing and attempting to convey words to the ladies in a most melodious and friendly manner that had all but the males smiling in self-satisfaction.

The prisoner entered the governor's house, briefly showing fear at the sound of the doorbell, but he quickly recovered and showed much interest at the pictures and artifacts presented to him.

He had often spoken the word 'woman,' referring to the word taught to him describing the convict prostitutes, and Padraig smiled, as when shown the picture of the Dutchess of Cumberland, he again uttered, "Woo-man!"

"Most certainly!" Padraig smilingly agreed.

As they walked through the governor's residence, he showed much interest, particularly as he peered out of a first-story window. Later at dinner, he showed great glee while dining on a mixture of duck and fish.

Before being shown to his sleeping quarters, the barber was called. His filthy hair was cut and his face was shaved clean. It was during this barbering feat that he took great delight in squashing bugs and other vermin crawling about, and ate them heartily, much to the disgust of those watching on.

And finally, he was dumped unceremoniously in a tub of hot soapy water to be scrubbed thoroughly from head to foot.

The following morning, he appeared in the community clad in a shirt jacket and trousers, much to the delight of the women yet again, but to the disgust of many of the marines.

Padraig was called to ascertain his name, but again could not follow the dialect that seemed somewhat different from the dialect of the ones who had befriended him earlier.

So, at the governor's suggestion, he was named Manly.

"Manly?" A few of the female convicts exclaimed when they heard this news. "Very manly indeed, what?"

Padraig and a few of the convicts were disgusted later, though, when Manly was handcuffed and a rope attached to stop him escaping. Manly, at first, was most amused at Ben-gad-ee, which he again called his ornament. However, he became enraged and immediately showed hatred for his ornament when he discovered its true use.

"A bloody prisoner in his own country, but for what crime?" was asked many times and particularly from the convict who was ordered to accompany him wherever he wished to go to, and even more indignantly by the male convict ordered to sleep next to him each night to block his escape.

In the days following, his eyes would wander to the far

shore where he would gaze at his tribe's people, and upon seeing their cooking fires, he would mutter, "*gwee-un*," which Padraig understood to mean fire.

Padraig was required to sit with him while he ate heartily, cooking his own fish from the fire he would build to do so, the purpose for which was for Padraig to learn and understand the words he used.

Three days after his capture, the governor ordered Padraig and some marines to take Manly back to his people to show them that the English meant him no harm. Upon seeing his people, he cried with joy, but his pleasure quickly turned to pain when he tried to leap from the boat to join his friends and family.

As the natives came closer and beckoned him to come with them, he pointed to the manacles that imprisoned him.

Padraig angrily offered his opinion. "I do hope you are so very proud of yourselves, English men. In their country, you defile them."

"Shut ya Irish mouth or swim back. Have respect for your king and country!"

"England is surely not my home, and your king will get none of my respect, not if this is how he treats countries he invades and their people he attempts to conquer!"

Angry words flowed until the boat officer intervened to calm the situation.

"You'll get yours, ya Irish bastard! I'll make sure of that," one of the marines mouthed as the boat began the trip back to Sydney.

Manly began to sob as he saw his friends waving good-bye. *Wee-rong* was a word he used while pointing in the direction of Sydney.

When they were close to the newly erected town, Padraig pointed and asked, "Wee-rong?"

Manly nodded his head vigorously. "Wee-rong! Wee-rong."

Padraig couldn't help but notice the irony of the word. *We are wrong*, he thought grimly, but he took comfort in knowing that if he'd had his way, none of these atrocities would've been committed.

*****

One year on from the time of the landing, much had been achieved in the new colony. Padraig had spent considerable time with Manly, and their friendship had developed. As Manly found confidence in their friendship, he explained to Padraig that his name was Arabanoo, which he pronounced Ar-ab-a-noo. When Padraig passed on this information to Watkin Tench and Governor Phillip, they agreed that Arabanoo would no longer be called Manly.

He enjoyed the company of the dogs and the cats the boats had brought with them, and while enjoying most of the new foods he tasted, he abhorred the taste of alcohol.

Padraig began to learn more words of the native dialect, and Arabanoo began to explain the customs and life of the peoples of the land around them.

Padraig had learned from bitter experience never to fully trust the English, and he felt that his new native friend had similar feelings. And so, in March it came as no surprise when Arabanoo learned of yet another English atrocity.

Sixteen convicts working on one of the brick kilns had snuck off and traveled to Botany Bay. They intended to attack the natives and take their food, fishing tackle, and weapons and then escape to the north.

The natives, however, had been watching and had attacked without warning, killing one convict and wounding most of the others.

One of the convicts, who escaped and returned to base, lied to the officers, who sent a detachment of marines, who were too late to repel the natives.

They did take the wounded back to Sydney where Governor Phillip was incensed at the story the convicts told him. The truth eventually came to light, and those who had survived were flogged.

Padraig and Arabanoo were made to be present at the flogging, which caused great distress to Arabanoo. Padraig tried to explain the vagaries of the English, but this did little to calm the fear of the imprisoned native.

This was enhanced when six convicts were hung for stealing flour as well as other foods and alcohol five day later.

With the memory of the swinging bodies still firmly in his mind, Padraig sat by the water's edge, and his thoughts returned to Killybegs and Donegal.

He imagined sitting in the tavern with his brother, Sean, drinks in hand, talking and listening to the tales of the fishermen. He imagined returning home to Kathleen and his little ones, watching his dog sleeping peacefully by the open fire. He smiled as he envisioned Kathleen shooing Sean off to the family home close by. And then finally, with her arm around him and with her beautiful smile gleaming at him, Kathleen leading him up the stairs to their bed.

Padraig sobbed and cried as those memories of her tender lovemaking engulfed his wretched mind.

Standing, he screamed to the startled gulls. "Kill me, God. Take me. Where are you, God? Take me to be with my wife and babies!" He slipped down onto the sand, alone and destroyed.

## Chapter 82

"I hate those bleedin' bags of shit!" Flash Harry exclaimed to his two friends leaning against the walls of The Stag's Head.

Harry was named for his style of clothing, which was considered most fashionable by his fellow criminals and was paid for by the proceeds of his team of youngsters, who were considered the best pickpockets in the East End of London.

Flash Harry and his friends were watching the horse-drawn carriage passing on its journey up to Essex and then on to Suffolk. They readily recognised the men in the carriage, who disdainfully sneered at them from the curtained windows, each impeccably attired and wearing his wig of choice, certain that these urchins, the lowest of English classes, hated them, and they, in turn, most certainly could find no affection or positive feelings for the dirty rascals on the mean streets of East London.

One of the men touched the tip of his nose with his scented handkerchief to ward off the smells that were so typical of that part of London.

"Scum!" Lord Humphries muttered.

"Never have I felt that our plan to rid us of these rat-bags is so relevant and so timely," Lord Bryant concurred.

"I heartily agree," said Humphries. "If James Cook, the good sea captain, did little else, he at least found a home for wretches such as these."

As the slums of London gave way to the fields and farmlands of Essex, Lord Carstairs puffed on his pipe and blew a puff of tobacco smoke through the open carriage window.

"I understand that there is an element of disagreement between Bolton and his wife," he commented idly.

"Not quite," Lord Bryant stated. "Lady Constance is most used to getting her own way, and as we fully understand, the House of Lords cannot and will not tolerate any contradiction or non-compliance to all the bills we pass."

"So long as she stays clear of our meetings with Bolton while we are at their home," said Lord Humphries. "We have too much planning and organizing to allow any disturbances."

And indeed, an hour or so later, the coach pulled to a halt outside the stately home of Lord and Lady Bolton, who greeted them with amiable enthusiasm.

"Welcome to you all, and please allow our butler to bring your bags up to your rooms. Afternoon tea will be served when you are ready." Lady Constance nodded to the butler.

"Your arrival is most timely. Look at our feathered friends that have also honoured us with their presence. The swifts and house martins have arrived early this spring. Maybe we can look forward to a long and pleasant summer."

"Tush, tush, my dear, I am certain our friends are not too interested in birds. We have much more important matters to attend to," Lord Bolton stated firmly. "Come, gentlemen, I have drinks ready in my study before we find what the cook has organized for afternoon tea."

When the five were seated, Lord Bolton spoke with a somewhat disdainful tone as he outlined the beginning of his presentation.

"It is certainly no secret my feelings toward our European

neighbours and the manner in which they have beaten us to the wealth of the American continents—the bloody Spanish conquering most of the Southern Americas and the French beating us to the north where we now have to fight and defeat the frog-swallowing swine. The Portuguese, not to be outdone, are also in the Central American mix. And we hear of the Dutch claiming land on the African continent, which should be rightfully British. How can we expect to teach these black savages just who is their true master, and of course, claim our mineral rights and the gold situated there with the bloody Dutch beating us to it? Plain downright disgusting and a pure example of how not to run Parliament!

"So ,what are we going to do in the Pacific?"

Bolton paused to sip from his brandy glass. "The first convict fleet is now well established in New South Wales, and we are preparing the second and third fleets to follow. I believe Commander Phillip and his men have done an excellent job in establishing our base there, but his intolerable attitude of fairness and his overdoing of what he considers right and just could cause my plans to go awry. Thus, I have insisted a much more hardened quality of men become part of the crews and armed forces on the next fleets to set sail.

"We are aware of the ignorant black savages who roam our new land and their inadequate weaponry and possible intent to halt our progress to settle and prosper there, not to mention claiming the gold and other precious metals that will be rightfully ours, quite frankly, gentlemen, we will not allow this to happen.

"With that in mind, my plan is to wipe out those that stand in our way. We must eliminate the natives and any others who show mercy to them and thereby halt our progress. Gentlemen, what say you?"

"They say it is the largest island continent on the planet," began Lord Humphries. "How do you propose we find the areas that are best suited to provide us with a profitable outcome? Then, how do we maintain the best results?"

Bolton smiled. "I'm sure you are all aware of the antics and the skulduggery my son, Robert, is rumoured to be part of or has instigated."

Four heads nodded in unison.

"Well, then, we send the lad with a group of cohorts out on the next available vessel to claim the best land to settle and farm, and then we send the finest prospectors to search for those areas best suited for mining gold and other precious metals." Bolton paused and smiled. "My son and his chosen men will then, shall we say, ensure there are no problems standing in our way."

"And the convicts! What will happen to them?" enquired Lord Bagshawe.

"That is our finest solution. We utilize them with payments accordingly to eliminate any risk from the black men by wiping them out, and of course, any loss to the convict fraternity is only more profit to us. Again, my son, who is rumoured to have little in the way of a conscience, will be ideally suited to manage this issue."

More and more questions were asked and answered, only to be interrupted by the butler who announced that afternoon tea was about to be served.

Lord Bolton glanced at the large clock in his study. "It is almost six o'clock; time to enjoy the wonderful dinner our chief cook has prepared. Salmon, pheasant, venison, and other delights await us, so I will finish our afternoon with my final thoughts on these matters.

"For each fleet of convicts we send to this new colony, we eliminate at least five hundred or more of our criminal element. For each group of ten fleets we send to the new colony, five thousand or more of the unwanted elements of society here in

England will arrive in New South Wales where we can utilize their disgusting talents to wipe out all who stand in our way. Those that the natives kill will even out a total loss of the blacks and the convicts united. That way there will be less work and risk for our own armed militia."

Lord Humphries nodded in agreement. "I say, Bolton old chap, what a marvelous plan. You certainly will have our support." Turning to the others, he asked, "What say you, gentlemen?"

The three other lords of England's realm stood and shook hands in gleeful agreement.

## Chapter 83

Mary Piles watched as he walked toward where she sat. His face, forlorn, torn, and lost in a myriad of tortured memories belied the man she had fallen in love with.

She had watched him stand tall in the face of the harsh and unfair judgment handed out to him in the courts of London, and again on many occasions since then, as he fought for fairness and indeed the lives of both female and male convicts. Most of the convicts liked him, or in her case, loved him for the man he had become in the face of the harsh and bitter life that was now their lot in this strange and foreign land.

Those that did not like the Irishman hated him for various reasons, all unjustified.

As he walked closer to where she sat, she whispered, "Padraig!" He appeared not to hear her. Instead, he seemed to be looking through her to some place only he knew of.

Mary had had a sad life prior to being sentenced. Abused as a child, she had been raped continuously since the age of eight. Or was it earlier? Birthdays were no longer days of joy. They were days of bitter memories. Her father had always laughed and stated, "'appy birthday, me dear. Look what ya daddy 'as for ya."

She couldn't comprehend then what he had produced from his trousers, but many, many times since she had found out and was forever reminded.

Growing up in London had been harsh. The only way they had food to eat was because of the money procured from the profession her mother had been forced into; either that or the money was stolen. And yet, Mary had defied all and grown into a slim, but well-proportioned lady who drew the attention of those somewhat better off, but sadly, those also whose company she tried to stay clear of.

"Padraig!" She spoke again, only this time louder.

He turned and stared at her. "Kathleen, is that you? Where are you?"

"No, Padraig. 'Tis only me—Mary Piles. You all right, Padraig? Please sit here with me."

He sat down, staring out toward the sea. "We lived near the waterside," Padraig said. His voice had a distant quality as he reminisced. "Well, not too far away. On good days, the water shone as if painted with the finest, clearest blue the heavenly painter could find. On stormy days, the waters, though rough and very dangerous, were my reminders of the safety that my family sheltered my brother and me from. And later, those ocean waters provided my brother a good living and food for the rest of our family, food that we all loved and enjoyed.

"Those waters eventually prepared us to fight the treacherous British that destroyed my entire family." He lapsed into silence.

Mary reached out and held his hand. She felt him flinch ever so slightly. "'Tis only me, Padraig. Please talk to me. Tell me what ails you."

Turning and looking into her eyes, Padraig began to tell her of his life and love for his now dead wife and the destruction of his family.

She listened, and though her upbringing had been far from happy, she could well understand how Padraig felt and the reasons for his deep and sad depression.

"Padraig, what will you do? How can I be a friend for you?"

"Mary, I understand and appreciate that you wish to help. But I want to be far away from here.

"I made an arrangement with Captain Phillip to release John Caesar if I helped them to gather more knowledge of these regions through my friendship with the local people. He has not honoured his promise, but instead has done more harm to them. Caesar has been brutally beaten again and again. I intend to help Caesar, and when he is well, we will disappear from here for good."

"But the soldiers will search for you and who knows what they will do to you both?"

"So be it, Mary. So be it," Padraig murmured softly. Slowly getting to his feet, he turned to Mary and gave her a sad smile. "I am going to talk to Captain Tench and ask if I may speak to John Caesar."

"I'll walk with you."

As they neared the new streets, Padraig was again amazed at the bustling activity. "I swear, each time I come here a new building stands. Mary, there is the officers' quarters. I must leave you now."

She looked into the sad eyes of the Irishman, and reaching up to him, she kissed his cheek. "I love you, Padraig; please be safe!" Mary turned and walked away.

"What ya want?" The words came from the guard outside the new wooden structure that now housed those who would determine the future of Sydney.

"I wish to speak to Captain Tench. He is expecting me." Padraig smiled at his untruth.

"Wait 'ere!"

"Lyin' bastard!" The guard snarled as he returned. "But the captain'll talk to ya. Go."

Padraig was led to a room where Tench and some other officers sat poring over blueprints and street plans.

"Ah, young Gallagher, I believe," Captain Tench smiled. "Come and be seated. What can we do for you?"

Somewhat bemused at the welcoming words, Padraig replied, "I was hoping I could visit my friend, John Caesar, if that is possible."

The officers glanced at Tench who replied, "Normally such would not be the case, Padraig. Caesar is still in irons due to his recent escape and recapture. However, as you have been a great help to us since our arrival here, and also as I am aware he is your friend, I will ask the guard to escort you to where Caesar is being held."

"Guard!" Tench called out. "Please take Mister Gallagher to where Caesar is being held."

"Yes, sir. Gallagher, come with me."

A short time later, the guard stood outside the wooden building. Producing a key, he unlocked the door.

"No point in lockin' it. He ain't goin' nowhere." He said this despite the fact that the door was locked, and he laughed at his little joke.

Padraig entered and stood staring at his friend, lying on the sandy floor with his leg manacled to an iron wall mounting. His clothing was shredded and still brown with matted blood. His face was bruised, and one eye was badly blackened. However, his spirit sparked when he saw who was standing in the light from the half-opened door.

"Padraig! That is you, I pray."

"Yes, my friend, your prayers are answered. 'Tis my very self."

Dropping to the side of John Caesar, he spoke quietly. "There is a guard outside who no doubt is listening to every word we speak. We must keep our words to a whisper."

Caesar then explained how since his escape he had traveled many miles to the north.

"I found another harbour inlet where the fish are aplenty. I lived with natives who were most friendly and indeed found myself in the nightly arms of one young lady who I could proudly boast would be at home in the company of many of the finest I have bedded." This he stated with a happy grin that did much to hide the damage to his face.

"However, these bastardly bloody British also found the harbour. They sailed in late one afternoon and landed close to the natives' camp. I lay sleeping after a fine lunch of fish and oysters and the attention of my lady. I awoke to the sound of gunfire, and as I ran out to witness the murder and savage beating of my new friends, I was felled by the baton of one of the bastards. Padraig, I could not believe my eyes when I came to my senses. The British had wiped out most of the male natives, and when my woman came to my side, they bludgeoned her to the ground. Those who had survived had run off into the bush.

"My friend, the cowardly British sons of Satan shits then started beating the women and violating them. I yelled to my woman to run to safety. I know not whether she escaped, as I was then smashed to the ground again.

"I remember little else other than waking while at sea and again when we landed here."

Padraig sighed. "What will we do? Where can we go? How can we escape from this hell we now live in, John?"

"Get me free, and I will take you," Caesar stated. "I will take you to where there are no British, only people we can call friends."

"Irish dog, ya time is up. Get on out 'ere. I'm lockin' the door!"

"I'm coming to get you out of here, my friend. Fret not," Padraig whispered.

Caesar nodded, this time with a broad smile on his battered and bruised face.

Padraig stood and watched as the guard locked the door and placed the ring of keys in the baggy pocket of his trousers.

The guard then turned, spat on the ground, barely missing Padraig's boot by inches, and walked out.

"Get well, my friend. You may be free sooner than you think." The Irish brogue reached Caesar through the wooden door as he lay in the gloom. But now he was much more contented.

Padraig walked back down the dusty new lane that separated the two lines of buildings on both sides of what would soon be the main thoroughfare of the township of Sydney. Since the camp had been moved closer to the mouth of the harbour, he hadn't realized that so much had changed. More and more he wanted no part of this place.

Deep within him, he knew that a new beginning was all around him. But the memories of his past and the tales that his parents and grandparents had told him about the invasion of the land he once called home echoed round and round within him. He saw only too clearly that the invasion of this strange country and the brutality toward those that called this land their home was created by those same invaders from England. Padraig realized he wanted no part of it. He could not understand how and why he had been found guilty of a crime he had not committed and then be condemned to be part of and a witness to such happenings. He wanted only one thing.

"God above! I ask of You, if you truly are the God I have been taught to believe and trust in, then please reunite me with those I love who are no longer with me.

"And please forgive me if and when finally I meet he who stole all those from me, and I take his life as he stole theirs. Then, God, I do ask that you understand."

"Padraig! Hey, Gallagher!" Padraig turned as the voice brought him back to the present.

"Captain Tench. Yes, what is it?"

"We would like to talk to you regarding some actions you may be able to assist us with. I can arrange some sleeping quarters for you and ask you to meet up with us in the morning. Shall we say an hour or so after sunup?"

Padraig thought for a moment or two. "Yes, Captain Tench. I will be there."

The humour was grand that evening as Padraig rejoined a large group of his convict friends who he hadn't seen since moving up harbour. Tench had allowed enough alcohol to ensure the mood stayed positive, and all were happy, apart from some heavy heads the following morning.

Padraig joined Tench, Commander Phillip, and a group of assorted officers at the agreed-upon hour.

"Ah, Gallagher!" Phillip began. "A number of serious problems are of major concern to us. Primarily, the increasing lack of food. A large number of offences have been committed by convicts thieving food from our food stores, and of course, they have been punished, some most severely. But that does not solve our problem. We understand that you have been most successful landing fish and sourcing other seafood. Also, your skills that you learned from the natives in locating fresh meat and wild edible plants have also not gone unnoticed. In plain truth, Gallagher, we need your help."

Padraig looked from Phillip to Tench and to each of the officers seated there. The irony of this meeting had certainly not escaped him, and the bargaining powers that now lay in his grasp began to mount as he planned his options.

"What do you have in mind, may I enquire?" he asked.

"We were of the opinion that an expedition to the north would be an option. Also, maybe inland to where we, ahem, captured you once before."

"And would I be going as a free man or as a convict?"

"Far too early for us to be granting that, I am afraid, Gallagher," came the terse reply.

*Of course*, Padraig thought. *Wanting and not giving.*

"I have an idea that may be of help," he said. "I know of waters full of fish and land to the north where wildlife abounds. I am willing to lead you there. You will need to prepare a boat that will enable us to be away for at least a week. I suggest we leave first light tomorrow morning as the weather appears to be reasonably settled right now."

"Agreed!" Phillip replied. "Captain Tench, I need you to organize one of our landing craft and three men to sail with Gallagher. You leave as agreed first light on the morrow."

"One more thing," Padraig said. "I would like again the opportunity to bid farewell to John Caesar later this evening. Would that be possible?"

"Certainly, Padraig. I will tell the guard that I have given full permission for you to do so. Shall we say around late afternoon or early evening?"

"Thank you, Captain Tench."

Padraig spent the rest of that day talking to some of the more recent native arrivals who had drifted in and out of the camp. He found Arabanoo with a group of his people down by the waterside. Together they sat, and Padraig managed to obtain much information about the land far to the north. Arabanoo was most intrigued, but Padraig was reluctant to give too much away as to the reasons for his questioning.

The late afternoon brought the usual activities of campfires and food preparation. Those who had cooking facilities, whether they lived in shacks or more palatial living quarters, also were in the process of preparing evening meals.

Padraig walked down to the dock area where the smaller boats were arriving from their day of work. He watched as the boat they were to use the next day was receiving its final preparation for the journey north. Water flasks and other equipment were positioned as only seamen know where all should be. As they stood to leave, two of the men smiled and wished Padraig the best. The other ignored him.

*Oh well, two out of three can't be all that bad.* Padraig smiled to himself, wondering what they would think in the morning.

Just before dusk, he went to where the guard had just been changed for the day. Much to his satisfaction, he noted that the surly guard from yesterday had taken over nightly duties.

"The bloody Irishman, is it? And what you want of me?"

"I understand Captain Tench has given me permission to take some bread and water to John Caesar while I visit him. When would it be possible for me to do so?" Padraig enquired.

"Not bloody now. I wanna eat, too, ya know. Come back later."

Padraig smiled. "Indeed, and to be sure, to be sure."

A slight breeze fanned the smoke from the dying campfires, and the last of the odors of cooked food gave evidence to a satisfactory end to another day. The sun was about to drop behind the tree line of the bush to the west.

Padraig walked to where Caesar was imprisoned and spoke through the wooden door.

"Be prepared, my friend, be prepared."

He then walked to the guard who spat another mouthful of tobacco at his feet.

"You again?"

"I need to talk to Caesar," Padraig stated.

As the guard rifled through the assortment of keys to find the key to unlock the door, he failed to notice Padraig pick up a metal bar conveniently left leaning against the cell wall.

As he unlocked the door, Padraig glanced around. All was quiet, and he could see no one other than two convicts walking down the road some distance away. He slammed the bar into the back of the guard's head.

He dropped without a sound. Padraig quickly dragged him inside the cell room where Caesar looked up and laughed outloud.

Trying each key and uttering an oath as each one failed, they both searched for the one that would unlock the manacle. With only two left, a cry of triumph echoed around the tiny cell as the lock snapped open.

Padraig helped Caesar to his feet, but as he stepped forward, he fell backward into Padraig's arms.

"Steady, my friend, steady. You take it easy while I lock this bastard in your place."

Ripping a sleeve from the guard's shabby uniformed shirt, he rolled it into a ball, and taking the belt from the guard's waist, he tied it around his head, securing the gag in his mouth to ensure his silence.

"Come, my friend, our vessel awaits us!" Padraig laughed as he again assisted Caesar to his feet.

Peering outside the door and seeing no one, they walked toward the dockside, passing only three other convicts who took no notice of them.

As they approached the boat, Padraig told Caesar of how everything had fallen into place. He helped his friend in and pushed the vessel out into the receding tide. As darkness fell around them, their escape went totally unnoticed.

Caesar swallowed great gulps of water and several mouthfuls of bread, and as Padraig raised the sails, John Caesar gained more and more strength.

By the time they reached the heads of the harbour, he was

able to assist Padraig as the vessel headed into the choppy waves. The moon, not quite full, gave enough light in the cloudless skies for Padraig to see that they had reached the open sea.

"Portside, John!" Padraig stated. "We now head north and to freedom."

# Chapter 84

The summer of 1790 was beginning with long days of extended sunshine with little or infrequent rain.

It was felt by the general populous that this accounted for the overall wonderful good feeling and fellowship, particularly to His Majesty as he announced to the seated lords of his realm that he would be ridding England of another thousand or so of England's riffraff and criminal no-goods. He would be sending them to the new colony of New South Wales.

"And good riddance, we say," were the overall mutterings and support from those at the House of Lords.

It was later that afternoon when Lord Bolton and his chosen circle of fellow conspirators gathered for their customary drinks of celebration.

"What say, old chaps. His Royal Highness has done us proud now, has he not?"

"New South Wales and the rest of that odd country are certainly up for those brave and daring enough to go get it."

Bolton watched and listened with cynical amusement. "So, Lord Rathbone, when do you plan on sailing?"

"What? Me go out there? Never. And dare I suggest, Lord Bolton, that you should have your scallywag of a son go out there and do your dirty work. Do you not agree?"

"Gentlemen," Lord Egmont interrupted. "Let us behave as

one would expect us to. I understand those connected to the new land of New Zealand, another of Cook's supposed discoveries, intend to name a mountain after me. But would I set foot on such a savage land? Never! Leave it to those foolhardy and stupid enough to put one's life in danger. As Bolton so rightfully points out, let them do the dirty work; we will claim the riches.

"And on that subject, Bolton, tell us more about your son, Robert. What the devil is he up to now?"

With a smile, Lord Bolton began. "Indeed! My good wife Lady Constance is forever fretful of his feisty behaviour. And contrary to general belief, he did not start that riotous incident in the Boar's Head. No, it was supposedly triggered by a common bar wench who commanded his attention in a manner practiced by certain ladies of the night.

"What she and the male were doing there was also a concern as the drinking establishment is not commonly used by scum such as those. Her man, husband, or whatever he may be, also a common thug, was incensed enough to challenge Robert over his attention to the woman. As the constable who was called to investigate the incident readily stated, all was most satisfactory, and the fool deserved to die. Thus, Robert was found not guilty of his death. Oh yes, a handful of guineas did manage to find their way into the constable's pocket.

"The outcome, of course, was that young Robert will depart from England once again, this time onboard His Majesty's vessel *The Scarborough* bound for New South Wales."

"We understand the wench went home with Robert and dutifully thanked him as only she knew how for ridding her of the fool," Lord Rochester concluded. This was accompanied by roars of laughter.

\*\*\*\*\*

Robert Bolton and his three friends were enjoying their ales. They had met at one of his friends' establishments in Knightsbridge. The Boar's Head was noted for its clientele being those of middle to upper class, and owing to the watching eyes of the man seated behind them, a feeling of nervousness would not leave him.

Reasonably well dressed, clean-shaven, and with a glass of ale in his hand, he in truth did not stand out from the regular pub goers enjoying an early evening ale or two.

His Irish brogue also did not raise too much interest from the barman who had served him.

He had learned that Bolton frequented some of the more nefarious drinking establishments as well as the more respectable ones where he had both business and pleasure interests.

He had been following Bolton from time to time, without arousing suspicion and had learned, not to his surprise that Robert Bolton had been ordered to leave England by his father.

Sean Gallagher was sitting with three recent arrivals from Cork. Their conversation ranged from the troubles back home to how their life might improve in London, when Robert Bolton walked in. With three of his comrades, he had ordered ales, and in doing so, he attracted the interest of a woman seated near them. She made little secret of her intentions as her hand drifted over various parts of Bolton's body. Suddenly, shouts of enraged blasphemies interrupted the normal clamor as a large overweight man appeared before them. Bolton grinned with obvious delight as he urged the fool to take further action, which, of course, he did.

Sean watched with great interest as Bolton then swiftly produced a blade and stabbed his knife into the gut of the drunken husband, then he sliced upward, and stabbed the man twice in the heart.

In doing so, memories of the man's enjoyment of murder

and cruelty flooded back.

*Man of the devil . . . son of Satan*, were thoughts that entered his mind.

Two days earlier, Sean Gallagher was extremely lucky in learning that his brother, Padraig, had been shipped off to the convict settlement in the Pacific. He had travelled to London to search for his brother based on the information given him by Throckmorton Squires.

By mixing with the Irish fraternity in the slums and anywhere the Irish worked or played, he had narrowed down two possibilities after finally finding where his brother had lodged when first arriving in London. Either his brother had been killed by Bolton or others, or he had left for another destination. Sean knew only too well that wherever Bolton was, Padraig would be close by or one or the other would be dead.

It was a suggestion by one of his new Irish comrades that Padraig could have been picked up by the constabulary as a vagabond that led Sean to the records of recently arrested and charged criminals. It was then that Sean found out that his brother was in a land far away.

In the days that followed, Sean pieced together all that had happened since his remarkable recovery from near death in the Atlantic. Money that Cohen had given him in Donegal had paid for his journey to England and then a bed in London. Quite proud of his investigative work, he had then learned by way of boastful chatter that Bolton was soon to journey to New South Wales, where he presumed his brother was a prisoner.

With his experience as a fisherman and a man of the sea, he had no problems signing on as a midshipman on the *Neptune*, also soon to sail to New South Wales.

But most important, he did not want to be too close to Robert Bolton in case his enemy and the killer of his family recognised him. To his relief, on the occasions that Bolton had glanced at him, no recognition was apparent.

Sean was now ready to leave London on the *Neptune* when it set sail in a week's time.

## Chapter 85

The first of June 1790 in the new colony began with a sad understanding of fearsome anxiety. The weather was wet and windy and woeful.

Over two years had passed without any contact or news from England. Food supplies were at their lowest, and morale in general could not have been worse.

Commander Phillip found that discipline and order were becoming increasingly hard to maintain. Both staff and convicts were continually bickering with each other, and his senior officers were continually being tested.

It was with huge relief then, that on the eve of the third of June, the cry of "Flag's up" rebounded around the settlement, bringing with it tears of joy and screams of happiness and joyous clamour.

Small and large boats put out to sea, and as the first reached the heads, the ship flying the colors of England came into full view.

The *Lady Juliana* had arrived.

She was carrying 225 new convicts who would join the Sydney colony.

On landing, the ship's administration was besieged with cries of "mail, please, letters!" from all who could get near. All previous ill humour was replaced with utter gladness.

As the following day progressed, the ships' officers were entertained by Phillip and those from the colony. It was stated that *Lady Juliana* had been at sea for over eleven months with many deaths occurring during the voyage.

The officers from the new colony of New South Wales were thrilled at the news from home with special thanks going to His Royal Majesty for his amazing generosity.

Each noncommissioned officer was granted an allotment of 150 acres. Every private soldier was granted 80 acres, extended to 100, if married.

His Majesty, in his ultimate kindness, stated that all were to be free of any costs or rents for ten years. However, after that period, His Majesty would be charging rents of one shilling for every fifty acres.

The good fortune continued when, later in June, three more ships arrived. *Neptune* had left England carrying 693. It was learned that 163 had perished en route. *Surprise* had arrived with 252. *Scarborough* had landed with 256. All told, 273 had died en route.

*****

Sean Gallagher watched as the *Neptune* approached the heads of Sydney harbour. He had been most intrigued by the changes in weather and was told that these were winter months. Winter, he knew, was a time of snow and freezing rain. How then were these days so warm in comparison? His thoughts were interrupted when the captain's orders came loud and clear to prepare to sail through the rougher waters of the entrance to the calmer waters of the inner harbour.

Soon, as many smaller craft sailed up to greet the vessel, Sean looked toward the settlement of Sydney and watched in anticipation as it came into view.

*Padraig, my brother, are you there? And has Robert Bolton found that you are here also?* These and many other thoughts flashed through his mind.

The ship finally dropped anchor, and then the activities of unloading passengers, convicts, crew, and the very much-needed supplies began.

Sean had been shocked at the treatment handed out to the convicts locked below deck. Those who had died on the long, hard journey had been blessed, it seemed to him. He could not fail to wonder whether his brother also had died on the first convict journey to this foreign land.

Finally, all the docking and deboarding tasks were completed, and he went to shore on one of the boats carrying the last of the supplies to land. He and a fellow crewman, also Irish, shouldered the final load into the storage sheds.

"Theys ya lot, me hearties. Follow on wi' me for a well-earned toast for all ya effort."

The welcoming words were just what Sean and John Murphy were dying to hear. The three men walked from the dockside toward town and were soon settled into a long first night in Sydney.

Sleeping quarters had been arranged in a room attached to where they were drinking, so a long walk home in a strange and foreign land was not to be a problem.

As members of the crew of *Neptune*, they came into regular contact with convicts who had been given relative freedom of the boat. Both Sean and John Murphy had become conditioned to the tales of misery told by the convicts they found time to chat with.

And so, merrily swigging pots of ale celebrating their landing, Sean was surprised to meet a more positive convict close by the table where they sat.

They learned that William Hatfield had been born and raised in Maidstone, but had been sentenced to seven years in the new convict settlement.

As the evening progressed and William, nicknamed Billy,

told of the brief history of the colony from the time of the first landing, Sean became more and more troubled at the numerous tales of floggings, short-term imprisonment, and executions.

How could he ask about his brother without raising suspicion?

"You are from Maidstone, Billy. Tell me—are there many Irish convicts here?" Sean asked.

"There are convicts from all over, and yes, Irish and all."

The evening progressed, and Sean learned more about the colony.

"And what about escapes? Do any try to escape from here? And if they do get out undetected, where would they go?"

"Indeed, Sean, in fact, we have had a run of escapes of late. Most get caught. But some are still on the run."

"Can't blame the poor lads for wantin' a bit of freedom," Sean said to build rapport with the convict, and then he took a swig to buy some time to think. Pondering on how best to ask about Padraig, Sean received his best news ever.

Wiping the cream off his lips, Billy continued. "Aye, and that's the truth and all. In fact, youse Irish never know when to quit, and the black buggers, also." Billy grinned. "A black man caught in England named John Caesar and one of your countrymen named Gallagher are still bein' sought."

Sean stared at Billy, hardly able to draw breath. Fortunately, he wasn't aware that Billy knew his surname was also Gallagher.

In a manner not to create doubts regarding his intent, Sean gained no further enlightenment other than to be greatly relieved and indeed thrilled to have come so far and to be so near. But where to next, and what could he do to find out more?

Sleep would not come. Sean eventually got into his makeshift bed sometime after midnight, and with the alcohol fueled snoring all around him, he finally succumbed and managed to calm his overwrought brain into an untroubled state.

Soon it was the dawning of a new day, and to the newcomers, squawking, chattering, and other peculiar sounds resounded through their ale- and cider-soaked heads. Those that were interested learned that these were the early morning calls of birds. To those nursing head pains from overindulgence, these sounds only intensified the pain.

John Murphy said, "To be sure, Sean, if they be bird songs, it will be the birds of Eire I will be preferring."

Sean found a bowl of water and went to find a place he could relieve his aching bowels. He was most eager to see what Sydney had to offer on this, his first morning in only the third country he had ever visited, and with a rapidly clearing head, he stepped out to greet this amazing new day accompanied by John Murphy.

The sun was shining in a cloudless blue sky, and the day was a bit chilly. But to Sean Gallagher and John Murphy, it almost felt like spring compared to the bitter cold of a winter morning in Ireland.

Together, they walked the streets, commenting on the work of both convict and tradesman in transforming the arid bushland into the foundations of England's new outpost in the Pacific.

Two women passing by noticed their bewilderment, and being interested in these fine-looking young men, who were obviously new to the colony, they spoke to them in friendly greeting.

"Good mornin'. Can we help you both?"

John Murphy, always one to take note of a pretty wench, replied, "Tis a cuppa tea we be needin', me dear!"

"Then follow us. We work where tea and the first food of the day are cooked. Though until the new boats arrived, you would be none too happy at what we were cookin'!"

Sean and John walked alongside the two women, asking questions and learning as much as the ladies could tell them. And soon after, both sat outside drinking from a large tin of tea and commenting on the happenings in Sydney.

"Look at that, Sean! He be as black as soot from the chimney." They watched as two natives walked past them.

Sean was totally unaware that Baneelon and his companion were friends of Padraig.

Sean was also unaware of the English treatment toward the convicts, but was soon to learn very quickly as the new convict arrivals were herded out from their new quarters and paraded for the arrival of Commander Phillip and assorted officers.

"Some of these convicts can barely walk, Sean," John Murphy said, and Sean only nodded in silent agreement.

The two Irishmen listened in amazement as they received their orders to commence work assisting the labor force in building the new premises from the materials unloaded from the ships arriving daily.

However, Sean was lost in a myriad of wonderings as to the whereabouts of Padraig, particularly, where and how could he reach him.

Then, to add to his confusion and to make his blood run cold, he sighted two new arrivals walking toward them.

Lowering his head he muttered, "The devil's servant himself—Bolton."

"What was that you say, Sean?"

Nothin', nothin' at all, John. Let's go see more of the town."

At noon, they both reported early for their shift on *Neptune*. And it wasn't until Sunday later that week when they were allowed back onshore.

During that time, Sean had decided to cast caution to the wind. After all, he had nothing to hide, and in truth, not much to lose.

He and John sought out the ladies they had spoken to earlier that week. They were both serving tea.

"Top of the mornin' to ya, me dears!" John greeted them. Sean spoke quietly to the lady pouring the tea into his cup. "Can I have a moment with you, or are you too busy?"

Elizabeth Hipsley smiled coyly at Sean. The Irishman, now tanned quite bronze from his time sailing through the tropics, with his red hair swept back, exposing his rugged good looks, inspired thoughts of lusty moments alone with him.

"Be back ta talk to ya once I serve those." She nodded to the other tables.

With a beaming smile, she returned and suggested they go outside to chat.

"Dirty bugger ya!" John laughed as they left.

Sean went straight to the point. "May I ask if you know Padraig Gallagher?"

"Padraig? Indeed. My friend Mary Piles adores 'im. No one knows where 'e is now. Took off with that big black one some time ago. But why do ya ask? Do you know 'im?"

The sadness on Sean's face implied enough for the street-smart Elizabeth Hipsley to understand not to enquire further. "Oh!" she whispered. "I think I understand. I will get Mary to talk wi' ya. Just you wait 'ere."

It wasn't too much later that she appeared again, this time with one who looked at Sean with sadness in her eyes.

"Hello, I'm Mary Piles. Elizabeth has told me you want to know about Padraig."

Mary spent the next fifteen minutes telling Sean of her love for his brother. She concluded by offering an even greater depth of her understanding of the grief and pain she felt he was suffering.

Sean pondered over these words and decided that he could trust Mary.

She listened as he told of his brother's love for his childhood love, Kathleen, and the subsequent loss of his wife and twin children. As he told of the murder of their parents and grandfather, Mary began to weep.

"I wanted to leave here and go with Padraig," she whispered. "But he . . . he would not take me. I chose to believe it was because of what would happen if we were all recaptured. I know, though, deep in my heart, it was because of his love for his Kathleen."

In the silence that followed, Sean had much pity for the English maiden. His love for his brother only deepened his resolve to find Padraig and together exact revenge for the horrific hurt inflicted by Robert Bolton.

"Do you know where Padraig and his friend went?"

"Only that they disappeared after dark and sailed for the north. Little is known of where they were heading or where they are living. Other than the determination of Phillip and his marines to find them and punish them, nothing much has been said about them since their disappearance."

Back onboard *Neptune* that night, Sean tossed and turned in his bunk, trying to find an answer to what he should do next. He had managed to obtain permission to ponder over the ship's charts. But with the vastness of what lay to the north and the scant information he had to go on, he knew he could never remotely find a solution to the whereabouts of his brother.

Sleep finally gave him solace.

## Chapter 86

Sean finally felt he had a solution to his problem.

He approached the captain of the *Neptune* and offered to stay on in the new colony, and in doing so, he arranged to swap with a sailor from the first fleet to take his place on the return journey. Thrilled at the option of returning home to England, there was an immediate rush from many, and soon Sean found himself a member of the new colony of New South Wales. Before Sean took his job onboard the *Neptune* in England, he used a fake last name so that he could remain under the radar, knowing that his brother was a convict, and also knowing that Bolton might be tracking the whereabouts of a Sean Gallagher.

There were looks of amazement at first from some of the officers who were bemused as to why someone would choose to stay on in the new colony rather than return to England, but as Sean explained, he had nothing to go back to. However, thanks to the king's generous offer, if he worked for Governor Phillip, he could obtain land and build a new life here in the new colony.

The warmer weather of September coincided with Commander Phillip venturing on a trip to Manly Cove.

Sean was summoned to be part of one of the boat's crew along with two of the Sydney-based natives. As the boat approached the sandy beach, they noticed a large hulk lying above the water line. As they sailed closer, it became apparent that it was the remains of a large whale.

Baneelon attempted to introduce the commander to a group of natives enjoying the remnants of the badly rotted mammal that had washed ashore. In the melee that followed, Commander Phillip was wounded in the leg by a spear.

Sean suddenly found himself in a situation where he was called upon to help the commander. His intervention and that of another crewmember and the subsequent success of the brief struggle that followed resulted in both being hailed as heroes.

The irony was not lost on the Irishman. What would be his brother's comments? He couldn't help but smile at the thought, and once again, he also silently thanked Hugo Cohen for his excellent training.

Sean's friend and fellow countryman, John Murphy, had departed for the return journey to England, so Sean turned to Mary and her friends for companionship.

Sean was somewhat smitten by Elizabeth Hipsley, and while his major focus was directed toward the concerns of his brother—well, he was a man after all!

To his credit, during the following two nights of somewhat noisy passion, Sean did come to terms with his conscience that it was for him to create an acceptable identity that would not arouse suspicion. And heroes, after all, were allowed to take advantage of their new status.

And in actuality, Robert Bolton had passed him by on three occasions without so much as a glance in Sean's direction. It was then that Sean decided if no news came regarding Padraig, he would allow his overactive inventive energies to take action.

Captain Tench and some fellow officers were going to great lengths to ensure that no outbreaks of violence were instigated by the English toward the natives, and as Sean was now a trusted member of the boat crews, he was continually called upon for boat duties when needed.

And so, as the winter faded into warmer September weather, Sean was again called upon to join a party journeying to the north shore. After rowing for some time, they eventually landed on the sandy foreshore. It was then the first time he had come face to face with a larger number of the Indians, as Tench called them.

Nanbaree, Abaroo, and Baneelon were distributing fish to their womenfolk and children. A bottle of wine was produced, and soon the good humour was flowing.

Sean found himself thoroughly enjoying the antics of some of the women as they at first spat out the bad taste, but with urging, began to swallow gleefully the first of the wine and more when it was provided.

Sitting with Baneelon, he tried to make his words understood, and in turn, he tried to understand Baneelon's attempts at English.

"Padraig, Padraig. You Padraig?"

Sean, suddenly amazed, tried to fathom the meaning of Baneelon speaking his brother's name to him with such urgency.

"Me Padraig?" he asked, pointing to himself.

Shaking his head, Baneelon said, "No, no, Padraig!" He pointed his finger northward.

Then, pointing his finger at Sean, he uttered a mouthful of words, then pointed at his ear, and stated, "Padraig!"

"Ah! I understand. I talk like Padraig." Sean pointed at his mouth as he said this.

Whether or not Baneelon did understand, he nodded his head vigorously. "Padraig friend" he affirmed, banging his chest with his clenched fist.

Frustrated that he could not learn more, but happier knowing that Padraig had made an impression on these strange people—and not surprised to learn that—but even more thrilled that his brother was somewhere on the continent north of Sydney, his only concern was how far north, and how could he reach him?

Later that night, he again spoke to Mary, telling her of his meeting with Baneelon.

"Padraig, your brother was one of the few of all the First Fleet to connect with the natives. He was very close to a number of them."

Sean suddenly felt a greater understanding of this strange new world and a clearer picture of how to begin his next moves.

*****

Robert Bolton sat with Commander Phillip. "Commander, the land my father, Lord Bolton, and I wish to purchase under the direction of His Majesty is as follows."

Laying out current maps and charts that showed both old and updated data, Bolton indicated the land he requested.

"Mister Bolton, your requests, to say the least, are somewhat extravagant. You are indicating many thousands of acres. And quite frankly, I am certain this vast region won't come under the guidelines set up by His Majesty."

"Commander Phillip, my father, Lord Bolton, and his colleagues, all supporters of your efforts here in New South Wales, and indeed, as peers of the realm and close friends with His Majesty, have already been granted approval and rights to purchase. I have been sent here to evaluate, approve, and settle the final agreements. I do hope you understand. I have here for your perusal letters that testify to the authenticity of my demands." He paused to emphasise his intent.

Phillip glanced over the papers and then handed them back to Bolton. "I will pass these on to my administrative people, and we will arrange a meeting with you accordingly."

In the days following the arrival of the second fleet, Robert Bolton investigated and explored wherever he was capable of traveling to. He believed that he had determined the most profitable areas to purchase with the least amount of bother and cost. He had most certainly seen that the land occupied by the natives was desirable acreage that he would definitely seek to claim, but as he had personally witnessed land owned by natives in other countries, and those then claimed by Europeans, he had little fear of opposition by the dark-skinned savages of New South Wales. In fact, he relished the thought of confrontation and how he would deal with it.

After conversing with most of the convicts recently landed and those from the First Fleet, he had gleaned from some that they would be most keen and very capable of meting out justice to any black man foolish enough to stand in his way. Those convicts with newly acquired consciences, he simply discarded. Fate had very definitely provided him with a private army at little or no cost.

Smiling and feeling at peace with all around him, Bolton watched as a group of those chosen sat swallowing ample mouthfuls of the grog he had brought to the gathering.

"Gentlemen," he began. "Enjoy the libations! There is more where that lot came from." He went on to explain in detail his plans to claim land within the guidelines set forth by the monarchy.

"But as convicts, your seven-year term has a few more years yet to run before you are free men. However, I can make life much more comfortable for you by obtaining permission for you to work with me. Those conditions will ease the burdens of your current convict life. And as it all concludes, you will have money to spend when your sentence is completed."

Outlining the foundations of his plans, Bolton was thrilled at the enthusiasm of his new companions.

"We may have some, shall we say, disagreement from the local natives, but I suspect you can deal to them."

Hoots of laughter and words of derision compounded his suspicions that these were well-chosen members of his private mercenary force.

"A pity bleedin' Caesar weren't 'ere, eh? 'E 'ould be inta this in a flash," Andy Knowlend laughed.

"Is this someone I should know more about?" Bolton enquired. "Would he wish to be part of our plans?"

"For sure, but he buggered orf. Long gone. Him and the Irishman Gallagher escaped some months back and took orf up norf."

Suddenly, a flashback memory of that face looking out at him from the prison wagon back in London shot through Bolton. His blood ran cold. "Irishman, you say. Was his name Padraig Gallagher by chance?"

"That it were, sir. That it were. He were on the same boat as me comin' out from ol' Blighty."

"You don't say," Bolton said in a noncommittal tone, giving no indication of prior knowledge to Gallagher, and as the conversation flowed, he guided questions in the direction of a more general interest so as not to reveal his devious motives.

He had managed to find a comfortable room for his lodgings in Sydney's new buildings, and later that night, he lay with mind racing as to where his enemy might be. He wondered if fate would deal him a good hand, and one day soon, he and Gallagher would meet again.

## Chapter 87

Robert Bolton had moved to Rose Hill with his convict team and begun work on the land he had acquired. With limited materials, but ample timber acquired from the plentiful bush land nearby, they soon established acceptable living quarters. At times, his convict work force reminded him of his cronies that he had brought to Ireland. That, in turn, brought back memories of his hatred for the Irish, and in particular, Padraig Gallagher.

But deep down, in the darker recesses of his mind, lurked a troubled feeling that he could not shake or find an answer to.

A few weeks back, the *Supply* captained by Captain Ball had returned, bringing much needed food supplies, corn and vegetable seeds, and as much essential materials that the ship could carry.

This coincided with the hanging of three more convicts, and it was there, while Bolton watched on with morbid enjoyment that he became more and more aware that eyes were watching him. From time to time, he would suddenly turn to survey others witnessing the men swinging to their final moments of life, but he could gain no further understanding of the reasons for his ill ease.

Bolton missed the comforts of his life in England, but in truth, he was finding the challenge of building foundations in the bush of New South Wales refreshingly different from other activities in his life to date. His house consisted of two rooms, one with a fireplace and brick chimney. Other buildings close by housed the convicts. While Rose Hill was predominately for male convicts, Bolton had used his privileged background to overrule these instructions and had selected three of the sauciest and prettiest women convicts to accompany him. The night and occasional daytime frolics with these three female convicts, who also handled the housekeeping and cooking duties, also lessened the yearning for London or other city life.

He had taken advantage of the country skills of Billy Kilby from Reading, and even without the rains that were very infrequent, they had still managed to harvest a fine crop of potatoes and other vegetables. With their allowances of pork and beef, the cook fed them well, in truth, better than he had experienced in Sydney. And there was no shortage of eggs or chicken meat as his fowls bred with happy abandon.

All in all, life in a timber shack in the bush on the vast continent of New Holland was not what he had expected, but his eye for opportunity saw much wealth to follow in the not too distant future.

From time to time, the natives living close by gave odd moments of concern, but it was an incident near Botany Bay that finally gave Bolton the chance to expedite his collection of firearms, which he had brought with him.

A gamekeeper named McEntire was speared and subsequently taken to Sydney, where, soon after he died, which gave cause to the governor to form a party to set out and capture the murderer and those willing to protect him and bring them to justice.

Bolton joined the group to march to Botany Bay where a number of tribesmen had gathered to meet those they knew would soon arrive to exact revenge for their actions. The orders were to capture and bring back the culprit and one other and to kill ten more.

This was to teach the natives that the laws of England must be obeyed, and all weapons such as spears and such like were to be seized and destroyed. Those slain were to be beheaded, and those heads brought back to Sydney as a lesson that in the future all natives must maintain a friendly and nonaggressive attitude toward those from England.

Bolton smiled in eager anticipation of the bloodletting that would soon follow. He had taught the Irish that they must obey the laws of the English. He would now teach these black savages a similar lesson.

After two days of wading through swamp water and heavy bush, the party arrived at the camp where they expected the aboriginals to be. Bolton was disgusted to find that the deserted campsite gave no clues as to their whereabouts.

"So, where are the bastards?"

"Gone," was the reply from one of the marines.

Dejected, the party began the return journey back to Sydney.

However, nearing the outskirts of the town, one of the marines spied two aboriginals apparently robbing a nearby settler's potato garden.

"Nab 'em!" yelled one of the sergeants.

However, the two were far too fast for the soldiers, and they escaped into the bush.

"'Tis good sport we are after, me hearties. An ale for the first what spots 'em."

And so the group set out after them with renewed vigor.

"Now for a wee drop of revenge," the sergeant called out, after eventually tracking them to their campfire.

He fired at a group sitting and eating. Yet once again, the men escaped, one wounded, but both still fleet of foot. However, two startled women remained motionless.

"Well, now, we do 'ave their lady folk. What say we 'ave some fun wiv 'em."

Bolton watched as the two women were brutalized and then their hands were bound and they were taken back to Sydney.

The next day in Sydney, Baneelon informed some Englishmen that the wounded tribesman had died from the musket shot. Disgusted, he retaliated by taking some of his tribal people to the harbour to rob one of the fishing boats of its catch. Unarmed, the Englishmen could do little to stop them.

Governor Phillip was outraged and set about exacting revenge.

Silently watching on, Sean Gallagher smiled grimly. He had seen similar actions in his homeland. He noticed Robert Bolton talking to a group of higher-ranking marines before walking away.

In the days that followed, Sean was most relieved to notice the absence of his enemy Bolton and subtle questioning confirmed that he had returned to Rose Hill.

With only the arrival of the *Batavia* in December and no sign of any other ships to work on, ship duties became scarcer. Sean began taking on extra work as a fisherman, and he enjoyed being back in the work he truly loved. He found great satisfaction in bringing back catches of fish unlike anything he had seen in the North Atlantic.

Making new friends among those he fished with, he learned more and more of this exciting new land.

But he was continually troubled by the complete lack of news regarding Padraig.

Christmas came and went, and the New Year celebrations ended with much humour and copious quantities of ale and wine.

His relationship with Elizabeth Hipsley was also becoming more of a problem as Elizabeth was falling for Sean's great sense of humour and his easy-going way of life. Sean, however, concealed his concern for his brother, and knew that when the time came, Padraig and only Padraig would dominate any decision to be made regarding their future.

Also, his wandering eye hadn't escaped the notice of Mary Piles, who continually warned Elizabeth not to fall for the Irishman's roguish charms.

Sean found the warmer waters of the Pacific most welcoming, and the friendship that developed between him and a selection of the convict womenfolk created a new form of entertainment, namely teaching them the skills of swimming and water safety.

*Cohen, where in the name of God are you?* He would ask in his thoughts as his mind went back to the swimming skills that the freedom fighter had taught them so long ago in Donegal.

It was on Monday of the second week of December when Robert Bolton approached Sydney for a meeting with Phillips and Tench. There had been concern raised as to Bolton claiming rights to land in Rose Hill.

"I understand, Mister Bolton, that currently you have laid claim to over two thousand acres," Governor Phillips stated.

"Indeed, I have," replied Bolton, "under an agreement already given to my father, Lord Bolton, and myself and on behalf of others associated with my father. I will be legally claiming another three thousand acres with intentions to look toward Parramatta and the northern country to lodge claims on land in those regions as well."

Pausing, with a smug smile he continued. "Surely you do not have a problem with partitioning a few thousand acres to a peer of the realm in so vast a country and only black savages roaming around pissing and shitting on it. We can utilize the land, farm it, and perhaps find mineral and gold deposits to create greater wealth for our king and country." Yes, Robert Bolton knew exactly what to say to leave Tench and Phillips bereft of valid argument.

After some moments, Tench said, "Indeed, I have seen the

agreements sourced by your father, Lord Bolton, and the king's council, but how far do you intend to travel, and how much land do you intend to claim?"

"As much as it takes, Captain Tench—only as much as it takes."

Phillips then asked, "How are your current farming operations faring, may I enquire?"

"Not so well, I regret to inform," said Bolton. "Our spring sowing has shown little response as yet, due, I am told, to the poor quality of the soil. However, this and the poor supply of rain has only dampened our enthusiasm, not our resolve. We can and will do better."

"I note that there are now close to 1340 male convicts and 133 female convicts living in Rose Hill. And an additional 100 troops and seamen have also settled there."

Suddenly, shouts and clamor echoed from the streets outside the governor's offices.

Both Tench and Phillip stood as the guard shouted through the doorway. "We got 'em, Guvna. We got Caesar and the bloody Irishman."

"Excuse us, Mister Bolton, we need to attend to an urgent matter," Tench stated.

Robert Bolton followed at a distance as Phillip, Tench, and a growing band of curious onlookers walked toward the waterside where three boats had landed on the sandy foreshore.

He watched as two bound men, ragged in appearance, lay on the sand, both somewhat bloodied and bruised.

The first was hauled to his feet and now stood facing the governor.

"John Caesar, I trust," Phillip began. "When will you learn not to try my patience with your ridiculous attempts at escape?"

Bolton's blood ran cold when the second prisoner stood and faced Tench and Phillips.

"Padraig Gallagher, I did think better of you. Guards, take them to the new prison premises, and ensure they are both securely locked down. We will address their fate tomorrow morning."

Stunned, but now so very excited, Bolton stared after them, his mind already working out the details of a plan as they were marched off.

## Chapter 88

Sean alighted from his boat. Laughing, he tossed a large fish to one of his friends standing in the sand by the boat.

"Ah, indeed, Billy Gunter. Ya surely don't catch fish like this in Bristol, now does ya?"

"And surely," his friend said, laughing in imitation mock Irish reply, "you don't catch fish like this in Donegal, now does ya?"

"Shut up the both of you fools," John Gould chided good-naturedly. "Let's load up this catch and get them up the town and drink to the success of a good day's fishin'."

Billy Gunter was a slightly built young man approaching thirty years of age and full of devilment. John Gould was reasonably well built and quiet spoken, and as a countryman from Exeter, was more reserved.

Billy and John had both been sent to the convict settlement for seven years each for theft and had arrived on the *Charlotte* and the *Lady Penrhyn* respectively.

All three had become quite close friends, and while conversation had from time to time focused on Padraig as the latest news, Sean had given no indication that he was Padraig's brother.

It was an hour or so later, as the three men sat downing the first of their ales, that Sean's thoughts and memories returned to the Atlantic Tavern in Killybegs. Celebrations of excellent catches from the waters off the coast of North Western Ireland came to mind and made him smile with bittersweet memories. Would he ever return home? If so, when?

The fading light of the setting sun gave cause for the lighting of the lamps, which gave the room a warm, ambient atmosphere. Sean looked 'round, watching the assembled drinkers and those just entering the newly built drinking establishment, eager to drink away the sorrows of the day or to celebrate the benefits received.

Half listening to the babble of the drinkers, he, at first, didn't notice the arrival of the two women until John Gould stated, "'Tis blind ya are, Gallagher. Two beautiful wenches and your eyes are elsewhere."

"Sean, how are ya?" Mary Piles enquired.

"Oh, I am sorry, Mary, and yourself Elizabeth. I was still on the boat catching fish." He laughed.

It was then he noticed the sadness in the faces of both women.

"Sean, will you walk with me?"

"What is it, Mary? What is it that saddens you so?'

Mary took him by the hand, and watched by his bemused friends, they walked outside, leaving Elizabeth Hipsley to tell the others the news.

"Sean, two escaped convicts were recaptured and brought back here to Sydney this day."

Sean stared at Mary, knowing in his heart what she was about to reveal.

"One of the prisoners was John Caesar, and Sean, the other was Padraig Gallagher."

"Are they alive? Are they well, or?" His voice faded as he stared at Mary, his eyes pleading for answers.

"Both are still alive, but neither looked well."

Mary went on to explain the wretched state of the two men when they were dragged from the boat, bruised, and covered with blood, and taken to the holding cells.

"Their clothing was hangin' from them in shreds," she concluded.
"They are here?" Sean asked. "Padraig is here, alive?"
Mary nodded vigorously, her eyes wide.
"That is all I need to know, Mary." Holding her close to him, Sean whispered his sincere and overwrought emotional gratitude as Mary went into much detail describing what she had witnessed.
"What will ya do now, Sean?" she quietly asked.
"Can you take me to where they are being held?"
"Of course, Sean, but ya must take utmost care. We will return to your friends and say very little, and later in the night, I will take ya to ya brother."
When they returned to their friends, the talk of the drinkers was only about the happenings of the day and the recapture of the escapees. Caesar, being black, and Padraig, being Irish, caused much derogative comment, but there was also much positive talk alluding to the contempt both had shown to the English judiciary.
Finally, Mary took Sean by the hand and whispered, "Now!"
No one noticed them departing. With the moon at only quarter light, they were able to make their way to where the prisoners were held unnoticed.
"Look, Sean, there are no guards," Mary whispered excitedly.
"I imagine they are very securely manacled to ensure no risk of escaping," Sean said in a quiet voice. "But we must still take care."
Peering through a small window protected by three iron bars, Sean whispered, "Padraig! Padraig Gallagher!"
Silence.
"Padraig, can you hear me?"
Silence.
Banging softly on the side of the wooden cell, he suddenly heard shuffling sounds. "Padraig, can you hear me?"

"Who is it? Who are you?"

"Padraig! It is me, Sean Gallagher, your brother!"

"Sean! My brother Sean! Never! Sweet God Almighty, is it really you? Please do not torment me so. Sean! Sweet Mother of Jesus, I pray to you, tell me this is truly my brother."

Mary Piles appeared by Sean's side.

"Quick, we must go. Soldiers are coming."

"Padraig, listen to me; you know my voice, brother. I will be back. I have so much to tell you."

Padraig whispered in the dark. "Please, God Almighty, I pray to you, tell me this is not a dream. How can this be?" Quietly, he wept until sleep overcame him.

Word traveled fast.

The early morning sun shone down on a gathering of convicts, marines, and officers to discuss the return of the escapees.

At 8:30 a.m., two burly guards slammed the cell door and escorted—rather, dragged—the weak and staggering men to the hearing.

Complete with white wig and robed attire of the English judiciary, Governor Phillip walked to the tables at the front of the crowded room. With Tench and other officers on either side of him, he began proceedings.

"John Caesar, Padraig Gallagher, you have been charged with escaping from His Majesty's legal holdings, where you were punished for your wrongdoings.

"You were each sentenced to serve seven years for your crimes. You were both warned of the severity of escaping from the colony. What do you have to say for yourselves?'

With blackened eyes peering from bloodied faces, both stared at Phillip.

"Well, what do you have to say? Gallagher, you first."

"Governor, it is useless protesting my innocence. I was wrongly arrested and wrongly charged for crimes I did not commit. And I will no doubt be condemned for stating the following. This land does not belong to His Majesty. You and your officers invaded this land.

"This land belongs to those you claim to be savages. You speak of the word legal, so I have a question for you. This land that you claim now belongs to His Majesty King George, did you ask the permission of those who protect this land, their animals, their fish and food, and their families?

"Does His Majesty King George agree that it is right to murder, maim, and steal from these people, rape and abuse their womenfolk, beat their children?

"Governor, you allowed me freedom, but only under your terms. Those terms were to guide you and your soldiers to steal more of the natives' land as you abuse them, even though they have yet to set eyes on you, the invaders, nor have they done you any harm.

"Did John Caesar and I escape? No! We left to warn those we could meet far from here to beware of the might of England. We warned them to prepare their families to fight or die! That is what I have to say, governor."

Not a sound broke the silence as Governor Phillip stared at the two convicts.

Then clapping of hands, followed by whistles, and hoots of glee from the assembled convicts greeted Phillip as he stood and thundered, "Silence! Or I will clear this room. John Caesar, what do you have to say for yourself?"

Attempting to smile through his bloodied whiskers, Caesar stated, "Padraig has said it all. I have nothing further to add."

"John Caesar and Padraig Gallagher, I have listened to your words," Phillip began. "Everything you have said is a complete insult to His Royal Highness King George III, an affront and most humiliating and cowardly attack for which I have to assess the seriousness and then pass judgment.

"You will appear before me on Friday morning, four days from now. Guards, take them to the cells."

As the onlookers parted to make way for the two being escorted by the guards, many passed their own verbal comments. These ranged from support to insults directed at the Irish.

Sean stood, hoping his brother would notice him, but to his deep regret and frustration, just as he moved closer, the guards shoved Caesar, knocking him into Padraig, who stumbled and nearly fell. As Sean pushed forward to help his brother to his feet, another convict jumped in ahead of him.

"Keep ya chin up, lad! We be wiff ya!"

Padraig smiled. "Thank you, John, you are a good man."

Padraig and John were thrown onto the clay floor of the jail cell, and the door slammed and locked.

Mary and Elizabeth suddenly appeared by Sean's side.

"I'm so sorry, Sean. What will ya do?"

"At this very moment, I have no idea. But at least I do know where my brother is now and I do know that he is very close by and I do know that I can speak to him again. But when? That will be the pleasure I greatly look forward to."

## Chapter 89

Robert Bolton's mind was awhirl. The ongoing news of the capture of the two escaped convicts was the talk of the colony. Since arriving back at his cottage, many thoughts and the beginnings of plans to deal with his enemy had crossed his mind.

As he sat staring out at the activities of workers beginning the day's activities, he idly listened to a conversation between two convicts building a stone fence outside the house he currently called home.

Peter Woodcock had witnessed the arrival of the marines triumphantly boasting of their capture of the escaped convicts Gallagher and Caesar.

He had been living with Padraig Gallagher prior to him being sent to the harbour head. Woodcock was, therefore, most concerned as to the treatment the Irishman had received and was very troubled as to the manner in which they had been manhandled and dragged to the governor. And, of course, now Woodcock was even more worried about the treatment being handed them as recaptured prisoners.

Bolton sidled over to the workers. "I say, gentlemen," he began, interrupting their conversation. "What is this you are talking about? Tell me more about these captured convicts."

Woodcock described the times he had spent getting to know

Padraig Gallagher, both good and bad times shared between them.

Bolton prodded for more information until he finally had what he considered to be the full story.

"Guv!" Woodcock concluded. "The Irishman, Gallagher, he bein' a friend an' all, would it be possible for me to go an' maybe meet up with him sometime?"

Expecting a negative response, he was most pleased to hear Bolton's reply.

"What say you go and sort out a pony and rig for tomorrow morning, and we can fetch some more supplies from the midweek market. While we're there, we can catch up with all the happenings as the prisoners prepare to face the governor."

"Done, Guv!" Woodcock replied with a wide grin.

Robert Bolton sat watching the men at work. The memories of his time in Ireland and the activities that had made him and the Irish families mortal enemies , and later his belief that the Gallagher family had stood between him and his claim for the young Irish woman he had fallen for, added more and more to the rage building within him.

"Padraig Gallagher, you wretched Irish bastard," he said quietly to himself, "you will die, and I relish the thoughts of doing harm to you."

Later that night, he lay in bed, listening to the snuffling and wheezing emanating from the nose and throat of the woman lying next to him.

"Bridget, why did you spurn me?" he whispered softly.

Through the swirling mists of his memories of their first meeting, Robert Bolton saw her, laughing and giggling as she visited the markets in Donegal. He visualized her in his arms, their bodies locked together in lustful passion. Even her sister, her twin sister, was no replacement for the perfection that was Bridget. If so, he would have taken her from that bastard Gallagher.

"Gallagher, you Irish swine, I will make you pay for what was taken from me." He spoke into the nightly gloom, stirring the woman beside him. "Be quiet!" he snarled, kicking her. But the combination of wine and overindulgent sexual activity had exhausted her, and she slept on. "Bitch!" he muttered and tried to fall off to sleep.

But it was well into the early morning before he succumbed, though not before he had finally decided on how to deal with Gallagher.

The noises of the workers outside woke Bolton. He angrily flung aside the woman's arm draped over his shoulder and rose from his bed. Walking to and opening the front door, he looked out at the workmen.

"Good mornin', Guvna. How does the day find ya?" Peter Woodcock smilingly enquired.

"Have you organized that transport to Sydney Cove?" Bolton demanded.

"All done, Guv, ready when you are."

Bolton walked back into the bedroom, struggling to come to terms with the new day. "You," he snarled to the woman. "Get up and prepare tea and breakfast. Now!"

It was midday when Bolton pulled to a halt outside the administration block at Sydney Cove. With buildings on both sides, the main street of the new town was bustling with activity. He entered the newly erected wooden structure where a number of officers and marines were in animated conversation.

He watched and listened as each voiced his opinion of the outcomes of the actions taken against the two convicts over the previous days.

"Who do ya wish to talk to?"

Bolton stared in obvious disdain at the man addressing him. "Is Governor Phillip able to meet me?"

"State your name and your business with the governor."

"I do not wish to discuss my business to one such as you. Tell me where I can meet Phillip."

"That will do, Sergeant," Captain Tench said, overhearing the heated debate. "I will take care of this matter."

"As you wish, Captain Tench," said the sergeant, and he walked off with disdainful backward glances at Bolton.

"Mr. Bolton, what can we do for you? Maybe you should come into my office."

Once seated, Bolton began. "Captain Tench, what, may I ask, will be the commander's decision regarding the two convicts on Friday?"

"Why do you ask, apart from, I hope, not morbid curiosity?"

"You may be well aware of my interest in locating land that could well benefit the future of this new colony as well as my business partners' investment in this enterprise."

"Indeed, Mr. Bolton, I am aware of this interest. What I do not understand is how this will affect the outcome of Friday's sentencing."

"What I'm wondering is whether a death sentence is imminent," Bolton said.

"Why do you need to know?" Tench replied with a hint of a smile.

"Well, if either or both survive and are released back into the community, I could use their knowledge, and possibly their guidance in settling those lands far to the north, but only with the commander's approval, of course. Then, I can advise the commander on how best to utilize these discoveries to create new farming opportunities for us all. This will benefit us with plentiful supplies of food, and of course, work for the convicts and newcomers soon to arrive on additional fleets."

"How do you intend to pursue this, providing, of course, the hangman is not utilized?"

"Very simple," Bolton said breezily, "but first, and only with your permission, I would need to talk to both prisoners to determine their opinion of the best lands they saw on their travels, but that will only be possible if they live. May I again ask, will they?"

"For what it is worth, Mr. Bolton, I am against any sort of death sentence for those two. They are far more valuable to us alive. And now, I am due to be at a meeting with Commander Phillip and others to discuss this very matter. I ask that you call back tomorrow, and I will tell you of our decision."

Bolton thanked Tench and walked out to the carriage where Peter Woodcock stood talking to a group of convicts he was obviously on good terms with.

Unnoticed by Bolton and watching with great interest stood Sean Gallagher.

*****

Victor "Crosseyed" Bates had been a very fortunate man, albeit, a man who had ruthlessly murdered many unfortunates on the dark alleys of London. Some said more than twenty; others stated many more.

Prior to his arrest in London, Bolton had met him on numerous occasions and had twice utilized his evil skills for his own nefarious work. He had lost contact with Bates, and it came as a shock when he found that Bates had been convicted of pickpocketing. Four weeks later, Bates was sentenced to seven years and sent to the colony of New South Wales.

And so, Bolton was most bemused when he recognised Bates as a prisoner, but a fellow Englishman in the convict colony of New South Wales.

Bolton had walked down to the water and sat watching

the dockside activities. It was mid-afternoon, the sun was blindingly bright, and it was still hot enough to cause Bolton much discomfort.

"Where are you, you bastards?" he muttered.

Finally, three men came into view and began walking toward him.

"Whatcha, Guv. Hot 'nuff for ya?"

Bates was tall and skinny and wore dirty clothing that hung from him.

His head was partially bald, with scraps of long straggly hair that emphasised the peculiar state of his eyes, which appeared to stare at the tip of his nose.

"What took you so long, Bates? I have been waiting here for an hour or more."

"Bloody arseholes ain't satisfied wif any ting we do. Anyway, we're 'ere now. What's up?"

"You trust these two?" Bolton nodded to the two men standing beside Bates.

"Do whatever ya want, Guv. Trust 'em as I would me own bruvver."

Bolton smiled grimly. "I thought you murdered your brother?"

"Oh yeah, forgot 'bout dat." Bates grinned in reply.

Bolton stared at them and began. "There are two men locked up, escaped prisoners, but I guess you are aware of this."

All three nodded.

"This is what I want, and here is how you can help me. In return, I will pay you considerably, or even better, I will arrange your transport to New Zealand or back to England. The choice is yours. All you have to do is break into the convict prison cells without being caught, grab Gallagher the Irishman, and bring him to an arranged place, the location of which I will tell you when you need to know. Is this clear? Do you fully understand?"

"As I understand, Guv, they are both due to 'ang on Friday. Don't give us much time," Bates replied.

"Should they hang, then the deal is off. However, if they are pardoned and returned to their cells, then we are back in business. Agreed?"

"Sure thing, Guv. Just leave it ta us," Bates concluded with a grin that only emphasised his ugliness.

Bolton left the three men and walked back to the township.

He was still unaware that he had been closely watched, and parts of their conversation had drifted to Sean's listening ears.

## Chapter 90

He walked under a group of trees. Even at midnight, his movements startled sleeping birds that immediately burst into a cacophony of angry resentment at being disturbed. Gradually, he made his way quietly to the rear of the cell.

"Padraig! Are you awake?"

"Sean! Is it yourself I am hearing?"

"Indeed, Padraig, 'tis I. But more to the point, how are you?"

"Worry not about me, my brother; how did you find me? How did you get here to this place that few know about, lifetimes away from our own homeland? I thought you were dead! And here you are! Is it safe to talk? Are the guards about?"

"Padraig, fret not. The guards are tucked up in bed fast asleep."

Sean listened to the sounds of the restraining chains as Padraig moved about in the darkness behind the bars. He could see nothing; only the sounds told him he was finally close to his beloved brother.

"What is it, Padraig? Is it truly your brother?" The voice came from inside the cell.

Sean listened as his brother answered the man's question.

"Sean, this is my friend, John Caesar, being held here with me; he can scarcely believe it is you. I've told him all about you."

"Padraig, listen to me. I must be quick. No one must know

of me being here and must never be aware that we are brothers. I have some important information for you that I think you'll find interesting. Brace yourself for this news."

Padraig listened in awestruck silence as his brother told him of Bolton and the plans that Sean believed their enemy had in store for him.

Finally, Sean concluded. "Padraig, I must depart for now. You can be sure I will be close at hand at all times."

"Sean, are you certain Robert Bolton did not recognise you?"

"My brother, in our struggles back home, the only time I was close to him, there was no confrontation. He doesn't have enough knowledge of me to recognise me or to presume that I hate him so. To him, I am simply another ignorant Irish peasant. Be safe, my brother."

In the hours that followed, Padraig told Caesar the stories of their times together in Ireland until finally they both fell asleep.

It was Friday morning and another cloudless sunny day. Sean Gallagher stood looking down the street of the new town of Sydney Cove.

In all, four streets of wooden houses and huts were the foundation of Van Diemen's Land's first settlement. Thirty or more houses stood on both sides of the main street, all built of wattle, plastered with clay, and topped with thatched roofs. They were reminiscent of homes in Ireland, Sean observed.

He stared at the governor's home. The house had been built by James Bloodsworth and was made of solid brick on a stone foundation, which certainly stood out from the other public buildings close to it. These were built of lath and plaster. A new brick storehouse had just been completed, over a hundred feet long with a house for the storekeeper.

He watched as work on the new barracks was suddenly halted. The time had come. He turned toward the cell blockade.

A sergeant with six marines appeared and unlocked the door.

Minutes later, his brother and Caesar were trundled out into the daylight, manacled. They were then marched up to the building where convicts, officers, and marines stood and watched as they were led into the overcrowded room. Sean stood listening to the obscene statements of some and the most welcome support of others.

Sean walked to where the three women stood.

"Good morning, Sean!" Mary gave him an affectionate hug.

"What do you think will happen?" Elizabeth asked.

Sean shrugged. "We must wait and see."

"Stand for the governor!" The command from inside the building echoed out into the street where they stood, announcing the commencement of the proceedings.

An hour or more of accusations, violation of the king's rulings, and total disregard for the honour and respect of the laws of the realm finally came to a completion.

"Padraig Gallagher, what do you have to say before I pass judgement?"

The crowd in the street was utterly quiet. Sean listened as his brother spoke.

"Governor Phillip, nothing I have said in the past or say now will alter my status. That is, in your eyes and the eyes of most around here, I am worthless Irish scum who has been found guilty of a crime that in truth I did not commit. I am in a strange land I did not ask to be sent to. In your eyes, I am guilty of the fact that I only sought freedom, freedom that my God willed to me, but you and your king choose to install restraint and take that freedom from me. Governor Phillip, do to me as you wish. I have nothing more to say."

"Silence!" The barked command was barely heard above the din that followed Padraig's words.

"John Caesar! What do you have to say before I pass sentence?"

"Governor Phillip, I can offer nothing more after those well spoken words of my comrade and friend. Do to me as you will."

Sean was astounded as he heard more and more support for his brother from most of those who stood around him. It appeared that many who thought of Padraig as nothing more than an Irish scallywag now saw him as one who stood as a fighter, a champion of lost causes—one to be applauded, not reviled.

"Padraig Gallagher and John Caesar, stand!" Silence again, as all waited eagerly to learn of the fate of the man from Donegal and his friend from the Caribbean.

"You have both been found guilty of the crimes as stated. These crimes demand the ultimate punishment. The verdict of guilt automatically calls for death by hanging."

Looking at the two standing, Phillip paused and then concluded. "However, I have decided to grant mercy on this one time and this time only. I now sentence you both to six months locked in the cells.

"I would also send you to receive one hundred fifty lashes; however, due to your physical condition, I will reduce this to seventy lashes each. This will take place on Monday morning in three days' time. These actions will serve as a deterrent to those foolish enough to attempt escape. Sergeant, take them away."

Sean listened, stunned, to the punishment soon to be dealt to his brother. The three female convicts stood next to him and supported him with encouraging words and brief hugs.

They watched as Caesar and Padraig were walked from the building back to where they would be locked away for the next six months.

"Sean, I am ashamed to be English. How can they do this?" Mary said in her soft voice, which today was laden with sadness.

"We will see, Mary. We will see."

Three days earlier, two American whalers had entered the harbour. They had been hunting the sperm whales that swam in huge numbers off the coast of New South Wales. Spermaceti, the oil found in the head of the sperm whale, was considered the finest and as such the most valuable of all whale oils.

These deep-sea whalers traveled back and forth from New Zealand, landing as much whale product as they could carry, before dispersing to their bases in America.

Two of the three whalers had hit extremely rough waters, causing major injuries to a number of their crewmembers. They arrived in Sydney Harbour to have repairs made to their damaged vessels and to find new crew replacements.

Sean Gallagher, with his Northern Atlantic fishing experience, provided the perfect solution for Captain Robert Oliver and his vessel *Lady Evelyn*.

He had met with Gallagher on the evening of the day of docking. Sean had agreed to sign on and to find suitable sailors to join the crew with him.

The *Lady Evelyn* would sail in ten to fourteen days.

Four days after, Padraig would receive seventy lashes from the cat o' nine tails.

## Chapter 91

Robert Bolton watched Padraig Gallagher as the verdict was reached.

The building used for these legal proceedings and other recent legal matters was positioned next to the governor's residence. There was seating for thirty people, including the officers and those with interests in the sentencing. Bolton had found a seat toward the rear of the room.

Both Caesar and Gallagher sat in chains at the right of the table where Phillip and his officers sat facing the public.

Suddenly, Padraig turned and stared directly at Bolton.

Bolton, at first, was startled as his enemy looked at him, but was then most intrigued to note that his enemy showed no alarm or shock at his presence.

*Could it be possible he has not recognised me?* he mused. *Surely, he would show some reaction to my being here?*

His concern was compounded when the two prisoners were walked from the room after their sentencing. Gallagher stared at him hard and long for those seconds in passing.

Bolton met with Victor Bates as the crowd dispersed. "I want him to die, and I want him to die in great pain, knowing that I am responsible," Bolton stated in a cold, flat tone devoid of emotion. "But how do we get him to where we can kill the bastard without Phillip and his officers meddling in our business?"

"We can burn 'im art! Set fire to the wooden wall and get 'im before the fire does."

Bolton stared scathingly at Bates before replying. "Perhaps a better idea would be to offer sufficient moneys to the guard to drop the key, perhaps."

"I got an idea, Guv."

Bolton turned to the tall blond-haired friend of Bates. "Yes?"

"I had a peep at the bars at the back o' the cell what looks out at the trees behind. I reckon we could harness one o' ya 'orses to the iron and pull 'em art dead easy. Whaddaya think?"

Bolton looked at the man and smiled. "I believe there is a brain somewhere in you lot after all. What's your name?"

"They calls me Whitey, Guv, on accounts o' me white 'air."

"Indeed, Mister Whitey, indeed. We could then stash the Irish dog onto the carriage and have him away in no time. Excellent idea. Let's plan the right time and make this happen."

*****

Padraig looked across at John Caesar lying on his makeshift bed.

"Well, at least our home has improved from what it was."

Caesar grinned and nodded his head. "And who knows, maybe venison and wine for dinner."

"I think not, but at least we can sleep in reasonable comfort, and who knows what may happen." His words faded as his mind reeled at all that had occurred in the last few days.

Their manacles had been taken from them, and they had been allotted wooden beds with blankets, all approved by Phillip on the condition that both would honour the goodwill of the governor and accept their punishment as demanded.

The seventy lashes each were to receive did little to faze either Caesar or Padraig as both had agreed that if they were given two hundred or more, then they would be concerned!

John Caesar drifted off to sleep in the lazy warmth of the early afternoon sun streaming in through the cell window.

Padraig lay and pondered as to what might happen in the days to follow.

The sudden and somewhat miraculous appearance of Sean had astounded him beyond belief, and all pain and misery was swept to insignificance as the possibility of miracles ran through his mind.

What had his brother envisaged? How could they escape and where would they go this time?

John Caesar had met and fallen in love with a native maiden far to the north, and his only dream was to return to her.

But his enemy Bolton! What was behind his sudden appearance? Padraig had no doubts he had been recognised by his mortal and deadly foe and equally had no doubts as to the Englishman's intentions should they meet again. He also had no doubts as to what he would do to Bolton if able to.

The horror of the memories of the murder of his wife, his twins, and his family suddenly engulfed him, and as tears filled his eyes and ran down his face, he tried in vain to seek solace. In the silence, he suffered alone.

*****

Sean Gallagher watched from a distance as Robert Bolton turned away from the three English convicts that had arrived on the second fleet.

He knew only too well of Bolton's desire to end the life of his brother. He was unsure whether Bolton would attempt to do so in the confines of the prison cell, or if he arranged Padraig's escape, so that he could have his evil way with him.

The fact that he was meeting and dealing with these three

gutter rats suggested the latter would be his choice of options. But how could he succeed in doing so, and what would be his next moves?

Sean knew that it was of the utmost importance for him to stay a step ahead of Bolton.

It was later that night that Sean again approached the rear barred window of his brother's cell. He was most certain that no one had seen him or was aware of his presence.

"Padraig!" he whispered.

Suddenly, a hand emerged from between the bars. "Sean, thank God you are here."

Brother held the hand of brother. And then, as Padraig's head touched the bars, Sean could barely make out the smile on the face of his brother in the dim moonlight.

"Padraig, I have much to tell you. You are obviously well aware of Bolton being at your sentencing this morning, and I have no doubts that he intends to kill you.

"I am certain that he does not know of my being here, so as far as he is concerned, you have no one you can turn to other than John Caesar. With his own ruffians to support him, he believes he has you at his mercy."

Silence ensued as each pondered Sean's words.

"Padraig, I have something that I am most reluctant to tell you. There never will be a time that is right, so I ask that you never judge me badly as I now reveal these words."

"What is it, Sean?" Padraig almost laughed. "What could be worse than the situation you now find me in?"

"My brother, you thought I had died, and, but for the grace of God, I may well indeed have done so, not to mention the excellent lessons of our beloved friend Cohen who regularly made us swim those harsh currents in the Atlantic Ocean."

"Aye, those were some cold, rough currents, weren't they

# SAVAGE *Sympathy*

brother?" Padraig said with a smile. "Go on."

Sean took a breath and said, "How long I spent in the waters off our coast, I know not. Eventually, however, I made it back to shore and too late, much too late, I followed your tracks to find you had departed for England.

"I will now tell you more of my experiences back home before following you to England, and when we have more time, I can tell you more, God willing, of course.

"I received information from Judge Throckmorton Squires, who, before he died, told me where I could locate the Bolton family in England."

"Before he died?" Padraig interrupted. "The good judge? How did he die? Or more to the point, what did you do to the English bastard?"

"I will tell you that and more later, my brother. But please, let me continue. I did travel to England, and I did find the Bolton home. And Padraig, I did find your children!"

"What! Sean, what did you just say to me? My children—my little ones? Sweet God in heaven, please do not lie to me, Sean. Please, in God's name, tell me this is true."

"Padraig, they are alive. Both, I am happy to say, were alive and appeared to be happy and well. Lady Constance, Bolton's wife, must have somehow found them and taken them back to England with her. The fact is they are safe and very much alive."

The sounds of his brother's sobbing nearly broke the heart of Sean Gallagher, and only the comforting words of John Caesar, who had heard all and quietly held and consoled his friend, gave Sean the courage to sit and wait to begin again.

Eventually Padraig spoke. "Sean, my brother! What can I say? You have traveled half the world to find me. You have given me hope that I could never have dreamed of. Now you have given me my life back; my every breath I shall now breathe will bring me one breath closer to holding my little ones again."

"I love you, my brother," Sean said. "But now I must leave you. I have much to do to get you both out of here and away from this hellhole."

Padraig looked at John Caesar and a slow smile stretched across his face.

"Much to do! Much to look forward to!"

"So be it, my friend," Caesar replied, and he was smiling so much, his face hurt.

# Chapter 92

The rain hammered down, and the streets of the new town became waterways for the torrents to traverse and eventually pour into the harbour waters.

Sean's smile was rueful when he spoke to his two fishing friends. "I had hoped to have at least another few days out there landing fish before I joined the crew of the whaler."

"'Tis a shame surely," Gunter replied.

"Ah, now, I remember well returning to Killybegs with a boat full of herring and the ales that flowed after." The three men sat under shelter reminiscing.

"Well, now, what a mess the rain has brought down. It's not like rain back home, is it?"

All three men smiled as Mary Piles and Elizabeth Hipsley joined them.

"Sean, can I have some words with ya?" Mary asked after the usual comments about the weather and general banter had subsided.

"Surely, Mary, let's walk over and get us a cuppa," Sean replied.

Seated with hands warmed around big steaming mugs of tea, Mary began. "Sean, when are you leaving us? What will become of Padraig when you're gone? I can't stop worrying about him."

"Ah, indeed, Mary, 'tis most sad I won't be seeing you until who knows when, maybe never. If all goes as I hope and pray,

I sail from here later next week. That is, if this bloody weather lets up, of course."

"And Padraig?"

Looking around for ears that might overhear, Sean leaned in close and said, "Mary, my brother and I have an enemy here who is the son of the devil himself. I have every reason to believe he and his cronies intend to bust Padraig out of the jail cell to murder him. I have some ideas that I believe will save my brother if indeed they try to do that. Otherwise, I will get him out myself somehow."

"And then?" Mary asked with no attempt to hide her sadness.

"I will get him onboard one of the whalers anchored off shore, and we will sail eventually to New Zealand."

"New Zealand?" Mary's eyebrows arched in surprise.

"A land I know nothing about other than it is peopled by warriors more ferocious than the natives from here. Hopefully, we can sail from there and return back home. It will be a long journey, but we'll eventually make it back."

Sean placed his hands around Mary Piles' hands to comfort her and went on to explain in greater detail all of his plans.

★★★★★

Captain Watkin Tench hurried through the pounding rain with one of the guards to the prison jail cells.

"Unlock please!" he ordered.

Entering the gloom of the cell, he addressed the two inmates.

"Good morning, Padraig—well, as good as it could seem to be, and to you also, John Caesar. Well, now, I see no tables or chairs, so I guess I will have to stand." He smiled at his attempt to humour the two men. "I wish to have some words with you; do you mind?"

John Caesar stared at him with a banal expression. Padraig

nodded and replied.

"I see no reason not to, Captain Tench."

"I was most displeased at your attempt to escape from us, in view of all the prior lenience we had shown you. However, that is not the reason for my visit. You may have noticed the changes since your departure.

"We now have close to 1800 residents, a mix of convict and non-convict in Sydney, and 1260 at Rose Hill.

"Our male convicts, as you are aware, are being utilized for labor, and the women convicts make the trousers, shirts, and other clothing needed for all.

"Aside from this, the commander and I, as well as our other officers, are most concerned at the variances in forest and general growing and farming soils overall." Tench paused to get a reaction from the Irishman before continuing.

"Padraig, your extensive travels, if I may suggest, would seem to have covered more ground than any other marine or convict in New South Wales—other than those who were chasing you!

"I have spent considerable time and effort persuading the commander to utilize your time and experience to lead us to where we can find more suitable and better soils and conditions to plant vegetable and crops in general. Also, your knowledge of the natives in these regions will prove very helpful, as more and more we are faced with their hostilities toward us."

"Little wonder, what?" Caesar commented with no attempt to hide his sarcasm.

Ignoring Caesar, Tench continued. "A new arrival to New South Wales, one Robert Bolton, has expressed an interest in expediting your services for his own purposes. I understand he and his family and company see major investment opportunity in land and mineral, and he has requested the commander release you to his care for you to lead him inland and to the north."

As he watched for a reaction, Tench was somewhat intrigued at the ensuing silence.

"Padraig, you seem to share little enthusiasm for remedying your plight and ending this situation you find yourself in. Pray tell, why is this? It is most unusual."

"Indeed, Captain Tench, you are right. Why should I trust and help those who have done so much to harm me and who have forced me to endure six more years of hell in this land I have been sent to?"

"But, Padraig, you were found guilty of crimes that you committed—you, Padraig! Our justice system is only carrying out its duty and obligation to punish you and others who commit crimes."

Padraig just stared at Tench with a blank expression. Finally, the Englishman turned to leave, and as he pushed the cell door open, Padraig spoke to him.

"Captain Tench, please stay. I have given your words some thought, and I wish to explain to you the reasons behind my contempt. It is not aimed at you. Indeed, I find you to be a gentleman and a man I can trust. In fairness to you, if you care to listen, I will explain why I was in London and how I was arrested."

Tench nodded and with almost a wistful smile replied, "Thank you, Padraig. I assure you, I do appreciate your words, and I will listen with great interest to what you wish to tell me. But first, I am curious about the words you use and the manner in which you use them. One could assume that you come from a privileged background."

"Most definitely not, Captain Tench! My mother and a very dear friend taught me the value of the spoken word. My friend, a man of Jewish persuasion and French by choice of country spent many hours teaching me how to speak French, and as he explained, I have a natural gift of memory and the ability to pick up the meaning and understanding of foreign languages with ease. But enough of that; my life began in Donegal some twenty-seven years ago . . ."

Padraig told the story of his life, and when he described how his family was murdered, Captain Tench appeared visibly shaken.

"Your family, friends, your children, all killed. You state that they were murdered, but surely, as I understand it, Ireland is under the rule of the King of England, and therefore has to abide by the orders of the king, and as such, you are all subjects of the realm. It is then right and just that you obey the commands of the king."

"If that is what you believe, Captain Tench, then it is futile for me to pursue this matter any further."

"You misunderstand me, Padraig. I do sympathize; in fact, I do understand your reasoning for your dislike, perhaps even your hatred of the English, but it allows me no reason to condone your actions."

"I repeat my earlier words, Captain Tench. There can be little, then, that I can do to help you."

"I am truly sorry I cannot go to the commander with a strong case to cancel your whipping and release you and possibly Caesar from further imprisonment."

"I understand," Padraig replied, "and I thank you for your concern."

"Padraig, before I leave, you mentioned once or twice that your purpose in going to London was to find the man responsible for the death of your family. You obviously know this man, and twice you let slip the name of a man who was with your wife at the time of her death and who was possibly also implicated in the death of her twin sister. The name you mentioned was Bolton. Not an uncommon name, but somewhat coincidental that we have with us here in New South Wales a Robert Bolton, and even more coincidental, he is requesting your release. This would put you under his control while you do what the commander and I wish you to do for us. Would you care to comment on this?"

As the sound of the rain intensified outside, Padraig stared into the eyes of Tench. "I have nothing further to say, Captain Tench."

## Chapter 93

Watkin Tench was very disturbed and secretly disgusted. He did believe Padraig Gallagher, and he sympathized with him.

During the previous night, he had tossed and turned, trying to sleep while envisioning losing his wife and children. As he pictured his father and mother being murdered before his very eyes, he understood the depth of hatred he would carry for the murderer.

Was Robert Bolton the man he now believed to be guilty of these horrific murders?

Stories and rumours had reached him regarding the violent and abusive manner in which Bolton treated the female convicts working for him at Rose Hill.

Sexual deviance was always a problem with the convict gangs, but to date, no accusations had been made against Bolton, who had obviously warned his victims of the seriousness of his vengeance should the matter be taken further.

Tench watched the preparations as the pillory was erected for the public floggings of Padraig Gallagher and John Caesar.

The rain had stopped, and as midday grew nearer, the temperature became hotter.

Tench glanced at a new instrument that measured heat, a thermometer made by an inventor named Ramsden, which calculated daytime heat on a Fahrenheit scale. Not normally bothered by heat, Tench felt uncomfortable as the thermometer read 104 degrees.

The pillory was near completion.

Then, the sound of voices grew louder, as the two convicts were brought to the place of punishment, as the governor called it.

Those that voiced approval, or in many cases, disapproval watched as John Caesar was walked up to the pillory. His shirt was taken from him, and his hands and head were placed into the half circles in the wood. The top portion was then brought down and locked into place. His hands and head looked down on those assembled below.

Herbert Watkins walked up the three steps onto the wooden base silently swishing the dreaded cat o' nine tails in his right hand. A large man with long arms that bulged with muscle, he smiled with malicious intent at the naked back of Caesar. "Well now, what 'ave we 'ere then? And it's seventy I have to gives ya then, is it?"

Those watching believed the man thoroughly enjoyed his work, and as Watkins had no friends, he therefore had no one who could testify otherwise. It would appear the only people he did speak to were those he thrashed into agony.

The crowd grew silent as he gave a practice swish with his whip and then the first of the blows fell onto the naked back of Caesar.

To John Caesar's credit, he did not cry out until the fourth blow. By then, the nine individual cords of the whip had opened up the first of the gashes in the skin on his back. By the time the tenth blow struck, Caesar was screaming in pain.

As Watkins prepared for the twentieth strike, he flashed the whip in the air and flicked particles of skin and blood over the watchers below him. He grinned at them and said to Caesar, "That be nineteen, and now for the twentieth!"

An additional forty-nine blows slashed into Caesar's back. Watkins laughed to all the onlookers and spoke to his victim.

"This be ya last, laddie, this time. I look forward to seein' ya again." And the final blow fell.

As Caesar was dragged from the pillory half-unconscious, Padraig was taken up and placed into the now sodden gaps where Caesar had been. Blood, sweat, and skin particles stuck to his own skin as he prepared for his whipping.

"So, it's the Irishman it is. Well, I have news for ya, laddie. I was only just warmin' up wiv ya friend. Youse gonna get the better treatment, cuz I hates ya bloody Irishmen!"

"Get on with it then, and enjoy your work," Padraig replied grimly.

Stunned at his stoicism, the crowd stood in disbelief, as Padraig Gallagher, with eyes closed, gave not a sound as the whip struck him for the twentieth time.

However, as the following fifty slashed into his back, strangled sounds emerged from his clenched mouth.

As the final blow fell, Watkins begrudgingly uttered, "Youse one tough bastard, here be ya last."

Padraig Gallaher was taken from the pillory and stood staring at the visibly shaken Watkins.

His back dripping blood and his hands by his side clenched in silent fury, he smiled up at the man who had tried everything to inflict pain and indeed worse on his victim.

"Better luck next time, then!" Padraig announced, and he fell to the ground unconscious.

Sean Gallagher felt the hand of Mary Piles slip into his. They were standing at the back of the crowd of assorted convicts, marines, and officers.

"Oh, Sean!" And she clung to him weeping.

They watched as the two convicts were taken back to

their jail cell.

*****

Bates and the man they called Whitey walked up to Robert Bolton.

"Well, Mister Bolton, sir. He's one, int 'e?" Bates said in reluctant admiration.

"One what?" Bolton replied scathingly.

"One very brave man to not scream out or cry," Whitey interjected. "I believe that is what my friend is trying to tell you regarding the Irishman."

Bolton looked hard at both men before replying.

"Then even more reason to find ways to make him cry when we finally get him into our hands, do we agree? And the sooner the better, as I will be returning to England in a few weeks, and I want all this completed before I depart. And don't forget, I'm the one paying you, so you'll keep your sympathies in check and do as I tell you."

"Right you are, Guv," said Bates.

"So what next?" Whitey still sounded somewhat begrudging. "Whaddaya want us ta do?"

"I have had a quiet word to the night guard. He also wants to return to London and is most happy to receive a few guineas to accidently leave access to Gallagher's cell. We will do a spot of damage to the door to make it appear as though the two prisoners were rescued from their jail cell by their friends. The only problem is that we will need to do it at night, but on a stormy night, when there will be no stray witnesses about. Any sounds of a struggle will be covered over by the noises of the storm. This bloody hot weather gives no indication of when the weather will turn in our favour, so we will have to be ready to act as soon as it does. Any further questions?"

"No, Guv. All sounds good," Bates said, speaking for the both of them.

✯✯✯✯✯

It was later that night when Sean called through the cell window to Padraig that he realized his brother was certainly not the man he knew in Ireland. The man who replied to his questions regarding his wellbeing was a vastly different man to the man he once knew. How his brother could take such a severe beating and still respond to Sean's concerns was beyond anything he had ever witnessed or heard of in the past.

He could hear Padraig, or was it Caesar, moaning in agony as he first listened to the sounds emanating from the prison cell.

"Padraig!" he whispered. "Are you well? Can you hear me?"

"Ah, 'tis my brother, is it? Could ya kindly come in here and scratch my back? I have an itch or two!"

"Ya silly bastard!" Sean replied. "We are all worried shitless about ya, and you give me this nonsense."

Sean didn't want to take too long talking, as he knew his brother needed to sleep, or at least attempt to. So the talk that ensued was all he needed so that he could depart on the whaling vessel, knowing his brother was as good as he could hope for.

As he softly spoke his good-byes to his brother, Sean had to smile at Padraig's reply.

"History will one day recognise and honour the men born and raised in freedom, the freedom that we will fight for and claim as our own—an Ireland free from English oppression. And then, these scars on my back will testify to our determination to win back that freedom. Good night, my brother."

## Chapter 94

Watkin Tench smiled at the diminutive figure that stood almost blocking his progress in the newly formed street of the new town of Sydney.

"Good morning, Mary Piles, and pray tell what is it that a fine young lady as yourself is doing impeding the progress as one so lowly as myself on such a fine Monday morning?"

"Captain Tench, I know 'tis not for me to question the commands and decisions of the commander, but why is Padraig Gallagher bein' treated so badly?"

"Well now, Mary, and pray tell, why this concern for the lad?"

Mary cast her eyes down and shuffled her feet searching for a reply.

"Padraig has done much to help us here in this new country. Is he guilty of what you say 'e did? Who knows! All I know is I think it is unfair the way he has been treated."

"Mary, there are times I also think that we all are being treated harshly. And in Padraig's case, maybe you are right. I soon depart for London, but before I sail, I will do what I can to help the Irish lad's situation."

"Thank you, sir. Thank you."

Sean Gallagher watched as Mary walked to the dining hall where she worked as a serving girl waiting tables. He noticed how her conversation with Tench had left her in a sad state. He walked toward her.

"Top of the mornin' me dear."

"Sean, ah, please make me smile. Say somethin' nice to me."

"Mary, I do have something to say to you. In fact, I need your help. Indeed, Padraig and I both need your help. Can we talk about it over a cuppa tea?"

While Mary busied herself serving those who had arrived to eat the first meal of the day, Sean sat sipping his tea. He was joined by some crewmembers of the whaling vessel soon to sail later that week.

Humorous verbal banter followed as Sean and one of the Irish lads teased the crewmembers from America.

The ship's captain, also American, joined them, complaining bitterly about the lack of coffee in the new colony. This amused Sean, as he had yet to hear of anyone wishing to drink anything that would make one cough.

As the captain stood to leave, he said to Sean, "Remember, we sail first thing Friday morning. If you and your fellow crewmembers are not onboard, we leave without you. Understood?"

"Surely, Captain, surely. We will be there," Sean replied.

The captain stood and headed to the exit, and Sean absentmindedly followed him with his eyes. In that moment, he noticed three men pushing their way through the door just as the captain attempted to step outside.

"Sorry, gentlemen," the captain uttered, and he paused to let them enter.

All three pushed past him rudely without any comment.

He shrugged and shook his head. "Englishmen! What else should I expect?'

Watching these proceedings out of the corner of his eye, Sean was relieved to see Robert Bolton and his two henchmen seat themselves at the rear of the room, far from where he was seated.

As Mary Piles approached him, Sean was confident that Bolton would not hear what he was about to discuss with her.

"Now tell me, ya Irish rascal, what is it you want of me? Me body maybe?" She giggled.

"Please sit, Mary." He smiled somewhat sadly as Mary adjusted her skirt and seated herself opposite him. "You are indeed a fine woman, Mary, and it gives me no pleasure to explain to you why my brother has not fallen for your very obvious charm and wondrous features."

"Sean!" Mary interrupted. "I already know. I cannot, no woman can ever replace the love 'e had for his wife. And that also makes me very sad. But what can I do? What can any of us do?"

"That is precisely what I want to ask of you," Sean said.

He then went on to explain how he hoped to get his brother out of the jail cell and escape with him from the colony.

He paused to take a sip from his now cold tea, and then looking at Mary over the rim of the cup, he said, "That is it. What do you think?"

"I'll do it, Sean, and I know Elizabeth will, too."

"But what of them?" She indicated toward Bolton, who was talking to his colleagues. "Don't cha wish you could 'ear what they are talking about?"

"I don't need to, Mary. I know exactly what is on their minds. For that very reason we need to be way ahead of any move they may make."

★★★★★

The sun had long set in the west, and the moon was not yet full and offered only partial assistance as Sean made his way to the jail cells. This intermittent light, compounded by the darkening clouds, gave him greater confidence that he would reach his brother undiscovered. The occasional sprinkling of light showery drizzle increased his optimism.

And so it was with considerable relief that on arriving at the cells, Sean noted that the guards had either retired for the night or had gone elsewhere.

Peering through the cell window, he whispered, "Padraig, it is me. Can you hear me?"

"Sean, Sean. It is you?"

Padraig thrust his arm through the iron bars. Sean grasped his brother's hand and an emotional silence followed.

"Padraig, do not worry. I will be getting you out of here. That I promise."

"But how? And when? And please, please Sean. Tell me more about my little ones. Are they being looked after? How soon can we go back to England to rescue them?"

"Padraig, be calm. Let us first get you out of here."

Sean then explained in detail about the whaling boats and when they were sailing.

And as he explained the imperative timing of how and when to get them both on the boat on Friday morning without the English being aware of their actions, Padraig finally relaxed and replied with his familiar chuckle.

"Ah, my brother, like old times, eh? Us against our enemies! But what of the bastard Bolton? I would dearly love to deal with him before our departure."

"Padraig, I would not be at all surprised if you do indeed meet him."

Sean then went on to explain how he had witnessed their scheming. But before they could talk further, John Caesar interrupted. "Hush my friends. Guards are at the door!"

"Good-bye, my brother!" Sean whispered, and he faded into the night.

The cell door opened, and a jar of water was thrown to them.

It landed on the dirt floor and spilled some of the contents as it hit the ground.

"Ah, dear me, such a bleedin' shame. Look at that, ya may have ta go thirsty 'til mornin'." The guard laughed as he slammed the door and locked it before settling down outside the cell door.

"I can only join you with your happiness, my friend," John Caesar said in a loud whisper to Padraig. "And I can only hope and wish you good luck, if and when you do escape, and sometime in the future become reunited with your children."

Padraig sensed a sad note in his friend's words. "But you will be joining us. You cannot stay here. Phillip will take out his revenge on you."

"You do not understand, Padraig. I do intend to run. And I hope to be reunited with my love when I get out of here and return to where I met her. But is she still alive? Did those Englishmen who recaptured me leave her alive? And more important, did they mistreat her in any way?"

Padraig nodded in silent agreement. "I understand, my friend. I truly do understand. I hope a miracle happens, and you find her alive and well and waiting for you."

Both sat silent reflecting on their past and the hopeful outcome of the days ahead.

## Chapter 95

Robert Bolton woke to another hot summer morning. It was Monday.

"I am heading into the town later today. Are you listening to me?" Getting no reply, he headed for the front door of the hut.

Staring out into cleared space before him, he emptied his full bladder onto scurrying ants that did their best to escape the flood that suddenly descended upon them. Grinning at the mayhem he had caused, he turned and headed back to his bed.

"I have a serious problem!" He stated to the still sleeping form of the female convict lying next to him. "There are some reasons I like this forgotten hellhole of the world. And I would like to stay on longer. And then there are reasons to hate this pathetic place with its naked, smelly ignorant savages. And yes, there are twenty-two less of them this morning."

Leaping from his bed, he went to the nearby table where three weapons lay. "And you, my bonny treasures, what say you, uh? You missed not one of the seven I slayed last night."

Bolton collapsed back onto the bed, giggling in a high-pitched stream of laughter, thus waking the woman next to him.

"What! Whatsa noise abart?" She rubbed her eyes. "Oops, sorry!" she muttered, apologizing for the barking sound that escaped her buttocks.

"Bitch!" Bolton snarled. "Go clean yourself up."

She returned and crawled back into the bed again.

"Now tell me, what was all the story abart yesterday. Didja kill a pile o' them black buggers?"

"We went hunting. You may remember a few weeks back, myself and some others went searching for perpetrators of crimes against His Majesty. It was mostly unsuccessful due to poor planning on behalf of a dim-witted marine sergeant. Well," Bolton smiled as he paused for suitable effect. "It takes the strokes of masters to put matters right, and I did.

"Under my leadership, we, that is, a mixture of marines and convicts and I, went to where a group of the savages were camping. They were leaping and dancing about, all painted up like nothing I have seen before. Making one hell of a racket, they were, so much so that we snuck up and fired on them from the bushes. I hit three with my first shots, and then as they looked for escape, we finished them off. All in all, I claimed seven; some I had to fire second shots into their ugly heads. Not bad, what?

"In future, these black insolent savages will have to come to terms that their future lies in the goodwill of His Majesty, and of course, those of us who will now take ownership of the land and what it has to offer.

"You will no doubt remember I leave for England in the weeks ahead. And I have one final matter to attend to before sailing."

He returned to the table and picked up one of the weapons. "See this one here, my dear? This is a staghorn and mother-of-pearl inlaid wheellock.

"This octagonal-to-round, pin-fastened, seventeen-inch iron smoothbore with a .52 caliber barrel is a killing machine that sent three of them to early graves last night.

"And this one . . . ahhh!" He smiled as he picked up the second gun.

"This is a Scottish flintlock only twenty years old. I actually picked this one up recently in America. It is said that this very gun, or one like it, fired the shot that commenced the American Revolution. Be that as it may. It fired the shot that sorted a problem I had over there some time back. Maybe you could take that as a warning and not be so bloody overbearing."

He smiled at her broadly.

"And yes, you do very well under those sheets, so keep up the good work. And finally, this is the third of my beauties!" Bolton picked up the final weapon.

He wiped it down with oil he kept by the table. He then poured a stream of black powder down the barrel. Then placing a cloth patch over the top of the barrel, he kissed the lead ball before pressing it down onto the patch. "Go to the heart of he who I hate," he whispered as he cut the patch and pushed the ball down the gun barrel.

Then, staring at the woman, who was looking at him with awestruck fear in her eyes, he stated with sudden fury, "The Irishman will not see this week out. I am sending him to hell."

*****

Bolton met with Victor Bates and Whitey later that afternoon. Pushing past the American who was exiting as they attempted to enter the dining hall, Bolton muttered, "Bloody Americans. They think they own everything!"

They sat with a mug of tea each that Mary Piles had served them.

"Thanks, Guv!" She smiled when Bolton tipped her for her friendly service.

She then did her best to catch some of their conversation without arousing their suspicion as she placed some cotton mats on the table in front of them.

The word *Irishman* and other words such as *the jail* did little to stem the increasing fears she had regarding their intentions.

Bolton paid little heed as she then went and sat with one she obviously knew.

However, a sudden nagging bout of nervousness hit him. He stared at Mary Piles and the man she sat with. He had his back to them, and while he could not determine what had aroused his concern, Bolton felt a growing feeling of dread. But as Bates and Whitey began asking questions, he shook off the feeling, and they began to plan.

When Bolton stood to leave, his last words to the two men emphasized the need for action. "I sail for London in two weeks or so. I want this done by Friday night, Monday next week at the latest."

"Yes, Guv, and our money—when do we get it?"

"On full completion of your assignment."

Bolton then walked out into the late afternoon sunshine.

It took him some time to locate the convict who had driven him into town, and in a foul mood, he made little effort to hide his temper. "Get me back home. Bah! Is that what I call it? Bloody place! Move it, damn you!"

The convict smiled to himself as he shook up the reins. "Certainly, Guv, your wish is my command."

## Chapter 96

Mary Piles watched Sean as he sharpened the blades of the three knives he had brought to where they prepared the food for the first meals of the day. The kitchen had been set up initially for the needs of Phillip and the captains and officers.

It had grown in size as lower ranks were given permission to eat there, which coincided with the officers' elite moving to more gracious surroundings.

Then, as more convicts were given kitchen and cooking duties, including some of the female convicts being utilized for table work, the establishment had grown to become not only the first eating establishment in Sydney Cove, but also a meeting point for the consumption of various brews and rums later in the day and the evening.

Sean had taken advantage of the various kitchen-sharpening tools and paused from leathering one of the knives and slid the blade down the side of his cheek. He smiled as he viewed the whiskered evidence on the shiny steel that certainly verified the keenness of the knife's edge.

"And do ya intend to use that?" Mary asked.

The smile on Sean's face diminished.

"I would prefer to be tellin' ya no, Mary. But with Bolton having his choice of many and us with no weapons other than these . . ." He shrugged in frustration. "If there is to be a confrontation, these blades will have to do. Hopefully that won't happen."

"Sean, what exactly do you intend to do? Do ya have a plan—I mean, after you leave?"

Sean turned and nodded at Mary.

"Two beautiful ladies will wander up to the jail cell guard if one is on duty. While the fool becomes engrossed with these two wondrous creatures, I will deal with him and obtain the keys. You know what happens next. I don't want to say it in case the walls have ears.

"All going well, we board the whaler and depart from these shores, and never come back."

Mary Piles smiled. "And these two beautiful ladies, what will happen to them?"

"As I have been told, Mary, these two ladies will be so painted up the guard won't be able to give an accurate description. Whores, I believe, will be how the fool will describe them."

"Me and Elizabeth are happy to help you Sean, but we will miss you both. We will miss you more than you will ever know. But as I asked earlier, will it be possible that we will meet again one day?"

"Who knows, Mary? Who knows?"

"Sean, I understand. But you do realize that Elizabeth is hopelessly in love with you, and you know how much I feel for Padraig, and yes, I understand his feelings for his wife, but she is gone now, Sean. Padraig can find someone new to love him. Me!"

Sean moved to Mary and held her tight to him. "Mary, I do know, and I do understand. I hope and pray that Padraig can and will find himself and forget all the pain and hurt he is suffering. And who knows, he may remember all you have done to help him. But for now?" His voice trailed off as Mary cried hopelessly in his arms.

*****

As the activities of the day came to an end, and the sun began to set, Sean met Elizabeth, and together they walked down to the beach. He sat with her gazing out at the ships and the incoming tide, and the gulls sat on the sand watching them.

She held his hand, and when she spoke, her voice was soft and quiet. "I have only this night and tomorrow night with you, Sean, and then I may never see you again. Which one of those ships over there will be that which I will forever hate?"

Pointing to a vessel that was obviously a whaler, he replied, "There she is, Elizabeth. But surely neither of us knows if these are our last two nights together. In truth, my dear, I have a feeling for you that I have never known for any other. But I am committed to rescuing my brother."

He wrapped a big arm around her narrow shoulders and pulled her close to him. "Please, let us love each other for these two nights, and as I know where to find you, let us both believe that one day soon I will return."

Later that night, as Sean lay with his head nestled against Elizabeth's breast, both exhausted after repetitive lovemaking, he knew with some element of grief that this night would indeed be their last together.

Earlier that night they had left the waterside, and noticing the guard talking to a passerby, had taken a chance to talk through the cell window to Padraig.

"All is going well, Padraig. We should have you out of here tomorrow night," Sean whispered.

Sean was again woken by the kookaburra calls announcing the beginning of the new day. Leaning over to place his lips on the cheek of the sleeping Elizabeth, he pondered whether this truly would be his last day in New South Wales. Rising, he walked to gaze out at the early morning sky.

Debating whether to dress and go outside or to return to the warmth of the bed and possibly a final tribute to their outstanding lovemaking achievements, Sean smiled as he watched stirring movements under the blankets, and he sagely chose the latter.

Afterward, Sean moved to his side of the bed and turned on his side, facing Elizabeth, his head propped in his hand. Smiling at her, he said, "Hope your Irish lackey didna let ya down. And hope I haven't wasted too much of ya mornin'!"

"Ah! I am bloody well late now!" Elizabeth laughed heartily. "And all thanks to you."

Then, suddenly recalling Sean's imminent departure, she added glumly, "I will see you later this morning, won't I?"

"Of course, my dear and most beautiful lady, of course you will."

Elizabeth jumped from the bed, and Sean heard the sounds of water splashing from the water pot, indicating the ablutions wiping out all evidence of the pleasures of the previous hours. When she was scurrying to the door, he arose and held her tight, not caring that he would make her a minute late.

"If only our lives were different," he whispered in her ear, "and we did not have to honour the commands of your king, I would not feel this total sadness of leaving you and the newfound love I have for you." Sean kissed her deeply and said, "Yes, Elizabeth, I will make time to be with you later this day and wish that this time would never end."

"Oh, Sean!" she replied, and as she turned and walked to the door, Sean heard the sounds of her weeping.

*****

Sean walked to savour a late breakfast, or as he glanced up at the now blackening sky, an early lunch.

He stopped to bid a happy day to an Irish convict, and as

they began some idle chatter, Sean noticed a buggy heading toward them.

Pretending to drop an item, he bent over to forage in the dust as the buggy sped past them. He arose to see the departing back of Robert Bolton.

Confident that Bolton had not noticed him Sean stood, and bidding farewell to his Irish countryman, he watched as Bolton stepped down from the cart and began talking to two recently landed convicts.

He quickly walked to the side of a newly built wooden building, and concealed in the alleyway, he saw the three men walk toward the jail cell area and onward to the waterside.

"What the hell are they up to?" he mused under his breath. "This I do not like."

Taking great care not to be seen, he walked to the dining hall, and upon entering, he scanned his eyes around and found Mary Piles. Gesturing with a head nod to an empty table, he took a seat, and she came over and served him tea, understanding his unspoken message. He told her briefly of what he had witnessed.

After Mary had spent a little time teasing him about his time with her friend, Elizabeth, she grew serious as Sean explained.

"I have no doubt that Bolton is also intending to do damage to my brother," he said. Looking at the darkening skies above, he concluded, "I would bet a king's ransom that he plans to take advantage of the threatening change of weather to get into his cell and kill him."

It was sometime later when Sean met up with his fishermen friends and chatted about the threatening weather that he mentioned his imminent departure.

"Ah, lad, we'll miss ya surely," began one when a sudden flash of lightning followed by a clap of thunder brought the conversation to a halt.

"I think 'tis shelter we be seeking." He laughed nervously.

"I certainly agree; let's head for Mary Piles and a cuppa tea."

As the storm intensified, Sean stared out into the streets watching as prisoners, soldiers, and officers ran to shelter.

*What happens now?* he thought.

When Mary and Elizabeth appeared by his side, Elizabeth enquired, "What'll we do now, Sean?"

"This rainy weather could be a blessing, or it could be a bloody disaster. We'll have to wait and see."

## Chapter 97

And then it hit him, like a branch full of snow descending upon him on a cold winter's morning.

Bolton sat upright in bed. He had been lying there, enjoying the afterglow of sexual satisfaction before turning over to sleep.

His convict bedmate had muttered some words about her long-departed brother. That had subconsciously awakened and reconfirmed all those suspicions that had been nagging at him of late. The brother! Yes! That was who he was. The man he had seen from time to time. And it was he who was sitting in the dining hall on the Monday those two days back.

He was a Gallagher. "The bloody bastard!" Bolton exclaimed. "He is the brother of Padraig Gallagher!"

His bedmate muttered some words about going to sleep.

"Shut your mouth, bitch!" Turning, he slammed his fist down onto her unsuspecting face. With blood streaming from her broken nose, she jumped from the bed, screaming and crying and ran from the hut into the night.

Bolton's mind flashed back to those days in Ireland.

Yes! That was him, as he recalled those moments of death and destruction instigated by his actions.

He could clearly remember being down on the Donegal sands as he saw the bloody bodies soon to be engulfed by the rising tides of the Atlantic.

It all came flooding back to him. And his blood ran colder as all now became clearer and clearer. "The bastard is here to help his brother escape!" He yelled this to the four walls, breaking the silence of the room.

Outside, he could hear the sounds of the weeping convict he had beaten. "Be gone, bitch!"

As silence once again descended around him, Bolton began to plan. *What day was it? Of course, Wednesday night, tomorrow would be Thursday! Damn this bloody country. I need to find Bates and his friend right now! But how? All my plans made on Monday now mean nothing. Or do they?*

Gradually, a calming influence overcame his very troubled mind. "Yes, yes, I can see it all now," he murmured in satisfaction. "But I need to be in Sydney Town first thing tomorrow."

Walking to the front door, he peered out into the darkness and called out sweetly, "My dear lady! Where are you? Come on back now; all is forgiven. All is good again."

Some moments later, the bedraggled and half-naked woman staggered back into his bedroom.

"Time to sleep, my dear, but maybe first . . ." He giggled.

★★★★★

Bolton woke and stared at the ceiling. Much calmer now than he had been during the night, he began to plan in earnest. But most important, he needed to get to the township most urgently. Arising from his bed, he walked outside to organize transport.

Onto the back of the buggy, he loaded his weapons, and he packed some extra clothing to conceal them. As an afterthought, he added a blanket in case he had to sleep the night in Sydney.

"Move it, and make it quick," he ordered the driver. "I have much to do when we get there."

As they traveled the winding dirt track that lead to Sydney Town, Bolton glanced up at the sky.

The morning had begun with clear sunny conditions. But as they made the slow journey to town, more clouds began to fill the eastern sky. And then, as they made their way into the clearings that indicated the outskirts of the town, the sky had darkened considerably.

By the time Bolton had located Bates and Whitey, the wind had picked up. They walked down the now well-traveled track that had become a dirt roadway that led to the jail cells.

A burst of recent disturbances had created overcrowding in the other three cells, but only Gallagher and Caesar were locked into their cell. The reasoning was that Padraig and John had too much outside knowledge that might well have inspired more convicts to attempt a successful escape.

As the three men passed the buildings, they feigned an appearance of walking down to the waterside.

Bolton nodded at the guard and received a curious glance in return as they passed by.

Looking skyward, he asked of Bates, "How much time do we have before it rains? Does the guard stay here at night if the weather turns savage, as it looks as though it might do?"

Whitey replied. "I was a guest 'ere when I was caught nickin' some food. Most nights there was no guard when I called art to 'im. But wiff 'em bein' so busy now?" He shrugged. "Who knows."

*Uncouth wretch*, Bolton thought. *The sooner I leave this uncivilized dump, the better.*

Suddenly, the storm hit. Almost without warning, the wind, with intense force, struck the surrounding trees. Foliage, tree branches, leaves, and debris flew into the faces of those running for shelter.

Lightning lit the sky amidst the darkening, almost black, clouds.

The crashing sounds of the thunder followed seconds later by multiple forks of lightning terrified those who were hit by timber and other materials not sufficiently secured.

Robert Bolton had been down by the water's edge when the storm hit, and he ran for shelter. He would finalize an attempt to break into the cell once he was safe and dry and had time to think.

As he passed the cellblock, he noticed the guard had also made the decision to head for safer options. He turned and looked toward a group of trees yet to be cleared as screams and panicked shouting followed a horrific flashing and crashing as an apparent lightning strike split a tree in two. Bodies that had hit the ground were frantically trying to stand and decide where to dash to for safety.

By the time Bolton, Bates, and Whitey had reached the town buildings, the streets were practically deserted.

"What the hell is this?" Bolton exclaimed, when finally they found the shelter they had desperately sought.

"I have never seen anything like that out there since I been 'ere. Worst yet!" said one of the marines who had arrived on the First Fleet.

"How long before it clears?" Bolton enquired.

"Who knows!" came the reply.

## Chapter 98

As suddenly as the storm began, it was over.

An eerie silence descended as everyone exited the safety of the buildings and surveyed the storm damage.

Sean stared up to the now rapidly clearing skies. The sinking sun still allowed sufficient light to show the devastation left behind in the storm's path. The once dusty, but clear streets showed the wrath of the subtropical storm violence.

Glancing up at the clock on the wall, he knew that time was no longer on his side. He had only ten or twelve hours before departing New South Wales.

That is, if the whalers had suffered no damage during the storm. He suspected they hadn't, as the crew was extremely experienced in sailing in horrific conditions, so all would have been secure and safe as they rode out the storm.

He and Elizabeth had packed a large bag with extra clothing for himself and his brother, as he knew that Padraig's prison garb would only create major concerns for the ship's captain. And of course, they would both need changes of clothing as they traveled to their whaling destinations.

He would collect that later in the evening, or in the early morning, all going well!

But first, he needed to check on the jail cells to see if they were still intact, and his brother had come to no harm.

Turning to Elizabeth and Mary, he told them of his plans and what he expected from them.

"But please, my dear friends, this will only work if the jail is guarded," he reminded them, and he gave Elizabeth a quick hug and left.

Working his way down the debris-covered streets, he eventually arrived at the cell area.

Acting as an interested passerby, he quickly observed he was not the first to show interest there.

A number of officers and marines, including Watkin Tench, had begun clearing branches and assorted rubbish from the area. Most interestingly, the four cells had suffered little or no damage at all.

Sean watched as Tench opened Padraig's cell and overheard both Padraig and John Caesar assure him they had come to no harm.

Suddenly both appeared, unchained, and stood stretching and flexing muscles as their cell was, Sean presumed, searched for interior damage.

He noticed that both still moved with a consideration to the damage done to their bodies from the whipping. He heard Tench make a comment to Padraig that food would be delivered to them as soon as the guards could organize what was available from the kitchens. Padraig responded with a chuckle as he and Caesar turned and walked back into the cell.

Lamps were lit as the marines and assorted convicts finalized the clean up and headed back to their quarters.

Sean could hear muffled voices coming from the cells as he approached cautiously, noting that apart from him, there were no other persons in the vicinity.

Moving silently to their rear cell window, he again spoke softly. "Padraig, can you hear me?"

"Sean!"

"Now listen very carefully. I will be back later tonight to get you out of here. We sail from these shores at first light tomorrow morning. I must go and prepare. But first, I saw you outside, talking to Tench. Are you able to handle any adversity should trouble arise?"

"Fear bloody not, my brother. I would take on the devil if need be."

"I hear people coming Padraig. I must go!" As Sean disappeared into the night, he thought of his brother's last words. "Indeed, my brother. And I wonder where that devil is?"

*****

Sean snuck away from the rear of the cell and gradually circled around to where he could watch the activities at the front of the four cells. Unseen, he witnessed the arrival of pots of food being taken into each cell. Guided by the light from the lamps they were carrying, the guards finally completed their task.

"Damn!" he muttered as he watched a guard pull over a wooden stool, seat himself in front of the buildings, and light up a pipe.

*How long will he be there, I wonder?*

Sean looked up at the now clear sky and the moon, which gave adequate light for him to define reasonably clearly the guard and the odd small cloud of smoke as the guard puffed away.

The moon's position suggested to the seaman's instinct that the time would now be nearing nine o'clock or thereabouts. If the watch normally commenced at eight o'clock, the guard, if he was there later in the night, could pose a problem.

Sean wondered why some nights there was a guard and other nights none.

"Why tonight, damn them?" he muttered to himself as he slunk away to meet the ladies.

"Are you certain you want to do this?" He asked this of Elizabeth and Mary when he arrived back to meet them as planned.

"If we do get caught or questioned, we just blame the drink!" Elizabeth giggled.

Sean watched most amused as his two friends began to prepare for their part in what he hoped would eventually result in the successful bid to release his brother.

Applying makeup and rouge and combing their hair, plus dressing in very revealing clothing that did little to hide their now most obvious womanly assets, his two friends appeared as ladies of the night.

Finally, Elizabeth asked, "What do ya think?" exaggerating a pose that certainly aroused Sean's interest.

"Get back into the bed!" he demanded partly in jest, but mostly serious.

"I hardly recognise you, Elizabeth, and you also Mary."

"Pages of our past," Mary replied with a hint of sadness.

"And you will be checkin' these out before you leave anyway, Sean!" Elizabeth laughed, plumping up her bosom with both hands.

Standing, and with a long drawn-out sigh, Sean nodded, knowing that would not be the case. "Now I need to get myself ready, ladies. I won't look nearly as good as you do!" Sean busily checked that he had all he needed.

Along with his bag of clothing, he placed on the table the three knives, their keenly sharpened blades catching and reflecting the light from the table lamp.

He laid out two axes about two feet in length each, and both with keen enough edges to shave facial whiskers.

He tossed from his right hand to his left a five-foot-long heavy steel pipe where at one end he had jammed the handle of a double-sided knife with the razor-sharp blades protruding in a most deadly manner.

Satisfied with the balance and the certainty that the knife would not dislodge, Sean grunted his approval and laid it alongside the other weapons.

He then began to change into different clothing. He strapped a wide leather belt around his trousers and his feet into a pair of ankle high sturdy brown leather shoes.

Placing a knife down the side of each between sock and leather, he jiggled them to ensure they would not damage his foot, but would be easy to draw if urgently needed.

The third knife he then wrapped in a rag and tucked down his left side secured by his belt.

Over his shirt, he put on an all-weather, long leather coat with deep inside pockets on both sides, ideal for hiding the axes.

The pipe spear he then slid down his right pants leg where the steel shaft gave a sudden cool, but agreeable feel against the skin of his hip and leg.

Elizabeth and Mary were putting the finishing touches to their facial transformations when Sean walked toward them—swaggered was more like it.

"Ooo, is this my man?" Elizabeth cooed.

Sean smiled and replied, "Well, if I am, then who are you?"

But then the mood changed when he said, "My dear and most wonderful friends, it is now approaching midnight; are we ready? Do we each know what we have to do?"

"Time will tell," Mary replied. "But if I may ask, why the axes and knives? Do you hate the English officers and guards so much that you will kill those that get in ya way?"

"In truth, Mary, I have learned there are many of your people I am most fond of, your two selves in particular. And I mean to do no serious harm to any guards or marines who attempt to stop me, other than to use whatever force I may have to.

"The weapons you refer to are for one so evil that if he shows his face, my brother and I will send him to hell! But let us go now. It is time."

Each picking up the rum bottles now containing water, the two women followed Sean out onto the dark street.

Making sure that no passerby saw and wished to confront two somewhat obvious ladies of the night, they made their way behind the buildings until they eventually stood across from the jail cells.

"There is the guard," Sean said softly. "We must be quick, as they may be changing guards soon. Time for your show, ladies."

With that, the guard who had been sitting and dozing quickly, stood up as two women walked toward him giggling and singing in an obvious drunken state.

As they neared him, one paused and took a long swig from what he thought was a rum bottle.

"'Ullo darlin'. Whatcha up to?" One giggled at him.

"In't he a liddle sweetee?" the other purred.

A big grin appeared on the guard's face. "What are you two up ta? Ain't seen you two 'round 'ere before. When did you arrive?"

"Just now, fool! We just got 'ere."

"No, I mean, when did you get 'ere to Sydney. No ship's been in for weeks."

"Ah! Gotcha. We was on the last fleet wot arrived, and we been up at Rose 'ill. But 'nuff o' that now. We is 'avin' fun. You want some?"

Mary and Elizabeth pressed their bodies close to the now standing guard. Mary tipped his hat off his head and commenced tickling his ear.

Elizabeth softly touched his chin and slowly ran her fingers down his chest until they reached his waist.

"Now wot 'ave we got darn 'ere, I wonder?" She giggled lightly, punching just below his belt buckle.

"When do ya finish up? Maybe we could go have some fun," Mary whispered in the guard's ear.

"In another hour or so, then I'm gone—hopefully wiv you two, what?"

Padraig could hear this conversation from inside the cell.

"John!" he whispered to Caesar. "I think it's time."

"I want first kiss," they heard one say.

"No, 'ees mine, ya bitch," the other one argued.

However, neither John nor Padraig heard the sudden blow to his head that knocked the guard unconscious.

"Quickly!" Padraig recognised the voice of his brother. "These have to be the keys."

After some scuffling noises, Padraig was ecstatic to see the door swing open, and there stood his brother.

Mary and Elizabeth stood watching silently as the two brothers held each other and then emerged into the moonlight outside the cell.

However, none had observed the three men who had crept up behind them.

"Well, well, well! What do we have here? A group of bloody ignorant Irish peasants and their harlots, I believe."

They turned to see Robert Bolton and his two henchmen standing there grinning.

A cloud that had partially shielded the moon moved, allowing the full light of the near full moon to shine on the pistol Bolton pointed at them.

## Chapter 99

Padraig stood staring at the killer of his wife and her twin sister, he who had murdered his parents and his grandfather.

Every second he had lived, every breath that he had breathed since his departure from Ireland, and the vivid memories of the man who had caused that misery and pain flooded back, engulfing him. And that man was again finally in his sight.

Sean quickly grasped his left arm and whispered from the side of his mouth. "Easy, my brother, be careful."

His brother's words of advice calmed Padraig, and he could clearly hear Hugo Cohen whispering in his mind.

*Remember all I taught you, Padraig, remember, remember, remember . . .*

"It has been some time, Gallagher, and you," Bolton spat the word, looking at Sean, "who I now recall as being his brother, have both caused me considerable bother for too long. But no matter; tonight you shall cease to be a concern, and your bones will lie in soil far from your homeland."

"'Scuse me, Mister. Wot's goin' on 'ere?" Elizabeth suddenly pushed her way between Bates, Whitey, and Bolton and pretended to sway while leaning on Bolton and pushing him against the cell door.

"Oo, look 'ere, youse got a gun. I like men wot 'as guns."

Bolton quickly stepped back to avoid her, but kept his gun pointed at Padraig, but then Mary bumped into him, and he tripped backward.

Staggering and not quite falling, Bolton stood fully erect again and laughed as both Padraig and Sean moved swiftly toward him.

"I could kill you now, but I want to enjoy your suffering more. Move again, and I will fire."

He glanced at Mary, and then moving his pistol to his left hand, he smashed his right hand into her nose. "You might have fooled him, but you didn't fool us," he said, indicating the unconscious guard. "I am well aware of who you are and that you bed down with Irish scum."

Turning to the brothers, he ordered, "Both of you move out of your cell, and you will walk in front of us very carefully down toward the water when I give the command."

To Whitey he said, "Tie that idiot guard up and stuff something in his mouth so he doesn't make any noise when he wakes up. It will appear that the Irishmen did it. And I can then claim credit for their demise when they are found very dead in the morning."

Whitey dropped to the side of the guard, and using the guard's belt, he did as Bolton ordered, finishing by ripping a sleeve from the guard's shirt and stuffing it in his mouth.

Bolton nodded his approval, then noticing the guard regaining consciousness, he reversed his pistol and slammed the butt onto the guard's head, sending him back into oblivion.

Turning to the two women, he then pointed the barrel of the pistol at them both and added, "And Whitey, lock these two in the cell when you're finished with the guard. Witnesses will testify that two prostitutes instigated the break-in with Gallagher here, and they will also be punished accordingly. The authorities will disbelieve anything they say, but will have no trouble believing our story."

Turning to Bates, he said, "Have your blade ready. If either of these two Irish fools tries anything, stab him, but only enough to do some damage, as killing them is to be my pleasure."

Pointing down the slope toward the water, he then added, "Now walk slowly in front of us. One stupid move and I shoot you in the back. Move it!"

Whitey grinned with gaps between his yellowed teeth, looking first at Mary who had blood pouring from her nose, then at Elizabeth.

Waving a knife in front of them both, he ordered, "You 'eard what he said. Get ya in there!"

As Mary walked through the door, dabbing at her bloody nose with the hem of her dress, she was suddenly aware of someone alongside her, who whispered to her from the darkness.

"It's me, Mary. Walk over toward the cell window and say nothing."

Elizabeth then walked in and joined Mary.

Whitey followed, giggling at Mary, whose legs he could see from the light shining through the cell window. "What say I 'ave a bit of a feel 'round, startin' wi ya tits, what?"

Mary then astounded Elizabeth by laughingly replying, "Go right ahead, and if ya got some money, we might go further!"

As Whitey moved closer to Mary, still with knife in hand, John Caesar came from behind him, swinging his left arm around the convict's neck, and dragging him backward. Whitey was taken completely by surprise, and he, therefore, lost his balance, which made it very easy for Caesar to grab his right arm by the wrist and force it back and up behind his shoulder blades.

Dropping the knife, Whitey emitted a sudden squeal of agony as his arm was dislocated.

Caesar then grabbed the knife and plunged it deep into the

convict's chest.

In the dim night light of the cell, the two women looked first at the shuddering body of the dying man and then in shock at John Caesar.

Finally, Elizabeth said, "You weren't serious about the fool playin' with ya tits, were ya, Mary?"

And then turning to Caesar, she said with obvious relief, "Thank you, John, thank you!"

"But John," Mary said, "Why did Bolton not realize that you were in the cell with Padraig?"

"I also wondered about that. I can only assume that his overpowering hatred for both Gallagher brothers clouded his judgement, or that I may well use the opportunity to get the hell from here as soon as possible. And he is certainly correct in that assumption, as I will be gone from here before sunup. But first, I must go to my friend's aid and see how I can help him."

*****

Padraig could hear the sounds of the breaking waves before they reached the waterside. Then, walking through the tree-cleared area before reaching the sandy beach, he could see the waves breaking high, almost to the edge where the trees once stood.

"Stop there. Now turn and face me," Bolton ordered.

Padraig and Sean stood side by side with their backs to the sea, staring at Bolton and Bates.

Bolton produced a second pistol, and pointing both weapons at the two men, he began to laugh. "Now, isn't this convenient. All that noise from the water to cover the sounds of your screams for help. Where shall we begin?"

As Padraig turned with his back to the sea and faced Bolton, Sean, who had been standing next to him, began to move slowly away from him to his right.

"Now, now! Not so fast," Bolton stated firmly to Sean. "You stay right where you are."

"Bates, use your knife on him if he attempts any nonsense."

Padraig listened to the sound of the crashing waves, but not the waves of the Pacific. He could only hear the sounds of the North Atlantic. And all he could see in front of him was Robert Bolton, standing over his beloved Kathleen, as she tried in vain to call his name, there on the cliffs of Donegal.

She lay there, in her disheveled state, her clothes hanging around her, as if emphasizing the horrifying actions of he who stood laughing in triumphant glory over her.

He heard the haunting sounds of an owl calling "more poor, more poor, more poor!" from the branches of a tree some distance away.

And then again, he heard the whisper of his Kathleen calling him. "Padraig, Padraig, where are you my love? Where are you?"

Padraig watched as Bolton stood laughing at him.

"You bloody ignorant Irish fool. I played with your wife before taking her life, and I claimed the blood of her twin sister, as I became the first to pleasure her. And now I intend to spill your blood."

He had felt no pain or discomfort from the wounds on his back, but the pain and anguish Padraig was now suffering was beyond any he had ever known. And staring into the eyes of his mortal enemy, he knew no bullet could or would ever stop him from attacking Bolton.

Sean, sensing what his brother was about to do, called out, "No, Padraig, he will kill you!"

"No, fool, I will kill you first!" Bolton laughed, as he pointed the gun at Sean's heart and fired.

Padraig watched helplessly as the force of the bullet knocked his brother backward, and in anguish, he threw himself down on top of his brother.

"Look at that, would you, Bates—one dead and the other soon to follow!"

Pointing his second pistol at Padraig's back, he was about to fire when a sudden sound caused him to turn. Bates had also heard someone behind him, and thinking it was his friend, Whitey, was shocked to find John Caesar coming at him with a knife in his hand.

Bolton glanced at Bates, as he crouched with his own knife in hand, ready to defend himself.

None saw or heard Sean whisper to his brother and grab his hand, placing it on the axe in his left side pocket.

Winded from the shock of the bullet hitting the axe-blade in his right side pocket, he muttered, "The bullet missed me . . . take the axe!"

Padraig pulled the axe head swiftly from his brother, and adjusting his grip to the axe handle, he stood to face Bolton.

Bolton turned his attention back to the Irishmen and was shocked to see Padraig almost upon him. Raising his second pistol, he fired.

Padraig's instincts had forewarned him that his enemy would fire his weapon, and his axe glanced against Bolton's arm just as he fired. The bullet narrowly missed Padraig's right hip.

However, as Bolton whipped the pistol back, aiming at Padraig's head, Padraig moved alongside him and slammed his right heel into the back of Bolton's right leg.

Bolton began to fall backward, but swung the now empty pistol at Padraig's head. Somehow, the barrel of his weapon did not totally find its mark and only glanced off the side of Padraig's head, knocking him off balance.

As he began to fall, Padraig turned in mid-air, and before hitting the ground, he swung his axe and the double-bladed weapon sliced into and through the Achilles tendon of Bolton's right leg.

Screaming in agony, Bolton dropped to the ground.

Padraig leapt to his feet as Sean also stood and looked around them.

John Caesar crouched, ready to strike at Bates, who, suddenly realizing he was on his own, threw his knife to the ground, and whimpering for mercy, he dropped to his knees.

Sean moved to his brother's side, and both watched in contemptuous satisfaction as Robert Bolton, writhing in agony, tried to stand, but fell at every attempt.

Blood leaked out from where the keen blade of the axe had sliced through the leg of his trousers and cut through almost half of his foot.

"So, Bolton, what have you got to say for your sorry self?" Sean asked as Padraig stared down at he who had caused him so much pain and anguish.

As Caesar moved alongside them, Sean pulled the length of steel with the embedded knife from his jacket and handed it to his brother.

Suddenly having his wife's killer at his mercy, so much confusion flooded through Padraig's mind. "Do I kill you, Bolton? Or do I make you suffer as you made me suffer?"

"Help me, Gallagher!" Bolton pleaded. "Please help me." He was lying on his back with his leg kicking in great agony.

"You now cry as I cried, Bolton. But in truth, I cannot kill you. Deep within me, I would be the same as you if I took your life. However, I can hurt you where you hurt my wife and her sister."

Padraig raised the spear above his head, and Mary and Elizabeth watched in grim satisfaction as he stabbed the blade deep into Bolton's lower abdomen.

Bolton screamed yet again, twisting and turning as he

wrenched the spear from his body, blood seeping through his clothes and running freely to the ground.

"Should you live, Bolton, I ask that you remember this moment. And as I now pray that my wife and family can rest in peace, you may well begin a life of agony. That is, if you do not bleed to death."

Sean placed his arm over his brother's shoulder, and turning to John Caesar and the two women, he spoke with obvious relief. "We had best be away from here before Phillip's men discover that Padraig and you, John, have escaped yet again!"

Padraig looked down for a final time at his enemy writhing in horrific agony. "May God have mercy on your wretched soul, Robert Bolton," he said, and then he turned his back and walked away.

As they headed toward the rendezvous point where Sean had arranged to depart later in the morning, they could hear a commotion in the direction of the jail cell.

"They have discovered you have gone," Mary said anxiously. "What will you do now?"

They neared the spot where the landing boats had been taken to higher ground, and Sean stated urgently to Padraig and John, "Quick, help me with this."

They dragged the vessel to a small inlet where the water was much calmer than where Bolton had taken them.

Suddenly, they heard sounds of men running toward them.

"Quick, into this hut," Sean said urgently.

Together, the three men and the two women moved into the darkness of the nearby workmen's building and crawled under some boat canvasses.

"The bastards could be anywhere!"

"Look, there in that hut. That'd be a place they could 'ide."

Padraig heard the orders, and his hopes of escape began to dim.

"Sergeant, we's need back-up. They's found a body bleedin' to death. They needs ya help!" The sound of the marines moving away gave Padraig hope once again.

Sean moved from under cover, and a few moments later, he called softly to the others. "It all seems clear now. But stay there for the time being to be certain."

John Caesar was at his side. "Sean, I'm going to take a chance and run for it. I am desperate to find news of my lady. And the longer I stay here, the greater the risk I will be captured."

"Yes, John. I understand. I wish you luck and God's speed."

Padraig and John Caesar held each other tight, and then Padraig spoke. "Go, my friend. I will never forget you. Please do not let them get you."

"I will die before I allow that." And silently into the night he disappeared.

Padraig and Sean sat with Mary and Elizabeth, listening and praying that as dawn approached, they could escape to the whaler and leave the colony.

It was just as the sun cast its first rays on the new day that they heard people approaching.

"Get under cover, Padraig. Move quickly," Sean ordered.

Padraig moved back into the hut and pulled the cover over him.

By now, Elizabeth and Mary had shaken their hair back to normality, and after splashing some of the seawater over their faces, they had scrubbed clean the rouge of the previous night's masquerade.

"Well, what have we here?' The voice of Watkin Tench startled them.

"Good morning, sir," Sean spoke quickly. "My friends are here to wish me well as I sail with the whaler yonder."

"Indeed. And by chance, you wouldn't have spotted any sign of two escaped prisoners?" Tench looked pointedly at Mary Piles.

"No, sir. Not all."

Tench then turned to two marines standing behind him. "You two! Search those two huts over there. I will have a look inside here."

Sean watched as Tench moved into the hut. It was not so dark inside the hut now that the sun had cleared the horizon, and the new day had begun.

In sudden fright, Sean saw Padraig's boot clearly showing from under a boat canvas.

Tench pulled another canvas from some equipment and said, "Nothing under there!" Then he threw the canvas over Padraig's boot, completely covering it, and stepped outside.

He then called the other two marines to his side. "I am now certain my suspicions are well founded. The Irishman and Caesar will most certainly have headed inland to the west. Come, we will organize a search party and follow them later this morning."

"Good day to you three. I wish you well, sir," Tench stated, and he turned to walk away.

Suddenly pausing and turning to Mary, he smiled. "Bid your friend a fond farewell for me, won't you, Mary? And wish him better luck in his next country."

When Tench moved out of hearing, Mary turned to Sean and said, "Why did he say that to me? Why didna he say it to your face?"

Smiling in great relief, Sean replied, "Because, Mary, he was not referring to me. He was talking about him hiding in there!"

## Chapter 100

"Well, ya made it right on time!" The whaler captain welcomed Padraig and Sean as they were helped onboard. "Go on down below, and get yourselves sorted. We're just about to pull up anchor and set sail."

The two brothers watched as preparations were made to begin the journey and their new life together.

"Well, my brother, we are truly united once more." Sean smiled at Padraig as the whaler's bow pointed toward the open sea and freedom.

Padraig looked toward Sydney Town and dwelt on the memories of those first days in what was to become the foundations of New South Wales and all that had happened to him since then, the friends he had made . . . the enemy he had dealt with.

"We are united again, indeed, Sean, and that we must treasure. But what will become of my little ones? I must return to England and find them."

"And I will be there to help you Padraig. We will do it together."

★★★★★

Mary Piles and her friend, Elizabeth, watched from the shoreline as the whaler finally disappeared from sight.

"I have never loved anyone as I loved that Irishman, Sean

Gallagher," said Elizabeth. "And now?"

Mary Piles turned to her friend. "I understand," she whispered. "And now, we must carry on our life here as if we never knew them." A tear dropped from her eyes onto the sand.

★★★★★

The surgeon finally completed his work.

He turned to those who had assisted in saving the life of the still unconscious Robert Bolton.

"He will never walk again without the aid of a walking cane. He will most certainly never be able to sire children or to utilize that!"

As the surgeon pointed to where the spear had done so much damage, Robert Bolton stirred. The screams that suddenly emanated from his tortured body startled all who stood around him.

"There is little else we can do to help him," the surgeon continued, as if nothing had happened. "It is now all over for him."

★★★★★★★★★★

*If you loved this book, would you please submit a review at Amazon.com?*

Printed in Australia
AUOC01n1742101115
271560AU00002B/2/P